GEORGE RYGA
THE PRAIRIE NOVELS

GEORGE RYGA
THE PRAIRIE NOVELS

Edited by
James Hoffman

Talonbooks
2004

Talonbooks
P.O. Box 2076, Vancouver, British Columbia, Canada V6B 3S3
www.talonbooks.com

Typeset in Century and printed and bound in Canada.

First Printing: August 2004

Hungry Hills was previously published by Talonbooks in 1974. *Ballad of a Stonepicker* and *Night Desk* were previously published by Talonbooks in 1976.

National Library of Canada Cataloguing in Publication

Ryga, George, 1932–1987.
    The Prairie novels / George Ryga ; edited by James Hoffman.

Contents: Hungry hills — Ballad of a stonepicker — Night desk.
ISBN 0-88922-501-X

    I. Hoffman, James II. Title.

PS8585.Y5A15 2004   C813'.54   C2004-900311-9

The publisher gratefully acknowledges the financial support of the Canada Council for the Arts; the Government of Canada through the Book Publishing Industry Development Program; and the Province of British Columbia through the British Columbia Arts Council for our publishing activities.

To Norma Ryga,
for her part
in these prairie stories

CONTENTS

COLONIAL PASSAGES
Re-Reading the Prairie Novels of George Ryga

Many will be surprised to learn that George Ryga wrote novels—about ten in all—and that they are as passionate and as peopled with captivating, contrary characters as any of his dramatic works. Certainly he is better known for his stage plays, especially *The Ecstasy of Rita Joe*. However, given his choice, Ryga would have preferred to be known principally as a novelist, for he considered the novel a more free form than either stage or media writing. In the novel he could transmute more directly and authentically the agglomerations of fancy and reportage that he had assembled over the years, the traces of his own growing up on—and off—the prairie.

He is, as we can see in these prairie novels, a writer of episodic fragments, a teller of tales, some tall and some truthful, and there are plenty of them here, as if every good story necessarily provokes another. Often they seem to sit together awkwardly, like the lonely dirt farms that he depicts on the resisting prairie, held together by the loosest of connections, the author apparently mistrusting the impositions of plot or character development. In two of the novels a nervous monologist rambles on to a silent listener, in the third a drifter recounts moments in his failed attempt to return home. All are told in the first person, all feature an obsession to tell their story through a mass of stories, each, significantly, positions the reader as a participating listener/writer and therefore as an active interpreter. Overall, in the multiplicity of stories told in each narrative, in the onrush of their telling, there is a feeling of incompleteness, of a lack of clear beginnings and endings, of narrative and thematic incoherence. At the same time, however, many of these are *necessary* absences: given Ryga's milieu and politics, his choices, structural and otherwise, contain their own articulations—of a world being re-read.

The three novels read well in tandem. They draw from the same large canvas of rural, depression-era Alberta. They have similar stark prairie settings, the same array of colourful, cantankerous homesteader and dirt farmer characters, and the same anxious voice of a narrator who has also played a prominent part in the events. All of this takes us in many pleasurable and revealing directions, both historical and mythopoeic, to a period of obstinate survival farming and boisterous, ethnically diverse community building, as well as to the more questionable aspects of colonial "settling" and "breaking" the land, in a place that was never unsettled or unclaimed to begin with. Told in a homey vernacular, by a speaker who could be anyone's neighbour, each tale evokes a time and place that is distinctly Canadian—and emphatically post-colonial.

The very notion of a "post-colonial" Canada is problematical. Long colonized by foreign powers, first by France and then by Britain, and lately neo-colonized by the United States, Canadians have only lately become aware of the deep complexity of their colonial inheritance, especially as they in turn have internally colonized the indigenous peoples, the French in Quebec, and, until recently, many other groups of immigrant peoples. Though long independent from direct foreign control, Canada has retained many of the forms and practices installed during its colonial past, particularly in the institutions, large and small, that regulate its orders of dominance such as the Indian Act, official biculturalism and multiculturalism, each regularly contested by First Nations groups, Quebec separatists, and people of colour. The familiar Canadian sense of social and cultural inferiority, that "authentic" culture derives from elsewhere, and that therefore local culture is devalued, continues to trouble Canadians' very notion of "nation" and "Canadianness." For the immigrant prairie farmers in the 1930s this meant confronting the psychological internalizations and complicit relations of the invader-settler: dispossessed of their homelands, their mythologies, and their languages, they both escape from and engage in crushing exploitation. Seemingly freed from imperial structures of repression in their former homelands, they nonetheless seem doomed to replicate the same rapacious attitudes and operations on a day-to-day basis in their new country. What can they make of a new homeland which appears so full of possibility even as it is represented to them as so appallingly empty?

Ryga engages precisely these issues. Rather than looking elsewhere for the content and models of his fictions, he looks inward, literally in his own place of cultural production in an emerging post-colonial society. His writing is spare, direct, intensely local; he places himself in the narrative; he assigns the reader a persona and challenges him/her to take a stance in, and with respect to, this community. He asks, "How can a writer construct a story to put forward both the possibilities and the contradictions of the prairie settler?" In their sum, these novels point to the work of a powerful writer, one intimate with his subject, creative in his methods, and sure of his politics. With the contemporary revival of interest in the construction of authentic culture, especially as it problematically exists in a post-colonial society like Canada's, Ryga's three novels, taken separately or together, are well worth a second look, an entirely new post-colonial re-reading.

When Ryga commenced full-time writing in Edmonton in the early sixties, he spent much of his time on a planned series of novels. No one can tell for sure how many he wrote in total: the number may be as high as ten, perhaps more, but some were lost during his family's move to Summerland, British Columbia, in 1963. The three prairie novels represent his first published prose works in book form—he had earlier published a book of poetry, *Song of my hands and other poems* (National, 1956). In total, Ryga had five prose works published, the other two being *Beyond the Crimson Morning* (Doubleday, 1979), reflections on his travels through China, and *In the Shadow of the Vulture* (Talonbooks, 1985), a fictionalized account of Mexican migrant workers in the Reagan era. Like the prairie novels, both of them were inspired by actual events.

The son of immigrant Ukrainian parents, George Ryga grew up in rural northern Alberta and began writing when he was a high school student. Even at that early age he followed two major impulses that drove all of his writing: a relentless need to record the deep attachment of ordinary people to the land, a kind of bardic chronicling of familial cultural inheritances and stresses imported to the new land, and a contrary assertion of the need for a post-colonial statehood, the land now a site for change and social progress. On the one hand, he casts those who till the earth as the natural, almost the original inhabitants, a mythic presence, the kind of hard-working stalwarts whose earthy, ineffable identity provides the rough contours of a national character. At the same time he chronicles how so many of these, the very same working class people he mythologizes, fail to live up to the promise of the land, too often amounting to little more than rapacious colonizers that continue to live in their European pasts, especially in the face of the potential for an emerging national mythology. The conflict of these impulses is behind the agonistic structure of many of Ryga's works, where desire for the land, struggle for it, and finally dispossession of it amount to his major thematics.

In his youth, Ryga wrote mostly poems, getting several published in the local newspaper, *The Athabasca Echo*. These typically memorialize the rugged life of his community's prairie settlers, those who toiled doggedly on the land, a life he knew well from his depression-era childhood in the hard-scrabble farming community of Deep Creek (now called Richmond Park), about twenty kilometres northeast of Athabasca. They speak, in close, personally felt detail, of the determination as well as the despair of the pioneer settlers in the Athabasca region, their motivations, their dreams, as well as their grinding poverty and endless battles with an essentially inhospitable land. Here he catalogues the many, many stories of everyday struggle—as though by their sheer enumeration a critical defining mass of narrative could be reached. For Ryga these many stories of individual conflict, so sparely told, amount to the invocation of a world that seems self-contained, deterministic, even as it struggles to become a metonym for a nation in progress.

In an early poem entitled "My Land," included in *Song of my hands and other poems*, Ryga writes:

> This is the land my father found—
> This is the land beneath whose ground
> Lie hearts that were so proud and strong—
> Lie men who hated greed and wrong.

This is writing that celebrates the simple, muscular nobility of people of the soil, the natural inheritors of a rural, timeless tradition; it also speaks of a higher calling, of the workers' collective ability to improve the world, to right its wrongs through sheer force of exemplary character. In his preface to the book, he speaks of the "young generation of Canadians to which I belong," of how this group must not only celebrate the land and the folk, but also "introduce new ideas and improve upon the work of the past," to contribute to "our vision of a greater Canada!"

Indeed, he soon learned that his writing could have a personal, liberating dimension: submitting an essay entitled "Smoke" (see *The Athabasca Ryga*, Talonbooks, 1990) to a writing contest, he won a scholarship to the Banff School of Fine Arts in the late 1940s. For two summers he worked with a number of important mentors, notably Burton James, a Marxist theatre practitioner who had worked at the Moscow Art Theatre and a political activist soon to be in trouble as Senator McCarthy hunted for communists, and Jerome Lawrence, author of a number of successful American radio scripts and several Broadway hits including *Inherit the Wind, Auntie Mame*, and *The Night Thoreau Spent in Jail*. These and other mentors taught him the rudiments of prose and script writing; more importantly, the power of writing to both invoke and challenge society. The young Ryga learned his lesson well: writing a poem critical of the Korean War, which was printed and distributed around Banff, he was visited by representatives of the Imperial Order Daughters of the Empire, the sponsors of his scholarship, who informed the unrepentant author that he would henceforth be ineligible for future grants—and future studies at the Banff School.

Returning to Canada from a highly inspiring, politically-charged year spent in Europe where he had attended several large youth rallies sponsored by international left-wing groups in the mid-1950s, George Ryga began to dedicate his life to writing. On the same trip he had also followed his impulse to idealize folk ways by making a pilgrimage to Scotland, where he literally walked in the footsteps of one of his favourite poets, Robert Burns. He had come home to Edmonton with a sheaf of notes, a rough draft of a novel, and strong memories of meeting world class writers—with several of whom he continued to maintain a correspondence. Within a short time he had published his book of poetry and was at work on the novel. The latter was his first completed major prose work, *The Bridge*, an apprenticeship novel that sets out the pattern and content of his later prose works: the innumerable, closely-witnessed scenes of prairie life connected by a young man's attempt to negotiate widely conflicting impulses. A representative selection from this unpublished work appears in *The Athabasca Ryga*.

Ryga began writing full-time in the late 1950s when he married Norma Campbell. Now with a secure home life, he could work part-time and between jobs (as a postal worker and hotel clerk) he could dedicate his time to writing. As he worked on his novels, he also completed a number of short stories that were sent to numerous magazines—collecting numerous rejection letters. Many were, however, eventually turned into radio or teleplays and broadcast on the CBC. He assembled ten of them under the title *Poor People*, hoping to publish them as a collection. These stories are mostly set in the 1930s Canadian prairie: they tell of a roaming, rootless worker; of a boy's search for a lost parent; of a rejected eccentric living defiantly on the edge of community; of the murderous result of a man's affair with the young bride of an elderly man. Like the prairie novels, they are told mostly in the (suggestively autobiographical) first-person. Stylistically experimental, each is sparely, dispassionately rendered, with little time spent on character motivation, imposing instead a biblical sense of right and wrong on his essentially existentialist characters, structured not unlike the folk tales of Gorky or Dostoyevsky that he was reading then. At the same time though, in his foreword to the *Poor People* collection, Ryga attempts to contextualize these tales in contemporary global scientific, social struggles, such as the recent triumphs of Walter Schirra's space flight and James Meredith's freedom march in Mississippi.

On the last day of 1962 Ryga signed a contract for his first novel. Longman's of Canada agreed to publish *Hungry Hills*, which appeared in a hardback edition the following year with a cover picture of a lean young man gazing at the reader against a stark prairie landscape. In 1974 it was re-published by Talonbooks, in a paper edition now with a cover picture by Bill Featherston of a sorrowing Aunt Matilda, prostrate on a churchyard grave. The novel is a fictionalized abstract of Ryga's own experience of depression-ridden rural Alberta, where his father had attempted to homestead on barely arable land, the spectre of mounting debts, financial ruin, and, worse, the fear of deportation, constant threats to his family's survival. As the farm work proved increasingly defeating and his health declined, his father fell into what Ryga characterized as a "black despair." Ryga's inherited destiny, as the only son of a paternalist immigrant family, was to continue the struggle, but, in part because of an industrial accident in which he lost several fingers of his right hand, his own struggle with the land was to remain a literary one.

The people who inhabit Ryga's prairie novels are largely immigrants like his parents who had fled to the Canadian west—in effect, to a European settler colony. Displaced from their own place of origin because of Imperial aggression, then seen by the British establishment in Canada as second-class citizens, they dispossessed the aboriginal peoples in turn, viewing them as their inferiors. The settlers are thus both colonized and colonizing, constructing for themselves a highly ambivalent identity. Where can they turn to find their real source of authenticity—to the "uncivilized" local or to the "old country"? Should they replicate European manners and values in their new place or should they (dangerously) "go native." Which language best describes this new landscape: an imported, imperially-inflected speech, or a local patois?

Seen in this light, the thrust of Ryga's prairie novels is to engage the difficulties of identity formation in a population severely alienated by the process of migration and resettlement. On the one hand, the prevalence of misfits and acrimony among the invader-settlers suggests a defining nature of the colonizing enterprise in which the settlers are doubly constructed within a discourse of inferiority—both in the homeland they left and on the Canadian prairie. On the other hand, the settlers, through the generations, are becoming indigenes themselves and are beginning to establish a genuine and authentic culture that owes less and less to the European culture from which they sprang as well as to the Indigenous cultures they have displaced. If the latter is the case, if the novels are read as an attempt to fictionalize the dialectics of post-colonial identity construction, then there are, as Ryga insisted there were, prospects for the construction of a productive, hybrid prairie culture. It is very important to note that the novels move chronologically from the dooming plot of *Hungry Hills* through the intimations of hope present in *Ballad of a Stonepicker* to the creative improvisations of *Night Desk*, from the pessimism of Snit Mandolin to the optimism of Romeo Kuchmir.

In *Hungry Hills*, Snit Mandolin, the protagonist, replicates the passage of the homeless immigrant to an alien land. Like the settler, he problematically wants both a new life and a replication of the old. He wants to return to the land of his childhood, to "live and work among my people," but he also has to contend with a land that had dispossessed him, that had sent him away an orphan. His first name suggests someone who is resentful at being wronged, his second an immigrant folk instrument—implying the question, "How will one already 'upset' be 'played' by his old/new homeland?" Badly, as it happens: the land and its inhabitants conspire once again to defeat him; worse than that, the deep hostility of these poor dirt farmers, their destructive social antagonisms, along with the complete lack of any heroic character or narrative closure in and to the novel, imply a general condition of settler failure, a portrait of the colonial experiment gone wrong.

Snit's Aunt Matilda, the lone family member remaining, is feeble and has allowed the farm to go to ruin; his only former friend, Johnny Swift, has become an outlaw; Mandolin himself, despite his avowals to "try a fresh start," is finally dragged into a round of violence and crime, finally realizing that "I had forgotten the harsh cruelty of the land and its people." Even before being driven away the first time, he had been an alien in his own community, a boy it had marked with deep family disgrace. *Hungry Hills* is a tale of endeavour without hope, of sickly, ineffectual parents, of cursing, inhospitable neighbours and conniving merchants, all of whom finally drive the boy again from their midst, "the bone of the outcast stuck in my throat." In the end, the settlers and their bleak surroundings become one as Johnny Swift, the destructive figure Snit mostly associates with, begins to define the landscape: "Life was Johnny Swift—nervous and jumpy, full of hates and mistrust. And Johnny Swift was the hills—nice and soft looking, yet hungry as a wildcat."

There are more than a few echoes of autobiography in these novels: in the homesteading environment of northern Alberta in the 1930s; in the struggle of Ryga's parents; even an oblique reference to his own Ukrainian grandfather, a passionate man and staunch atheist, in the character of Aunt Matilda; as well as Ryga's own sense of familial obligation to his mandate, as only son, to continue "working" the family farm. If there is one autobiographical side to the story, it is the author's attempt to rationalize his own leaving of the land by determining it as essentially inhospitable: abandoned—in the atheistic cries of both Matilda and Swift—even by God. Told in a dispassionate, spare manner, the narrative implies that, while the prairie folk life contains the potential for a construction of a distinct post-colonial culture, the cultural contradictions inherent in it are too overwhelming, too inflexible, resulting in disaster for too many of its inhabitants. There is no attempt to attribute the suffering of these people to the absence of the original inhabitants, the aboriginal peoples. *Hungry Hills* is, in the end, a powerful tale in which the settlers have no recourse but their ongoing, Sisyphean struggle, not only in physically "breaking" the earth but also in negotiating their broken relationships to the land, to their language, to each other, and, by implication, to the absent aboriginal owners (of whom we hear so emphatically in Ryga's popular stage plays *Indian* and *The Ecstasy of Rita Joe*).

Ballad of a Stonepicker also draws from the same milieu, but in his second novel Ryga finds a more colourful, even hopeful, landscape—partly because for this work he cobbled together a greater variety of disparate tales. He also lessened the dark impact of *Hungry Hills* by choosing not to construct a strong, central plot, one which would necessitate narrative closure—thus positing a tentative and preliminary resolution to a complex, post-colonial experiment. This work was completed in Summerland and first published in 1966 by Macmillan of Canada; Talonbooks then re-published it in 1976. *Ballad of a Stonepicker* is actually a compilation of short stories, some written much earlier in Edmonton, intended for publication first as individual short stories, then as a collection of linked short stories, *Poor People*, and, later as a short novel under the working titles, *A Forever Kid* and *Recollections of a Stonepicker*. As Norma remembered, "He had about his tenth rejection and we couldn't afford any more stamps so we discussed that and decided the best thing to do was to make it into a book ... the only way to do that was to have a couple [of characters] that wove all these stories together and that was how the these brothers came to be."

The two brothers in *Ballad of a Stonepicker* represent the profoundly divided position of the immigrant prairie settler who is both attracted to and repelled by the project of "settling" the land—which in its unreceptive state refuses the alien forms of materiality and commodification of the colonizing settlers. So while one brother leaves the farm and the other stays to work it, neither prospers. For both, indeed for all characters, the act of settling the land involves various forms of twisted desire. Images of the misguided, the misfit, and the sexually transgressive, thread through the novel: Andrew, driven crazy (and marked) by the sun; Freddy the idiot, driven crazy by a girl (whom he scars); Hunch-backed Joe (disfigured), obsessed with building a church, only to have it cruelly taken away; Clem, the honest blacksmith, ruined (made destitute) by a prostitute. In this environment ownership of the land is questionable, businesses do not thrive, and violence is endemic.

More interestingly, there is the increasingly creative presence of the author himself in his second novel. In *Hungry Hills,* Ryga is partially present in the persona of Snit Mandolin, who could be seen to represent the more rural side of Ryga, the side which needed to imaginatively return to its roots and consider alternative outcomes, had he remained to work on the family homestead. In *Ballad of a Stonepicker*, Ryga's identity formation resides in the two brothers, one staying on the farm, attempting to fulfill a destiny different from that of *Hungry Hills*, the other leaving for advanced education and travel in Europe. This latter side of the persona, that of Jim, can be read to represent Ryga as a writer, a "great student," the one who left the farm and travelled (like Ryga) to Europe. But this attempt to access and work with the imperial centre provides no escape from the colonial condition either: his journey ends in apparent suicide, the surviving brother recounting, "He was a young man who lost one world and never felt at home in another."

Ryga constructs the story as more than simply a survivor's rant: the narrator speaks to an interested listener/reporter, so by implication the story will be retold from different and, for the first time, from other perspectives: from a transcendent "outside." The listener/reporter is positioned as an urban, educated person who may or may not re-read/re-write the truth of the stories being told by the brother: "You tell me—you look like you had a half-assed education! Or don't you know nothing about things that hurt, frighten or mix us up?" However viewed though, the brothers' agonistic, love-hate relationships, both of them tied to the land yet displaced by it, together amount to Ryga's complex response to the dilemma of a questionable colonial inheritance. There is now at least the possibility that these stories can be objectively and creatively re-worked, re-read, in a more affirmative post-colonial light.

Night Desk was written from notes Ryga made in the early 1960s when he worked as a clerk at the Selkirk Hotel in Edmonton, a low-end establishment frequented by a host of colourful characters, including a garrulous fight promoter named Nick Zubray, the model for the character Romeo Kuchmir in the novel. Ryga made an arrangement with another desk worker to cover some of his duties, which left him time to write on the job. Bringing his typewriter, he copied Zubray's monologues almost verbatim. Again, as in *Ballad of a Stonepicker*, the novel is almost plotless: a linked series of first-person anecdotes. And again, there is the usual lineup of eccentric/misfit characters. In the first versions of this novel, then entitled *The Last of the Gladiators*, there is an exotically dressed Count, an admiral, and a poet. The night clerk is a fellow named Jigs who not only also takes notes but also becomes involved with the other characters, to the point of going to the gym to work out with Kuchmir and his wrestlers.

In its final form, however, Ryga pared down the characters: gone are all the colourful figures except Kuchmir, who talks incessantly while the character of the clerk is restricted to listening. What is new in this third novel, however, is Ryga's direct insertion and interrogation of himself in the story. In a written "Prologue" (his only novel to have one) he admits, "I am in the story somewhere, but not through choice or design. I was only drawn into the vortex, as were others, of his consuming restlessness." Beyond that, what tidbits of seeming autobiography he leaves the reader with are probably spurious. He implies, for example, that he neglected his duties as a clerk and was dismissed, a fact disputed by Norma who recalled that in the spring, when there were fewer personnel required, it was usual to lay off a number of employees, Ryga among them. Nonetheless, the author himself is implicated autobiographically; he grows, over the course of these three novels, to occupy a position of increasing interrogation.

In a very conscious way, *Night Desk* continues where *Ballad of a Stonepicker* left off. Again the reader is presented with a monologist, but now he is more colourful, multi-layered, and occupies a more potent, determinative role in the stories. Like Ryga himself, who has cited his own racial and cultural origins of fiery Mongolian horsemen (see chapter one of my book, *The Ecstasy of Resistance: A Biography of George Ryga*, ECW Press, 1995), Kuchmir's heritage is "a mishmash of Tartars, Mongols, Cossacks." The character doing the listening, recording and writing, too, is more complex. The clerk/recorder could be a re-imagination of Jim: he has recently fled from university (and will soon be in flight from the night desk); and like Jim he only speaks marginally—briefly in the prologue and silently in the story. This can be read as a figure of Ryga himself, who also attended university, left, and now is a writer. He of course is the *real* speaker who articulates the stories against the imagined responses and rewritings of a silent witness: himself. As the stories multiply, the character and role of the interpreter-interrogater increases, thereby enabling the opportunity to re-read these stories in post-colonial terms.

In colonial narratives, the colonized subject is usually figured as silenced, in contrast to the colonizer whose authority extends over language—and therefore knowledge. Kuchmir certainly demonstrates, in his non-stop monologues, and in his locally-inflected narratives and combative tone, control over language. He constantly contests traditional colonial discourses and power structures. His speaking position is less determined by a distant authority, by allegiance to a standard, "correct" English, than by the realities of local colloquialisms. Even the clerk "speaks" subversively, since by recording Kuchmir's every word, he demonstrates the potential not only to master but to mark the discourse for rearrangement, for remaking it with local variations and to legitimize it by "writing," for the first time, the essentially oral "tradition" of the local. His deliberate muteness becomes a potent form of transformation, especially as we *know* it is Ryga himself creatively constructing a new kind of post-colonial character who can gain control over the paralysing and defeatist (colonial) contradictions of his life.

Of the three novels, *Night Desk*, in the commanding figure of Romeo Kuchmir, most effectively—and dramatically—constitutes the potential of the post-colonial settler. In him the role of the settler becomes more flexibly creative: whereas Mandolin in *Hungry Hills* and the stay-home brother in

Ballad of a Stonepicker were narrowly bound to the land and therefore restricted in their capacity to respond to colonial stresses, (the first overwhelmed and the second merely surviving), there is an irresistible, life-affirming energy in Kuchmir: "Dance until your feet hurt an' your skin glows like stars in the night." A "night person," he identifies positively with the marginalized other; as a "fighter" he defies the institutional authority of church and state; as a self-proclaimed actor he models the performative characteristics of an emerging hybrid culture.

Indeed, Kuchmir's exuberant, monodramatic voice lends itself to another form of re-reading: live performance. Ryga dramatized *Night Desk* for the stage. At the request of a Summerland performance group, Giants Head Theatre Company, Ryga condensed the script to about thirty typed pages. Under the title, *The Last of the Gladiators*, the Company performed the work along with Michael Cook's *Quiller*, giving the whole parenthetically Canadian production the title *East of Ryga, West of Cook*. Giants Head, named after a mountain near Summerland, premièred the play locally in June 1976, with David Ross as Kuchmir, then performed it in Vancouver at City Stage Theatre. Ken Smedley, the director, later played Kuchmir himself in the 1980s, under the title *Ringside Date with an Angel*.

Significantly, although Ryga writes of depression-era prairie farmers, there is little overt reference to the considerable socio-economic and political unrest of the 1930s—surprising for a writer schooled in Marxism. There is barely a mention of specific historical droughts or crop failures, nor any reference to the politics of the unemployed, public assistance programs, shrinking grain markets, the decline of incomes (Alberta had the second highest drop in per-capita income in Canada in the 1930s), nor to the many progressive agrarian movements (the United Farmers of Alberta, Social Credit, and the Co-operative Commonwealth Federation all had their origins in Alberta). These merely hover in the background, Ryga's interest being in tracking the everyday realities of a people encountering material and identity dislocation. The lack of a specific politics among these characters is telling. The contradictions of their lives are enormous, arising as much from their position as colonizing settlers as from a deteriorating world social order—contradictions beyond the capacity of the socio-political movements of the day to either effectively interrogate or resolve.

The harshness of Ryga's prairie landscape derives from its resistance to an assumed domestication. His fragmented family homesteads delegitimize colonial possession as a natural right; the presumed bonds within families are disrupted and the project of prairie settlement remains, in these novels, an imagined one. Yet at the same time he offers the roughhewn energy for survival and self-determination, as a possible ground of origin for an authentic post-colonial culture. In the very isolation of the prairie settlers, geographically and politically, in the calculated dis-ordering of their stories, and especially in the nascent vigorous dialogue between speaker and listener, between reader and re-reader, Ryga offers the possibility of an authentic prairie culture. His deferral of temporary solutions becomes, in these novels, a strategic political position in the anti-colonial struggle that so powerfully marks all of his subsequent work.

HUNGRY HILLS

ONE

The faded board swinging in the wind said "Elsie's Coffee Shop & Eats." I could have drunk a river, I was that dry, so I entered.

I dropped my bag inside the door and looked around. All the tables were littered with crumbs of food and coated with the same grey dust I could taste between my teeth. One table near me seemed less soiled than the others, and I sat at it.

Elsie didn't know me. Three years is a long time, although I remembered her very well. The cop had stopped for a drink and bought me a sandwich then—a sandwich of stale bread with bits of leathery chicken inside it.

She hadn't changed. Still the same mountain of woman with a dirty white apron cutting into the folds of her stomach where it tied, and the same brown dress, bleached down her sides from the sweat of her armpits. The wart on her thick upper lip was crowned with the sprig of dark hair I remembered. She stood, watching me with a vacant, hostile stare—the back of her head propped against the mirror which covered a considerable portion of the wall behind the counter. I stared back at her, remembering.

Three years ago, Corporal Kane and the welfare man had stopped here. We sat at a table further in—the furniture was rearranged since, but then there was a table in that corner. I sat between them, facing the street. The windows were just as dirty then as now, and the weather as hot.

"What you got for your boy friend to drink?" Kane half-hollered at Elsie. Her big face got red, and she scratched under a breast with her thumb.

"I don't got no boy friend," she said thickly. Corporal Kane slapped his knee and laughed—that heavy laugh of his which ends up in a girlish squeal, and sounds crazy coming from a big guy like him.

The welfare man, a Mr. Webber, or Webster—can't remember now, because he was one of those people you don't remember by name—had grey hair and a small grey-black moustache, and he didn't speak much.

When my knee brushed against his, he moved away in the car, because he wore a new brown suit which had such a press in the pants you could cut your finger on the crease. And I was pretty dirty.

Elsie sighed and moved away from the mirror. She fished around under the counter and came towards me, holding a moist cloth in her hand.

First she picked up the full ash-tray from the table in front of me, and emptied it into another, equally full, at the next table. Then she wiped it clean with the cloth. Using the same cloth, she wiped my table. When she finished, the table had the smell of stale tobacco ashes and soap.

"Wot ya want?"

Her voice sounded like it started in her stomach and came up through a towel in her throat.

"A coffee ice-cream."

"Ya go to hell!" Her face was still flat, but her eyes were getting angry. She turned her face away from me and stared out into the dusty street.

Nothing much had changed. The broken window of the hardware store across the road was fixed since I last was here. The bank next door had a new sign out—"Imperial Bank of Canada" it read—but the building was still the same as when Stanley Muller operated his blacksmith shop within its walls. So the new sign reminded me of new shoelaces on a bleached old pair of boots.

Folks had funny stories to tell about Stanley Muller—he came from Poland or Germany, and never learned to speak English too well. After five years in Canada, he tried to get his citizenship papers. At his court hearing, he was so nervous, what little English he knew he lost.

"Your name?" the magistrate had asked.

"Blacksmith," Stanley had said.

"Your occupation?"

"Muller."

Everyone laughed. Even the magistrate smiled.

Yet Muller might have become part of my family if he'd lived long enough. Maybe I'd have been able to move into town with him, away from the hills. But all that is gone now.

Another summer, hot and dusty as every summer I remembered. The same strong, hot wind. Here in town, it came past the grain elevator down the wide open street, carrying fine sand and a litter of paper and dead leaves, which it brushed across the dirty window of Elsie's coffee shop with a delicate scratching sound. I watched, and saw a large grey cat with a lame hind leg appear from the narrow space between the bank and the hardware store, and cross the street toward the café. The wind raised the fur high on his back, giving him a lethal appearance, which his sticky, tired eyes belied.

"How long's it been since the last rain?" I asked.

"Ya want somethin', or ya just aimin' to rest, goddamn you!" Elsie suddenly turned and planted her beefy red hands on the table before me. Her eyes were watering with anger, and her voice had become quite crisp and strong.

I only had coffee ice-cream once—Pete made some for me. I liked it, because it left a nice, lingering taste in my mouth long after I had eaten it. But ...

"I'll have a Coke."

Elsie waddled away to the cooler, and returned shortly with the drink in a bottle, which she thumped down hard on the table. This violent handling made it fizz and run over, making a dirty brown puddle on the table-top around the bottom of the bottle. I was fascinated with this mess, and tipped the bottle back and forth, enjoying the sucking, snapping sound I made breaking the surface tension of the liquid.

"Hey! Cut that out! Yo're givin' me a headache doin' that!"

Elsie had retreated behind the counter into the same posture and place at the mirror that she held when I first entered the café. She was getting salty.

I wondered if all women without men suffer the same way. My Aunt Matilda was one long headache after Muller went his way. I couldn't scratch in the same room she happened to be in without giving her a headache. A spoon dropping, or a board banging in the wind, and she'd dig her fingers into her hair and press like her head was a lemon from which she was squeezing juice.

What would she be like now?

Soon, I would be seeing her again. Yet until this moment I hadn't thought of what sort of person I would meet. Would she know me now? I was big—fully grown, and I knew everything I had to know. I stared at the Coke bottle and tried so hard to remember. Her voice—her face—these I recalled well. But I had lost the feel of her—the separate sounds and shadows of a presence. She had travelled a long way on her strange, confusing road.

A hard, dry, tight-lipped woman my Aunt Matilda was, with narrow hips and the thin, bone-hard arms of a boy. The skin on her neck and face was mottled by brown specks, like the speckled shell of some chicken eggs.

"Too much sun she gets," my mother used to say in that jealous way of hers. "If she washed herself in skimmed milk every second day, she'd soon get rid of that."

My mother had opinions, but no audience, for she was tuberculous and confined indoors most of the time. Which was unfortunate, for I remember her as a gentle, bewildered person with wonderful bursts of fun in a retiring, hungry existence. But the law of our household gave authority only to those who worked in the fields, and so Aunt Matilda was always the dominant one of the two women.

One summer Aunt Matilda took up with Stanley Muller, the blacksmith. It was ten miles from our farm to town, but Aunt Matilda walked, sometimes four nights in a row, returning with the first glow of sun in the mornings. She was tired, hot and happy, and would begin her daily chores without breakfast.

"Aunt Matilda's been gone all night. Don't she sleep?" I used to ask my mother.

"Sure she's slept—with her back to the coal sacks, for she ain't that strong or big!" my mother would reply, then she would laugh and slap her knee with her thin hand.

One Sunday, Stanley Muller came to visit us and eat dinner at our table. He had something wrong with his chest, for his breath sang like an organ. And he had black pocks on his forehead and nose, where fragments of flying coal and steel dust had imbedded deeply in his skin. He sat next to my aunt, on a bench which was too small for them, and they wriggled much to keep their seats.

"Ven you have to sharpen ploughshares, bring dem to me. Stanley do for noting." Muller spoke to my father, who shyly lowered his head over his plate. Then Muller ate, his large hand enclosing all but the prongs of his fork. I remember watching him cut meat with the edge of the fork, and butter his bread by drawing the prongs lengthwise across the slice, which produced a lovely, rippled design. I wanted to do the same thing, but when I reached for the butter dish with my fork, mother caught me by the wrist and drew my hand back.

Aunt Matilda walked some way with Muller when he left that evening. When she returned, my mother and father were having tea, and she joined them.

"What you want to take up with a guy like him for?" Mother chided. "He don't even speak English good."

My aunt picked her teeth with her thumbnail and looked at my mother thoughtfully. But she didn't say anything.

Strong as he was, Stanley Muller died that summer. The story went that he had a drink of cold water while he was hot at his anvil, and the drink gave him a chill to his chest. For two weeks he lay on his straw cot. Aunt Matilda took food to him, but he would not eat. The front of his smithy was open, and farmers came, bringing ploughshares and axes for him to sharpen. But he never relit the fire in his forge.

Now they have made a bank of his building.

"How much better if it had been me instead of him!" Aunt Matilda cried at the burial of Muller. My mother hushed her to be still, and father wrung his hands and glanced over his shoulder to see how many of the neighbours heard.

It was a terrible thing of my aunt to say—young as I was then, I felt the full weight and pain of her words. And as I watched them shovelling the earth over Muller, I was numb with despair.

So much I could now remember of Aunt Matilda in love—how she would surprise me by grabbing at my arm and pulling me to press tightly against herself. Sometimes I would come into the house and find her kneading her thin lips as she studied her face in a broken sliver of mirror. When I cleared my throat to make my presence known to her, she would giggle and shoo me off with a wave of her hand.

"Run away and do something! You're worse than your father used to be!"

After the tragedy of Muller's death, she sort of caved in on herself and didn't laugh any more. Her face got thin and old, and I remember how her hair started to grey. Our house was small and thin-walled. At nights, I often heard her crying in her bed and tossing from side to side.

My father became worse—he took to talking to himself, and our home became an angry, nervous place.

I began straying from home, not wanting to go back even for food. Some days, I would just walk down the road past Whittles' store, until I got tired. Other days, I would visit one of the many farms up and down the road from us. There were always kids to play with—there were more kids in the countryside than hogs and cattle put together—kids big and small, lame and straight, all sitting in the sun, waiting for something to do.

I kept leaving our place because there was nothing to do at home. Nobody cared if I dressed or washed, and I was never shown how to do chores. Now my aunt and my mother changed for the worse. With my father, it didn't matter.

"Go ask Jim to split some wood, and I'll bake bread." My mother rose from bed one afternoon, hot-faced and wheezing, and spoke to my aunt.

"I'll get it myself," Aunt Matilda said testily. "Your Jim would water the garden on a rainy day!"

Mother didn't argue. She merely went back to bed, and remained there until the following day. Her ever lengthening spells in bed did not disturb me then. I was really pleased, for when she was wakened during the day, she would rise blue with meanness and demand to know why she could not be left in peace. If she woke by herself late in the afternoon, she was peevish about being allowed to sleep the day away. As for my father—memories of him had always been dim. A mild man, with down-bent head and repentant eyes—afraid of folks, and avoiding even us.

But there is no pity among the poor.

One afternoon, I strayed further than usual—over to the Hardy's place. There were two boys and a smaller girl—nice kids to play with, for they didn't call me names. We tore around through the yard and out into the fields, where we upset the cows enough to make them move away from us. Fred Hardy, the father of the family, whistled to us, and we saw him wave at us to come in. We were all hungry, and ran a race to see who would get to the house first. The two boys beat me, and their sister was left some distance behind. When the boys reached the door, they squeezed past their father and went in. I started to follow, but was stopped by Mr. Hardy's hand catching me at the neck.

"Ya plannin' to eat, then stay all night?" he growled at me. "Go home, ya little bugger!"

So I went home. It had always been the same—even when my father lived, I had nobody to take my part. The bone of the outcast stuck in my throat all through childhood.

"Look at him, will ya! He ain't afraid of the night! He's got the heart of a thief—even looks like a thief! Just look at his eyes, and the way his teeth stick out. Isn't that a thief if ya ever seen one?"

"The way he fights, too. Tore my kid's lip to here, when he was called a little pig for not washing his face."

This was when the neighbourhood went out of its way to pick on me. At best, they were no meaner than Mr. Hardy had been. But I was a boy, and when I became lonely, I would go to people's homes uninvited. I didn't leave until I was asked to or told to go home.

Yet it wasn't something I understood then, and I was happy despite it all. I still am, for what difference would it make if I wasn't? Who would hear me?

After Muller's death, my aunt and I grew more distant, for she was also beginning to die, as I was coming to life. We never came together, yet there were moments when I came close to invading her world, as she must have invaded mine without my being aware of her.

One night, I had overstayed at someone's house, and was ordered home when the children were called in for bed. I went out on the road, kicked dust about with my bare feet. The earth and sky were still grey with twilight. When darkness fell, I began making my way home. The road I took led past the cemetery—and as I neared the burial ground, the early moon rose, silvering the grass and dusty road with a soft, comforting light.

I had no fear of the cemetery, for I had no misfortunes with it any more peculiar than I might have had with a pasture field. Also, I was spared the terrifying tales wiser adults sometimes improvise for children in a closer family than mine. Anyway, as I neared the cemetery, I heard a voice, and stopped to listen. Yes—I heard it again, coming from behind the willow hedge which bordered the grounds.

I was curious, and crouching low, I tiptoed off the road and up to the hedge. Pushing aside the willow branches, I peered through.

There, clear and sharp in the moonlight, was my Aunt Matilda, lying on top of Stanley Muller's grave. She was so near I could have spoken to her. She was lying on her stomach over the grave, her cheek pressed into the mound and turned away from me.

She held her kerchief in her hand, and waved it frantically up and down. She was saying something—something pleading and sad in the cooing tones of a pigeon. I got scared and chilly, and moved away towards the road. Then I ran all the way home ...

"Did you know my Aunt Matilda?" I asked, and Elsie stirred her massive bulk. She gave me a mean look, then turned her attention back to the windy street outside the café.

"Wot?"

Leaving a dime on the table, I got up without tasting the Coke she had brought me. I no longer had any stomach for refreshments. So near to home again, and a hot excitement had begun to creep through me.

It was late afternoon now, but the sun still burned like a furnace. The wind from the hills was good, even though it was full of smells of hot leaves and parched grey earth. It was all so familiar—the smell of home—all a part of other summers I remembered; hot sun, dry winds, and a thirst which only a great rain could quench.

Even from the simmering street, bordered with grey clapboard buildings, I could see the hills beyond the single grain elevator which split the landscape. How blue they were! How peaceful and silent, falling away like great abandoned anthills. Small tufts of trees and brush clung to the valleys, but the hilltops were bare, rounded and wind-blown. Beyond this first range of hills was home. There the land was flatter, and shielded by taller trees and windbreaks to make farm land from which the hardy could eke out some sort of life.

I started to cross the street, and the wind struck my chest full force, billowing my shirt out behind my back. It was a cool, pleasant sensation, for my clothes were damp with sweat and had stuck to me.

A clatter broke the silence of the street, and I turned to see a team of lathery horses appear from the corner back of the livery stable. They approached me at a fast trot. I jumped towards the bank, out of the way, and watched.

I knew the horses—Pete and Jenny, the plow nags which the Swifts owned. I looked up at the standing driver, who was lashing the animals with the tail-ends of the leads. Sure as hell! It was Johnny Swift!

"Hi! Ya goddamned, rubber-legged hammerheads! Hi!" Johnny's voice had grown stronger, but his language hadn't changed. He had been the only kid I knew who could make a dog cringe with a verbal scolding. Kids only played with Johnny Swift when there was nobody else to play with, for he was rough.

"Johnny!" I shouted.

I could see his face plainly as he neared me. Big beads of sweat stood out on his temples and cheeks, trickling to dry in the dark fuzz on his jaws. These dark streaks made him appear older than he really was. His head was uncovered, and his long hair was a wind-twisted mess. He looked up and saw me. For a moment he didn't recognize me, then suddenly he yanked hard on the reins, bringing his team to a rearing stop. Dust swirled around the wagon and rose in a thick cloud.

"Hey—Snit! Is it really you? How ya doin' boy? Goin' outa this damned town?" He shouted with pleasure, and a loose smile creased his cheeks.

I ran over to the wagon and stepping on a wheel spoke, swung myself up on the seat beside Johnny, and we were on our way. I looked back and saw the dust lifted by the wind envelop the bank building. Only the new sign showed through the cloud. This struck me as peculiar, and I giggled.

With a vicious lashing at their backs, Johnny had the horses at a gallop before we left town. The wagon jolted and bounced over the deeply rutted, dust-covered road, and I had to clutch the wooden seat with both hands to keep from falling off. Johnny was standing all the while, his filthy clothes slapping around him. I noticed his trousers were worn completely through at the seat, and on his feet he wore boots of different sizes and colours, and no socks.

When we passed the grain elevator and were out in the country, Johnny sat down and allowed the horses to break gallop into a trot.

"Good to see ya, Snit—ya rotten little bugger! How ya been, anyhow? It's been what? Three—naw, goin' on to four years since they took ya away. Whatcha come back for? This ain't no place for a man. Ya'd been better off wherever it was ya were. What'd they do—put ya in jail, or something?"

"Naw—a welfare home."

"A *welfare* home! What in hell is that?" Johnny's brows crinkled suspiciously. I grinned.

"Well, it ain't a Sunday school. More like a jail, except it got no bars across the windows."

Johnny relaxed, and brushed his sleeve awkwardly over his temples to wipe the sweat away. He also wiped off the dirt, and I marvelled at how white and soft his skin was under all that grime and filth.

"Boy! That's more like it." He sighed. "Sure wish I knew a guy who'd been to jail. Sort of makes a man outa a kid, I hear."

"What's new hereabouts?" I asked.

"Nuthin'. Same old place—same old hills. Same old two-bit farmers, and each one hungry as a bitch with a dozen pups. Nuthin's new." Johnny looked down at his feet, and seeing his mismatched boots, pulled them under the seat so I would not see. I did the same with my feet, for I wore a newish pair of black oxfords, and suddenly felt ashamed of them.

"Ya still living with yore old man?"

"Yeh," Johnny nodded. "He don't like me none, but I don't like him neither, so we get along all right."

He became quiet after this. But I felt, each time I looked away, he was watching me, trying to figure me out. Once, I glanced at him sudden-like, and caught him staring at me and my clothes. He grinned with embarrassment.

I had forgotten how a human being smells in poverty—the musty smell of sweat and old clothes, and hair and feet that don't get washed. This was the smell of Johnny—the smell of yeast and horses. I began to wonder if it wasn't all a bad mistake. Maybe I should have done what Pete suggested.

"Christ, but some folks'll be surprised to see ya come back, Snit!" Johnny laughed bitterly. "They signed a petition that long to get ya packed off—an' I know every name that went on that paper."

"I don't want to know, Johnny!" I was startled at the sharpness of my voice.

"Hey! What's eatin' ya? I just wanna be friendly. Ya gonna need friends bad when ya get back, I'm tellin' ya!" Johnny said peevishly, his moon-face setting hard as he turned to me.

"I'm sorry. I'm kinda beat." I was miserable. The sun burned into my eyes like two jets of a blowtorch. I bowed my head, and Johnny was silent for the rest of our drive.

Ten miles—but the ride was without end or time. It was a silent ride now. Folks in the hills don't talk much, and I was back in my hills and of my hills—I could never lose that, any more than I could lose my staggering, long-stepped country walk. You are born with these things and you never forget them. So I had been away three years, but I had no more to say to Johnny Swift than he had to say to me. I did not want to know the names of the folk who had *signed against me*, because I was not returning for revenge. I was returning with a presentable set of clothes on my back, a jacket on my arm, and a cheque in my pocket—and I was returning to live and work among my own people.

To occupy myself, I milked my thumbs and tried to recollect all I knew of Johnny Swift. I felt Johnny was still watching me, and also trying to remember.

Johnny's folks had no use for him as a kid. They figured he was too lazy and careless to amount to anything. And he was, at that. It was spoken about the neighbourhood that old Walter Swift lived by 'the Book and the axe,' and his family went to pot for it. Johnny had once told me the old man actually *did go* to bed at night with a Bible in his hand and an axe by the bedside— to accommodate the devil in case he came a-calling during the dark hours. Johnny had been a dodger. When he left his spade in the potato patch and jumped the fence to go larking the rest of the day, old Walter Swift took it off on the mother for bringing the boy up wrong. She was a pious, shivery little woman who died while I was still here.

"Sadie died of a sorrow for that punk boy—God bless her!" Walter Swift had stopped by for water, which he shakily held to his lips in a dipper when he spoke.

Aunt Matilda turned red and jumped him.

"Sorrow, hell! You clubbed her to death, you goddamn animal!" she shouted. Swift never did drink his water. He threw it and the dipper back into the bucket.

"Just ya don't go cuttin' me none, Matilda Mandolin! Just ya don't go cuttin' me, ya blasted heathen bitch!" He hunched over and his hands shook like he was going to nail my aunt one. Then he turned and left our doorway.

When I told Johnny about the incident the next time I saw him, he laughed.

We were now close to home. Whittles' store stuck out of the landscape like the awkward heap of old lumber it was. As we passed, I strained to see through the soiled windows into the shop—to check against my memory the rough board shelves of dusty clothes, canned vegetables, flour bags, cattle salt, tobacco, and dried fruit. I could even remember the smell of the store now—the paper-and-grass smell of aging dry goods, strongly laced with the odour of the kerosene barrel which occupied the middle of the floor. But I could see nothing, for the sun was over the roof now, and the windows were blank and glazed like the eyes of a dead cow.

"Ya gonna stay with yore aunt?" Johnny asked. I was surprised to hear his voice after the many miles of silence between us—as I was surprised by his question. It had never occurred to me to wonder if I would stay with my aunt—I was returning home, and home was the place my aunt lived in. Now I wondered.

The farms we had passed seemed uncompromising and deserted some-how, grey and stark as the hills against which they were outlined. Almost hostile, and the further we drove in, the more uncomfortable I felt. I took my time answering Johnny, because I was no longer certain of the answer.

"Yes," I finally said.

Johnny grunted and faint lines crinkled his brow.

"She ain't been much since yore old lady went, Snit. You wouldn't know her much now—looks like a scarecrow, and acts batty as hell. Even the farm ain't much any more." I laced the fingers of my hands, and my palms felt sticky against each other.

Next would be the church, and then, a short distance off, our farm.

"Johnny," I spoke too quickly, "do you think—well, is it right for me to come back?"

"I couldn't care less. I just think yo're crazy."

"That's not what I meant. What will folks think—my aunt—will she want me back, ya think?"

Johnny thought on this for a while.

"I don't know." He squirmed as he spoke and scratched at his neck. "How can I tell what the hell folks think? Nobody's dyin' to see ya back, that I know. Folks don't like ghosts croppin' back—especially ones they ain't so sure of. But don't ask me. Go talk to Whittles—or yore aunt, if ya can get any sense outa what she says."

"What ya mean—folks ain't sure of me? Don't ya know why I'm comin' back?"

Johnny pulled the horses to a stop and looked into my face. There was suspicion in his eyes now, and a strange hostility which seemed so much a part of the hill country.

"No, I don't know why yo're comin' back," he said. "You tell me."

"I been gone a long time," I began. "I done some good things and I done some bad things. But I want to make a start somewhere—anywhere. I'm on my own now, nobody's got anything against me. The way I figured it, I may as well go back where I come from and try a fresh start there. So I hitch-hiked in from Edmonton, and now I'm on yore wagon just short of home by one hill. That's all there's to it."

"Yo're comin' here—to make somethin' of yore life?" I could tell Johnny didn't believe a word of what I said. I nodded. "What ya gonna start with—yore teeth?"

"I've got some money."

"Ya think the bit of dough ya got is gonna bring rain and good times here?" Johnny laughed a hard, tight giggle. Then he laughed louder, until he clutched his stomach and bent over his knees to catch his breath. When he looked up, there were tears in his eyes, and I felt sick and frightened.

"Boy, that's the best one I heard yet!" He wiped the tears from his eyes with the back of his hand, then reached for the reins to drive on.

"Just a minute," I said, "I'm getting off now. Think I'll walk the rest of the way in."

"Suit yoreself—yo're welcome to ride, but then it's yore shoe-leather, so if ya wanna walk, then walk," Johnny said, fighting to keep a grin back. I jumped off the wagon, and he drove off, trotting his horses now. I waited until the dust he raised settled, then followed after him on foot.

The earth was hot, and soon I felt the soles of my shoes burn with the heat stored in the dusty road. I felt wretched and thirsty. Somehow, my arrival home was not what I had expected. I had forgotten the harsh cruelty of the land and its people—the desperate climate which parched both the soil and the heart of man. There were no friends here—there never would be.

Now I was returning, with clothes which somehow still remained clean and out of place. But I was returning as a burden to those with whom I had to share a place on this earth—burden to what remained of my family, and a burden to the conscience of a community which had once banished me. I had already made Johnny Swift resent me. There would be others.

I was now alongside the church. It was desolate and parched, with white-wash on the siding showing only under the eaves, where the walls were shielded from the sun and weather. The rest of the building was grey and decaying. The door sagged and was held closed by a length of rope and a peg. The windows were cracked and taped with strips of paper in grotesque patterns, like veins in the eyes of a man who has worked through a night without sleep. The churchyard was overgrown with dandelion and quack grass, and the gate had fallen and grown into the earth.

Now on a rise of the road, I could see my old home in the distance. It was desolate and grey, and I felt I could go no further. I turned into the church-yard, and making my way around the building to the shady east wall, sat down to rest. I unlaced my shoes, and removing them to ease the pressure on my swollen feet, lay back into the stringy grass.

TWO

I sprang to my feet in a panic, for momentarily I had no recollection of where I was. The sky overhead was a blue-black sheet, punctured by stars, and the outline of the hills was now murky and strange. I could not tell how long I had slept, or whether it was the deep twilight of evening or of morning I had wakened to. Reaching for my shoes, I brushed my hand against the grass. There was no dew.

Recollection came quickly; I remembered the afternoon and my ride with Johnny Swift. I walked around the church and onto the road. The air was warm, and heavy with the odours of dry decay. Once I was on the road, I peered towards the farm where my aunt lived, but could see no light. I tried to moisten my lips, but my tongue was swollen with thirst and my throat felt parched. I had to find someone to talk to—to give me food and water. Without thinking, I approached my aunt's farm at a run.

In moments, I was there, standing by the roadside, trying to pick out the path to the house, for it was overgrown with mingled grass and I could no longer see the fence and gate which at one time surrounded our yard. I gave up, and stumbled to the house, tearing the grass which caught at my feet.

The house was silent, dark and lonely as I neared the front door. But familiar odours reached me as I came closer, and they were comforting—there was the scent of rotting wood, washed with lye and beef-fat soap. This was Aunt Matilda—she smelled that way herself. Over to one side of the yard, I picked out the outline of the waterpump over the well—which again conjured childhood visions of an old man deep in thought. And the old laundry tub still hung grey against the dark, weather-beaten siding of the house.

I tried the door and found it locked. I knocked, gently at first, but there was no reply. I knocked again, louder, until my knuckles ached.

"Aunt Matilda? Are you in? It's me, Snit. I've come home. Let me in!"

Have you ever known a sleepless night—a night so silent you could hear the footsteps of a spider through it? I strained, and heard a sound, deep and far away in the house.

Then suddenly the door creaked open, and I smelled a sour, fevered face close to me.

"Snit! What do you want with me? Why did you come back? Get out! Go away and leave a poor woman in peace. I don't want to ever see you again—nobody wants to see you! Now go!" Her voice was so fierce it sounded like a burst of compressed air.

"Aunt Matilda—it's all right! I know you're all by yourself, and I won't bother ya none. I've just come visiting. Let me in—everything will be all right again!"

But she didn't move.

"Nothing will ever be right again, Snit. Never again! I can't hold you back with my hands. You've grown some. But you're not wanted here any more by me or the folks hereabouts." Her voice sounded tired and distant now. Then she walked back into the house, leaving the door open.

I hesitated a moment, then followed her in.

Only three years had gone by, but the face staring at me across the pine table in the light of the kerosene lamp had aged by ten times those three years. It was frightening—saddening. Her eyes were dead and tired, like those of a dog peering into a sudden bright light after coming in from the dark outdoors. Her hair, too, had turned a yellow-grey and hung over her shoulders and face in sticky strands. The brown-flecked skin of her face and neck was crinkled and dry, like a piece of ancient chamois cloth which had been rolled into a ball when wet and allowed to mildew. She wore a dark, nondescript outer coat, which showed signs of having been worked and slept in, and which had ragged ends on the sleeves and along the bottom. Yet she seemed in place in that kitchen, where the stove had food cooked onto it and the walls were soiled and cracked.

Aunt Matilda's hands trembled violently as she pushed a cup of tea across the table to me. They were such thin hands, and the sinews showed through the parched, fallen skin.

"Don't stare at me like that! I can still count to one hundred," she said, and grinned.

Her teeth were long, thin and badly decayed. Then, for no reason at all, her eyes lit up quickly, and I bent my head down. I was home, and things I had forgotten and learned not to fear began flooding my memory.

"I know you can, Aunt Matilda. Is the land in crop this summer?"

She glanced at me suspiciously and her tiny, tragicomic mouth set firmly. She lifted her cup to her lips without answering. But she was splashing her tea, her hands were trembling that violently now. I watched the hot liquid trickle down her wrist and underneath the ragged sleeve of her coat.

I had been taken away from my mother and my Aunt Matilda. At the "home" it was rumoured I had been taken because of insanity in my family. Yet when I asked Mrs. McGilvray any questions about it, she just stared at me and gave no reply. So I used to lie awake at nights, thinking—thinking about my father and the frogs. It didn't make much sense. And still it did—for when I tried hard to recall my father, and my home and the hills where I had lived, I would remember the frogs as well.

My father was afraid of frogs—he was afraid of many things. There was a slough of stagnant water on the boundary line with the farm north of us. In the spring and early summer frogs croaked all night through, and father sat up with the light on and his eyes wild with fear. He walked about the kitchen a lot on those nights, with his hands cupped over his ears and keeping us awake with his pacing and muttering. Not that it bothered me much, for I got used to this, just as I got used to going to bed on a hungry stomach.

He had been a quiet man, with a little sprig of brown moustache under his nose. Every Sunday morning, he trimmed his moustache with scissors, and if my aunt or mother saw him and laughed at his vanity, he would get so embarrassed as to leave the house and sit in the yard until they apologized and called him in.

He was so shy—so completely helpless. He always sat on the bench nearest the door in church. If he walked along the road and met a neighbour coming towards him, he would be the first to step out of the road, and with his head bent low in confusion, wait until the neighbour walked by. We always owed money to Tom Whittles at the store—everybody did. My father would not go near the store, for he felt Whittles would pick on him—which he did—and humiliate him. So my aunt did our buying, and infrequently, when she felt like going out, my mother.

There was the Hallowe'en night when all hell broke loose in the country-side. My aunt didn't allow me to go out, so I lay in bed and planned what I would do to her when I got big and strong enough. I'd starve her and beat her, that's what I'd do.

Outside, the kids were setting up a lot of noise, yelling "Monkey Mandolin! Monkey Mandolin—come out and play!"

This was me they were calling for, but inside the kitchen my father and mother were arguing. He was supposed to go to the barn to finish his chores with the cattle and horses, but he felt all the shouting was against him, and he was afraid of getting stoned or hit by a kid.

"You damned coward!" I heard my mother shout at him.

"Leave him alone, Nellie—you're as foolish as he is," my aunt said in a quiet voice, but mother kept right on.

"All right—I'll get the boy to protect you!"

"Snit!" she called. "Get up and take your father to the barn. He's scared of the dark!"

I got up and went into the kitchen, avoiding my aunt's eye. Then I took my father by the hand and led him outside. He was crying, or it sounded like it, for his head was down and I couldn't see his face. I walked to the barn with him, and the kids didn't do anything, for I was set to lace the dickens out of anyone who picked on my pa.

He wasn't a good farmer, but he kept us as well fed and dressed as the next man. But he was wasteful in a lot of ways. He had a horse he doted on—a bay stud which he fed all year round on oat and barley chop. Other folk only used these choice feeds when they worked their horses. In the winter, the animals had to fend for themselves by pawing away snow and eating what they could find beneath.

My father used to harness the bay to the stoneboat and go out into the field to load stones and haul them against the fence until the field was clear of rock for one season. Each year it was the same, for every summer you plowed up as many stones as you had picked off the land the year before. Sometimes I would run out to help him. If he didn't see me coming, I'd find him talking to the horse as he worked. He also talked to the horse as he dressed him down for the night in the barn. I got quite a kick out of standing outside the barn door in the moonlight, listening to him apologize to the horse for working him so hard, and promising him all sorts of pleasant things "soon"—when times got better.

"He's just a kid—a kid who grew a moustache," my aunt would say to my mother when they thought I wasn't listening.

"Oh, God!" my mother would sigh bitterly. "Why don't you take him, if you feel so soft for him?"

Aunt Matilda would laugh in a high, terrible way.

"It's too late, Nellie! You shoulda thought of that fifteen years ago!"

Without any warning, the bay stud got colic and died. My father buried him on the hillside where he had led him to die. When he returned to the house, he sat down at the kitchen window and stared and stared into the yard. I remember how he held his chin in his hand, his fingers reaching up and hooked over his lower lip until his teeth became dry and dull in his face. When Aunt Matilda came into the house and saw him, she scolded him for sitting around, and asked him to go with her into the garden and help out with hoeing potatoes.

He wouldn't move, even when night came.

A couple of days of this, and we were all pretty worried about him. Mother and my aunt tried everything, but he just sat there and stared into the yard.

"Leave him alone, Matilda," my mother said with a hard laugh. "Just wait until he wants to eat, and we'll see if he gets anything for behaving like that—trying to scare us!"

Saying that didn't help, for pa didn't seem to miss his meals. He wouldn't even look at the tea Aunt Matilda made and held under his nose.

Mother went to bed, where she remained, coughing and moaning all day. In the evening, she rose and approached father.

"If only mother was alive—she'd know how to deal with you!" she shouted, stamping her foot.

Father looked up, dropping his hand away from his chin. For the first time I could remember, his voice was strong, and he looked hard into the face of my mother.

"I been thinking, Nellie," he said. "We did something awful wrong. All the fires in hell won't burn it out of you or me … "

I never heard him finish what he was saying. Mother closed her eyes tight and pressed her hands against the sides of her head. Then, quick as a cat, she let go and jumped at me. She grabbed me by the arm and jerked me to my feet and away from the table, which surprised me, with her being so sick and all. She steered me to the door and ordered me out.

Aunt Matilda followed and led me down the road towards the church. She put her arm over my shoulder as we walked, and in a soft voice which was as sad as it was gentle, told me not to listen to what folks said, because folks like us were given to doing peculiar things sometimes, and talking like people with the fever or drink in them. We walked a long way that evening, and I felt very close to my aunt. I took the hand she held over my shoulder, and squeezed it with both of mine.

When we came back, mother had gone to bed, and I was surprised to hear my pa whistling cheerfully. He was sitting in front of the kitchen stove now, oiling up the old rifle he used for scaring owls in the scrub. Then he put a shell in the gun, and holding it over his arm, walked to me and Aunt Matilda. He patted me on the head and went out.

"Where you going?" my aunt asked, almost in a whisper. But father was gone.

Like a person in a dream, my aunt moved to the kitchen table, where she sat down. Then she stared into the lamplight, her face twitching something awful. I spoke to her, but she didn't hear me, so I went to bed.

Mother and she went to look for him in the morning. They found him with his face in the frog pond. They kept me home when they buried him, so I never did see what he looked like with the back of his head blown off ...

I will never forget how it hurt to have my first tooth pulled. But the death of my father did not leave any disturbing pain with me. His life had given me no particular joy or sadness, and like the ghost he was, he neither took anything nor left anything with me.

"I'm only glad he came to his senses long enough to end it this way. Who would have taken care of him in a few more years?" mother said to Aunt Matilda over supper one evening. My aunt glanced at me, then opened her lips to say something. But I never heard her thoughts, for she nodded her head and remained silent.

Aunt Matilda worked the fields alone after this, for mother was not a woman of the land. She hated the soil—the hot, dry summers, and the cold, windy winters which kept folks around the kitchen stove for warmth months on end. The harder Aunt Matilda worked, the less she spoke. I never helped, for she didn't ask me, and I did not volunteer, choosing instead to spend my time drifting around the neighbourhood and waiting for the next day, in hopes it would bring some exciting, interesting change.

It was the summer following my father's death that mother confined herself to bed as an invalid, and I lost interest even in her.

Some four miles to the east of us was a ravine which cradled a stream during the spring, when water ran off the hills from winter snow. The life of the stream was short. Two weeks after break-up the land was dry, and with no run-off to replenish it, the water in the stream-bed disappeared. Across this ravine, on a flat, windy bit of land, stood an old log schoolhouse which had been put up by some Norwegian settlers long before my time. Years ago, the stories have it, these people gave up trying to make a living off the dead soil of the hills, and emigrated back to the land of their ancestors. But the school was kept open.

I went to this school for one year—just long enough to pick up the alphabet and a raging hatred of the long-armed teacher, Miss Bowen, who always picked her ears with a hairpin while contemplating my punishment for coming late each morning. Not that it was all my fault. I had never been brought up to tell time—one day didn't crowd another, so hours were insignificant. Besides, we didn't have a clock in our house.

I dropped out of school earlier than other children of our parts. Some of them went two years.

There was an inspector of schools who lived in town. Each fall, he drove out to our community, calling on each of the farms here. He argued and shouted at our folk to send the kids to school, or he'd make trouble. But our people were suspicious of him and said they wouldn't. In a very official way he would then write down the names of all who resisted learning, and then before he left he threatened he'd see what he could do about it. He always said that, and nobody paid him any mind until he came around the next year. My aunt and mother didn't argue; they just walked away from him. But others argued and told him why they wouldn't send us to learn.

"We don't raise kids for school here!" folks would shout at him.

"A kid don't need to learn t'read and write for to be able to grow potatoes and oats! Give a kid a bit of school, and he stops obeying his elders and betters. Next thing, they run off—an' who's gonna take care of us when we get old?"

Maybe the school inspector was impressed by this argument, for he never did make trouble among us.

If there was such a thing as a meeting-place for our folk, then I would say it was the church. Here everybody congregated on a Sunday, and there was much singing, shouting and "hallelujahs"— all sweaty and hot, with their hands threshing the backs of the benches in front, and the floor creaking under pounding feet. Reverend Nigel Crowe was the preacher in our church. He lived in town and came out to preach his sermon, often arriving a day earlier so he could stay over with Tom Whittles at the store. They were good friends—even resembled each other in appearance.

Reverend Crowe was as bald as a stone on top and heavy around the stomach. He had large, bushy grey brows that twitched and jumped when he got worked up during his sermon about any sort of sinning.

"Why were the children of Israel punished?" he would thunder, his brows bouncing.

"They was sinnin'!" A churchful of feet would slam and hands would clap together.

"Why are we punished with the vengeance of drought?"

"We is sinnin', *sinnin'*, SINNIN'!" The voice of the congregation rose in a chant, and fifty frightened, gleaming faces leaned forward and stared at Reverend Crowe.

Quite often, the reverend got so fired up with his own preaching, he'd step down from the pulpit and walk right among his congregation, asking the same questions and getting the same answers.

"Where does the Almighty send the sinners?"

"To hell!" the congregation would shout back, a quaver of fear in their collective voice.

"And what happens in hell?"

"We burn—we burn!" A moan now, and scarey enough to give a kid the creeps.

After the sermon and the singing, Reverend Crowe would walk with Tom Whittles over to the store. Many of the folks were still excited by the church service, and would follow, hoping somehow that the minister would say more to comfort or fever them up. Tom Whittles wanted folks to follow, for it meant he'd be able to sell stuff in the store. So he'd argue mildly with Reverend Crowe as they walked. And close at his heels the country folk followed, listening hard.

Tom Whittles was a religious man. He resembled the minister in his baldness and fatness, although he lacked Reverend Crowe's shaggy brows and his voice was thinner. But he kept a Bible on his store counter at all times, right next to the weigh scales. He'd finger the Bible as he poured peanuts to sell to kids, cheating like the devil by pouring the nuts on the furthest end of the scale tray to make more weight. I discovered this trick long before I knew how it was accomplished. On a balanced small see-saw I placed a half-pound tin of tobacco against a half pound of peanuts I got from Aunt Matilda. The tobacco easily overbalanced the peanuts. Tom Whittles sold a lot of peanuts in his store, and I often wondered why Reverend Crowe didn't mention this sort of cheating in a sermon. Maybe he didn't know about it.

Yet, as I have said, Whittles was a religious, industrious man. Besides running his store, he knew how to build chimneys in houses. So he had more money than anybody else, and being alone without a family, he lived and dressed better than even Reverend Crowe. But he had a streak of hard meanness in him. One incident has remained fresh in my memory, because somehow what happened has a bearing, I feel, on all the events which followed.

Shortly after Stanley Muller died, Aunt Matilda had a way of suddenly getting mad at everyone and everything about her. She'd flare up and sound off on things which didn't concern her, and it used to upset my mother if it happened in a public place. This day was a Sunday, and I recall how Aunt Matilda fidgeted and twisted in her seat in church during the sermon, her face hot and her eyes dark and bothered. Folks sitting on the other side of her turned and stared at her, for she made small sounds under her breath while everybody was trying to hear Reverend Crowe.

After the sermon, Reverend Crowe moved down through the church to the back door, where Tom Whittles stood waiting to shake his hand. Folks rose and crowded outside. As always, Tom Whittles and the minister began walking to the store, followed by the usual crowd of people from the congregation. Before we were even out the church gate, Whittles was questioning the minister on Scripture, and Reverend Crowe was replying in a firm, strong voice.

"What's he saying?" Aunt Matilda was crowding forward to be alongside the two men.

"What's got into you, Mat?" mother caught my aunt's arm and tried to hold her back.

"I just want to know what they're saying. I don't think either of them know what they're talking about!" my aunt said sharply. Mother looked at her hard.

"Be quiet and don't go making a fool of yourself!" she warned.

Aunt Matilda pressed on, however, and was among the first to get in when Whittles unlocked his store. By the time we came in, she was leaning on the counter, watching the storekeeper and Reverend Crowe, who were both behind the plank partition.

"I see what you mean, Reverend Nigel," Whittles was drawling, as he opened a bag of money to put into his change drawer. "Anyway, that was a right good sermon you gave this morning, and may the Lord hear it and take kindness upon us and you for it!"

"Thank you, brother Tom," Reverend Crowe replied, straightening his shoulders, for even though they spoke to each other by first names, the minister showed no intense warmth to the storekeeper while the store was full of people. He was still the preacher, just stepped down from his pulpit.

"Amen," someone in the back of the store echoed. One of the women asked about the price of lard at that moment.

Then, out of the blue, Aunt Matilda stopped all conversation.

"There is no God!" she exclaimed, her lips trembling and her eyes bright and sharp. Mother pushed in beside her and told her to mind what she was saying. Aunt Matilda pushed her away with an elbow.

Both Tom Whittles and Reverend Crowe turned with surprise. As for the rest of the crowd, you could hear a pin fall in that shop. The woman with the lard still held the package high over her head, and her arm froze there.

Whittles was the first to regain his senses. Looking over the heads of the folk in the store, he cleared his throat. Then he fixed a mean stare on my aunt.

"What did you say, you black-faced harlot?" he almost shouted, his voice high and thin. The preacher's brows began twitching with nervousness.

"There is no God!" Aunt Matilda spat out the blasphemy for the second time, and there were gasps of horror around us. But my aunt paid no mind. Looking straight in the eye of the storekeeper, she said in a dangerous voice, "You call me that name again, and I'll scratch your damned eyes out, Whittles!"

She looked like she could do it, too.

Whittles got scared then, and backed nearer to the minister. But at the same time the folk around us began to chide and scold Aunt Matilda; and when the noise picked up, mother got me and my aunt each by an arm, and steered us outside.

Mother did a powerful lot of coughing as we walked home that morning. She kept saying to Aunt Matilda that she had gone and fixed us all up proper with her big mouth and thoughtless ways. Then she said she knew what folks were thinking, and it was well enough to leave things as they stood.

At that point, Aunt Matilda stopped and turned to mother. As she spoke, she kicked road dust to one side with her foot.

"If there is a God, why don't He take pity on us and give us what the heart wants most? Why don't He give us some rain and a garden of flowers—just once? Why? Because there ain't no hell for us who live in this hell here—and as for the other place, it's all a nice story and nothing more!"

Which was talk way over my head, so I walked on by myself without listening to what mother had to say in reply. They argued all the way home.

Next Sunday, folks avoided us at church meeting, and whispered and pointed in our direction when they thought we weren't looking. For the first time in my life, I felt hot and choked up among all these people and all the secret things they thought. When Reverend Crowe started in singing and waving his hand to get everybody in the congregation singing with him, I said to mother I wanted a pee, and sneaked outside.

The church ground was small, and by the time I got out, there were about six other kids standing around trying to get some action going. They were pushing against one another, and one kid was grinding on the toes of a smaller with his heel, trying to get the kid to fight. When they saw me, they all made a circle around me like I was something strange and new.

"Fee! Fee! Fee! Yore aunt's a bad-un, and she ain't got no right staying around here in a chrishun community!" It was Mickey Rogers who said that. Mick was a kid who lived one farm north of us, and whom I could lick hands down any time. I started for him, and the circle broke and scattered. When they were at a safe distance, they all shouted like a bunch of magpies.

"Go home, ya little bugger, and take yer aunt with you, if ya know what's good fer her!"

"We'll get ya, Mandolin!"

Mick got out the gate and on the road, so I gave up chasing him and started walking back into the church.

"Yah! Yah!" he shouted, with his dirty hands cupped over his mouth. "They'll take ya away to a little bastard home! Yuh'll see—they're makin' a paper on ya! Ya'll see! The Mandolins are bad-uns!"

"The Mandolins are buggers!" the other kids started to singsong, and I was glad to get back into church and over to my aunt and mother.

THREE

A few weeks after, one of our cows broke pasture. Before I brought the cow back and my aunt finished repairing the damaged rails, we were late for church. Mother was waiting in front of the house, and when my aunt signalled we were ready to go, she pouted and said she didn't know whether she should be seen arriving late in church.

"Don't argue—come on!" Aunt Matilda growled, and mother came without further complaint.

Reverend Crowe was already in his sermon when we entered the church. But when he saw us, he lowered his book and became silent. Mother became embarrassed and almost tripped over her feet as she hurried to be first in our seats, for all eyes in the congregation were on us now. I felt my aunt go tense and tight beside me. My own hands became sticky and cold, for I had never known this sort of interruption in a church meeting before. As we took our seats, I looked up and noticed the hands of Reverend Crowe were trembling, although he was standing very stiff and erect, and staring hard at Aunt Matilda. He cleared his throat, and the church congregation stirred with excitement.

"Matilda Mandolin—will you stand up and come before the congregation!" Reverend Crowe suddenly ordered, his shaggy brows a heavy straight set below his temples.

My aunt swallowed hard, but did not rise. I could feel the hot breath of the congregation as everyone leaned forward to close in on us.

"What for I come up?" Aunt Matilda asked in a thin voice.

"To beg forgiveness of the folks and God Almighty for your sinfulness and blasphemous ways."

"And supposin' I don't?"

A slow colour was rising to the preacher's cheeks. He was glancing around over his congregation, as if looking for someone to help him.

"I'm warning you, Matilda Mandolin," he said, but his voice wasn't as firm as he would have wanted it to be. "I'm warning you—I've discussed this matter with the church elders. You're being given a chance to clear yourself, and you had better do so right now. The Lord don't take no tomfooling with the likes of you!"

"Go kiss my ass, you Bible-thumping bastard!" Aunt Matilda said fervently. Rising to her feet, she upped and left the church, with everybody staring open-mouthed after her. Without thinking what I was doing, I rose and followed her, leaving mother behind. She was already in tears, and bent low in her seat to hide herself. I didn't want to watch my mother cry, any more than I wanted to stay cooped in the church, waiting for folks and Reverend Crowe to start burning over what my aunt had done.

Aunt Matilda ran all the way home. I called to her to wait as I ran after her, but she didn't hear me. When I got in the house after her, she'd closed herself in the bedroom and locked the door. I heard her sobbing.

When mother came home, she looked pale and tired. She had a red welt across one cheek, where someone had hit her with something sharp. From this day on, the differences between my mother and my aunt became as marked and strong as the changes of night and day. Aunt Matilda became fighting angry, staying away from the house and involving herself in hard work around the farm. My mother sort of gave up trying for anything any more. She got thinner and less anxious to rise from bed in the mornings. My aunt and she seldom spoke after this, except to argue or complain. At first I was worried about mother, when she wouldn't get up some days at all, not even to eat. Aunt Matilda didn't seem anxious about her, and soon I forgot to worry, for it seemed like things had always been this way with us.

There are so many answers I want to find to many questions which no one ever explained to me. Maybe folks in these parts have it in them to be suspicious of two husbandless women living together. Or maybe they never liked us—just let on they did in other times. We used to have neighbours who called in once in a while to chew stories with my aunt and mother. Then, there was nobody calling at all. I found more and more folks chasing me off when I went calling on kids to play with. The only people who paid any notice to us at all were odd drunks driving home in wagons from town late at night. They would stop on the road by our gate and yell across the yard to my aunt, asking if she was lonely enough to let a good man in. Whenever this happened, Aunt Matilda would come tearing out of her bed and out into the yard, shaking her fist and threatening damnation on the drunks if they didn't leave her alone and go their way. The drunks would laugh like whinnying stallions, and then with wagons clattering they would drive away.

Across the road from us, but with their buildings on the other side of the hill and out of view from our yard, lived the Shnitkas. They had a whole bunch of kids, with one boy my age. His name was Harry, and he was smaller than me because he had rickets as a baby. He used to collect feathers, which he kept in a tobacco can. I saw him prowling around our field one day, searching for magpie feathers. Since he would no longer play with me, I ran over to torment him. He was a funny kid, with a nose always running; and when he spoke, his words came out muffled as if his tongue was tied to the roof of his mouth.

"What you got there?" I shouted, as I bore down on him. With no trouble at all, I took the feathers he had gathered away from him.

As I said, he was smaller, but he tightened his fists and came at me. I grabbed him and threw him over on his side. He got up, crying with anger and hurt.

"We'll fix ya! We'll fix that witch of an aunt of your'n and yore muvver, too—we'll fix ya good. We'll fix ya special!" he shouted at me, and then ran away.

We didn't go to church any more, so even our Sundays had nothing exciting happening. Mother stayed in bed, waiting for death. Aunt Matilda spent long days working in the fields and garden. They didn't ask me to help, and I didn't. One day was like another to me, and they were all boring and depressing. I walked around the yard kicking stones back and forth. Some folks drove by on the road during a day, but none of them waved to me, so I couldn't be bothered even waving to them.

Then there was the day old man Shnitka came over, his face hot and dirty, and his eyes bothered by something terrible.

"Where's yore mother?" he asked.

I pointed over my shoulder to the house. He began walking in the direction I pointed.

"She's sick in bed," I said after him. He stopped and shuffled his feet in the dirt uncertainly.

"Where's yore aunt, then?"

Without replying, I ran out into the field to get Aunt Matilda. When we returned, Shnitka was still standing in the yard, in the same place I had left him.

"Well?" Aunt Matilda brushed her hair back, and looked at our neighbour suspiciously.

"I come to tell ya," Shnitka faltered, his gaze fixed halfway up my aunt's stomach, because he was a shy man and could look no one directly in the face. "There's a paper making the rounds in these parts. I didn't sign it, Matilda, because I don't go for this sort of thing at all. So I come to tell ya, before it's too late."

"What ya talking about?"

Shnitka looked at me, then at my aunt. Then he turned away from us and stood facing the fields to the north.

"They is signing a petition to take the young-un away from here!" he blurted, pointing a thumb in my direction. "Paper says you and his mother are not quite all there in the head, and the boy's gonna grow up like that and be bad. Don't say to anybody I came atelling ya—I don't want no trouble with my neighbours."

Without another word, Shnitka walked away, crossing the road to his own farm. My aunt stood there with her mouth open. Looking up at her, I saw that the colour had left her cheeks, showing great blotches of tan on her thin face.

"What's it mean, what he said?" I asked.

"Nothin'—just talk. Folks have to have some talk, that's all. You go in, or this sun will melt your brains," she said, pushing me towards the house.

Soon after, there came an afternoon so hot and sticky that Aunt Matilda stayed home in the shade.

"Let the place go to pot—I'm not aimin' to roast alive!" she said. This had been the day she was to go out in the fields and pinch off thistle blossoms to prevent the weeds from going to seed. She and I were sitting around the front door, watching flies drowsily examining the door-frame. We both saw the car, which bumped its way along the road and came to a stop at our gate.

"Look!" Aunt Matilda exclaimed, then shouted over her shoulder, "We got company, Nellie—in a car!"

Only the school inspector and the police drove a car in those days, so we were pretty excited. Mother came out of bed, and the first thing she did was comb her hair for the occasion.

Both doors of the car came open at the same time. Out of one stepped a mountie with yellow-striped blue breeches and a tunic red as fire. It was too hot for a hat, so he didn't wear one. Out of the other door appeared a tall, grey-haired man wearing a brown suit. He carried a large briefcase under his arm. They stopped momentarily, glanced at our house, and approached.

As I said, our door was open for coolness, and these two men came right in without knocking. Aunt Matilda rose to put on water for tea, and mother quickly sat in the chair she had vacated to be nearest the door and the men.

"Howdy. I'm Corporal Kane, and this is Mr. Webber," said the policeman, grinning quickly at nobody in particular.

Mr. Webber stood in the doorway. There was a long silence, for they didn't ask any questions or state the purpose of their visit. Instead, they searched our house—not searching by walking around and turning things over, but snoop-searching, examining the floors and walls, and craning their necks to see into the bedrooms. They both looked up to see into the cupboard when Aunt Matilda opened it to get the tea. I was watching them, and getting sore, for I never have liked snoops.

After they had seen into everything possible to see from where they stood, Corporal Kane looked down at mother and grinned a friendly smile.

"I'm sorry, but which one of you ladies is Mrs. Mandolin?" he asked.

"She is!" Aunt Matilda snapped without turning from where she stood at the stove. "You're not paying no friendly visit, so whatever's on your minds, get on with it!"

Corporal Kane coughed to clear his throat, and his face turned red. My aunt's rudeness left him with nothing to say, and he turned to his companion, pointing to my mother at the same moment, as if to say, "Do something—here she is!"

Mr. Webber stepped into the room now.

"Mrs. Mandolin, we'd like to have a word with you—privately."

He looked at me, and then at Aunt Matilda. I rose to my feet, but Aunt Matilda didn't even turn, and I could see they weren't going to push her none. I didn't want to miss a word of what the mountie and Webber had to say, so instead of waiting for mother to order me outside, I crossed the kitchen into my bedroom. I closed the door behind me, then pressed my ear against it to listen.

First thing, I heard them ask Aunt Matilda to leave the room. Quick as a whip, she replied with a dirty suggestion about where *they* could go if they wanted to.

The voices of the Corporal Kane and the other man were no longer polite now.

"Mr. Webber is from the Provincial Welfare Department, and we didn't drive all this way to listen to nonsense. Just remember that!" Kane raised his voice.

"Please, Matilda—don't get us in trouble with these folks," my mother begged.

After this the questions began, hot and fast. How much was my mother earning from the farm, and how much were we spending on food and clothes? Why wasn't I made to go to school? And were we in the habit of making trouble in the community? Did we go to church without missing a Sunday—and who was parson in our church? What happened to my father? Were my grandparents normal, or had they been to a hospital for observation? Had anybody still living been to a hospital? After the first few questions, mother began to cry.

Aunt Matilda took over the answers. Of course grandpa and grandma had never seen the inside of a hospital! A tree had fallen on the old man, and grandma died in bed of old age—and would they get the hell out and mind their own business instead of bothering folks who were busy.

Mr. Webber had a voice about as sympathetic as a rusty hinge. "We're just doing our job, madam. You understand we have to—a petition was sent to our department about—"

"A petition? You know where you can stuff your goddam petition!" Aunt Matilda was really going on.

Suddenly, my door was yanked open by the policeman, and I was pressed so tightly against it listening that I went sprawling into the kitchen. The cop took hold of my collar and lifted me to my feet.

"Let's go, Roy," he said to the welfare man, still holding me. "I've got the kid, so let's beat it. This broad is driving me buggy."

With a shove, he pushed me outside the door, and began steering me for the car. I fought like a cat, and almost broke free of the corporal. But Webber closed in and caught me by the other arm. Against the two of them, I could only bite and kick, but I couldn't hold back. When they held me at the car, and Webber reached to open the door, I looked back at our house. Through the open kitchen door I saw my mother sitting at the table, her head buried in her hands. But my aunt was right behind me, her eyes wild as she bashed Corporal Kane this way and that about the face with her hard little fists. She had already given him a pretty mean scratch over his left eye.

"Uniformed punk!" she shouted at the mountie. He was mad by now, and letting go of me with one hand, he hit my aunt with his fist across the mouth. She fell down by the car, both her hands clutching at her lips, and blood oozing out between her fingers.

The two men threw me into the car, and drove off quickly, with the car heaving and tossing over the bumpy road.

The lamp sputtered. Home. Slowly, my good Aunt Matilda was getting over the shock of seeing me back. A little smile came to her lips. She reached out with the pot and poured me another cup of tea.

"Did they hurt you bad, boy?" she asked, as if sifting my memories with me.

"No—not where it shows or matters particularly," I replied, and wondered if she had a bed for me to sleep the night. The door to what had been my room was open, but it was pressed against the floor with the sag of the house. Yet I hoped that inside, the room might have been preserved— that something of me had not been forgotten and neglected.

I woke during the night and sat up, thinking it was time to get up and get ready to open the coffee-shop. As I moved, the noisy bedsprings creaked fit to wake the dead, and I heard Aunt Matilda groan in the next room. I became alert and aware of my surroundings, and it gave me a great feeling of sadness.

There was silence now, except for the faint rustle of the settling house. My room was in darkness, and smelled of vegetables and dust. Only a pencil of moonlight showed through a chink in the wall. I reached for it, and playing it on the palm of my hand, imagined I could feel it tickle me.

There had been only one stop when they drove me away—at Elsie's in town, where they bought me a sandwich of stale bread and leathery chicken, which I could taste even now. Then out of town on the black tar highway to Edmonton and the orphanage.

They didn't call it an orphanage, they called it a welfare home—The Merciful Redeemer Welfare Home; but after a while I found I was the only one who had a living parent. The place was run by Mrs. McGilvray, a fat, cross-eyed woman who looked like a tired cook.

Across the road and three blocks to the east was the school in which we were to get our learning. In it there was a reminder of the home. Aged and water-soiled plaques saying "God Bless Our Home" hung on the walls of both buildings. I later learned that they had been embroidered and framed by a Polish kid who became a sailor. But that was a long time ago.

After school, we were to come directly to the home. We were then to repay the generosity shown to us, and also build our characters, by growing potatoes on a twenty-acre field which surrounded the main buildings. Those of us who did not want field work were given the alternative of staying indoors and scrubbing miles of floors in corridors and dormitories. This work was done by hand in a kneeling position, and I didn't know of a boy who could take it more than three evenings in a row without limping badly with bruised knees.

"You are now among nice, Christian boys, like yourself. Stay out of trouble, and you will be happy here. Supper will be at six o'clock," Mrs. McGilvray had said to me even before I was through the gate, where she met me.

"One other thing," she added, as I followed her to the dormitory. "We do not allow our boys to talk about where they came from. We just want them to be happy."

She turned then, and with her one good eye on my face, took me in a half-hearted hug. Her clothes smelled of turnip and sweat.

The boys didn't talk about their pasts—but not because Mrs. McGilvray had ordered them not to. Most of them had been in the home so long they just didn't remember anything so far back. Lying in bed when the lights were out at night, I would tell the boys who shared the big dormitory with me about the hills, and about my aunt and mother—even about Johnny Swift and the Shnitka kid across the road. The boys listened, asked questions in whispers, and never told on me.

For the first few days, I was shown around the buildings, and made to clean up the kitchen and our sleeping-room. Then came the time to decide whether I would take duties indoors, or out in the fields. Dave, an older boy who shared the room we slept in, advised me to ask for field duties. He was a tall, thin, blond-haired fellow with a sad face. I liked him right off the start, because he never spoke rough to anyone, and always stopped to help the smaller kids when they were behind in a job. Mostly because Dave worked in the fields himself, I asked for field work.

It was a smart thing to do, for here we got the benefit of fresh air and sunshine. Nobody worked very hard, for we were supervised by a Mr. Swanson, an elderly man who had something wrong with his back and could not walk around much. I soon learned to work away from where he sat or leaned on his cane watching us, and to go where the others were digging and spading. Here we could talk, and work slower.

Once one of the boys leaned on his spade and began picking his nose.

"Here," Dave said angrily to the kid, "don't stand there doing nothing, or we'll get Mr. Swanson in trouble, and they'll get someone really tough to supervise us. Don't take advantage of a man that's easy—there ain't that many of them around."

Dave never talked about himself, so I knew no more about him than what he did and the few things he said, yet I remember him so well even now, and feel proud of having had him as a friend once. If only he had done what I later did—together, the two of us would have done great things.

We were made to pray before supper, and any of the boys caught mumbling their prayers instead of showing genuine devotion were deprived of their pudding after the meal. So we learned to pray loudly and with zeal.

A few weeks after I was in the home, I felt restless, hot and closed in. At the risk of waking the others in my room, I rose, and putting on my clothes went downstairs through the dining-hall and outside. It was cool outside, with a light wind blowing from the south. I thought first of just walking around the garden, but there was a chance Mrs. McGilvray might still be up and see me, so I scaled the fence around the grounds, and was out on the road. I knew I was breaking a strict house regulation, but figured I could make it to the highway junction and back without being missed.

I was nearing the intersection where our street met the main highway, when a gasoline truck came roaring around the right-of-way circle. He was coming too fast, and halfway around the circle one of his rear wheels hit the outside curb of the concrete ring which bordered the island. The truck lurched and swayed, but continued driving on. The safety hatch on its tank trailer snapped open with a pop I could hear, and a sheet of gasoline sprayed the street. The truck driver hadn't noticed, for in a minute he was gone down the right-of-way into the city.

I could smell the gasoline now, and hurried forward in the darkness. However, before I reached the intersection, a car came in the same direction the tanker had taken. As the car passed over the wet street, one of its passengers must have tossed a lit cigarette out of the window, for no sooner had the vehicle cleared the intersection than the street burst into flame with a dull *whoosh*. I was fascinated by the heat and light the burning gasoline made, and was hardly aware of cars drawing up from all directions—the shouting and hurrying of people in a panic.

"Pull the fire-box—hurry!" someone shouted from a distance, and someone near me shouted back, "Where is the alarm box?"

One of the people in that crowd must have known the location of the box, because a fire truck soon appeared, with lights flashing and siren slowly wailing into silence. The darkly caped firemen played a hose on the street, covering the burning gasoline with a milky foam. It was all over with, and I was just about to leave, when a firm hand gripped my shoulder and turned me around.

It was the fat cook of a house-mother at the welfare home, Mrs. McGilvray.

"What are you doing out here?" she hissed through her teeth, and her left eye looked hard into mine. I opened my mouth to explain, but couldn't get the words out.

She pressed my shoulder hard now, and I nearly shouted with the pain. Then she led me down the road back to the home. When we reached the grounds, she unlocked the gate and motioned me through. I waited for her as she locked up. When she pocketed the key, she stepped in front of me, and very casually, as if it were part of the locking-up procedure, she struck me across the face with the back of her hand.

My eyes felt as if they would fly out of my head, and I felt dizzy and sick to the stomach.

"You pig! You big, dirty, overfed, ugly old pig!" I screamed at her when I felt steadier on my feet.

She struck me again, this time a double-handed blow over the head, and I fell to my knees. She sure knew how to hit. Try as I would to cover my head with my hands, she always found an unprotected part of my cheeks or temple at which to slap and punch. I was dazed with pain, and my nose ran as if my head had sprung a leak. I took my hands off my head and reached for her leg. Getting a firm hold, I sank my teeth deep into her ankle. I thought I heard her shout, but I'm not sure, for everything began spinning, and I fainted.

I was not allowed to school the following morning or for three mornings after, as my face was cut and swollen. But she woke me with the others all the same. I was taken off field work and ordered to clean the hallways leading to the central washrooms. I scrubbed, but when the day ended I could not eat, for even walking made me ill to the stomach.

As I scrubbed and rescrubbed the same floors day after day, I plotted my escape for the time when I felt strong enough to do so.

My opportunity came on the fourth night following my beating. It was easy. Our sleeping quarters were on the second floor of the building, directly over the dining-hall. Mrs. McGilvray had her apartment behind the dining-hall, alongside the kitchen, and facing into the field, away from the road. From her apartment, Mrs. McGilvray put out our lights at nine o'clock on days preceding school, and at ten on Friday and Saturday nights. As this was a Thursday, the lights went out early, but I lay wide awake, listening to the whispers of the boys in my room.

I had wanted to tell Dave of my plans, to urge him to go with me. But I was afraid he might betray my intentions. Yet there had been moments during the evening when I felt he must know. After supper, he had wandered away in the direction of the north porch, which had been rebuilt into a small, cold library. I went after him, but in the reading-room a group of boys had gathered, and there was no privacy.

Now it was night, and the lights had gone out. I lay in the dark, listening, and trembling with fear.

"Quiet, you guys, I wanna sleep." I tried to make my voice sound weary. Soon the whispers died, and there was such a silence I could hear the roar of traffic on the distant highway.

I was able to count the sleepers in my room—almost tell them apart by the sleep sounds they made. I thought perhaps Dave might be awake, suspecting I was leaving.

"Dave." I formed the word with my lips, but could not bring myself to say it.

I waited for about a half hour to make certain they were asleep before I stirred. Then I got out of bed and dressed very quietly. Taking my shoes in my hand, I tiptoed to the window and pushed it up. It made a scraping sound and I flattened against the curtain. Two beds down, someone mumbled and turned. Afraid I was detected, I quickly climbed over the sill of the window and jumped out, landing in the soft garden earth outside. The dining-room window opened on the garden, and glancing inside I saw the light under the door of Mrs. McGilvray's apartment. There was no time to waste, so I went across that garden at a gallop. Only after I had scaled the fence did I stop long enough to get my shoes on and laced tightly.

And after that I ran—faster and longer than I had ever run before. I ran through back lanes, blindly and in a panic of fear—going to no particular place, just running away from the last one as fast as I could. I ran over people's lawns and between houses. Fortunately, I met no one in my flight, or the entire city would have been alarmed by me.

And as I ran, I cursed. I cursed the fat cook of a house-mother. I cursed my aunt and my mother, and Tom Whittles, and the preacher, and the under-handed pig of a cop, Corporal Kane. I cursed the grey-haired man in a brown suit who didn't like dirty kids. One day! One day I would look them up, and then they would know what it was like to be taken from the hills and brought to a welfare home where they beat you and made you work like a slave!

There was no end to the city. Like one huge cement anthill, it stretched forever. And yet, I ran out of it—out of the lawns and row houses, the lonely street lights that looked down at me like filthy old men, the rickety ware-houses with bottled-up anger in their small windows. I was on the highway, running from the last street lamp, with only the long white lines showing on the hard road before me. Still running, I pointed my finger and shouted at each white marker on the road. My chest was burning and my lips cracked with thirst.

I stopped and sat down on the pavement to rest. I could go no further this way. My head wobbled, and my shoulders pressed hard on my body. Loosening my shoes, I wiped my forehead with the sleeve of my shirt.

Behind me, the glow of the city rose into the sky, yet I had lost any distinct, individual light. I then turned to look down the highway into the countryside. Some distance away, I thought I could see a faint light twinkling. Feeling terribly thirsty now, I got up and walked towards this light.

FOUR

I walked past the strong-smelling gasoline pumps and pushed open the door of the brightly lit coffee-bar. The man was turned away from me when I entered. He was wiping glasses and arranging them on a shelf. One of those bony, thin people he was, with a shirt that hung loose off his sharp shoulders. His pants were buckled tight and crinkled all around him as if they were pulled in by a drawstring. I sat down on a stool at the counter and waited.

He turned a long, hungry face to me and his eyes widened. They were soft eyes, almost like those of a woman, and blue in colour. I noticed with surprise how out of place his heavy lips were in that sharp, dry face.

"Yessirree, son?" he spoke, but I only stared at him stupidly. I thought he smiled ever so little, and then he walked away and filled a glass with Coke and ice.

"You been hit by a car, son?" he asked, when he placed the fizzing glass in front of me.

I shook my head, for my throat was dry and hot and I couldn't make a sound. He returned to his work, and I drank the Coke greedily. When I finished, I felt cool and good again.

"Thanks!" I said. "Thanks a lot!"

He continued with his work. Only when he had put away the last glass did he turn again and walk toward where I sat. He wiped his hands slowly, looking me up and down carefully as he did so.

"Now, where you going and why?" he asked in a firm voice. "You'd better tell me all about it before I call an ambulance and the cops, or just take it in my mind to kick the shit out of you for trying to pull a fast one on me."

I told him the story, but only from the time I was brought to the orphanage. I didn't feel he needed to know about the hills where I was raised, or about Aunt Matilda and my mother and pa. Even if he had wanted to know, I couldn't explain to him, for I no longer knew the truth of what I had seen and lived through. But he didn't ask. After I finished my story, he lit a cigarette and looked at me a long time. Yet he wasn't examining me any more—he knew I had not lied when I spoke. He was just thinking.

"How old are you?" he asked, after a few minutes so silent I could hear the buzz of the tube lights in the ceiling.

"Fourteen."

"Kinda big for your age, ain't you?"

"My ma used to say I growed like a weed."

"What's your name?"

"Snit Mandolin."

"Snit—that's a nice name—different, too. Mine's Pete—Pete Olson." He leaned forward towards me, and his clear, woman's eyes were excited.

"Listen carefully, Snit. They'll be looking high and low for you, because they're responsible. But"—his face broke into a broad, crinkly smile—"I ain't one to help keep an animal or a kid caged against its wish. I can't do much for you, but if you want to stay with me here and help out, you're welcome to. I can't pay you wages 'cause the place don't bring that much in, but you'll get food and clothing, and if business is good, there'll be a little extra. Also learn a trade for the time you're old enough to step out on your own. Means a lot, that. But mind, you're not to talk to anyone about yourself, or I'll have my neck in a noose good. Just say I'm your uncle or something, if anyone asks you. But best you don't talk at all."

Pete had two gasoline pumps in front of his place, and a garage for minor repairs and servicing. Back of the garage, adjoining the kitchen, was a little room in which he kept small auto parts and dry confectionery. I slept on the floor of this room the first night. The next day, Pete brought me a cot and bedding. I helped him move the other stuff out and get the room cleaned for my own.

Working for Pete was hard, and the hours were long. He had a home in the city, so I was left alone when the garage and coffee-bar were closed for the night. He was his own boss, yet he seldom closed before midnight, and was open before eight in the morning. But I enjoyed working for him. He taught me how to operate the pumps and count change on gasoline and oil sales. Then he taught me to change tires and do quick tune-ups on a sluggish carburetor, as well as oil changes and lube jobs. I worked hard and learned quickly. Before winter came, Pete seldom had to go outside to help me.

One afternoon things were slow for a few minutes, and I joined Pete in the bar for a coffee. A big car came on the tarmac, but it stopped short of the pumps, so I waited for the driver to come in. He was one of those guys who can always find ways of giving you trouble—a fat, red-faced, round-bellied guy with mean eyes and a soggy cigar stuck between his teeth. That's the type who breathe down your neck when you're trying to work, and who always pretend to know the other fellow's job inside out.

"Ya got a mechanic on duty?" he asked loudly as he came through the door. "I got a wobble in my front end, and I wanna adjustment."

Before I could catch myself, I turned and took a fast look at his gut-bag. I couldn't choke back a grin, so I stuck my face back into my coffee mug. Pete saw the look on my face, because he coughed hard before he could reply.

"Mr. Snit will see to your car." Pete nodded in my direction and winked.

"That kid! G'wan—I wanna mechanic—some joe who knows one end of a car from the other!"

"Mr. Snit is a very capable mechanic," Pete's voice became pretty hard. I looked up, and saw that his face had set like he was sporting for a fight. Fat Boy backed down.

"Aw, awright. But he better do a good job."

I didn't mind the fat bugger breathing down my neck as I jacked up the car and started in on aligning his wheels. I worked fast, but carefully, for I wanted Pete to be proud at having trusted me. When I finished and brought the car down, Fat Boy grunted and took it for a run up and down the tarmac. He stopped on the far side, on the highway entrance, and called me over.

"Say, kid—you're all right! Works like a charm! Say—that guy sure stuck by you when I got salty. What's he like—y'know—sweet on ya? Ya can tell me, I got an open mind. He is a queer, ain't he?"

I didn't know what the hell he was talking about, but I didn't like the oily smile he was giving me. I didn't know what to say, so I just stood there looking at him. He got pretty uncomfortable, and his face became redder.

"Awright, so it's none of my business. Here—betcha he don't pay you much. Here! This is for you—don't tell him I gave it to ya!" He pulled out a wad of money from his pocket, and peeling off a five-dollar bill, stuck it out to me. Then he went into the coffee-bar to pay the repair charge to Pete.

I didn't tell Pete about the tip, and it sort of bothered me. I put the money in a cigar-box which I kept under my bed, along with other tips I got from folks from time to time during the three years I stayed and worked with Pete. But if Pete knew, he never let on, for which I was grateful; but it still bothers me not telling him.

Pete was good on getting me things. Once a month, he use to bring me a new shirt or sweater, or a new pair of slacks. I took good care of these clothes, and wore the garage coveralls almost all the time. A few times he bought me books, but as he never read himself, he wasn't much on these. The ones he gave me were baby books, with pictures and big type you could read a block away. At Christmas time, when calendars came from his suppliers, he used to tack them up himself in my room, and it gave a lot of colour. Almost felt like my room had been repainted.

We didn't talk much, for most days we were apart and busy, and at nights I wanted to get to bed first off. Mornings, I got up before he came in, and I would light the fires under the coffee urns for him, as well as grease and heat the hotcake iron. A fleet of trucks coming in from Saskatoon would pull in between eight and nine each morning, and the drivers would come in for breakfast. Pete had his hands full getting the breakfasts prepared before the men arrived, so I ran the pumps and service garage on my own in the mornings.

Pete appreciated my getting things set up for him in the coffee-shop. Each morning he'd wag his head with surprise and smile at me as he took his coat off and put on his white apron.

"Snit, you're quite a boy for get-up-and-go in the morning! Tell you what—one of these nights we're gonna lock up early and go on the town—just you and me."

And he lived up to his promise—about a year after I was with him. We closed up at six and I changed into my neat new clothes. Then we drove into town to see a picture called *How Green Was My Valley*. The thought of going into town no longer frightened me. We even drove past the welfare home, and I pressed my face against the car window to see into the fields. A group of boys were burning leaves, and I saw Mr. Swanson among them, leaning on his stick and watching. But the boys were too far away and I couldn't tell if they were new ones, or the fellows I had known. Then we were in the heart of the city, and Pete parked his car across the street from the theatre.

I ate three boxes of popcorn during the picture, and felt thirsty and sad. Pete just lay back in his seat and slept right through the movie. When I had seen the cartoon and news for the second time, I woke him, and we went to the coffee-bar in the theatre lounge, and Pete treated me to a strawberry milkshake.

"Good picture, wasn't it, Snit? Sure beats me how they can think up all them stories—and then you see them like that and could swear you was there and lived it all." He yawned.

"Yep," I said, and drank my milkshake. I was sort of hoping he might take me to his home so I could see what it was like. But he didn't. After I finished my drink, he drove me back to the garage and we never went out again.

Then came the third summer—hot and windy. Business was lighter than usual, and when our mail came, I watched Pete gloomily study his many bills, then toss them into a box behind the coffee counter.

"Jesus Christ! If a war don't come soon, the whole country's going to go bust!" he'd growl as he poured us a coffee each. Few cars stopped at the pumps any more, which made me wonder—where in hell do people buy their gas and oil when times get bad? The same number of cars were still passing by on the highway, yet our business was down. I asked Pete about it.

"Credit," he said. "The big guys can afford to give credit. You know—'Fill 'er up now, and pay me next month.' Me, I can't give no credit even to myself."

Pete was a funny sort of guy when he got to talking. The way he figured it, a war would fix everything just right.

"Ya ever been in a war, Pete?" I asked, as I swallowed from the steaming coffee-cup, and then wished I hadn't, for it was like a furnace outside and the coffee burned all the way down my throat. Pete looked at me surprised-like.

"Me? In a war? Are you kidding? I couldn't fight my way out of a wet paper bag!"

"Then what for you want a war?"

"I dunno. It always seems to straighten things out. I dunno how these things work—it's the Jews that run the world—they got it all figured, and they work it just right for themselves. It's guys like you and me that's got to suffer."

"Ya ever known a Jew?" I asked on my second swallow.

"Naw—I never met a Jew in my life. Why did you ask that for?"

When the wind and heat got bad, a lot of dirt and dry weeds got blown on the tarmac around the pumps. I used to sweep up at first, but it didn't do any good, for the wind just carried the muck back as soon as I finished. Hosing the place down with water would have helped, but Pete didn't want the expense of pumping any more water than he had to have for the coffee-bar. So when the weather got really hot, I used to go into my room and lie down to get away from the sun and dust.

I was lying stretched out on my bed one afternoon, rubbing the toes of my moist socks back and forth across the bedrail and thinking of nothing at all. Pete had been coming and going without a word to me lately. He'd show up for a few hours in the morning. Then the telephone would ring and he'd answer it. Just like that, off would come his apron and on with his tweed sports coat.

"Keep the homestead together, Snit! I got some business in town!" he'd shout over his shoulder as he ran for his car. He'd gone off that way this morning.

So I lay in bed, thinking of nothing at all when I heard Pete clear his throat, and I looked up to see him standing in my doorway. His long face was wet with sweat. He was worried and uncomfortable, and kept his eyes down on his feet.

"Snit," he said, and bent down to brush some lint off his pants, "I guess I better tell you now as tomorrow. I sold the business."

I didn't understand what he said for a moment and just grinned back at him. Then it hit me.

"What ya mean? Ya mean you and I aren't gonna be here no more?" I said, jumping to my feet.

Pete really got bothered, and turned away from me as if to go out.

"Yep," he said over his shoulder. "I'm thinking of moving on to the coast and buy a little store some place. Hours are too long and lonely here, and I'm not a young man anymore. You'll do all right, Snit. You're bright and handy with your hands. Betcha anything you'll get another job like nothing at all."

"But Pete! I wanna go with you—can't I?" I was scared clean through.

He didn't say anything, but I could tell by the way he hung his head and rested himself with one arm against the door-frame that he didn't want me any more.

"When I gotta go?" I asked.

"Any time you like."

He turned towards me, and it sort of shook me to see the tears in his eyes.

"I got something here for you, Snit—not much, but it's all I can afford, and it'll help you."

He fumbled in his shirt pocket and brought out an envelope, which he handed me. Without thinking on what I was doing, I opened it right there and then. Inside was a cheque for three hundred dollars.

I didn't even thank Pete. I didn't remember to. With everything in my life suddenly turned inside out, I had no way or desire of telling or showing Pete what I thought. It was no good my hanging around watching him close the station down, so that same day I got my things together and packed for him to ship out.

"Where you planning to go?" he asked me over breakfast the next morning. I was dressed in a white shirt and my pants were nicely pressed. I had laid them out under my mattress and slept over them during the night to take the wrinkles out.

"Think I'll head out for the old home place."

"What? Into the hills?"

I nodded.

"You're stupid!" Pete was staring hard at me. "What you gonna do in that hell-forsaken place? I hear you can't even grow potatoes there!"

"That's a lie!" I argued. "We used to grow lots of potatoes—and barley so tall I used to get lost in it as a kid."

"Big deal!" Pete laughed. "I can drive you around to a few garages I know, and we'll find you a job for wages in no time at all. Put in eight or nine hours a day, and you're your own boss with money in the pocket and no worries in the world. Come on—finish your grub and we'll take a drive."

I was going back to the hills or nowhere at all, and I told Pete so. He rose from his stool, threw his arms apart, and blew a long whistle of air through his lips.

"Suit yourself—you're a man now," he said. Then he loaded what things I could carry into his car, and drove me through the city. When we reached the highway leading to my home town, I told him this would be far enough, and he stopped the car.

"Good luck, Pete!" was all I could say to him.

"I'll ship the rest of your things by bus. See ya!" He turned in the middle of the highway and drove back into town.

About an hour later, I hitched a lift with a gravel truck which was going right through to my town. By this time the wind had come up, hot and dusty. I slept much of the way, one of those neck-sore sleeps with my head thrown back over the dirty shoulder-rest of the seat. It was a ride on clanging tools and with crushing bumps, but I didn't mind, for I was going home and I was tired.

When we reached town, my head ached from the heat and my throat burned with thirst. Across the street, swinging in the wind, was the faded board sign, "Elsie's Coffee Shop & Eats."

I had arrived.

Aunt Matilda was suspicious as hell of me.

"How long you figuring on staying?" she demanded over breakfast. "And why did you come back?"

I didn't really know, so I said nothing and kept eating with my face pretty close to the table. She left her chair and rummaged about in an old coffee tin which stood on a shelf above the stove. She came back with a soiled piece of paper, which she unfolded as she sat down.

I had been watching her all morning, with shock and fear, for in the light of day her appearance upset me as much as it had when I first saw her last night. What little flesh was left in her face had knotted and dried into short cords, as if she had been roasted by some fire, put out into the sun to dry, and then roasted again, until every drop of moisture in her body was evaporated.

This wasn't my Aunt Matilda—I never met this woman before. She wasn't even a woman. Yet with a heavy heart I knew there was no mistake, for if the aunt I remembered was no more, it was only because she had become what my mother and father had become in the end—broken on the earth like pieces of rotten wood by the cowardly greed of these hungry hills.

"This here paper, boy," she began, "was the will your mother made out before she passed on. I ain't got no quarrel with anyone, but she didn't know what become of you, or if you were ever coming back. So when we got her into town with the last attack, she called for the preacher Crowe and for a policeman to be her witnesses. The preacher didn't come, but the policeman made out this paper which she signed."

My aunt stuck the paper at me, and it trembled in her weak hand.

"Read it!"

I didn't want to read it. I knew what it said, so I pushed her hand away from me.

"With her own hand your mother signed this paper, and it says that this land and everything on it belongs to me, her sister," Aunt Matilda now had the will close to her face. "So if you're thinking of making any claims or moving me out, you'd just better know where you stand, Snit Mandolin!"

She leaned toward me, staring hard into my face.

"You've changed, Snit. You don't even look much like us Mandolins, and I don't like it. I don't know you no more."

The cold hostility and fear were fading from her eyes. But just as quickly, they became fired and intense with a hidden fever.

"Listen to me, Snit!" she said in a hoarse whisper. "If you wanna work the place and help me out, I won't be saying anything to you, or asking you to go! Just so long as you don't intend making trouble. I don't want no trouble. But if you try starting anything first or behind my back, I'll grind you into dust! D'you understand?" She slammed her dry, small fist hard on the table. I looked at her, and saw that she was scared—real scared. I rose from my bench and walked to the door.

"Where you goin' now?" Aunt Matilda demanded in a shrill voice.

"I don't know," I replied, and stepped out into the sun-baked yard.

I wanted to have a smoke. Pete had given me cigarettes from the coffee-shop for nothing. I smoked very little, but now I felt I needed something to cheer me and take my mind off this desolation and suspicion. I crossed the yard to the road, and turned in the direction of the store.

The road felt quite warm under my feet even though it was still morning. My shoes sank into the loose dust, and became ashen-grey after a few steps. The sky was a roof of hot lead. There would be no rain this day—if anyone had asked me for an opinion, I would have said there would be no rain the rest of this summer. Yet the fields had some greenery to them—and the barley, though short in height, was turning a pale golden colour. But the pastures were dry and wilted.

I saw cows wandering over the parched earth in search of grazing grass, swishing the sandflies off their backs with their tails and mooing sadly. I had never seen cattle so bony and hungry-looking before.

Short of Whittles' store, the road dipped and rose through a slight hollow. The air was cooler here, and I began to walk faster. A red-faced farmer, with a high thatch of grey hair on his head, was walking toward me with a shovel over his shoulder. He was grinning as he approached, but when he came near enough to see me, the smile faded from his face and he turned away from me. After I passed him, I turned quickly, and saw him hurrying away without a backward glance. I knew him—George Webster. "The Law of the Land," folks called him. That's because he always used this expression in an argument. Like the time Shnitka's Jersey cow broke pasture and wandered into Webster's yard. Webster tied a rope around its neck and led the cow back to Shnitka.

"The law of the land sez ya gotta keep your stock fenced in proper, Shnitka," Webster warned. "Don't let it happen again!"

George Webster had spent all his spare time wandering up and down the road to our community. He was a sort of one-man maintenance outfit, filling in deep ruts in the road and covering culverts with ditch clay so's the rain wouldn't get at them to rot them. In the spring he was busiest, for then he used to open up ditches to drain the run-off water.

"Ya must be a rich bugger, all the money ya make from the gov'ment on road work," someone would say.

Webster would look hard not only at the person who said that, but at the neighbours who stood around listening with grins on their faces.

"There are those who do their best to make life better, and there are others," he would say in a big voice. "I do what I can, and I do it for nothing. But the law of the land says all men are rewarded for their labours, and one day I will get paid."

"Maybe they'll give you a pension when you get old and shaky, and you'll end up being a somebody after all!" they would laugh, and Webster would walk away. Not because they made jokes at him, but because they spoke of old age, and George Webster was afraid of growing old. It bothered him. When Reverend Crowe gave a sorrowful sermon on the waste of passing life, folks listened thoughtfully, with their heads bent low. Except George Webster, who scratched at his heavy red neck, and ran his fingers through his white hair in fear.

He used to play catch-ball around the store on Sunday afternoons, and some mornings he could be seen running fast down the road, trying to keep the juices of youth high in his body.

He didn't marry, although folks had a story about how he tried. The story went that he used to buy magazines and answer the ads from lonely women that they contained. He was supposed to have received a letter of reply from some woman in Three Rivers, Quebec, in which she enclosed a picture of herself riding an elephant during her missionary days in India. My mother had seen the picture.

"She looks nice and young, but the picture itself is very old," mother said. "Besides, what's Webster want with a woman who rides elephants?"

Whether Webster had these same thoughts, or whether he had other thoughts of his own, he did not mail-order himself a wife, but remained single.

In my own way, I had felt pleased to see him. He was one of the many objects, dead and living, of home—like stones by the roadside, broken fences, cattle losing tufts of winter fur, a man limping with weariness, or a bunch of weed blown in a ball across a field. Yet he had not been pleased to see me, and this both amused and bothered me as I approached the general store.

A kid who grows up without a proper home or family grows up quickly. Early in life I had learned that a loud noise attracted attention from folks around me, those who liked me as well as those who didn't. So I pounded my heels hard on the short board walk that stuck out like a dry tongue from the doorway of Whittles' store in the direction of the road. The building was old and warped, with clapboard siding which had never been painted and was now the colour of the surrounding fields. I pushed the door open with difficulty, for it dragged on the floor.

I saw Whittles at the far end of the counter which stretched the length of the store. He was placing bars of laundry soap on a shelf. Even turned away from me as he was, I noticed he had become heavier since I last saw him.

I slammed the door shut with a bang, and Tom Whittles turned with a frown on his round face.

"Where in goddam hell do you think—" he began to say, then he saw me and the colour left his face. His lips were still open, but instead of speaking, he lifted his arm and pointed a pudgy finger in my direction, as if accusing me of something, or trying to order me out of the building.

"I wanna package of Exports," I said quietly.

For a long while he didn't move. Then the colour began creeping back into his cheeks and temples, and he took a step towards me, his finger still pointing in my direction.

"Gimme some cigarettes." I started to get sore. "Come on, I haven't got all day."

He reached the part of the counter directly in front of me now, and with a crooked smile twisting his face, he reached out to shake my hand.

"Snit! How are ya, boy? Sure glad to see ya back—so big and strong-looking! Boy! Ya've sure grown some!" His words tripped over one another like a bunch of clumsy pups learning to walk.

"Boy—will folks hereabouts be surprised and pleased when I tell them you're back, Snit! And wait 'til Reverend Crowe hears the news. Ya'll be a great help to us now, coming back from where it was ya were! Folks hereabouts, or what's left of them, have sorta drifted away from parish life!"

He turned to get my cigarettes. He was so rattled, the veins on the back of his neck twitched. To rattle him double, I paid him for the cigarettes by giving him the cheque which Pete had paid me with, and which I still had not cashed.

Tom Whittles picked it up and examined it closely, shaking his head with disbelief.

"I can't handle that, Snit—I haven't got stock in the store worth that much. Pay me some other time when ya've got smaller money," he said, handing the cheque back to me. I dug around in my pockets and found the right change for the cigarettes.

Whittles came from behind the counter to see me to the door. I was about to leave when a thought came to mind.

"Say," I said, turning around, "I just remembered something! Reverend Crowe—that's the guy! He was the preacher who looked like you, and who busted his ass to get me sent away—also drove my Aunt Matilda nutty with his holy baloney."

The grin Whittles had managed to work up blew off as if I'd slapped him in the face. For a moment I thought he was going to burst into tears. He looked just like a big, fat kid who'd taken one helluva beating, and had nobody to tattle to.

"If ya'll be seeing Reverend Crowe soon, then tell him I said he can go fuck himself! And you, Whittles, go fuck yourself too—twice!" I yanked the door out of his hand and slammed it as hard as I could.

Out on the road I felt good, like I could take on anything and come out a winner. Everything was sawdust and fear here in the hills. With three hundred bucks in my pocket I was accomplished, grown up and rich—and nobody was ever going to spit in my eye again.

The sun was rising fast now, and the morning had become hot and dusty. I walked off the powdery road, and found the tufts of grass growing near the ditch much cooler and more comfortable to the feet. When I reached the boundary of my aunt's farm, I did not go towards the house, but cut off to approach the buildings from behind, and so have a look at the fields.

These no longer reflected Aunt Matilda's industry. The land was badly plowed, and the barley she had sown was late and parched with improper cultivation. Weeds grew everywhere, and what harvest she would get this year wouldn't even pay for the binder twine she would have to purchase. I skirted the first hill and made my way to the pasture. There were only two cows, skinny and unfreshened. She had fenced off one corner of the pasture for the two horses she must have bought since I was away. They were in very bad condition, and were just now losing their winter shag. Worst of all, the four animals appeared to have had no water for a few days.

I opened the pasture gates, and they trotted towards the house and the watering-trough.

Walking after them in the direction of the farmstead, I tried to reckon on how much money would be required to get the farm functioning again, but all my planning only depressed me. I could easily see the three hundred dollars I carried being swallowed up with hardly a thing to show for the bother.

If only it would rain, then any gamble might pay off. I would get nowhere discussing my plans with Aunt Matilda, for her mind was dimmed now. There was no telling how she would react or how the best plans would be shadowed by the private terrors with which she lived.

The sky was milky, with a sun so hot it burned my naked arms and face as if a hot iron was held near the skin.

If only it would rain …

FIVE

I was tired, but I couldn't sleep. So I found a very old copy of the *Family Herald and Weekly Star* in the rubbish under my bed and brought it to the kitchen to read. Aunt Matilda is sitting in front of the kitchen stove, peering at the flames which showed through a crack in the burning chamber. She was rocking back and forth in her chair, nodding her head to a maddening, constant rhythm. The heat of the stove combined with the warmth of the sunscorched walls to make the room almost unbearable.

I opened the buttons of my soggy shirt, and putting my feet on the kitchen table, settled down to read. My aunt turned her face from the stove and studied my feet for a while, then her gaze moved to my face. I could feel her looking at me—her stare seemed to give off a peculiar heat of its own, which made the moisture run from my hair down the back of my neck.

"Whatcha staring at me for?" I muttered, but got no reply. I looked up at her, and noticed with shock that her eyes were blank and mirror-like, almost like the eyes of a cat peering into light. She hadn't heard me—I don't think she was even aware I was in the room. All the same, I felt uneasy and brought my feet off the table.

There was a knock on the door, and I almost jumped out of my chair. Aunt Matilda also came out of her reverie, and a scowl darkened her thin face.

"You expecting someone?" she asked me suspiciously, but made no move to open the door.

"Yeh, yeh—I'm expecting the Prime Minister to drop in for a cup of coffee!" I said testily, for I was finding her moods and suspicions just a bit wearing. She was queer, in a way which scared me and made me mad all at the same time. The knock came again, stronger now, and Aunt Matilda rose to her feet. Wrapping her head scarf about her shoulders, even though the night was a living heat, she left for her bedroom, closing the door after her.

I felt bad for having spoken mean to her, and got up to go after her and apologize. But the knock came again.

"Hi, Snit—ya sleepin'?" Johnny Swift stepped through the door I had opened, and blinked his eyes at the kitchen lamp.

"Sit down." I waved my hand to the chair Aunt Matilda had sat in. He was sweating in great beads which rolled down the sides of his face and gathered in the pink folds of his throat.

"How ya doin', kid?" He grinned up at me as I found two cups and poured tea for both of us. He drank his cupful with one gulp and pushed it out for a refill.

"You gonna bugger up your liver drinkin' that fast," I said.

He looked at me with surprise. "I didn't know that. Where's a guy's liver anyhow?" I didn't know. He drank his second cupful with less haste and sat back in his chair and rolled himself a cigarette. "Anyone else in?"—he motioned towards my aunt's bedroom. I nodded and he scraped his chair nearer the table.

"Snit, whatcher plannin' to do here?" he asked almost casually as if it didn't concern him, but his voice was low and secretive now and his eyes were excited. "This backwoods farm don't even buy ya clothes for yore ass."

"I reckon it don't at that. I just haven't made up my mind about anything, Johnny." He took a long puff on a cigarette, watching me, then he leaned forward in his chair, his eyes narrow.

"I wanna talk to ya, Snit—but ya gotta promise nobody don't hear what I say. I got a few things goin' for hard cash, but ya gotta keep as tight as a nail in a board about it—like my old man. He has a good idea what's goin' on, but I told him I'd snap his head off his neck if he squealed, and he don't tell anyone the time of day since. So ya gotta promise to keep it under yore hat!"

The lamplight flared between us for a moment and then fell to its faint yellow glow. In that light, I got a very good look at Johnny Swift. When I rode in from town with him a few days ago, I had somehow thought his face still had the softness of childhood about it. But I was wrong, very wrong. The soft babyish fat I thought I had seen about his cheekbones was gone. In its place he had the loose flesh which comes of not sleeping properly.

He seemed round and deceptively gentle, but his deeply imbedded eyes were sharp and hard. Yet this was a contradiction of his manner, which was boyish and awkward. His easy, mischievous smile—the fine fuzz on his cheeks and all the dirt—suggested a good-natured boy. But sitting across the kitchen table from me now was another Johnny Swift—a darker man who was growing up below the surface of skin and cloth.

I had seen his face before, on a spark-plug salesman who came to the garage one day and sold Pete three cartons of defective plugs, which we had to spill into a garbage bucket when car owners we sold the first sets to returned with complaints. This same salesman was arrested ten months later attempting to hold up a supermarket in Calgary. I saw his picture in the paper—a nice, round-faced, jolly sort of fellow you can grow up with and never know a thought going through his head.

"You know me, Johnny. Whatcha got in mind?" I asked.

"It's this way, Snit," Johnny looked sideways at Aunt Matilda's door. "Ya can't make any pocket dough growin' barley, milkin' cows or raisin' stupid hogs. An' if ya don't have hard cash in yore pocket, ya don't have a goddamn thing! Now you've been around. Them places ya been to ain't no church picnics—although it's in jail a guy really gets to know which end is up. That damned Tom Whittles is blowin' his wind about how he seen a three-hundred-buck-cheque on ya. When I heard that, I thought to myself, 'Old Snit's been around—he knows the ropes!' So I come down to talk to ya, and see what I could do to help ya."

His cigarette had gone out. As he relit with another match, which he struck against the leg of his pants, I noticed his face sweating until his cheeks seemed to crawl with moisture. His jaw was closed tight, and little muscles in the upper parts of his throat twitched with nervousness.

"I got some cash, Snit. I ain't got no three hundred bucks like you got. But I got some stashed away that my old man nor nobody else in these parts knows about—because I'm smart, and I ain't gonna show my hand and have questions asked about me. Ya understand, don't ya, Snit?"

I didn't know what the hell he was talking about, and told him so. He cleared his throat and leaned forward until I could feel his hot breath on my face.

"I'm in moonshine, boy—right up to here!" he said in a voice hardly more than a whisper, and indicating his neck with a dirty finger.

"What are ya saying? Ya making and peddling the stuff?"

He nodded with a sly smile.

"How in hell—don't the mounties get on to ya?"

Johnny wiped his brow with his arm.

"Ya're damned right they know it's being made and sold in a pretty big way. But how they gonna nail me? I got a good head on me—they don't know who makes the stuff. So they're sittin', waitin' for me to make a wrong move. They can't get me movin' the stuff out, 'cause they'd have to go through every wagon of cream cans and potatoes the local yokels haul into town. If they missed on the first wagon they searched, they'd miss on all the others—you know how word travels when somethin' happens! An' the day they start searchin' wagons, Johnny Swift's wagon is gonna turn around and go home. Oh no, Corporal Kane has more upstairs than to go searchin' folks. Ya know what's he waitin' for?"

I admitted I didn't.

"They're waitin' for me to flash the cash. Ya know—like goin' into town and buyin' a pair of expensive horses at my age—or a better piece of farm machinery instead of the second-hand junk everyone here deals in. The cops know how much a man can buy farmin' gumbo in the hills, so if someone one day shows up with a couple hundred in pocket, they got him marked just like that! Then all Corporal Kane and his clucks gotta do is wait a coupla days—then take an easy drive to yore place one night and nip ya distillin' the stuff by the creek. Then bingo—three hundred bucks in fines, or ya go to jail, and some punk cop gets a pat on the head!"

"I still don't see what yore driving at." I was getting sore, because I didn't see what he was leading up to.

"I could use ya, Snit." Johnny's face was white now and strained with worry. "Folks know ya came with cash on ya—Whittles seen to that already. So why don't ya give me a hand in turnin' out and hawkin' the damned stuff? All ya gotta do is carry the cash on ya, and do any buyin' we make. Cops get nosy, and folks say, 'Oh yeh, the kid's been away three years and come back with a wad—lucky bugger!' So the cops get their noses off ya. Meanwhile, we save up and work as anybody else does durin' the day. When we got enough saved up, we light out and start some business of our own—and ta hell with the hills and all the ass-holes in 'em! Nobody can touch us then! Whatcha say, Snit?"

Everything he said came so hot and fast I had to think about it for a while, trying to foresee difficulties for us in a partnership of this kind. His ideas made sense all right. The land wouldn't grow wild grass in a dry year, least of all proper grain. As far as my future here with my Aunt Matilda went, I had about as much chance as a hog in a stonepile. Even trying to fatten the cattle for milk or meat was pretty hopeless and would chew up all the money I carried in no time flat.

"I'd like to think it over, Johnny," I said. "How do you think we gonna get on with one another—like, who's to see we don't try to do one another for the money we make?"

Johnny seemed disappointed.

"I dunno, Snit—whatever ya think is best by us is okay with me. I ain't aimin' to cheat ya. Ya wanna go fifty-fifty, we can split anythin' we get. I got some supplies but that don't matter—I ain't gonna charge ya for comin' in."

I could see Johnny was being pressed for someone to cover up, and I could drive any sort of deal I wanted. But the fifty-fifty split seemed okay by me. Johnny was as sweaty as an old horse now, what with not being sure if I was going along or not. He got up from his chair and came toward me with an outstretched hand. I shook it, and found his palm dead and sticky.

"Snit—if ya back out, ya promise ya won't say to nobody I saw ya?" he asked.

"Naw—don't worry!"

"Ya don't think the old crow heard us, do ya?" He pointed with his head to my aunt's bedroom door.

"Naw—she's out of it, probably asleep."

"Okay, Snit. Think it over and keep yore lips shut. I'll be out on the road tomorrow at this time, and ya can come and tell me what ya aim to do."

He left in a hurry, forgetting to close the kitchen door behind him.

I blew out the light and went outside to have a piss. The night was warm, and frogs croaked from the pond like they croaked all through my childhood. Only now I could smell the pond for what it had become—a small puddle of rotten, heavy mud. A slight wind blew across the hills from the west, and it had the same dry odour of scorched vegetation I had first noticed when I came into town on my return.

Only now it seemed stronger.

Next morning I ate a bowl of coarse cereal, and rose from the table immediately after to go out into the fields.

"Whatcha doin' now?" Aunt Matilda looked up from the table. She hadn't touched her food. I felt raw and edgy, and in no mood for company over an after-breakfast coffee.

"Nothin'—just goin' out," I said over my shoulder.

"If you're over for anything with Johnny Swift, then mind your step. He's a bad little bugger," my aunt warned.

It was still an early hour, but a brisk wind had started up. The short grain stalks had the dew blown off them even though the sun was still low over the hills to the east and the fields were in shadow.

I hadn't been able to sleep much for thinking about how I would work the harvest this summer. As I walked through the field, I pinched the forming heads on the barley and oats, but discovered only bran. The odd time when my thumbnail cut into a forming kernel of grain, it was pasty and small, and would not pay for the cutting and binding of it, not to mention the cost of threshing. I could see no other way out but to cut all the grain for hay and save money and labour later. In this way, it would at least provide the cattle and horses with roughage for the winter ahead.

When I reached the pasture, I tried to catch the horses. But I was strange to them, and they gave me a strong chase around the field. Both of them had halters on their heads, but no sooner I got within reach of their heads, they would snort and run from me. I finally cornered the older of the two—a large-hooved and lame Percheron. As I led him out of the pasture and towards the farm buildings, the other one followed. Quickly I got them into the barn and harnessed. On the way out, I took them to the well and gave them water. The well was in the yard in front of the house, and Aunt Matilda saw me. She came out and approached me, a puzzled expression on her face.

"What are you doing, Snit?" she asked sharply, her hands clutching at her coat.

"Hitching the team up to the mower and cutting down the grain for hay. It won't pay to keep it out there growin'," I replied.

"Snit Mandolin!" she exclaimed. "You get them harnesses off and stop your mucking about!"

"Listen, Aunt Matilda—I wanna tell ya—"

"Don't you go tellin' me nothing I don't know! There'll be rain in a few days, and the crop will come out strong and good as ever—so don't go ruining things! There'll be rain—you know there'll be rain! An' what right you got to go cutting *my* grain down without my say-so? I didn't ask you to come around with your high-flown ideas. I'm born to the land and worked to put that grain down while you were city-slickin' about! Now just take them harnesses off the horses and clear off—you hear me?"

She was shaking all over with anger, her eyes burning like she had a powerful fever, and her yellow-white hair hanging in loose strands about her bony shoulders. Her withered little hands were clenched into tight fists, which she raised toward me. She was of the land, all right—she proved it to me, for I could never feel this strongly about the goddamned dust and everything that grew out of it. But I also knew she was wrong; she was like a blind dog walking into a building which is burning up, not realizing every step in the direction he chooses brings him one step nearer to death and destruction. I thought of the bony, hunger-mooing cattle in the pasture.

"Shut up, Aunt Matilda! Get back into the house and stay there!" I didn't raise my voice, for I wasn't angry with her. I just had to get past her.

She stared at me in an odd sort of way, with her mouth open as if she were planning to say something, but didn't know where to begin. Then a cloud came over her sparkling eyes, and she turned quickly and went back into the house.

I led the horses back of the field shed, where the old mower had been left in a jungle of pig-weed and thistle. I examined the blades and found them rusted from exposure to the weather, but as I didn't have a file or sandpaper to clean them with, I proceeded to hitch the horses to the machine and try working it in the condition it was. When I pushed the clutch in, the mower did work, but it was hard pulling for the horses.

The farm had little sown to grain—only about forty acres in all, and half of the fields were hills, where the soil was sandy and hot and nothing except the hardiest weeds grew. So I cut the lower patches where there was some ground moisture and the grain grew as tall as a foot in some places. But it was slow work, for I had to stop often to rest the badly fed, lathery horses.

When the sun rose high the sand-flies blackened the air, giving the horses as much bother as pulling the sluggish mower did.

I scraped some grease off the mower axles and dabbed the mess around the noses of the animals, to keep the flies out. But it didn't do much good, and the horses suffered, with me not able to help them.

It took the best part of the day to get the cutting done. By now the lame Percheron was limping badly, and his smaller companion was dropping behind. But with the falling of the sun low over the hills to the west, the air cooled, for which I was grateful, because my neck and head ached with heat exposure. Then I cut through the last swath, and disengaging the mower, turned the stumbling, snorting horses toward the shed where the machine had been stored. Unhitching them, I led them back to the barn to remove their harnesses and brush them down. I found a bucket and went to the grain bin to get some oats for them.

The bin was empty, and the floor was littered with mouse droppings. So I took the horses back to pasture, and watching them walk away to graze, low-headed and weary, I cursed the futility of life.

"Goddamit!" I thought aloud. "If Johnny Swift got an easier way for a man to live in these parts, then I go the way of Johnny Swift. A man's gotta eat to live, and there won't be much eating from the work I do on this farm!"

The house was in darkness when I approached. Inside, the kitchen stove was cold and still held the pans and dishes of the morning meal. I lit the lamp and kindled the stove, then washed my face and head in cold water. Then I set about making a supper of fried eggs and tea.

The door to Aunt Matilda's bedroom was closed, and when I opened it, I saw her lying face downward on her bed.

"I got supper done," I told her. "Come on and eat with me."

She began sobbing into her pillow, and I approached her.

"Don't you hear me, Aunt Matilda—supper's ready."

I shook her by the shoulder, and she turned, fixing her red-rimmed eyes on my face. Then she rose quickly on an elbow and spat at me, after which she dropped her head back into the pillow and continued sobbing. I jumped back, feeling a disgust and a pity for her.

"I done what I thought was right—there's no other way," I stammered, but she lifted her hands to cover her ears.

I lost my stomach for food, and hurried outside and up the road to meet Johnny Swift.

The road was dark and silent. I stood listening, but all I could hear was the chirping of crickets on the hillsides.

"Johnny! Where ya hiding?" I called, but got no reply. I couldn't wait any longer—I had to find Johnny, so I ran north towards the Swift farm.

Johnny's place was two farms down from us, next to the Rogers', whose land bordered on Aunt Matilda's. Rogers and my aunt did not share a common boundary fence, however, for the road allowance ran between these two farms. The road itself had never been cut through, for the land on the far side away from the highway on which I hurried was wild, and nobody ever had reason to explore on the west side of all the farms which hung on the market road.

I was aiming to run all the way to the Swift farm, but I only got as far as the road allowance, for Johnny was waiting for me there. He was riding a horse, and holding another by the lead.

"Johnny!"

"Where in hell ya been this long? Thought ya'd never come," he said peevishly. The horses were restless, and turned circles on the dark, dusty road.

"I come as fast as I could."

"What's yore answer, Snit—ya comin' with me, or ain'tcha?" Johnny leaned towards me, but I could not see his face.

"Sure, I'm with ya, Johnny! All the way!"

"Get on!"

I mounted the spare horse. Before I could ask him where we were going, Johnny turned off the road into the overgrown road allowance, and rode west at a fast trot.

Johnny's still was set up in back of his father's farm, in a heavy clump of alder which grew where a bog had been in wetter years. It was impossible to walk through this jungle from the field side of the Swift farm, so we had to ride a detour some two miles long over the road allowance and then back to the bog through an abandoned farm which was now overgrown with bush.

"Why in hell didn't we walk through Rogers' farm?" I asked Johnny as I pulled my horse alongside his.

"Too risky," he said, glancing back over his shoulder. "Never know when Rogers might be creepin' around his farm—lookin' for mushrooms, maybe!"

Johnny laughed at his joke, but I didn't see anything funny. As soon as we left the road allowance and began back-tracking over the deserted farm, the horses seemed to follow instinctively a faint path through the waste and shrub. Reaching thicker bushes, Johnny stopped and dismounted.

"Okay, Snit—we tie the nags here and go the rest of the way on foot. Gets pretty soft ahead." And he led the way for the remaining distance.

Then we reached the place—a scooped-out hollow, completely overhung by alder branches. It was pitch dark here, musty and heavy with the smell of yeast and fermentation. Johnny lit a storm lantern and quickly draped a sack over it, so that only a thin panel of light shone on his equipment.

"Cripes! What a set-up!" I exclaimed, seeing the still and the fermentation cans.

"Yeh—nothin' can go wrong! Even if somebody was stupid enough to come here, he'd have to walk right in on my factory to find it. An' look at them branches, Snit—ya see any stars through them?"

I looked up, but could see nothing through the heavy alder branches and leaves.

"Even if the cops was birds they'd never spot me!" Johnny said with pride. Then he set about lighting a fire under the nearest fermenting-drum. As the flames caught, I saw his face in the flickering light. It was soaking with sweat, which gathered in little pools at the edges of his tightly closed lips.

He stood up and handed a bucket to me. "Here. About ten steps back through there ya'll find a water-hole. It smells like shit, but it's cold, and we gotta have cold water for the cooler. Fill up the bucket, and I'll set up the gear."

I found the pool all right, and Johnny hadn't exaggerated about how stagnant it was. When I returned, he had set up everything and was working a low, well-controlled fire under the distilling drum. I emptied the water I had brought into the cooling trough, and stood by watching him.

"Ya gotta have the fire just so. Make it too low, and ya steam all the booze off. Too high, and it pukes the yeast all through the fuckin' lines. Get the empties under the line."

I placed one empty gallon jug under the end of the long copper pipe which stuck out of the far side of the cooler. I then set a couple of other jugs beside the first one. After this I waited, while Johnny fanned the fire and used the same leafy branch to break up the smoke.

It took over an hour for the mash to come to a boil, and for the first trace of liquid to show at the end of the copper tube. When the first drops of alcohol formed, Johnny threw down the branch he was waving and feverishly crouched down to watch the whiskey drain.

"Come on, baby!" he whispered. "Ataboy! Faster, and pure as tears! Come on, baby!"

I too was burning with excitement now—the hot feeling that something was happening to turn my life into a new and happier time.

It was still dark when we finished distilling, but a lot of work remained to be done. Even though the drum was boiling hot, Johnny worked at disconnecting the tubing, cursing softly as he burned his hands. Finally he got the nut undone, and we rolled the hot drum to one side off the stand. Johnny crouched down and disappeared into the underbrush, returning a moment later with a shovel.

"Hurry up—dig a hole!" He handed the shovel to me. As I dug into the soft earth, he unscrewed the top off the drum. The smell of the boiled mash was sickening. I turned my face away and choked for breath.

"C'mon—what's the holdup? This ain't no fancy party, Snit—we got to git outa here before it lights up!" Johnny's voice was threatening.

When I opened a hole about a foot deep and two feet wide, Johnny said that would do, and he worked the drum toward me. When he had it over the edge of the hole, he turned it over and drained the mash out of it.

"Cover it, quick!" he whispered thickly. "I'll wash up and reload."

I was fascinated by his organization and timing. Slow and clumsy as he seemed, he was a transformed person here in his moonshine den. Very quickly he had the drum scraped and sponged, and was refilling it with ground grain which he had hidden previously in a sack under some moss. He rolled the drum back on its stand, and then dumped a bag of sugar and some dry yeast over the crushed grain. He disappeared in the underbrush again, this time returning dragging a cream can full of fresh water. He emptied this water into the drum, and then stirred the mixture with a stick.

"If ya wanna drink, then wait until ya get home. I had to bring this water in my arms, ridin' a horse. If ya think that's fun—ya'll get a chance to do it next time," he said grimly.

A few more shovelsful of dirt, and I finished covering the refuse. Johnny was already winding up operations by reconnecting the distilling pipe to the drum. But instead of replacing the steel screw-on cap on the drum itself, he merely tied a piece of cheesecloth over the top.

"The stuff's gotta breathe while it ferments," he said, looking up to see me watching him.

While I drained the water from the cooling trough, he cleaned up the area around the drum by replacing the shovel and cream can into the under-brush. We capped the two jugs of moonshine and put them in the empty grain sack. Johnny stamped out the last traces of hot embers under the stand; then he hoisted the sack over his shoulder and, motioning to me to follow him, led the way back to where he had left the horses.

"Goddammit, Snit, it's later than I thought it was!" he swore as we came out on the road allowance. "Let's git out on the double before some early shepherd finds us here!"

Despite the brush and treacherous ground of the abandoned farm, we galloped back towards the settlement. Dawn was coming fast now, and even before we reached the first bend in the trail and were heading directly east to where our ways would part, the sky was turning grey. I could faintly pick out the outlines of the hills around us, with their narrow fields and clusters of brush and wood.

At the main road I dismounted and gave the bridle leads to Johnny. I was startled to see how pale and moist he looked in the ghostly grey light of early morning. He was also irritable and in no mood to hang about.

"Go home, Snit—hurry up! An' hang yore shirt on the fence to air, or the smell of it is a giveaway. I'll call fer ya later today on the way to town. Got to get some groceries. Git the hell indoors! I'll see ya later."

I stood for a moment watching his departure, and taking a deep breath of the dust his horses had thrown up as he wheeled them sharply and trotted away in the direction of his farm.

Walking the remaining distance home, I felt very tired. I didn't want to undress, so instead of going into the house, I walked into the barn. It was still dark in the building. I fumbled trying to locate the ladder leading into the hayloft. When I did find it, I pulled myself up.

There was still a layer of old timothy hay in the loft. Finding the first convenient spot, I lay down and fell asleep almost immediately.

On the way into town, Johnny brought me up to date on the history of the countryside. He told me of those who died, and he told me of those who had found a new foothold on life, and of the others who failed in spirit and health. He also told of those who had married, colouring his observations with his own cynical attitude towards life and love. There were some girls who had become unwed mothers, and these gave him great amusement.

"Lots of hot potatoes here, Snit boy!" He roared, and slapped his knee so hard the horses jumped forward and almost toppled me off my seat. "They'd give it to a trapper, and they'd give it to a cowboy!"

He laughed again, nudging me in the side with his elbow.

"Y'ever had anything to do with a girl?" I asked.

"Naw—that stuff's not fer me. A woman only ruins a man. If she don't give him a pile of kids, she gives him other troubles," he said darkly.

"What kind of troubles?"

He looked down and dragged his feet back and forth across the floor of the wagon before answering.

"Hell, I coulda got married if I wanted to, Snit—any time I wanted to, I coulda married. But what's it get ya? Ya get married to one of 'em, and they start to bugger around with some other guy. Jesus, I get mad when I think of it. I could kill the whole goddamned bunch of 'em for it!"

"Ya sound like that preacher Crowe," I growled.

"Don't mix me up with no preacher, if ya know what's good for ya!" He was getting sore. "I don't believe in no God!"

"What makes you sound like you know what's right and wrong about everything?"

"All right! So I don't know nothin'. But I got my eyes open—I see what I see. If ya want to go around thinkin' folks is made of holy shit, that's yore tough luck! Me, I look out fer myself—and don't ya forget it!"

He got pretty gloomy after that, and we didn't speak for the longest time.

The two whiskey jugs were wrapped in a horse blanket in the back of the wagon. I turned to look at them often, worrying if they should overturn and smash. Johnny seemed to have forgotten about them altogether.

We were passing a farm which was distinctive in that it had a fence around the front yard. A man was at the well, drawing up water for a flock of noisy geese. Johnny saw him, and grinned.

"Hello, Joe—waddaya know?" he called.

The farmer took one hand off the bucket rope he was pulling and waved to us.

"Who's he?" I asked.

"Joe Skrypka—ya must've known him. He married a French girl from the other side of town—hell, I guess that was after you were gone," Johnny said cheerfully, as if our argument had never taken place. "Yeh, she had quite a time of it—I figured it would drive Joe to the bug-house."

"Was there something wrong with her?"

"Yeh—she had cancer, and never told Joe about it. It was only after she had a kid Joe found out. Too late to do anythin' by that time."

"Is she still around?" I asked.

"Naw—she died over a year ago. Joe's old lady is takin' care of the kid. Sure changed Joe."

"What ya mean?"

"Well, he went sorta crazy after that. Figures his old lady is his wife—even calls her Jeanette, which was what his wife was called. Some of the neighbours told the old woman she should get him packed off to a nut-house. But she figures he can't do no harm bein' around, and if he was taken off, the farm would go to pot—so ya got yer choice!"

"Cripes!"

As we passed the next farm, a dog bounded out after us. He ran alongside of our wagon and set up one helluva racket barking. Johnny had been driving this far, but now he passed the leads to me. Then quickly leaning over the edge of the wagon, he caught hold of the dog's tail.

The dog yelped with fear and pain, and Johnny lifted him off his feet and began swinging him in a circle round and round over his head. The horses got jumpy at the noise over their backs, and I had to hold tight to keep them from breaking into a frightened trot. When Johnny got the howling dog into a fast spin, he let go of the tail and the poor devil went sailing over the edge of the road, across a barbed-wire fence, and head-on into a thicket of scrub willows on the other side.

"That's one sonofabitch won't bother me no more. Been waitin' to do that fer a long time, but never had anyone around to hold the horses from boltin'," Johnny said with satisfaction as he took the leads from me.

The hot air seemed to rise from the pores of the earth, to meet the burning sun overhead. Holding on to my seat with both hands, I tried to keep my head from nodding, for the low rumble and the jogging of the wagon were putting me to sleep. Johnny must have been bothered in the same way, for he stopped talking until we got into town.

"Hey, Snit!" He stabbed at me with his elbow as we lumbered down the main street. "I'm gonna have ya hang onto our money. But don't go showin' it to anyone. Ya just hold onto it, and keep count on how we spend it, but don't go flashin' no bills, Y'understand?"

I nodded, and Johnny steered the team towards the Grain Growers elevator.

He drove right on the scales in the building and let out a shout. In a moment the fat, stubble-bearded elevator agent came out of his office, scowling with heat and sleepiness. When he saw Johnny he smiled a dirty, rotten-tooth smile.

Johnny just sat, as if he didn't see the man. The agent first walked to the door of the elevator, and took a long look up and down the street. Then he walked to the back of our wagon, dug under the blanket, and took out the two moonshine jugs. He again looked out into the street, then furtively carried the jugs into his office. When he returned, he carried two identical but empty jugs under his arm. He placed them in the back of the wagon where the other two had been. Then coming over to Johnny, he dug into his pocket and gave him a handful of money.

"Get going, ya little bastard!" he said by way of parting, and hurried back into his office. We drove out of the building. As we reached the sunlit street, Johnny passed the money to me. I counted thirty dollars and pocketed them.

"Is that all there's to it?" I asked with wonder.

"We're homefree again, boy," Johnny said with satisfaction, although I could tell he was nervous as hell, the way he kept looking up and down the street. There were a few people about, but nobody paid us any interest.

"What's the score with prettyboy—he a bootlegger?" I asked, thumbing back at the elevator.

"Look, Snit—he don't ask me no questions, and I don't ask him none. It's best that way," Johnny said philosophically.

We pulled up at the hardware store and the horses snorted to clear their noses of dust.

"I want ya to do somethin', Snit," Johnny was staring past me, but talking fast and clear. "We only got a few months left for brewin' the poison. I got lots of copper pipe stashed away, but I can't go buyin' too many cream cans without someone gettin' suspicious. Especially since folks know I don't keep no milk cows. But it's different with you. Go and get two or three big cans, the eight-gallon kind, and we can expand our business. They won't make as good brewin' drums as the screw-top I have, but I got that one at an auction, and luck don't shit twice in the same place. Okay?"

I understood, and went into the store while Johnny waited for me. I got the two cream cans all right.

"How often you going to need these?" the hardware man asked as he reached up to pull them off a display shelf.

I almost got panicky, but his back was turned, and he didn't see me.

"Uh—once a week." I tried to sound as cheerful as possible.

"You got better luck than most other farmers in these parts, son—hardly any of 'em selling milk or cream this summer."

"I got some alfalfa hay from last year. They sure milk good on alfalfa!"

He wrote up a sales bill and I paid him. Then I picked up the two cans and made my way out. I glanced up and saw the bank sign next door, and a thought came to me.

"You wait here," I said to Johnny as I loaded the cream on the wagon. Then I went into the bank. Even here there was a delay I hadn't expected.

The girl at the wicket took Pete's cheque and went to the manger's office at the back. A moment later she returned.

"Mr. Mandolin, would you be able to call back in about a half hour? We'll have to telephone Edmonton about your cheque."

"But why? What's wrong?"

"Oh, there's nothing wrong. Only, it's a personal cheque and we must find out if the account it is written on is still in existence. Perhaps twenty minutes ... "

We left the horses in the shade of the hardware store and walked around town for a while. Pretty soon we got thirsty, and stopped outside Elsie's place. She was asleep as always, standing with her back to the mirror. The sun burned through the unshaded windows, and Johnny cursed.

"Damned if I go in there and roast for a cup of her slop!"

He rapped his knuckles sharply against the café window, which made Elsie jump and shake her fist at us. Johnny laughed, and we crossed over to the bank.

The cheque was good, and as I counted my money, the girl at the wicket watched me.

"If you'd like to deposit some money in an account ... " she began to say, and I hesitated. But Johnny nudged me from behind.

"Don't leave no money in a bank, Snit! Don't ever do it!" he said grimly.

"Why, Johnny? No sense carting all this cash around."

"Yore crazy if ya leave it here. Everybody knows yore business then. And look at this damned place—could go up in smoke anytime, and all yore money with it! Banks are all right fer them as needs 'em—but I'd stay outa them if I was you!"

I didn't want to argue with the girl listening to us, so I thanked her and we went out.

The sun was a great red ball of dry heat when we started for home. Once we were out of town and no one to see, I took my shirt off. It didn't feel any cooler, but it amused Johnny.

"Jesus!—What'ya do—wash yerself all over every day? Ya look like ya was powdered all over, so white and clean! Betcha smell like a woman!"

And he nudged me in good fun, and laughed one of those laughs that bubbles out of a man's nose. I had a lot to say to him about this subject, but what was the use? So I endured, and kept silent.

August came, and still the weather continued dry and hot. The fields baked and cracked in many places, in long, snaking crevices many inches deep. The smell of dry leaves vanished from the wind, and a new, weaker scent, as of old leather, replaced it. Some forest fires had started far to the north, and we had a few cooler days when the smoke overcast the sky, screening out the sun.

I got the hay cured and stored in the hayloft. Also, I worked on some of the fences which needed new posts and wire-mending. I even persuaded Aunt Matilda to give up on the garden, for every plant had been scorched and dead since June, yet she had been persisting in hoeing and watering the wasted earth.

"Nothin' ever dies altogether—there's always a seed or root that lives, Snit. If you were a proper farmer, you'd know that yourself," she argued, before she finally gave up hope herself.

On one of my trips into town with Johnny, I purchased a load of feed oats from the elevator, much to the agent's surprise and Johnny's annoyance. Johnny was no farmer, and looked on my attempts to preserve and improve farm animals as a fool's dream.

"Whatcha wastin' money on a couple of bone dry cows fer? Cost ya more to fatten 'em than they're worth!" he chided.

He was right, but I felt sorry for the animals, but how could I explain this to Johnny Swift?

When we pulled into the yard and unloaded the oats into the feed shed, my aunt came out to see what we were up to.

"Why glory be!" she said. "How much is this costin', Snit? You didn't go borrowin' money from folks, didya?"

Johnny snickered, and began shovelling the grain into the shed.

"Here, now—let me give a hand!" My aunt climbed on the wagon, and turning up the frayed cuffs of her coat, took the shovel from Johnny. This was the first time I had seen her cheerful since my return.

Inside the barn, in one of the stalls at the very back, my father, or some-one before him, had stored a small, single-cylinder John Deere stationary engine. When Johnny left, I pulled the motor out into the yard to dismantle and clean. When I got it together again, I filled the fuel tank with lamp kerosene. It took some time to start, but when I got it going I found it still worked reasonably well. Using it for a source of power, I was able to grind the grain I had bought.

That same evening, Aunt Matilda enthusiastically began feeding the two cows and caring for them properly again. She curried them, and they shied away at such unfamiliar attention.

She talked to me as I stood watching her. "You're a good lad, Snit. You've got a good heart and your head's set on right. I'd kinda given up hope when you took to chumming about with that good-for-nothing Swift boy—figured he'd take you for what money you had before the summer was over. Worse still, I figured he'd start movin' in on me. He's a bad one, Snit—I don't know how a soul deals with someone like him."

"Johnny's all right, Aunt Matilda. He ain't no better nor worse than other folks in these parts. Everybody gets pushed into some kind of shape when times get tough—and ya know yourself times couldn't get no worse than they are."

"Bad times don't make people bad, Snit. People do queer things that maybe they'd rather forget later on. But it don't make them mean and bad. Somehow the bad ones start that way, and don't ever change."

"Then yo're saying everybody's good and kind as hell around here, and Johnny Swift is the one black bird in the country?"

My aunt didn't reply. She had stopped currying, and was watching me. Her little mouth was set angry, and her eyes hard.

"Look," I continued, "I ain't got no quarrel with Johnny Swift. But I got a lot of quarrel with Tom Whittles, and the parson, and all them good folks that busted us up."

"Have you?" my aunt cut in sharply.

"What's the matter with ya?" I raised my voice at her. "Look at what they done to pa and ma! Look what they done to you! I was scared of ya, when I first saw ya! That's what all this nice, neighbourly treatment we been getting done to you."

"We done it ourselves, Snit—don't you see?" There were tears in Aunt Matilda's eyes now. "We done it long ago, and other folks had no part of it—it started long ago, when two sisters and a brother came on this farm. There was no proper life for anyone when the work was done. But instead of going out and doing what we shoulda done, saving ourselves for a good life, we turned ourselves inside out, killing everything we touched until we didn't know what was right or wrong any more. Your pa and ma paired off, and you were born. I was one of the outside folks then, and I hada start taking care of things. I coulda been like your ma—could've come and gone in the same way—just like your pa did. I was saved for a taste of life—but it come too late, Snit!"

I stood like a man that's been hit hard on the head but can't fall down. I thought of nothing—nothing at all. The only feeling I had was as if suddenly the soles of my feet had burst, draining all the blood and warmth out of me. When I became aware of my surroundings again, it was dark, and I heard Aunt Matilda weeping softly near the feeding cattle. I moved towards her, and lifted her to her feet.

"Has everybody known this—all these years?" I asked her as I held her close to myself.

"Yes, everybody has known."

"And nobody told—when the time come they sent out a petition."

Aunt Matilda nodded.

"We didn't do right by ourselves, and we didn't do right by you. Maybe it was best you got taken away. But you ruined it by comin' back. Why did you have to come back?"

I didn't know.

"I reckon we all have to go some place—and outside of Pete's garage, this is the only spot I've ever lived in," I said for want of something better to say.

"You're not sore about—everything?"

"No, Aunt Matilda; I'm not sore."

"You're not hurt too bad?"

I didn't say anything.

"All them things I said when I wasn't thinking, Snit—I take them back. If you're thinking of staying on with me, I'd like to talk to you—"

"It's late, Aunt Matilda—yo're tired. Let's go in."

There was nothing to discuss about my presence on the farm. I was going to pay my own way, but at the same time I didn't feel rooted here, and I would make no commitments.

Then there was Johnny. She must never learn of my association with him, for she was a good and honest woman—and for that very reason I could no longer trust her.

Our nights were busy. There was little to do on the farm, so Aunt Matilda did not miss me while I slept during the days. I had taken to sleeping in the barn hayloft, so that she would not become concerned or suspicious about my movements. The way I figured it, even if she caught me sleeping, she would think I was lazy or bothered by the heat.

Johnny was a terror for brewing. Each night he would haul in more containers of various sizes and shapes and fill them with mash for fermenting, until we had enough of the stuff going to produce about fifty gallons of moonshine. We had worked out a system for placing away so much fresh mash per night, and when the fermentation matured, distilling the containers in rotation. Because of this extra volume, we soon ran short of the finely ground barley and wheat which we used for raw mash.

"What we gonna do?" I asked, when we emptied the last bag of prepared grain.

"What we gonna do? I'll tell ya what we gonna do. I'm gonna see that punk elevator guy, and get him to grind and mix some grain for us. Then I'm gonna get him to put it into bags, so nobody don't get nosey," Johnny growled, puffing drags on a cigarette.

The elevator agent wasn't willing to go along and get himself involved with us any deeper. Johnny got mad, roaring mad, and his face in a sweat, he lowered the boom on the bootlegger.

"Look, ya swine!" Johnny turned white as he stood up in the wagon to stare dangerously at the agent. "We ain't got much to lose—a coupla hundred in fines, which we can afford to pay. But if ya want trouble, ya'll be flat on yore ass without a job. So ya gonna play along, or do I see the cops and turn ya in?"

The agent's eyes bugged and he swallowed hard.

"All right, boys." He nodded and spoke in a choked-up voice. "All right— just cool off and be sensible, an' we can get along nicely, I'm sure. Come back in a coupla hours, and I'll have the grain ground and blended fer ya."

Things remained pretty quiet until we got the first heavy distilling done and delivered. When it hit the market, the police started moving, and folks got awful jumpy. Not that Johnny or I were afraid. I kept the money at home, buried in a quart jar under a floorboard in the corridor of the barn. As it turned out, the cops didn't even question Johnny or me, for I had cashed in my cheque, and nobody thought of trying to figure out what I was spending, where, and on what supplies. Even if someone had, the chances of pinning me were slim, for word was getting about that Snit Mandolin was setting his aunt's farm on its feet.

I saw Corporal Kane's car driving about the hill country, stopping here and there at farmsteads where he threatened or jollied farmers into telling anything they might know.

Kane tried other tricks, like cultivating informers to watch and listen for him. Tom Whittles was the first of these rats to show his hand. He'd been treating me very politely since the first visit I paid to his store on coming back—and by now I didn't mind him so much. I wandered down to his place one afternoon for lard and tobacco. After making out my order, he placed his beefy hands on the counter and leaned towards me, with a peculiar look on his face.

"Ya seen the way Corporal Kane's been driving around the last week?"

"Yeh—sure seems like a busy boy, don't he?"

"Well, maybe he's got cause to. Snit—the cops are worried about the moonshine they're sure is coming out of these parts. Maybe we should all be worried—it's givin' the district a bad name."

"So what ya think we should do—bleed for the district?"

"Oh no, don't get me wrong. What folks do is their business. But it's still terrible what bad likker does. Last dance the other side of town was flooded in the stuff, and almost resulted in a knifing. Corporal Kane told me so himself. Terrible, isn't it, how some folk will stoop for that lousy dollar!"

I was tempted to say something at this point, but changed my mind.

"I wonder," Whittles continued as he wrapped my purchases, "I wonder if old Dick Campbell has something to do with it? It's a dry year, and he's putting up a new barn. Doesn't it make ya ask where he got the cash to be so ambitious with his future as to be building a barn, and his bill here unpaid since last January? And his kids' asses bare to the sun for lack of clothes."

"I don't see where it's any of your'n or my goddam business what old Dick Campbell does at all!" I said flatly, and picked up my package.

"To be sure! To be sure!" Whittles blushed and lowered his head. "It's just that I was wondering—everybody's got a right to wonder, Snit. Folks have strayed from the Holy Word and good life something fearful the last while."

I slapped my parcel down on the counter, and clenching both fists, waited. One more word—just one tiniest remark, and I'll lay you out flat on the floor, I thought. Even with his head down, he was watching me, for he froze as he stood, not saying a word, not moving a muscle. I left.

When I met Johnny that night, I told him about my conversation with Whittles. Johnny blew his roof.

"If that lousy bastard don't want his rotten store to go up in smoke, he'd better keep his snout outa other folks' affairs—or he'll get what's comin' to him good!"

I agreed, and we got down to a busy night of work.

Business was booming, and all things accounted for, we figured on making about four hundred apiece to the good before the leaves started falling off the trees and we'd have to close shop or find a new location for our still. At least one thing we were grateful for—coming into late August, the nights were getting longer, and we could put more hours into our work.

We had to change our routine as well. For one thing, we had to dispense with Johnny's horses, because the marks of traffic on the blind road allowance were beginning to show, and it would be only a matter of time before the police or one of the neighbours would notice fresh hoofprints down a road which had never been used. So we began moving back and forth on foot, crossing over Rogers' farm, crouching low and following the hollows, our backs raw from the weight of water and grain containers. In the morning we would return, carrying the lighter load of distilled moonshine. The biggest danger we faced now was being seen by one of the Rogers family. Fortunately, Rogers didn't keep a dog, or we'd have been in real trouble. His fields were brick hard from the heat and bad cultivation, and our footsteps didn't show.

Yet I was scared, real scared, each time we came out into the open.

"Johnny—what if suddenly we should walk smack into old man Rogers or one of his kids?"

"Don't worry—they'd never talk!" Johnny snarled at me.

"Whatya mean—they'd never talk? Ya just tell me whatya mean by that."

"We ain't runnin' no Sunday-school, Snit—not by a long shot. We ain't gonna be nailed by no barley-chewin' hick! Just ya remember that! Now shut up and let's go!"

It was this sort of thing that scared me terribly, and I prayed to myself that old man Rogers would stay out of our way, for his own sake.

One night we were working hard, and both steaming from the effort. Johnny never changed his clothing, and with the way he sweated I was finding the smell of him as hard to take as that of the fermented mash I had to bury each night. So I called a stop for a cigarette to sort of purify my immediate surroundings.

Johnny went for the idea of a break. He rolled himself a smoke from the tobacco I carried, lit up, and crouched awkwardly by the fire.

"Pretty good, eh?" he said, and grinned up at me.

I didn't know what was pretty good to his mind at the moment, so I just grunted and continued smoking.

"Snit, I gotta talk to ya." His face pulled up serious-like suddenly. "I been thinkin' about the money we're makin' and how best to use it. Ya know, we gotta slow down some time, or that bugger at the elevator will lose his nerve and squeal or back out. Then where we gonna be? I don't know where else to unload the stuff, even if we didn't get caught ourselves if he threw in the towel."

"All right—what plans ya got?" I asked.

"Well, I been thinkin'; maybe you and I could toss in together and spend it on some—some investment. Somethin' that'll pay off even more in a few years. We could buy a farm with eight hundred, fer instance—or if we find someone who's really havin' hard luck, we could maybe buy a coupla farms."

"Yo're no farmer, Johnny—so what ya gonna do with a coupla farms—or even one farm?" I argued.

"I don't mean buyin' to farm. What I meant was buyin' them to rent or resell when times and prices get better."

I couldn't keep back from laughing.

"Who's gonna buy land from us here? Even in good times?"

"I don't worry about that none. How much ya think a farm pays in taxes each year?" Johnny kept right on.

"I dunno—forty, fifty dollars maybe—less if it's really bad land."

"So—we pay the taxes, maybe even invest in some machinery, and start raisin' crops that don't need rain every goddam day to grow. I don't farm, but that don't mean I'm stupid. What ya say, Snit?"

I figured I'd have to think it over more. It hadn't occurred to me that our moonshining couldn't go on forever, and sooner or later we'd have to plan our next steps. Yet I wasn't sure Johnny's idea was all that good. So we returned to work, and I dismissed our discussion from mind for a few days.

Every Sunday was meeting day at the church. Sunday was the one day of the week Johnny and I knocked off from work. We weren't religious—we were just tired.

"How long's it been since ya been to church?" I asked my aunt cheerfully over coffee. She looked at me with the expression of a person roused from sleep, but not wakened. I laughed, and she lowered her head the way she held it whenever she sat across the table from me lately.

A knock sounded on the door, and before I could rise to open it Johnny walked in. My aunt did not stir.

"Hi, Snit!" Johnny was excited and his face was glistening. "Snit—I wanna talk to ya—come on outside!"

I stepped out after him and closed the door.

"Snit!" Johnny grabbed my sleeve. "Get some money—maybe a hundred bucks, and come on to church. I think we got a real deal on the go. I got gassing with my old man this morning—first time we spoke this summer, an' I learned somethin' everybody's been keepin' quiet about."

"What in hell ya talking about?"

"They's plannin' to close the church up!"

"So what's that gotta do with me?"

"You'll see. Grab some cash and come on!"

"I don't reckon Reverend Crowe is gonna be all that pleased to see me."

"Fuck Reverend Crowe! Come on!"

There was no making sense out of Johnny, so I went into the house for a quick shave and a change of clothes. I even buffed my shoes, which was pointless, as they would be grey with dust before I got more than a few yards down the road. My aunt looked up once to watch my preparations, but there was no interest in her eyes, for which I was grateful.

When I stepped outside again, Johnny was sitting on the grass, staring at the house door. He reminded me of a barnyard dog.

"Jesus!" he said when he saw me, but I hurried away to get our money from the barn.

Some people had already driven past and others were walking to church as Johnny and I made our way to the road. I saw Johnny's dad go past, sitting straight and severe on the wagon Johnny and I used for hauling whiskey into town. The Rogers family went by on foot, led by the father and mother, and followed by Mickey, who had grown into a fairly tall guy since I saw him last. Then there were the folks from the stonier land further north, all of them walking, for they were really hard up. We were not particularly sociable people in the hills. No two families went to church together.

"How does anyone go about getting married here?" I asked Johnny as we walked with our faces to the parching sun.

He looked at me with surprise. "What in hell anybody wanna get married for?"

I laughed out loud, and Johnny stopped to stare at me. "Ya gone kooked or somethin'? What's the matter?"

"Nothin'—ya just answered my question, that's all!"

He watched me from the corner of his eye, shook his head, and didn't say any more. The road in front of the church was crowded with wagons driven half into the ditch, and the horses tied here and there to the fence. Folks were moving through the gate, and Johnny and I fell in line to enter the churchyard. I looked up at the church, with its cracked and dirty windows which were like the eyes of some tired, diseased animal. Reverend Crowe did not tend to the building, and no one in the community took it on himself to do more than sweep the floor for a wedding or a funeral.

Tom Whittles had opened the peg-and-strap fastening on the door, and stood to one side, beaming like one of those porcelain figurines which clutter every auction sale. Now Johnny and I stepped aside. We both had the same instinctive dislike of being crowded in a building. Whittles saw us and waved, but we both ignored him.

The Reverend Crowe arrived at the gate, and those parishioners who were still lingering in the churchyard hurried into the church. The preacher was dressed in a crinkled suit which had once been grey, but now appeared colourless and sun-bleached. He hadn't changed much from when I remembered him—he'd gotten a bit heavier maybe. But the eyes and shaggy eyebrows were the same, and his face showed no signs of further aging. He looked in our direction as he walked by, and seeing me, he stopped. The shaggy eyebrows twitched a little and he moved forward, as if to shake my hand, but reconsidered, and resumed a quicker pace into the church. Johnny and I followed, and behind us came Tom Whittles, still beaming.

Three years had not altered the preaching form of the Reverend Crowe. His sermon was a strong echo of other days, his voice dropping into drowsy depths, then suddenly soaring with hellfire and damnation. He prayed for the destruction of sin—he prayed for everlasting life for the righteous—he prayed for rain—he prayed for a happiness on earth which I found disturbing, for it was so stern and barren a promise.

His words had an astonishing impact on this poor, superstitious and illiterate folk to whom he was giving spiritual guidance. They moaned and wrung their hands with agony when he roared at their sins, then a moment later they glowed and a sigh of happiness passed like a breeze through trees when the preacher subsided and spoke of the rewards of suffering. Then everybody sang; and despite myself, I joined in as lustily as the next person:

> The B-I-B-L-E
> Yes, that's the Book for me!
> I stand alone on the Word of God,
> The B-I-B-L-E

A ray of sunlight flashed off the collection plate which was now being passed through the front benches, with Tom Whittles standing in the aisle, never taking his eyes off it. I decided now was the time to leave. I was stopped in rising from my seat by Reverend Crowe slapping his hands loudly together.

"Brothers and sisters!" He stepped down from the pulpit, and his voice dropped from its dramatic preaching tones to an ordinary, conversational sincerity. "As most of you must know by now, we are experiencing terrible difficulties with this church."

I glanced at Johnny, but he was leaning forward, listening intently to the preacher.

"I do not wish to take more than a few moments to explain, so I shall get to the root of our problems right now—money! Brothers and sisters, we have no money, and if the collection doesn't rise above the pittance it has been every Sunday this summer, this will have to be the last service I shall lead among you. It just doesn't pay for me to come all the way here from town for the small sums you collect for me."

There was an anxious murmur from the body of the church and faces strained towards him. I looked around, and realized for the first time how deeply ingrained was this building and faith in the lives of the hill-folk—like the homes they built and the clay they worked with a horse and a hope of some harvest. It was comforting, but at the same time it was frightening to me, an outsider.

"We just can't afford to give no more, Reverend!" a plaintive voice shouted from just behind me.

The preacher threw his arms apart and looked at his congregation helplessly.

"Then what can we do, brethren?" he asked.

This wasn't my problem, so I began sliding along the bench to leave, when I noticed Johnny holding up his hand to catch the preacher's eye. Crowe saw, and nodded.

"Well, Reverend," Johnny drawled, his eyes half closed and his hands in his pockets, "Seein' as the church needs money, I reckon the church should get money—whatya think?"

He stopped, and you could have heard a handkerchief drop in the building.

"What do you propose, John Swift?" The preacher was shaken, and had to clear his throat.

"What you propose? It's you needs the cash, an' Snit Mandolin an' I got it—how much ya need?"

I closed my eyes and leaned forward, trying to keep my nerves from churning up my guts. I felt every face in that church turning to me.

"Come on—how much cash ya need?" Johnny's voice was getting thin and angry.

"Tell him, Reverend—let him help us if he wants to!" It was the plaintive voice from behind me again.

I looked up, and saw that Reverend Crowe's face had become white and tense. He was glancing back and forth across his congregation, and I could tell he was scared of what he saw.

"All right, all right—we're still in meeting!" He silenced the murmur that was rising from the crowd now. "I think a hundred dollars would see us through another year."

Johnny raised one leg and placed it on the bench behind him. A little smile played on the edges of his lips.

"Tell ya what Reverend—we'll give ya fifty bucks. But since that's a lotta money, and seein' as anythin' could happen to the buildin' the way it is, Snit and I gotta do one thing to protect the buildin'." Johnny's voice was still thin, but now it had a trace of insolence.

"Fifty dollars isn't enough to—" Reverend Crowe began.

"Take it, Reverend—we'll raise more somehow!" It was Mrs. Rogers who now rose to give her opinion.

"Sure Reverend! Let's keep the church open!" somebody else called from the back of the building, and there was a murmur of approval.

Tom Whittles hurried to the preacher's side and whispered something in his ear. Reverend Crowe looked up at Johnny.

"What else was it you wanted to do beside give us fifty dollars, Mr. Swift?" he asked suspiciously.

"Well, Reverend, tomorrow I'm aimin' to go into town, an' I'm gonna buy a brand new lock, which I'm gonna put on that door!"

"No!" Tom Whittles shouted, raising his fists in protest.

"Sit down, Whittles! It's little enough ya done to keep the place lookin' respectable! Maybe it's time we got some youngsters to look after our church!" the plaintive voice behind me shouted.

"Yah, Whittles—ya was never put in charge o' this church!"

There was a real uproar now, and Whittles gave up. Reverend Crowe walked away, stopping alongside his pulpit, where he stood, holding his hands over his face.

A burly neighbour in front of me turned.

"G'wan, you guys—pay the Reverend his fifty bucks so's he'll keep comin' back! An' Swift, it's a good thing you gave Whittles a kick in the ass."

Someone behind me, rising to go, squeezed my arm and mumbled in my ear: "Glad ya turned out right after all, Snit. Maybe God don't forget some of us after all."

I felt both elated and weak in the stomach. Johnny bumped against me.

"Let's get the hassle over with!" he growled, "Pay that sonofabitch and let's get outa here!"

He pushed past me and I followed him to the pulpit. My hands were shaking something awful as I counted out the fifty dollars and gave them to Johnny.

"You're not serious about that lock bit, are ya, boys?" Whittles shoved his way between us.

"Here's the fifty, Reverend, I wanna receipt," Johnny said to the preacher.

"Listen boys—I wanna talk to ya," Whittles kept butting in.

"Forget it, Tom—don't make a bigger fool of yourself." Reverend Crowe took his hands off his face, and spoke to Whittles. The preacher looked aged, tired and beaten all of a sudden. He turned to Johnny.

"Whatever you're up to is your business, Swift. But one thing I want to know—what's Mandolin's connection with all this?"

"Snit an' me are partners, Reverend. Whatsa matter—can't two guys help out the church without you hollerin' murder? Or do we gotta try see about gettin' a new preacher?" Johnny was boyish as he said this. If he'd got himself cleaned up a little, he'd have looked like an average highschool kid.

The preacher gave both of us one long, hard look—almost a sad kind of look, then he wrote out a receipt on the back of a hymn sheet.

"Boy! Have we got luck by the tit! An' we're gonna hang on like two hungry cats!" Johnny slapped his knee with excitement once we were out on the road and walking home.

"I don't see what we got except fifty dollars' worth of friends. An' we need fifty dollars more than friends!" I complained.

Johnny laughed one of those good, long laughs which brought tears into his eyes.

"Trouble with you, Snit, is ya don't look ahead. Ya gotta think big to be big!"

"What the hell ya talkin' about?"

"Ya'll see soon enough. Hey—let's forget it's Sunday and do some work tonight. I gotta get that lock tomorrow, an' I don't wanna go into town empty."

We had reached Aunt Matilda's place now, and I left him, saying I'd see him tonight.

SEVEN

We did work that night—harder than we had worked any night before. When the first touch of grey showed in the sky, we had eight gallons of moonshine ready and crocked.

"Let's get outa here!" Johnny said, as he stamped out the embers of our distilling fire. We split the moonshine into two lots, four gallons to a sack. Then, hoisting a sack each over our shoulders, we left the bog and began crossing Rogers' farm towards the road.

I had no idea what time it was, but the sky seemed lighter than on any morning before.

"Christ!" Johnny swore. "Anybody on the road could see us comin', it's that bright! Run, Snit!"

Crouching low, we ran, following the beds of the faint dips in the land. Johnny was ahead of me, panting under his heavy load and the strain of running. I broke into a cold sweat.

"To hell with it, Johnny—let's go straight for the road!" I was ready to risk anything, just to get off the open field as quickly as possible.

Johnny turned on me.

"Ya just try it, ya yellow bastard! I'm gonna open yer head with a stone if ya do! What ya so scared fer? Nobody seen us yet!"

We moved forward again, but I saw that Johnny was no longer crouching as low as he should have. Ten minutes later, we were in the scrub bush alongside the road. Johnny threw his sack into the centre of a willow bush, and then lay in the grass, his arms and legs thrown wide apart. I put my sack behind the bush, and then flopped down beside Johnny.

"Holy crackies!" he exclaimed, his mouth opened wide for air, and his eyes turned upward into his forehead until only the whites showed. "We run—we sure run! We musta run a hundred miles, Snit, I feel that tired!"

"What we gonna do with the crocks?" I asked, glancing back at the willow bush.

"Leave 'em there. I'll go home and hitch up the horses. When I come past here, I'll pick 'em up and throw 'em in the wagon."

"It's a lot of moonshine, Johnny."

"Ya're not just whistlin'! This is it, Snit—the big one! We get rid of this load, and we got 'er made!" His eyes swung back into focus, and he sat up. The tiredness was gone from his face, which became bright with excitement.

"See ya in half an hour."

We both rose and parted. I ran all the way home. At the pump I stopped to wash myself, then went to the barn to change my shirt. In about a half hour I heard Johnny's wagon on the road. Aunt Matilda was still asleep when I left.

We arrived in town well before noon. The streets were deserted except for the bank manager, who stood outside the bank, studying the sky as he puffed on a short, stubby pipe. He glanced in our direction, then went in.

"Just look at that guy—he's got all the money, an' he don't do no work," Johnny said sarcastically.

"Oh, I reckon he's gotta work for his living same as everybody else," I commented.

"What ya talking about? He steals, that's what he does—an' he don't even have to go out to steal. Folks bring it in fer him!"

"Fer Christ's sake, Johnny—folks who leave money in a bank know what they put in, an' they know how much they take out," I argued.

"How they know? Who's so smart can remember everything in his head?" Johnny brushed his knuckles against the sides of his lips.

"I never kept money in a bank, but the way I understand it," I explained, "the bank gives ya a book, and each time ya put money in or withdraw, the girl marks the figures down, an' gives ya a count on what ya got."

"Like hell!" Johnny stuck out his chin like he was setting to argue all day. "They're crooked same as everybody else—'cept they're smart, too. They don't run no place that size to help ya count yer money! Don't give me that bull!"

"The way you figure it, everybody living runs a racket—there ain't nobody honest in the world. Is that the way ya see it, Johnny?"

"Ya gonna tell me different?" he snapped.

"Go to hell!"

I wanted to get away from his thick head for a moment. We were passing the hardware store, and I jumped off the wagon.

"Where ya goin'?" Johnny shouted.

"I'll see ya at the elevator. I'm gonna get that lock for yore church."

"Let's get it on the way back," Johnny called, but I ignored him.

The hardware store didn't carry any proper door locks for under ten bucks, and as I reckoned fifty dollars was more than enough to spend on that church, I picked out a strong padlock for three and a quarter. Then I made my way down the street to the elevator.

I didn't walk fast, thinking that Johnny could get rid of the moonshine and meet me coming back. When I neared the elevator, I noticed the horses standing with the wagon on the ramp, but Johnny wasn't around. Suddenly, I was afraid—afraid so it dried my mouth, and I started running.

When I got to the ramp, I saw Johnny kicking at the office door.

"Johnny—what's wrong?" I shouted.

"The goddam, rotten, scum eating pig!" Johnny cursed in a high voice. "He's locked up—run out on us! I'll kill the dirty bastard!"

Again that fear—this time knotting up my guts like a bad cramp.

"Come on, Johnny! Let's get outa town!" I called, as I climbed quickly on the wagon.

"I'm not goin' nowhere until I find that rotten pig!" Johnny drove the heel of his foot against the door.

"Johnny!" I shouted, and he turned to me, his face white and sparkling with nervous sweat. "We're in trouble, man—bad trouble. We gotta get outa town!"

"Ya think the cops are onto us?" He tried to keep his voice low now.

"If they ain't, they're gonna be. Come on!"

I struck the horses forward, and Johnny mounted the wagon at a run. Once he was on the seat beside me, he took the reins from my hand.

"Now go slow," I urged. "Just drive outa town slow and easy, like nothin' was wrong."

"Ya fuck yerself slow!" he spat at me. Then rising to his feet, he lashed the horses, and we went through town and out into the hills at full gallop.

I staggered to the back of the wagon, and crouched where our crocks lay covered by a blanket. They were rattling against each other, and I was afraid they would smash. I began packing the blanket between them. Johnny shouted at me, and I looked up.

"If yore aimin' to dump the whiskey, I'll kill ya!" He was roaring mad again. "We're savin' our whiskey—ya hear me! So keep yore hands off it!"

"Cool off—I'm just coverin' the crocks better, goddam ya!"

Johnny scowled, watching me with distrust. When I finished and returned to the front of the wagon, he sat down and pulled the horses back into a fast trot. It was hot now, with the sun shimmering over the fields and hills, and not a breeze to blow away the oppressive air. The horses were lathering fast.

"Pull in, Johnny—ya'll kill the studs." I felt sorry for the animals.

"They ain't my horses—so why the hell worry!" he snarled.

I don't know whether it was my nerves, or whether some feelings had been building up in me for quite some time, but suddenly I had enough. Reaching out, I yanked the reins from Johnny's hands and pulled the horses to a stop. Then I dropped the reins and stood up.

"All right Johnny," I said as quietly as I could. "Let's step down on the road."

"Yeh—what fer?" he drawled, his eyes half closed.

"So I can kick the shit outa ya proper!"

"You! Ya haven't got the guts or brains to stand up to me!" He laughed hard, and began rising to his feet. But I didn't let him get up. I drove my fist down hard on the back of his neck, sending him sprawling on his side across the seat. He covered his head with his hands, and when he looked up at me, his eyes were big and scared.

"Cripes, Snit—what's got into ya?" The arrogance was gone from his voice now.

"Ya comin' down, or aren't ya?"

"I didn't think ya'd do it." He sat up and shook his head. "I never thought ya had it in ya. All right, I'm chicken—I ain't gonna fight. But I'd never do what you did, Snit—just ya remember that. I'd never hit ya when ya wasn't lookin'."

I didn't feel bad for having clipped him like that. He'd been asking for it since town. Yet we couldn't fight now—we were both too deeply in trouble to fall out. So I thought of making the first move to patch things up. But I never got the chance

"Holy smokes, look!" Johnny cried frantically. I looked up, and saw Corporal Kane's car approaching us from the front.

I felt sick, and glancing at Johnny's face, I knew he felt the same way. I pulled the horses over to one side to let the mountie pass. But instead of driving by, he stopped some distance ahead of us, and poking his head out the window, waited for us to drive up.

"Hi!" he called. "You boys wait a minute—I want to talk to you."

He stepped out of the car and approached. I pressed my hands hard against the reins I held to keep steady, and Johnny slouched forward, with his head low over his knees.

"Let's see—do I know you guys?" Kane asked, glancing first at Johnny, then at me.

"You're the Swift boy—what's your first name?"

"Johnny."

"Oh yes, Johnny. And I've seen you before somewhere—what's your name?" He looked up at me.

"Mandolin."

"Mandolin—Hey, you're the kid got sent off a coupla years ago! I remember you. When did you get back?"

"I been back all summer—didn't ya know that?"

Kane grinned, and dug a thumb behind his belt.

"Was I supposed to know?"

I looked straight ahead and didn't reply.

"Your team?" he asked, indicating the wagon.

"No. Belong to Johnny's old man," I said.

"How come you're driving?"

"We take turns." The answer was as stupid as it sounded, and Kane broke into that laugh of his.

"Jesus Christ!" he said. "A couple of backwoods pansies!"

I cleared my throat and looked down at him. Kane's laugh wore off, and he hooked the other thumb behind his belt.

"Sorry, Mandolin—I was just thinking aloud. Which way you going now?"

"We're just coming in from town, and going home. What ya wanta know?" I asked impatiently.

"I just want to find out what's going on around here, and who's doing what—that's all. Anybody see you in town?"

A wild idea suddenly came into my mind.

"Yeh," I said, trying to keep my voice from sounding too eager. "Johnny an' I went in to get a lock fer the church—we're caretaking the old place now. The guy at the hardware store seen me."

Kane seemed satisfied, and began moving away. Then suddenly he looked up.

"Can I see what you bought?" he asked, his eyes narrowing. I shoved the reins in Johnny's hand, and reached under the seat for the package, which I opened to show the cop. He glanced into the bag and shrugged.

"Okay—I guess you can go. Oh—got anything in the back of the wagon?"

"Jus' some sacks to keep the wagonbox from rattling," I said, and held my breath for dear life. For a moment I thought he would go back to look. Then he turned and went back to his car.

"See you again," he called over his shoulder.

I never seen Johnny so scared and whipped as he was when Kane drove away, and we both looked at one another.

"That was good talkin', Snit—I never coulda done it," he said feebly.

"We're just lucky so far. What we gonna do now, Johnny? We gotta get this wagon back to yore old man—what we gonna do with the likker?" At the back of my mind I couldn't help feeling Kane had us tabbed somehow. At least, he was getting awfully close, and he could spring a search on me or Johnny at any moment. Whittles would certainly do his bit to help get us in trouble.

Johnny began to roll a cigarette.

"Snit," the drawl was returning, "don't ya worry none about stashin' the moonshine—it's that elevator bastard I wanna find now."

"He ain't gonna stash no moonshine on us!" I argued.

"Naw," Johnny lit his smoke. "Ya know where this stuff gets put? I'll tell ya—it's goin' into the church!"

"What!"

"Sure—that's why we gave money fer the privilege of lockin' the place up. I was figurin' on storin' our equipment in there fer the winter!"

"Holy—Yo're crazy! What about folks an' their Sunday services?"

"To hell with their Sunday services! Ya think they're really so hot-up about goin' every week? Close up the church fer the winter, and by summer they got twice as much prayin', singin' and shoutin' stored up! It's good fer them!"

"But it's wrong, Johnny. We got no right doin' that to folk!"

"Ya wanna get caught then? Be different if a guy could get into jail for a year—learn a lot that way. But if Kane gets us with eight lousy gallons of moonshine, he'll fine us and run us outa the country. I got me pride, an' it don't make way fer no lousy, Bible-thumpin' hill hick!"

In a short while we were at the church. Pulling the horses off the road, we watched to see if anyone was around. The road and surrounding fields were deserted. I then found a stone to use as a hammer, and began fastening the padlock on the church door, while Johnny busied himself with lugging the moonshine crocks into the church. In a short while it was all over with, and I snapped the lock shut. Then I gave one key to Johnny, and pocketed the other one.

"That stuff don't stay in there a minute longer than it's gotta," I said, sitting down on the grass with my back to the building.

"Sure, Snit—soon's I figure out what that bootleggin' bastard is up to, we unload."

"How soon's soon?"

"Tomorrow—maybe the day after. Kane's hot, an' we gotta take it easy. What about tonight—we gonna brew some more, or ain't ya with me no more?"

"I dunno, Johnny," I said wearily. "I just don't know."

I was crossing the yard to the house, when I looked out to the fields and saw Aunt Matilda bringing the cows in from the pasture. I waved to her, but she didn't see me. Waiting for her, I pumped water into the drinking trough for the cattle and rolled myself a cigarette.

"Was you in town again?" Aunt Matilda asked as she came up to me. The heat was wearing her down, and she was tired and aged looking.

I nodded.

"Wisht I'd known—you coulda got some salt for the cows. They're salt hungry."

"I'll go to Whittles' store an' get a block of salt from him," I said. Aunt Matilda looked off to one side.

"Are you in some kind of trouble, Snit?" she suddenly asked. "You can tell me if you want—I won't go spreading it."

"Whatya mean, Aunt Matilda—what kind of trouble ya think I'm in?"

"That cop as took you away a couple years back—you remember him? He stopped here today an' asked where you were, an' if you stayed on the farm days and nights that I was sure of."

"Whatya tell 'im?"

"I said you was a good boy, Snit—that you worked hard an' never strayed where I couldn't see you. Whittles was with him, but he stayed in the car."

"Whittles!"

"What's it mean, Snit? Are you doin' something you shouldn't be doin'? It's Johnny Swift, isn't it? I don't wanna bother with what you're doin', but I gotta know what to say if the cop comes around again." Aunt Matilda looked at me with worried, clouded eyes.

"It's nothin'! I been breaking the law all right, but I ain't gonna be breaking it no more—that's fer sure, Aunt Matilda. First, I gotta straighten some things out!" I was mad fit to burst.

"Whatya gonna do, Snit?"

"That Tom Whittles—we ever done him wrong? You tell me—did pa or ma or you or me ever get in his way?"

"No, we never done anything to Whittles."

"Yet he been riding our asses Christ knows how long! What for? He been fightin' us all along. We ain't fightin' people, Aunt Matilda—that's been our trouble. But after today he ain't gonna push no Mandolin around no more!"

"Snit—now you listen to me!" Aunt Matilda came after me. "Don't you go roughing him none. I don't want you goin' to jail on account of Whittles—leave him alone."

"He ain't worth going to jail for. Now let me be!" I pulled my arm out of her grasp and made for the road.

When I reached the store, I was all in a sweat, with my clothes sticking to my skin and itching me, for I had walked fast, and the sun still rode high in a cloudless sky.

Rogers was in the store, along with an old bachelor who farmed some four miles north of us. They were talking to Whittles, but when I came in, the two farmers looked at me and became silent. Whittles ignored me altogether, and with his elbows on the counter, carried on with what he was saying:

" … wake up in the morning, and first thing ya do is mark another date off yore calendar—'cause ya got no one to talk to, an' no way of knowing whether it's Thursday or Saturday. If ya wanna be a bachelor, Dan, ya go into business. But on a farm—nothin' doin'!" Whittles was saying to the old bachelor.

But neither Dan nor my neighbour was listening to him. They were both watching me, peculiar like.

"I wanna block of salt and some cigarette papers," I spoke to Whittles. He didn't move or look in my direction.

I hadn't counted on anyone being in the store. What surprised me even more was that the same folks who would have chewed Tom Whittles up in church yesterday were now on his side. I could see that by the look Rogers and Dan were giving me. I waited for a long moment, feeling a chill spread across my back, for if I gave ground now, I was licked and could think of packing out.

"Ya deaf or something?" I rapped the counter with my knuckles.

Tom Whittles moved his jaw slightly and spoke in a low voice. "This store is closed to Mandolins, Swifts, and all other kinds of cop-fearing, unchristian bastards who happen around here. Now git out and don't ever come back through that door again!"

Right next to where I stood was a pile of twenty-pound bags of rolled oats. I grabbed one of them and threw it with all my strength at Whittles. He ducked behind the counter and the bag struck the shelf behind him, ripping open and bringing down a shower of canned goods around him. The store-keeper came up with a scaregrin on his face, expecting to see me leaving the shop. But instead he almost caught the next bag I threw at his head.

"If I gotta bring down yore goddam store before I get service, then that's exactly what I'm gonna do!" I said as I let fly with a third bag.

"Hey, kid—smarten up!" Old Man Rogers lifted one hand for peace and stepped towards me.

"You keep outa this, ya gutless, crawlin' weasel!" I had another bag of oats in my hand now, but instead of sending it at Whittles, I brought it down over Rogers' head. He yelled and fell awkwardly to the floor. Dan, the bachelor, went out the door like a shot.

"Hey—help me!" Whittles shouted, when he saw Rogers rise to his feet and likewise head out the door.

"Ya still wanna see how tough and bad I can get? Ya wanna go tell Corporal Kane what I can do to ya? Go tell him—next time ya lay down to polish his boots. But ya ain't gonna push a Mandolin around no longer—no, no! You just ain't gonna push anyone around no more!"

I was wild with anger. Everything I had ever seen or felt that hurt or humiliated took form in this whimpering, scared man in front of me, with his back pressed against a shelf of groceries—his hands stretched out to push me back as I approached. The solid citizen—the self-righteous dispenser of laws—the detached animal, without nerves or longing—the untouchable.

"Ya wanna know something else, Whittles? Sure—Johnny an' me are in moonshine—we made enough moonshine to drown everybody here. Sure—we're dirty an' mean an' bad clean through—an' ya know why? Because we gotta live! An' a man gets mean when he's gotta live an' the Lord don't provide him with nothing to work with. Now ya know, Whittles—but ya ain't gonna tell Corporal Kane! No, yo're not gonna tell nobody, because if ya did, I'd come back—sooner or later I'd come back—an' ya know what I'd do?"

"Snit—please! I don't want trouble. Let's talk this over like men." Whittles' voice was cracked up, and sounding like that of a kid.

"I'd kill ya—that's what I'd do!"

I was right on him now, and he sort of shrank in front of me, his head trembling against a ledge of the shelf behind him.

"Snit—for the love of God—don't! I don't care what ya do—or what anybody does. Just let me be—I'm gonna mind my store an' not bother with cops, folks or religions—whatever ya say, but let me be!" Tears rolled down his cheeks and he started to babble.

I walked out, forgetting about the salt and the cigarette papers. I was surprised to see how low the sun had fallen, and then this great tiredness hit. Like tons and tons of weight it settled on me, making my feet feel like they had grown into the earth for hundreds of years—that's how hard it was to walk. I was washed out—inside and out. No more angers—no more fears. I just wanted a grassy spot to lie on and sleep away the rest of my life.

Turning into the yard, I saw Johnny standing in front of the house, with Aunt Matilda guarding the doorway. I shook the weariness out of my head and began walking faster.

"Where's the salt?" Aunt Matilda called out when I got within talking distance. I stopped and stared at her with disbelief. It was her voice—suddenly so strong and vibrant, like it had been once.

"Well, where's the salt?" This time she snapped at me.

"I—I forgot!"

"Gimme the money an' I'll go get it myself!" She came towards me, her back erect and her face sharp and alert.

"Or don't we buy at Whittles' no more?" she asked in a lower tone. "Ya didn't—mess things up?"

"No—no, we still buy at Whittles'." I dug into my jeans for some change. She faced Johnny.

"An' listen, Swift—if I catch you around here when I get back, I'm gonna take a stick to you—you hear me?"

That was it—she was mad! I hadn't seen her mad like this since I came back—and now, once again, she was the aunt I used to know.

"You know what he tried to do?" Aunt Matilda spoke to me, but glowered at Johnny, who had turned away from us. "He tried to move in on us! You heard me, Swift—say to Snit what you gotta say, then clear off!"

And she marched off to the store.

"The lousy bitch-cat!" Johnny swore, when Aunt Matilda was out of hearing.

"What happened to yore face?" I asked, seeing Johnny's left cheek cut bad.

"My old man did that with a piece of two-by-four. Snit—I got no home." There was an unpleasant whine in Johnny's voice.

"How come?"

"That fuckin' cop was over to see my old man—him and Whittles. That Whittles, Snit—he's out to fix us for what we done to him in church. He don't know we're in moonshine, but he put a bug into the cop's ear, and between the two of them, they give my old man a scare. So when I came home, the old man's got a two-by-four in his hand, and he says get out!"

"Whatya do?"

"I figured he was gassing off, so I give him lip, and started to unhitch the horses. Next thing I know, I get this two-by-four across my face. Jesus, it hurt! But he got it good, my old man. I knocked him down an' then I put the boots to him—the old sonofabitch! He started dirty, so I fought dirty, too!"

"How bad didya hurt him?" I started to get frightened.

"Most of his teeth's loose or out, but when I poured a bucket of water on him, he got up by himself. He's sick, but he ain't gonna die by a long shot. But when he got up, he looked at me a long time, like he never seen me before. Then he says to me, 'Take whatever clothes ya got now, 'cause ya ain't comin' back.' He says, 'I'm gonna load up my gun, and when you step on this farm again, I'm gonna shoot ya dead!' He'd do it, Snit—the way he said it, he'd do it!"

"Great!" I said. "It's like we ain't got enough trouble already—now ya beat up yore old man. He can get you put away a couple years for that."

"Let him try! I ain't scared of jail!" Johnny snarled back.

"Sure—yo're the big hero. Whatya gonna do now?"

That put him back on the ground, and he started walking back and forth, twisting his hands over one another.

"I dunno, Snit. I ain't got no home no more—no place to go. I was thinkin' since you and me are together, maybe ya could fix it so I could stay with ya until I find somethin'."

"This farm belongs to my aunt—and she sure don't want no truck with ya. When she hears about what happened between you and yore old man, I wouldn't take no chances on yore even visiting here any more."

"Hell, Snit—ya can talk to her. Why talk? Just tell her that's the way ya want it, an' she'll listen to ya. Who in hell is she anyway, except a screwy old woman!"

"No, Johnny—we got no right pushing Aunt Matilda."

Johnny stamped his foot and turned on me, his lips drawn back like he was set to lace into me.

"I'm gettin' tired of ya, Snit—good an' sick an' tired! I'm gettin' so much of ya, I wanna puke, that's how I feel! Ya gonna play my way, or ain'tcha?"

"What's your way, Johnny?"

"The hard an' straight way. No turnin' around—no lookin' back! All or nothin'. I got no love fer no one, an' no one don't care about me. What I want, I aim to get. An' I gotta have a place to sleep and somethin' to eat, or things gonna start happenin' fast. Yo're the only friend I got, Snit—ya gotta help me, because I helped you!"

I didn't know what to do. I wanted to help him, but now I was afraid— afraid of losing a home the way he had. Worse still, I was afraid of losing my aunt, just when I was so near finding her again. All this Johnny would never understand, for he had his own values on what folks did and thought—and this was the difference between night and day with us.

"I'll do what I can, Johnny." I spoke anxiously, because I had no idea what I could do for him. "If only ya can find a place fer tonight, I'll try and rig up somethin' fer ya tomorrow. Maybe I can get Aunt Matilda to see the score, and leave ya here for a spell. Hang on, an' I'll get some food for ya!"

"Bring it to the church—I'll wait for ya there." Johnny was watching me to see if I meant what I was saying. "I don't wanna face that bitchy aunt of yores again today."

I thought of something.

"Hey! Take along a hammer an' nails, so's if anybody sees the door open, they'll think we're repairin' the church," I suggested.

"Nobody don't see that door open with our whiskey inside. I'll wait outside the church," Johnny said grimly.

"Then let's pour the damned stuff out and forget about it! I don't wanna get no deeper in trouble than I'm in now!" I nearly shouted at him.

"What?" Johnny glared at me, and his lips drew back again. "Maybe ya'll want to forget we got gallons of mash brewin' in the bush, eh? Ya wanna chicken out, maybe?"

"Look here, Johnny," I wagged my finger at him, "I'm not goin' back into the bush to brew no more moonshine—no sirree. I gone far enough with ya in this, but from now on ya do yore own brewin'!"

"Why, ya rotten—" Johnny swore, his eyes buggin' with disbelief. "What about the eight jugs in the church—ya aimin' we should spill those?"

"What else can we do now?" I argued. "The bootlegger skipped on us, an' with no wagon, how we gonna get into town? Maybe I could pull the two horses outa the pasture without Aunt Matilda knowin'—but that don't settle anythin'."

Johnny stared at me for a long while, dark circles of hate forming around his eyes.

"All right, Snit—that's all right. But I wanna tell ya somethin'—one day, you an' me are gonna settle. An' ya ain't gonna have no big fist to help ya, like when ya clipped me by surprise in the wagon. Ya ain't gonna have no aunt fer excuse neither, because I'm gonna settle with ya where I'm gonna get everythin' ready fer myself, an' in my own time—in my own way. Ya jus' remember that.

"Maybe I'll keep brewin', maybe I won't—I'll think about it. But them eight jugs is gonna get sold, Snit! If ya wanna help me, then we split like we split all along—if not, I'll sell them myself. What ya gonna do?"

"I'll help," I said, coughing to clear the hard knot in my throat. "When we gonna move them?"

"Tonight," Johnny replied.

"But how?"

"We gonna carry them into town on our backs, that's how. If we gotta wait a week at the elevator fer that pig to show up, we gonna wait. He an' I had a deal, an' he's gonna live up to it." Johnny's voice was menacing. He walked past me towards the road.

"Soon's the sun goes down, ya meet me at the church, or I'm movin' the whiskey out alone!" He spoke without turning.

"All right, Johnny."

I went into the house and sliced some bread and dry sausage. Then I wrapped the food in a piece of paper. It was hot and musty in the house, so leaving the door open, I sat in the shade beside the well pump, leaning my head against the cool casing.

I was tired, worn out clean through. Life was Johnny Swift—nervous and jumpy, full of hates and mistrust. And Johnny Swift was the hills—nice and soft looking, yet hungry as a wildcat. I was afraid of him, in a different sort of way than I was afraid of Corporal Kane or Tom Whittles, for those two had purposes which stuck out clear enough to see. But Johnny was a bit of everything gone wild. And because he was wild, I felt this evening I could no longer face the storm he was creating around me and everything I considered mine.

EIGHT

Johnny was anxious to go at sundown, but I insisted we wait until darkness, to give ourselves the least chance of being spotted on the road. We had divided the moonshine into two gunny sacks, four gallons to a sack, with handfuls of dry grass packed between the crocks to keep them from banging together. Then we carried them behind the church, away from the road. After that I smoked, while Johnny ate the food I had brought, and we waited for the night.

Night was long in coming. Even when the sun settled behind the crest of the westerly hills, its red rays burned in slight wisps of cloud overhead, throwing a disturbing glow over the countryside.

"Jeez!" Johnny muttered. "Look at it—just like the world was on fire. It mus' be hot up there. No wonder we don't get rain."

I grunted and closed my eyes.

"Makes ya wonder about guys who fly in airplanes—must be screwy to go up there. Ya ever see a guy who been up in an airplane?"

I hadn't.

"I'd never do it. Makes me dizzy just to go up in the hayloft," Johnny grumbled.

The last bright light in the sky faded, first becoming a leaden grey, and then dark. A night-hawk groaned as it swooped down, and caught a mouse in the field only a few yards from where we sat. Johnny and I rose to our feet.

"Jus' one thing," I said as we prepared to leave. "If something should happen, like somebody see us or Kane waiting for us up the road, I ain't takin' no chances, Johnny. I grab the first rock handy and smash the jugs. They can't nail us with the moonshine spilled."

Johnny's face darkened with anger, but he didn't argue.

"All right, Snit—but nobody'll see us, an' I don't aim for Kane to catch us."

We hoisted the sacks to our shoulders and walked around the church to the road. My load was heavy, and the round crocks bit into my shoulder and back. But we had ten miles to walk this night, and I vowed not to speak of any discomfort I felt, and to ignore any complaint Johnny might make. Johnny must have felt the same way, for once we were on the road, we moved forward at a fast walk, neither of us saying a word to the other.

Whittles' store was in darkness as we walked past. Suppose the bastard is watching, and gets ahead to warn Kane, I thought. Then I remembered our row earlier in the day, and I felt pretty certain he'd be too scared to do anything, even if he did see us. He'd tell *somebody else* to go report to Kane—but time was on our side now. Three hours from now we'd be in town, and that would be the end of that.

Two miles down the road, my shoulder had become numb, and I was waiting for Johnny to suggest we call a rest. From the field to the left of us a dog barked, and instinctively Johnny and I fell apart to crouch in the ditches running along either side of the road. We waited for about five minutes. The next time we heard the dog bark, he was some distance away, and we both rose to resume our walk. We had shifted our sacks to the other shoulder.

"I could drink a well dry, I'm that thirsty," I said.

"Why don't ya have a swig from one of the crocks? The bootlegger pig ain't gonna stick no fingers in to see if all the jugs are full," Johnny suggested.

"Don't be crazy—I don't wanna die!"

I had said that as a joke, but I felt Johnny watching me.

"Snit, I know how moonshine's made—good moonshine an' bad. That stuff yo're carrying is the best a guy can brew."

"I didn't mean nothin'."

"Two years ago my goddam old man brought home a quart of real poison," Johnny continued. "It killed a dog Rogers had—bugger used to come and pee against our well. The old man used to shoot after him—never even nick him. So one day he stuck out a piece of bacon, an' the dog come. The old man brought him into the house, uncorked the quart of moonshine, and poured about a cup down his throat. Then he let the dog go, but he never made it outa our yard. Kinda dropped his head into the dirt once or twice, then rolled over an' died."

"Served him right—shoulda knowed better than hang around yore yard."

"That's not the point," Johnny argued. "It was bad moonshine—coulda done the same to a man."

"What—kill a man?"

"Sure. The old man took it back to the 'legger he bought it from. Said he'd turn him in to the cops. He should've, too."

"Whatya mean, bad moonshine?" I asked.

"Stuff's been doctored up—like a cup of quicklime to a gallon, or a dash of formalin. Makes a guy go hairy, or lay him out with one drink. Get enough of it inta yore guts, an' you'll go blind or die."

"No guy would buy stuff like that!" I was rattled by what Johnny had said.

"Sure they buy—guys who drink hereabouts ain't got money, Snit. They'll buy anythin' with a kick. If it's got two times the kick fer the same price, they'll buy. Ya ever seen a guy starved for likker?" Johnny stopped to shift his sack to the other shoulder.

"No."

"Boy, I'll tell ya, it's somethin'! They get thin and weasel-eyed, an' start shakin' so they can't hold anythin' in their hands. Then they get friendly as hell, or mean. That's when they gotta go out an' get booze quick. My old man gets mean."

"Yore old man ain't a boozer, Johnny."

Johnny laughed, hard and dry.

"He ain't, eh? Ya wanna go back and walk in on him right now. He'll be sittin' on his bed about this time, with his shoes off—spittin' on his hands, an' fingerin' his axe. Or maybe he'll be singin' his goddam hymns—that's just before he starts bawlin' like a kid with his ass spanked!" Johnny spoke bitterly.

"What about his church-goin', and dedication to the Good Life as he calls it?"

"Hell, Snit, he's been tryin' to scare himself outa the habit. A guy like my old man gets scared awful easy. He's a bad one—ends up by scarin' the hell outa everybody else, an doin' nothin' to help himself."

We walked in silence for the next mile. The moon rose, orange and warm. We could see the road plainly under its light, but it deepened the shadows of the fields and roadside. My back was beginning to ache, but Johnny didn't seem to mind. He was sweating a lot, and when we walked close together I could smell the heat and sour odour of his clothes. But he was like a machine now—just walking like he'd never stop.

"Ya ever felt sorry for your old man?" I asked—not that I wanted to know, but I had to talk to keep my mouth moist.

"I hate the bastard clean through." He said that quickly and quietly, like it never left his mind, even when he was thinking of something else. I didn't want to talk. I tried to figure out how far we'd gone—how many miles were left to go. I even argued with myself, like using my left eye against my right—why didn't we take Aunt Matilda's horses and ride them? Would have saved our feet. Or why carry the stuff into town anyway—seemed like asking for trouble. What if the elevator agent didn't show? All this for nothing ... Then I would see the direction of Johnny's thinking. He carried a lot of money in the gunny sacks—maybe it was a risk, but one we couldn't take tomorrow.

I looked up, and in a field we were just approaching I saw a thin cow drinking at a trough.

"Johnny, I gotta get some water." I pointed to the cow.

"Hey—that'll sure be good! Be nice to dip my head in that trough!" Johnny exclaimed, and dropping his sack into the ditch, he began climbing the fence.

"Don't ya go sticking yore head in the trough before I get a drink!" I called after him.

"To hell with ya!" Johnny was over the fence now and running towards the cow, which lifted up its head, then turned tail at seeing him come like that. I tried to catch up with him, but before I reached the trough he already had his head down and was swishing it through the water.

"Rotten, bloody pig!" I swore, grabbing him by the hair and pulling him back. He blew a spray of water out of his mouth and laughed. I had to force myself to lean over the trough. When I did suck up water, I had trouble swallowing, for I imagined it tasted of Johnny and all the muck of his face and hair. Johnny was still laughing when we returned to the road.

"I gotta hand it to ya, Snit," he chuckled as he lifted his sack to his shoulder. "I didn't think ya was gonna drink that water at all. Guess there's hope fer ya to become a man like the rest of us!"

"Shut up!" I barked at him.

"All right—I didn't mean nothin'. Don't get rough with me—we got a long way to go yet, and we gonna need all our fightin' strength if we gonna get to town at all." He walked away from me. I followed, deliberately letting him keep in front, because I didn't want to row with him.

The higher the moon rose, the paler it became. Johnny still carried his sack over one shoulder, but I found myself shifting shoulders frequently now. Once Johnny turned and waited for me to catch up. I shifted the sack twice as I walked towards him.

"Christ—ya keep swingin' that thing like yo're doin', an' ya'll get sore arms. Kinda looks like old Snit ain't gonna be able to make it!" There was a sneer in his voice.

"Go to hell!" I growled, and swore I wasn't going to shift the sack unless he did, even if it cut right into my shoulder. We walked, the dust rising to our nostrils and not a sound to distract us. I thought of things I'd seen and done, and then I didn't think any more.

"Hey!" Johnny suddenly called near my ear. "Whatsa matter—ya gone to sleep? Ya been walkin' like ya needed all the road to get where yo're goin'."

"Don't worry none!" I snapped back at him. I guess I must have dozed, because I looked around, trying to reckon how far we'd walked before I blanked.

"Another half hour, and we're there," Johnny said. His voice was tired. I looked at him, and saw the moonlight glistening off his skin. His mouth was open and slack with weariness. Grudgingly, I had to admit he was pretty tough when it came to taking a test this way. I had to turn away when he stopped to unlace his boots and scrape out the dust which had packed inside, for they had hardly any soles, and he must have walked the last few miles in quite a bit of pain.

When he cleaned his boots, I rolled us each a cigarette. When I gave him his and struck a match to it, I noticed him watching me with an amused expression in his eyes. He didn't goad me, though, for which I was thankful.

Reaching the top of the next rise in the road, we spotted the few lights of town.

"There she is—damn her rotten heart!" Johnny shouted, and we hurried on. I didn't ask Johnny what he planned on doing. Instead I just followed him.

On the outskirts of town, Johnny left the road, and we made our way in a semicircle until we came near the highway which approached from the opposite direction. Here Johnny stopped.

"There's scrub bushes we can sleep behind, 'cause morning's a long way off," he said. "But I wanna be near that elevator when that sonofabitch gets there!"

"There's no place to hide near the elevator."

"We can go *into* the elevator," he suggested.

"Whatya talkin' about? It'll be locked tighter than a thief's house."

"Let's take a look." We moved forward again. There were no street lights near the elevator, so we came from the shadowed side without fear of being seen. Staying close to the walls of the tall building, we reached the ramp to the scales. The doors to the platform were lowered. Johnny climbed the ramp and tried the doors, but they were locked.

"Hey!" I called in a whisper. "We could hide under the ramp!"

The ramp rose at an incline from ground level to a height of about three feet, where it was joined to the elevator itself. Under it was a jungle of weeds and grass. Johnny jumped down beside me and peered where I pointed.

"Yeh! We could sleep like we was in God's lap. Come on!" Pulling his sack behind him, Johnny parted the growth of grass and disappeared beneath the ramp. I followed after him.

I dozed for a while, then woke up and couldn't go back to sleep for Johnny's snoring. I'd never heard a guy snore like he did. He lay on his back, his mouth wide open and his eyes only partially shut, which was pretty frightening to see. When he took a breath in, he groaned, and when he blew it out, the sound coming out of his throat was a gargle with voice to it. I jabbed him in the ribs, for I was sure anybody passing on the street would hear him. He only ground his teeth, and a few minutes later he was snoring again.

So I kept poking him, and hoping morning would come soon.

With dawn, the air became chilly, and I took the jugs from my sack, laying them side by side in front of me. Then I used the empty gunny sack for a wrap around my shoulders. Johnny slept with his chest bare and arms thrown wide apart. I touched the skin of his neck with my finger, and was startled to feel how warm he was.

Hunger was twisting in my belly like a living thing, and I rolled myself a cigarette to numb my appetite. In the cool morning air, the cigarette tasted impure, so I snubbed it out after one puff. At that moment I heard footsteps approaching from the direction of town. I shook Johnny, but his head bobbed from side to side and he continued sleeping. The footsteps came nearer, and I shook Johnny harder. Then the footsteps struck the edge of the ramp. Putting my hand across Johnny's mouth, I rolled over him and held him down. His eyes opened with alarm, and he reached for my throat. Awareness came quickly to him, and he relaxed. I sighed and released him.

The footsteps overhead reached the building now, and we heard the rattle of keys, and the heavy groan of the elevator doors being pushed open.

"It's him!" Johnny whispered thickly, his face flushing with excitement. Rolling over on his stomach, he crawled out from under the ramp. I followed him.

The elevator agent was drowsily unlocking the door to his office when we caught up with him.

"Hey!" Johnny called to him. "Been tryin' to reach ya—where ya been?"

The agent turned so fast with surprise the keys went flying across the scale deck, and his office door still locked. He was both mad and frightened.

"What the hell you guys doin' here?" he demanded gruffly, his eyes fixed on Johnny.

Johnny was good natured and smiling, fumbling awkwardly with his hands. But I noticed the nervous sweat beading on his forehead.

"Brought in some more stuff—been waitin' for ya all night," he said, stretching as he spoke.

"I don't want none of the stuff—whatever yo're talking about. Now get out." The bootlegger bent over to pick up his keys, but Johnny caught him by the shoulder and jerked him up.

"Whatya mean ya don't want the stuff? We got eight gallons fer ya!" Johnny was still smiling, but he was holding tightly to the bootlegger's shirt.

"Eight gallons! What the hell ya think I run—a likker store! Naw, I'm not buyin' anymore—I'm outa the racket. You guys are poison." The agent tried to pull himself out of Johnny's grasp. "Come on—leggo!"

"Ya not buyin' anymore? Sure, yo're gonna buy the eight gallons like a good boy. Snit, open the door to this pigsty. We're gonna take our friend in, an' we're gonna find a crowbar and work the sonofabitch over so's his own whorin' mother wouldn't know him. Sure, he's gonna buy!" Johnny jumped behind the bootlegger, catching a stranglehold under the fat agent's chin. I grabbed for the keys and unlocked the office door. Johnny was already working him backwards into the room. I glanced out to the street of the town. Nobody in sight.

In a moment we had him in the room and thrown into a chair. I slammed the door shut. Among the litter on the dirty office desk which occupied a corner of the room, there was a tackhammer. Johnny got hold of it, and releasing the bootlegger, stood over him. Both he and the bootlegger were breathing hard.

"Now—ya still gonna chicken out—or we gonna have to work ya over?" Johnny was insane with hatred. He was spitting his words out, and by the way he stood poised, I was afraid he might just attack the agent without thinking twice about it.

"Cool off, you guys—there don't have to be no trouble." I spoke to both of them.

Johnny half turned his face to me.

"Shut up, Snit! Ya got nothin' to do with this—it's between him an' me! Look at 'im, shakin' with fright! Bet ya figured I'd get scared first after what ya done. Johnny Swift don't get scared away by yellow pig cowards!"

The bootlegger's eyes were swimming in tears of fear.

"I'm scared, Johnny—ya bet I'm scared!" he babbled, watching the hammer in Johnny's hand. "What's got into ya, man! I'll buy—I'll buy yore likker! Just don't act like ya was aimin' to kill me or something, Johnny! Fer Christ's sake, put away that hammer!"

Saying this, he lunged forward to grab the hammer, and Johnny swung to strike. I jumped in between them, pushing the agent back into his chair, and Johnny away to the table.

"Ya rotten weasel!" Johnny cursed, glaring at the bootlegger.

"Break it up!" I shouted. "He wants to buy, so sell the damned stuff and let's get outa here. If ya came for revenge, then I'm outa this. In fact, I'll go and bring Kane down here to straighten you guys out!" I said to Johnny.

That sobered both of them.

"All right, Snit—I'll leave the bastard alone. Go bring the moonshine in, an' I'll collect off him."

"No rough stuff?"

"Naw." Johnny was quieter now, and his face had turned pale and sick. "But I'm hangin' on to the hammer till ya get back, just so's he don't try no monkey business."

There was still nobody on the town street as I brought the whiskey out from under the ramp, and placing all eight jugs into one bag, dragged it up to the scale deck, then into the office. The other sack I left where I had slept with it under the ramp.

The bootlegger stared at the sack I had brought in.

"Take my word for it—there's eight gallons there," I muttered at him.

"Sure, boys—I trust ya!" He seemed considerably relieved now that he was in no danger of physical harm. "I was just gonna tell ya it wasn't my fault ya found the elevator closed the other day—"

"Shut yore fuckin' mouth!" Johnny's temper flared.

The agent cringed back into his chair until his double chins made two white collars around his throat.

"He paid ya?" I asked Johnny.

"Yeh, he paid."

At the door, Johnny turned and dropped the hammer on the floor. He stared a moment longer at the bootlegger.

"Ya can thank Snit yore head ain't bust in two, ya double-crossin' snake! Just remember, Snit ain't always gonna be around to save ya—an' I'll get ya then!"

"Why don't ya leave me alone? I don't ever want to see any of yore damned whiskey!" The man was actually in tears now.

"Aw fer God's sake, Johnny—let's get outa here," I complained.

Johnny slammed the door shut and we walked out into the street. The sun was higher than the town buildings now, throwing cool shadows diagonally across the white dust of the road. Neither of us spoke until we reached Elsie's place.

She was sweeping when we came in, but once we were seated at a table, she dropped her broom to the floor and waddled towards us. I looked down and saw that her feet were in a pair of heavy woollen stockings, with no shoes on. They were huge feet, with ankles that seemed waterlogged, they were so thick.

"Whatcha want?" she demanded, looking first at me, then at Johnny.

"I ain't eaten," I said. "I'd like a coupla eggs and some coffee."

She looked at Johnny.

"The same."

She still stood looking suspiciously at us.

"Ya punks really wanna eat, or ya just playin' around?" She spoke gruffly. "I ain't got much in food here, an' I don't wanna cook if yo're just jokin' with me."

"We're not jokin'," I assured her. "We ain't had anythin' to eat since some time yesterday."

"How many folks has?" she growled, but she seemed satisfied we weren't larking her, for a moment later we heard the crackling of a hot greased pan in the kitchen back of the café.

Johnny handed me the money he had collected from the bootlegger.

"Count it out, so's he don't get away with nothin', or I'm goin' back an' see the dirty, lousy—"

"Lay off the guy. We're finished with him, an' I don't see no cause for houndin' the bugger the way ya been doin'," I said as I counted the bills.

"Bootleggers is the lowest," Johnny said vehemently, as he leaned forward with his elbows on the table.

The money was right.

"An' ya know what's worse than an ordinary bootlegger?" Johnny was staring at me. I said I didn't.

"It's a bootlegger that tries to do ya!"

"He didn't try to do ya—he just chickened out!" I argued.

"The way I see it, it don't matter what the reason is—a guy like that gotta be kicked around some to show him who's top dog, I'm disappointed in ya, Snit—the way ya took up fer him."

"Whatta hell ya sayin'! I didn't take up—ya'd a killed him if I hadn't stopped ya."

"So what—he's just a goddam bootlegger. You an' me, we work our hands to the bone, makin' stuff to sell. He just buys, turns around an' sells—don't ever get his hands dirty; an' I betcha he cleans up more on a gallon than we do! Then he chickens an' we coulda ended up in jail on accounta him. I don't mind goin' to jail, Snit—but not for that lousy bastard!"

"Sure, Johnny—I agree with ya. Now shut up." Elsie was approaching with two plates of food, and I didn't want her to hear our conversation. She plunked the plates in front of us.

"Now wot was it ya wan'ed to drink?" she asked, her arms akimbo.

"Coffee," I replied.

"I gotta pot of tea that's still warm, if ya wan' it," she said, and coughed.

"All right, Elsie—tea'll be fine."

"Youse guys is easy to please," she muttered, and made her way back to the kitchen.

Johnny cut a small part of egg with his fork and nibbled at it.

"This is good!" he said, and began eating greedily.

The café door opened just then, and I glanced up. Corporal Kane entered, his face drawn and his eyes sleep-angry. He saw us and came over.

"The cop's here," I warned Johnny in a low voice, but he didn't seem to hear me.

"You guys sure made it into town early this morning," Kane said sourly. "Mind if I sit down?"

"Go 'head—it's a public place," Johnny muttered without looking up. Kane glanced hard at him, but Johnny was bent over his plate, finishing the last of his breakfast. As Kane pulled up another chair, Elsie came around with the teapot and two cups. She placed the tea on the table, then looked at Kane through vacant eyes.

"Whatcha want?"

"I'll have a cup with the boys," Kane nodded at the teapot. Johnny took the lid off the pot and peered in.

"I dunno—there ain't much there," he said. Elsie took the pot and went back into the kitchen with it. Johnny grinned at me, then composing his face, looked at Kane.

The mountie was drumming with the fingers of one hand on the table, while he draped the other over the back of his chair. He was staring at Johnny.

"Well, what's new, co'poral?" Johnny asked with a straight face. "Catch any bad guys lately, or any moonshine makers?"

The drumming stopped, and Kane leaned towards Johnny. "Just keep talkin' Swift—and I'm gonna pull you in so fast you won't know what happened to you! Then maybe we'll get to the bottom of this."

"Johnny's only kidding," I butted in.

"You keep quiet—I'll talk to you later," Kane snapped at me. Just then, Elsie brought the tea back, also a cup for the policeman. Then she propped herself at the nearest table, and stood, with her arms folded, listening.

Kane turned his head to see her.

"That'll be all!" he said crisply, and Elsie backed away, her mouth slightly opened.

"Boy—she's sure scared o' ya," Johnny marvelled. "Think she makes moonshine in the kitchen?"

"Where were you last night?" Kane asked Johnny.

"Oh, I been around." Johnny poured himself a cup of tea.

"I'm asking you a question, Swift. And I'm going to get an answer out of you if it's the last thing I do. Where were you last night?"

"Maybe I was home in bed." Kane was mad, and the cheek was going out of Johnny.

"You weren't home at all. I've just come back from an early morning drive to your place." Kane began drumming on the table again.

Johnny had just lifted the cup to his lips, but he dropped it hard on the plate. His temples broke out in sweat.

"I saw your father," Kane continued in a soft menacing voice. "He's a sick man, Johnny—a badly hurt man. I could see you get three months for that."

"I don't care—I done nothin' wrong," Johnny blustered.

"And a couple of lashes," Kane continued, still drumming with his fingers, Johnny winced, and looked up at me helplessly.

"It ain't so—the old man musta done somethin' to hisself to get me in trouble! Ask Snit—he knows everythin'." Johnny was staring at me with the expression of a helpless, trapped animal.

"He's right, corporal," I lied. "Johnny was with me all the time. He never saw his old man."

Kane looked at me, and his lips parted in a hard smile.

"Maybe I can accommodate both of you, then. It would have taken two guys to beat up the old man like that—no one person would have taken so much time and work to do such a perfect job. You ever seen a man with one ear missing, and his teeth broken out of his jaw? He's staggering around now, trying to get his cattle watered and out to pasture. He could pass out any time from loss of blood. In this heat, he could die before anybody got to him to help. You know what could happen to both of you if he died?"

"Cut it out!" I tried to keep my voice down. "Why didn't ya bring him in for a doctor to look at him? Ya want him to die?"

"He's the same kind of person as your aunt, Mandolin—worked hard all his life, and hasn't even got a respectable shirt on his back to show for it." Kane kept boring into me. "Raises a kid to help him, and one day he gets jumped by one or two good-for-nothing punks who bust up what's left of his health. He can't even afford a doctor—you understand? And how's he going to eat with no teeth? Tell me!"

"I got nothing, same's Johnny an' everybody else in this bloody place! Why don't you leave me alone?" I argued desperately.

"You got nothing, eh!" Kane turned in his chair, "Look around you. See any other hill farmers eating in this café? Folks from over there don't eat in cafés—even a place like this. They bring sandwiches and eat on their wagons, or where nobody sees them. Where were you last night?"

"What ya aimin' to do to us?" I asked.

Kane poured himself a cup of tea before he replied.

"Well, I could do a number of things. I could book you in for attempted manslaughter. Or I could pull you in on suspicion of moonshine-making, then call in a few more officers to round up enough evidence to make a charge stick against you, or whoever is producing. I'm not stuck for ideas on what I can do to you."

"Then why don't ya?"

Kane put his cup down and thought for a moment.

"I've been here a long time," he said slowly. "When I first came here, you must've been pretty small kids. There was moonshine made and sold then. I've caught more moonshine-makers than I can remember—but there's one guy I've never been able to catch—the person who handles the stuff. The moment I start to move, he vanishes into thin air."

Johnny fingered his cup now, an ugly grin spreading over his lips.

"Ya tryin' to make a deal?" he asked.

Kane clenched his drumming fingers into a fist and glanced at Johnny sideways.

"I said nothing of the sort," he said coldly.

"Yeh, yeh—I know. But all this baloney about my old man an' the lashes—that's just talk, eh?"

Kane remained wooden.

"All right—I was sleepin' last night, but I wasn't sleepin' good an' had some bad dreams—ya wanna hear about my dreams?" Johnny's face was a study in excited treachery.

"Johnny, what the hell ya doin'?" I tried to stop him.

"Sit down!" Kane ordered me.

"Like I say, I was dreamin'—an' it come to me that the elevator agent was bootleggin' like a sonofabitch. Betcha, if yo're lucky, ya might find some jugs in his office right now. But like I said, I was only dreamin'—so don't put the bite on us fer nothin'! Ya know how it is when a guy sleeps bad!"

"Ya rotten bugger!" I shouted at Johnny, but he wasn't listening to anything I said. He just sat there, grinning like a satisfied idiot.

"Look," I said to Kane. "It's all wrong. Me and Johnny was moonshine-making, all right. He's got no call to—"

Kane was on his feet now, smiling at Johnny.

"Thanks, Swift—thanks a lot. If your dreams mean anything, forget I saw you. And you, Mandolin," he turned on his heel to face me, "Keep your damned nose clean, or I'm going to bring you down to size so quick you won't know what happened! I don't like crooked missionaries!"

He left in a hurry.

I moved to the counter to pay Elsie. Johnny was behind me, but I didn't want to see his face again. Elsie took the money and stared at us through half closed eyes. Then in her wheezy voice she said, "If you guys got trouble with the frigging cops, then don't come around here any more. Ya hear?"

"Good old Elsie, the Borden cow!" Johnny said from the doorway and laughed. I left as quickly as I could, but not before I heard Elsie shout after us, "Punks!"

Out in the street, I stopped and counted out half the money we had made on the last moonshine sale.

"Yore share—ya rotten bastard—ya good-for-nothin' prick!" I spat the words into his face, as I handed the cash to him. He took the money without batting an eye.

Then he sort of slouched on one leg and said in a matter-of-fact voice, "You an' I are through workin' together, Snit. I done the right thing—it was us or that bootleggin' snake. But it ain't us no more—now it's me myself. Ya been goin' against me a long time, Snit, an' I'm gonna hit you too if yo're against me. Just ya remember what the cop said—keep yore nose clean, or him an' I gonna get ya into plenty of trouble."

"I see. Well Johnny, ya can collect the rest of yore money any time yo're ready. An' then I don't ever wanna have anything to do with ya."

"I thought ya was gonna fix me up with a place to sleep and somethin' to eat until I got myself looked after." I couldn't believe it, but he said that with sincerity.

"Ya got money—go buy yoreself some groceries an' set up housekeepin' in the church. Ya wasted fifty bucks of our money on that damned place as it was—so ya might as well get some benefit for it. I won't!" I started to walk home.

Johnny didn't buy groceries. He followed me, always a few paces behind. If I walked faster, he did, too. Then if I slowed down, I'd hear his footsteps become slower in the dust behind me. After the first few miles, it began to bug me.

"Whatcha followin' me like that for?" I turned to him. "Go ahead an' walk in front of me."

He was smiling, his eyes hard, but his face soft and boyish. He just stood there, waiting.

"Go on! Go ahead!" I spoke again. But he just stood there. I began walking, and I could hear him, still the same distance behind— still following at the same pace. My skin began to feel clammy, and pulling my shirt out of my trousers for cool air, I began to run. And behind me, I heard him run.

This is ridiculous, I was telling myself. He's got a right to follow—so forget about it and act like nothing was wrong. But I was getting panicky. Ahead of me was a broken branch lying partly in the ditch. Reaching it, I suddenly stopped, and catching hold of it turned on Johnny.

"I'm gonna hit ya—sure as hell!" I warned him. He stopped, smiling and scratching his ear. "What's the matter—ya forgot how to speak?"

He continued scratching his ear, and suddenly his smile broadened to a grin. Catching a good hold of the branch, I ran towards him. He turned and ran. I threw the branch, but it fell short of hitting him. I stopped, and he ran only a few more paces before glancing over his shoulder, and seeing me give up the chase, likewise stopped. His hand went up to his ear, and he began scratching again.

"Damn you!" I shouted at him. The sound of my voice, thin and metallic, alarmed me. What the hell's happening to me? I thought. I can't let him get me down. He's after me now for breaking away from him, same as he was after the bootlegger.

I began walking again, hard and fast until the calves of my legs ached with strain. And still behind me I heard Johnny. He began whistling—not any special tune, just whistling, high and low without any pattern or beat. It was a senseless, small sort of thing I could have ignored—probably had ignored, for he must have whistled that way before when we drove the wagon or made moonshine in the bog. Yet now it was a part of the heat and dust of the road. A part of the sun-scorched hills and dead grass around me. Even a part of the thirst which hurt my throat so that I couldn't swallow the pasty saliva in my mouth.

"Damn! Damn! Hell and damn!" I started to curse to myself. Whatever brought me here, anyway? I could have had a good job in the city, with decent clothes and money in pocket. Here I had nothing to look forward to—just an aunt who let me stay so long as I was needed and could make my way, a bad name with the police, and more trouble with Johnny Swift than I could cope with.

We were alongside the church now.

"Hey, Snit!" Johnny called, and I turned to him. "Ya gonna fix it up with yore aunt so's I can sleep at yore place? I gotta have some place to go!"

He was about ten yards away from me, and the white dust between us was dazzling. He was squinting at me, his mouth set and sober. I stared at him for a while, trying to figure if he was meaning what he said, or still trying to make a donkey of me.

"Come on, Snit—yo're not gonna let me down. I helped ya once!"

"Why didja tail me all the way like that?" I asked hesitantly.

"Whatcha talkin' about—tailed ya where? Cripes, yo're getting as kooky as yore aunt, Snit! How about it, Snit?" I turned away, remembering what he did in the café.

"No, Johnny—like ya said, you and I are through. Ya gotta take care of yourself, and I gotta take care of myself, too." I started to walk away.

"Then yo're not gonna help? Is that the way it is Snit—ya become a yellow, double-crossin' bastard? Is that the way ya wan' it? All right—I'll get squared with ya for this. I'll get ya when ya ain't lookin', like I'm gonna get every sonofabitch who gets in my way!"

I put my hands up to my ears and fled towards my aunt's. Johnny was still shouting after me, but I didn't want to hear anymore.

NINE

In the afternoon shade of the house, I waited for Johnny to call and collect his share of our money. Aunt Matilda brought me a cup of tea.

"Somebody comin'?" she asked, following my stare down the road.

"No nobody's comin'," I said. She stood around for a while, leaning one arm against the wall.

"Been losin' hair. Stuff comes out by the handful."

I looked up and saw her biting her lip with embarrassment. Her hair was combed back—severe and old-fashioned, but clean and combed.

"Say!" I mocked. "Ya goin' dancin'?"

"Oh, shut yore big mouth!" She pretended to be angry, and turning sharply, went indoors.

I waited, and overhead the sky deepened and darkened, but Johnny didn't come. I didn't worry about him—not in the sense that I was concerned about his having money. I just wanted him to come so we could divide our earnings, and part. I wanted no further ties with him, wanted the chance to stay out of his way and not create any great bitterness. I was afraid of him in a way I could not understand.

"You want supper, Snit?" my aunt called through the open door.

"Naw—it's too hot to eat."

"If ya want anything, say so now, or I'm goin' to bed."

I was staring down the road, watching closely to make sure, for through the shimmering heat of the evening I thought I saw somebody approaching.

"I been talkin' to you, Snit!" There was annoyance in my aunt's voice. A moment later, she appeared at the door. I was standing up now, looking hard down the road.

"What's the matter? Your eyes are bugged like you was seein' a ghost," she said, scratching the small of her back with a thumb.

"Somebody's comin'," I pointed.

"I thought you said nobody was comin' tonight." She followed the direction of my gaze. "Kinda looks like two somebody's comin'. I'll heat some tea."

There were two people approaching, but even at a distance I knew neither of them was Johnny. At the entrance to our yard they turned in. One of the men was old man Shnitka, smiling and looking sideways with shyness. He was hunched with age and hard work, and the hair straggling from under his threadbare cap was grey. When he smiled, his teeth showed as short, rotten stumps which failed to come together.

"Ay, Snit! Ay, Matilda! Good to see ya healthy—good way to be!" He greeted us some distance from the house. He almost tripped, he was that awkward and bashful.

"This here's some more of the folks hereabouts, Nick," Shnitka introduced us to his friend.

This man was a stranger. He was old, with skin crisscrossed with wrinkles, and small shiny dark eyes that stared out from under bushy brows. He had a thick, long beard of an iron-grey colour, and his hair was long, like that of a woman. He wore no hat, and the clothes on his body had been discarded by other men. In his hand he carried a violin with only two strings, and a bow.

"Howdy." He nodded, and giggled a secret sort of giggle, like a man who's doing something bad behind an outbuilding.

"Nick here can make rain," Shnitka said offhandedly, then poked a long finger to scrape inside his ear. "Don't cost hardly nothin'—just two bucks."

"He's gonna make rain—fer just two bucks." Aunt Matilda mimicked Shnitka's voice and mannerisms. "Just like that—fer two bucks he's gonna make rain. How much flour an' sugar can you get for two bucks?"

"It ain't much," Shnitka said feebly, staring at his feet as he spoke. "Besides, everybody's goin' in."

"Everybody?" I asked.

"Sure—everybody down the line so far, except Tom Whittles, but Tom don't need rain in the same way us farmers need it."

"How's he make this rain?" Aunt Matilda asked sharply.

"Well—" Shnitka got real upset now, and swivelled this way and that on his heels. "Nick fiddles, and the rains come. Ask him—he made it rain everywhere else."

"Yessiree, folks—I can make it dribble just so much, an' I can make it come down in torrents—whatever's your choice!" The rainmaker stepped forward, talking loud, with his eyes closed and his arms thrown apart. "The secret's in my magic violin! Yes, my violin can open the heavens to those who wish it. You cannot go wrong. Up in the cosmos, something has gone wrong—the balance between good and evil had been disturbed, and it will take the sympathetic vibrations of my violin to restore the harmony to proper order."

"He's mad!" I said to my aunt.

"Can you make it rain, say right now—just to give us a sample of what's to come?" my aunt asked innocently. The rainmaker took exception to what she asked, for suddenly he opened his eyes, and quivering with anger, shook a fist in front of her.

"You are making it hard for me, woman!" he said in a rising voice. "You are making it hard for your neighbours and friends—have you thought of them? Poor folks, suffering and crying for rain, and you stand between them, like a harlot in the temple! For shame!"

"Hold on now!" I stepped in front of him. "We didn't call for ya, but since ya come, ya'll have to show respect and decency fer us."

"Phah! Respect and decency you want! Just two lousy bucks, and you can share the good fortune of all!"

"Now now, Nick—these folks don't mean no harm. Matilda was just curious, she don't understand all there is to know." Shnitka sidled into the argument.

"Cripes, Snit—we gotta do somethin'. Reverend Crowe's been prayin' fer rain, and it don't come. Folks has gotta help themselves."

"Waste no more time on these heathens, my good man." The rainmaker dismissed my aunt and me with a wave of his hand. "There are other folk to see, but I warn you, these two have hurt our chances of a proper rain!"

"Now Snit, Matilda—let's look at this sensible." Shnitka was shaky and fearful.

"Did you pay him two bucks?" my aunt asked. Shnitka nodded.

"Then take your money back an' stop makin' a fool of yourself!"

"Ya don't understand—ya got no kids, Matilda. Even this late, a rain would still make hay of the grain, an' give us somethin' to keep our stock on. There ain't gonna be no milk at our place this winter!" Shnitka's voice was whining with anxiety. The rainmaker stamped his foot angrily and began walking away. Then he stopped and turned just long enough to lift his fiddle to his chin and play a few bars of a squawky and unnerving melody.

"That'll put a curse on your farm, an' maybe on others near yours! Don't blame no one but yourselves for being so cheap and reckless as to cross me!" he shouted, and made for the road. Shnitka still tried to argue, but seeing the rainmaker leaving, he gave up and followed.

"The nerve! Did you ever hear of anything like that? People—hell! Sheep show more sense than our folk," Aunt Matilda said with disgust, and went indoors.

All the same, I glanced up at the sky. It was perfectly clear and dull with heat.

Night was filling the hollows now. I waited a while longer, then decided that Johnny would not come, so I rose and walked to the barn and my hayloft bed.

I thought, as I tossed and turned that long night. I thought how pleasant it would be to live where a farm produced a living, where a man could work with a tractor in reasonable conditions and see plants which grew tall and strong. Where there was no more fruitless labour in working the soil by hand, or tormenting horses until they were just as weary and sick as the men who drove and guided them. Where there were proper schools, and a kid didn't have to begin working the moment he stood upright. Where there was no fear and no want to twist and damage the soul and body of man.

This wasn't farming—this wasn't even living. It was penal servitude to the blasted hills and desert-making sun; yet men clung to the soil like flies to a cadaver and wouldn't let go.

I had grown into the habit of sleeping late since working nights in the bog. Waking, I heard Aunt Matilda pumping water for cattle in the yard. Even in the shade of the hayloft, the air had the feel of being well warmed by the sun. I struggled to my feet and hurried down the ladder and through the barn into the yard.

My aunt was at the well, slowly working the iron pump handle and watching the drinking cows without interest. I came up to her before she saw me.

"Why didn't ya holler? I could've done this earlier," I said sourly.

"No bother—nothin' to do anyway. You could cook an egg in the dust, the sun's that hot."

I could feel it burning through my shirt and tingling the skin of my shoulders. Dipping my hand into the water trough, I scooped some cold water and rubbed it on my face and neck. It felt good, for a moment, and I came completely awake.

"You should wipe yourself with a towel. Your skin is getting dry and crinkly as everybody else's here," Aunt Matilda observed, as she again worked the pump slowly.

"Ach!" I grunted. "Just gets towels dirty, an' it don't make any difference. Ever see a cow use a towel after a rain?"

"It's been many years since I saw a cow in a rain," she said sadly. I thought of the rainmaker who came last night.

"Hey—what's gonna happen to the guy with the beard when he skins all the farmers and the weather don't change? I wouldn't wanna be in his shoes!"

My aunt thought about this for a moment.

"He'll hightail it outa here at night. But he won't really have to. You heard him talk—he could talk our Crowe to a standstill. He'll have something to say to save his neck. Never knew a guy talk himself into trouble that couldn't talk his way out again. Talk is a big thing. We never learned to talk, Snit—never learned how to defend ourselves, or explain how it feels to be us.

"I seen it happen even worse. Your folks and I lived close to North Battleford before we came here. Used to be a big Ukrainian settlement there. Those of us who didn't speak their language called them dumb bohunks—the silent ones. They worked hard, stayed outa trouble and lived on next to nothing. Then one day we heard that twenty young men among them—chosen to speak for everybody, themselves and us—had left on foot to go to Regina and ask the Government for better prices on grain and livestock, or else give us relief.

"We stopped calling them names after that, Snit—because it takes a lot of guts and figuring to reach a point where folks that suffer make a decision to speak up as best they know how."

"What happened to those twenty guys?" I asked.

"They got arrested for vagrancy and each got a month in jail. Then they came back."

"Then nothin' happened at all."

"That's where you're wrong, Snit. A lot happened—but I didn't understand it then. For one thing, the whole community started to work and think together—not like here, where one neighbour don't know another, an' every family is afraid of itself. They really got through—used to come together into the schoolyard on Sundays, and everybody would talk and argue about how we needed better roads, an' fertilizer for the fields, weed-killers, and all that sort of thing. Then the Ukes used to sing, playing their mandolins, an' the girls dancing. Or there'd be some good softball games. We were all poor as hell, but when you laughed it made it easier."

"Why didya leave—why in hell come out here?" I asked with amazement.

"I dunno—pride, I suppose. You see, Snit, in North Battleford, we suddenly found ourselves the outsiders—the silent ones. Twenty men walk away to tell the government who they are an' what they want, and suddenly you find everything you took for granted was just so much hogwash. It wasn't enough to stop calling them names—we would have to eat crow, and then run like hell to catch up, instead of standing still like we'd done for a long time.

"We didn't try, we moved to where no one we had known would learn how we made out. Your dad heard about this place, where land was cheap to buy and there was supposed to be enough rain and good soil. So we sold everything we had an' came out to Alberta. We sure got what we asked for, as far as finding folks like ourselves went. Jesus Christ, I wish I could die!"

"Don't talk like that, Aunt Matilda!" I approached to touch her hands on the pump. "We're holding our own against the weather, an' we'll do better next year. Besides, yo're getting healthier an' happier. I never seen ya this good since the old days!"

She looked up at me, and her face was so sad it brought tears to my eyes.

"Sure, Snit—I been looking better an' feeling better, too. I been fighting time to pay back for soaking up your money an' work. I can even stand back an' get sharpish with my neighbours for not trying—but it's all a big, foolish lie, Snit. It's all over for me now. You know what's the worst thing a person like me can do?"

I didn't know, and I said nothing.

"I'll tell you, Snit. It's to leech on—like for me to leech on to you, drawing on your goodness, strength an' sympathy—an' to go around pretending that youth was never gonna leave my bones, an' death an' the end of all dreams is only for other folks. Giving it a name—love! Then both you an' I getting sick of the word, but saying it every day to each other to make sure."

"To make sure of what?"

"Me to make sure you still respected my cheap pride, an' you to live up to your responsibilities—or what you figure are your responsibilities."

"Aunt Matilda, yo're talkin' nonsense."

She was still looking at me, fighting so hard against tears. Her lips were thin and trembling, yet she stood erect and proud, like nothing would knock her down—nothing she saw or lived through.

"I gotta die, Snit—same as anybody else. But I ain't gonna die easy. My conscience won't let me!"

"Ya ain't alone—I'm with ya. I don't want to hear anymore!"

"But you've got to listen, Snit—you've got to understand. Once you've made up your mind, there's no turning back. I don't want no love from you—nor any respect. As a family, we didn't do nothin' to deserve it. But you got to think—your life is too dear to throw away on a useless old woman like me, or a piece of hilly, rocky land!" She was pleading with me now, and I wanted to push her away from me and run. Instead, I tried to change the trend of conversation.

"Has Johnny Swift come calling for me?" I asked. She knew she was beaten, that I was fighting back against her attempts to open me to herself and myself. Rubbing her hand over her eyes, she turned away and began pumping more water, even though the cows had drunk their fill and were walking away to pasture.

"No," she said. "He didn't come calling. You're still mixed in with him, Snit? He's no good at all—he'll only bring you trouble."

Her voice was tired, old.

"Ya figure he's like that rainmaker that come last night?" I asked.

"He's worse. The rainmaker is a bad one, but he comes an' goes. Johnny Swift stays, living off people he growed up with. Folks who work got feelin's for one another. Johnny don't have no feelin's—he's like a dog gone wild."

I left her and went out to the road, looking toward the church. I thought of maybe taking the money and going to Johnny to split what we had. But the idea of going to Johnny, alone, made me uneasy. Besides, if he wanted his money bad enough, he could come and get it—damned if I was going to kowtow to him any more.

Aunt Matilda was warming a pot of coffee when I came into the kitchen. I sat heavily at the table and cradled my head in my arms.

"What you want for breakfast?"

"Nothin'—just a cup of coffee. I got a headache," I replied.

"It's salt you need, boy. Weather like this a body sweats a lot—an' if you don't put the salt you lose back into you, sickness sets in. You want some salt water?"

I looked up at her.

"Ya leadin' me on, Aunt Matilda?"

"No. Here. I'll make a glass, an' drink half of it to show you it's all right— then you drink the other half."

She busied herself preparing the solution of table salt and cold water. After prolonged stirring, she lifted the glass to her lips and drank half of it, passing the remainder to me.

"Here, Snit—make you feel like a new man. Ever lick on your hand when you been sweatin'? You gotta put all that salt back into you."

I took the water down with one swallow and almost gagged. She quickly came up with the coffee.

"Johnny an' I are through, Aunt Matilda." I told her. She was listening, but her face was bent down over her cup.

The salt water did cool me and cleared the mist from my head. As we drank coffee, I told her most of everything that had taken place—about Johnny's fight with his father, and him wanting to stay with us for a while. About the ratting on our bootlegger that Johnny did to the cop, and about making up our minds to call it quits. Through all my telling, Aunt Matilda didn't once look up. She just sat there, looking down at the table and sipping her coffee like it didn't matter what I said.

"Ya heard me, Aunt Matilda?" I asked angrily when I finished, for I wanted her to know I understood and was fully responsible for what I did.

"Yes Snit—I heard you!" She lifted her head to look straight at me, and I was surprised at the sharpness and anger of her voice.

"Well," I said, rising to my feet. "I'm gonna go out and close the pasture gate. While I'm there, I'll check the fence and replace any staples that are loose. If anybody calls, you'll know—"

"I know exactly what to do if Johnny Swift calls while you're gone. Your dad's gun is in my bedroom, along with three shells which never got wet, so they should work!" She rose and getting hold of the coffee pot, walked briskly to the stove with it.

I stopped off at the barn to collect a hammer and a few staples, then went into the fields.

The fence was still in fairly good shape. In the dry earth, the posts showed little signs of decay. But the wire was hanging loose here and there, so I stretched and secured it against the posts, taking my time. Hot as it was here in the sunlight, it would have been just as uncomfortable for me in the house.

It got on well into the afternoon, and I was nodding, wishing I had a cap to wear, for my head and neck ached with exposure to the sun. For some time now I had been aware of a low hum in the air, like a motor running fast somewhere in the distance. But I didn't give it much thought.

Then suddenly the air changed. Instead of the soft, hot breeze, a gust of wind came up which had the feel of ice in it. I shivered and straightened up, glancing at the sky. On the entire southern horizon, a dark grey bank of cloud was advancing quickly. The wind came from the same direction, and it was cold.

I watched, thinking with disbelief that the long-awaited rain was coming. Yet even as I watched, I realized it was not rain. The cloud twisted and spread, as if bursting from within, and the low hum I had been hearing now became a thundering grumble. The wind turned stronger and colder. I clutched my shirt tightly to my body.

The cows had been lying in the pasture, chewing their cuds. They now rose as one and approached the gate. In the other part of the pasture, the horses whinnied and with tails high also ran towards the gate. I still kept my eyes on the fast-moving cloud. If it wasn't rain—what was it? Instinctively I knew—hail!

The first pellets of ice were falling now, steaming where they touched the parched earth. Once I opened the gate the horses galloped directly for the farm buildings, followed by the cows, which ran in their fast, clumsy manner. I followed behind them, running as fast as I could, watching over my shoulder. About three miles to the south, the disaster had hit the countryside, for I could now see the wall of the storm. Larger bits of ice were falling around me. One piece struck my cheek like a wire whip, and brushing my face with my fingers, I saw it had cut my skin enough to bring out blood.

"Hi! Hi!" I screamed full-voice at the animals before me. They shared my sense of panic, for breaking into full gallop, they raced without hesitation directly into the shelter of the barn.

Turning off for the house, I had to cover my head with my hands, for the hailstones were becoming bigger and more numerous, and fell to the earth with a stunning speed. Aunt Matilda was standing in the open doorway. She was pale as death, and her eyes were wide with fear.

"Thank God you made it, Snit! I thought you might have fallen asleep—out there, in this—no one to help you or see you!" She squeezed my arm. Then she stepped into the kitchen, leaving the door open.

"To hell with what happens out there—the cows an' horses are under the roof, an' so are we—nothin' else is worth worrying about, Snit." She spoke with relief and happiness in her voice.

"What's this all mean?" I asked vaguely from the doorway, where I was still standing, watching the gathering fury of the storm. Aunt Matilda made some sort of reply, but I didn't hear what she said. With a thundering wallop, the hailstorm hit our farm.

In seconds, our front yard was a thick mat of broken ice, on which wave upon wave of other hailstones fell with a sound like that of breaking glass. A shred of poplar leaf, whipped along by the high wind, appeared out of the storm and stuck itself to the frame of the open house door. I looked at it, bleeding its green juices, and I was afraid.

"Will the cattle be all right?" I shouted to Aunt Matilda over my shoulder.

"So long's they stay in the barn, they're all right. Heaven help them if they wander out."

Then, just as quickly as it came, the storm was over. I stepped outside, sinking to my ankles in the sheet of broken ice which covered our front yard, the fields beyond, and the soft hills of the countryside. The sun had come out now, making the landscape blinding with reflected light. I was staring, searching for I know not what, hardly conscious of the cold wind which still blew, numbing my skin.

"Come in an' have some coffee," my aunt called. "What's happened has happened. No point in catching your death of cold out there. Close the door after you."

I came in, still too stunned and dazed to collect any thoughts into sensible order. Out there—a blanket of sharp ice, with everything that grew from the earth stripped and killed. Nothing left—no grass for the cattle, no hay for the winter ahead—nothing at all. I had never lived through anything like this before, and the fear I felt was paralyzing.

"How are folks gonna make out?" I asked dumbly, staring into the cup of dark, steaming coffee Aunt Matilda placed before me.

"We ain't made of powder that blows at the first puff of wind. Folks have lived through all sorts of things—hail, blight and sickness. They'll make out some way or other. Who knows, maybe we'll get twenty lads to go see the government, and tell them we gotta have help this year. You're worried, ain'tcha?"

I nodded.

"We got enough hay to see us through the winter, an' you got money besides. An' *you're* worried! What about folks like Shnitka? He's got no hay, no money—an' he's got a flock of kids to feed. You think *he* ain't worried? But it's no use us tellin' each other our problems—we gotta act, or suffer in quiet." She began to mix some batter violently.

I couldn't drink the coffee, so I rose and walked to the door to look outside. The hailstones were melting quickly now, and patches of dark earth showed on the hillsides facing the sun. In front of the house, a steaming puddle of water was spreading from the melting ice of the yard and the water falling off the eaves.

The cattle and horses had emerged from the open barn, and with tails half raised were sniffing at the white covering of the yard. I heard a rooster crow from the direction of Rogers' farm, but otherwise there was a strange silence, broken only by wind and gently running water. It was as if nobody had lived here before—as if one disaster of nature could make the earth forget sounds of hammering, shouting children, and cursing, working men.

I walked to the barn to get some money from safekeeping, for I would have to go for groceries and tobacco as soon as the hail melted on the road. When I lifted the floorboard, I found the jar in which our money was kept floating in a pool of water which had seeped under the building. Not being able to find a better hiding place for it, I carried the jar back to the house.

Aunt Matilda's face dropped with surprise when she saw the jar and its contents.

"Is that—all yours?" she asked with disbelief.

"No, half of it belongs to Johnny Swift," I said.

"All bad whiskey money." She shook her head, without taking her eyes off the jar where I placed it on the table.

"It'll keep us alive an' eatin'. I don't care what colour or smell money has—s'long's it buys things. Ya know as well as I where it come from, so don't bug me no more!" I spoke angrily to her now, but she didn't appear to be listening. She was still looking at the jar, and shaking her head from side to side.

"I gotta go to the store fer tobacco and grub. Might as well take Johnny's share to him as have him tryin' to get past ya to see me here."

"You might as well. Johnny Swift ain't settin' foot on my land. That's more money than I ever seen all my life. Lotsa kids gonna go hungry because you got that money in your hands, Snit. You wouldn't have had it if it weren't for Johnny Swift. No, he ain't ever gonna set foot on my land."

"I would've had it, too!" I tried to keep from shouting at her. "How else was I gonna live? Sure, I woulda gone to moonshining, Johnny Swift or no Johnny Swift!"

"No, Snit—you wouldn't of done it." There was a sad, hard look on her face as she glanced up at me.

"Go to hell! Ya got less sense than I give ya credit for!" I turned away from her, and opening the jar, counted out Johnny's share of the money. I replaced what was left in the jar and handed it to her.

"Here—hang on to it while I'm gone. An' don't go spendin' it foolishly." My hand shook with nervousness, and I tried to sound joking, as if we hadn't argued at all.

But Aunt Matilda was working over the stove now, and paid me no mind. I stormed out of the house, making certain to slam the door so hard behind me as to make the windows rattle.

I stopped for a moment in the yard, watching the cattle and horses, which were restlessly circling near the pump. Then I looked further, to the scrub border of Rogers' farm, and above that to the bog and the hills beyond. Everything was grey and stark, and steaming in the low sun. The wind blew from the south, and I buttoned my shirt high against its icy bite.

The dust of the road had turned to a pasty mud, which crept up my shoes and onto my ankles. Long before I was anywhere near the church, I had to leave the road to scrape the mess off. Then I walked in the shallow water and floating ice of the ditch. It was cold, and my feet were wet, but I was walking faster.

The lock on the church door was hanging freely in its clip, and the door, blown open by the storm, was swinging in the wind.

"Johnny—It's me—Snit!" I called as I turned into the churchyard. There was no reply, and I hurried across the yard and into the building. It was empty.

"Johnny!" I hollered again, walking around to the back of the church. Returning to the gate of the churchyard. I studied the softened earth for footprints. There were none. He had left before the storm, if he had been there at all that day.

Taking to the road again, I continued to Whittles' store. The wind was turning warmer now, and what hailstones remained in the shady hollows were fast becoming water. All the grass along the fence lines and in the fields was broken and flattened to the ground. Shrubs were stripped of leaves, which floated as bruised bits of greenery in the pools. It was a depressing scene, and yet there was a feeling of exhilaration in the air, for the ground had been watered after many dry seasons, and the scent of moist earth was sweet.

At Whittles' store, I cleaned my shoes again before going in. In the dim light of the shop, I didn't look for Tom Whittles before closing the door behind me. When my eyes got used to the faint light, I saw Johnny standing behind the counter at the far end. He was eating from a loaf of bread and a tin of fish, which was lying in a pool of spilled oil on the counter before him.

"Hey!" I said, "I was lookin' fer ye at the church. What the hell ya doin' tearin' into the grub? Where's Whittles?"

Johnny's shoulders sort of sagged into a crouch, and his eyes were sullen and dark as he watched me. He continued eating, using his fingers to lift out bits of fish from the raggedly opened tin, yet never taking his eyes off me.

"I asked ya—where's Whittles?"

"He ain't here," Johnny replied through a mouthful of food he was chewing. Then he sort of smiled as he rolled his tongue over the front part of his teeth. But the expression in his eyes didn't change. I came closer to him, and it was then that I saw that his right shirt sleeve had been torn away.

"What's happened to ya?" I asked, pointing to the torn part of his shirt.

"Nothin's happened to me!" Johnny snarled, and particles of chewed food sprayed out of his mouth. "Whittles ain't here, an' I don't know where he's gone!"

"Then ya got no right taking over like this."

"Sure I got a right! I bought the store from him. From now on, I'm runnin' this place! Y'understand?"

He was telling me all this in a sharp, shouting voice, yet the amazing thing about him was that through all this he was eating, stuffing great wads of bread and fish into his mouth. A thought came to me suddenly, and a chill rippled down my back.

"Johnny—he ain't in there, is he?" I pointed to the back of the store, where Tom Whittles had his one-room living quarters.

His eyes narrowed and brightened feverishly.

"What ya drivin' at, Snit? Come on, boy—what ya drivin' at?"

"Nothin'. Only it seems kinda funny Whittles would sell on short notice, and then go away without seeing anyone. Ya sure ya don't know where he went?"

"No!" It was a tortured shout that seemed to come through his whole body.

I stepped back in alarm.

"Yo're feelin' all right, ain'tcha, Johnny? Ya don't sorta black out like ya can't remember anythin' ya do or say? Ya can tell me, Johnny—we been good friends." I talked quickly, feeling for the doorknob behind me.

His face had now become a cunning mask, as still holding a hunk of bread, he began moving down the counter towards me. When next he spoke, his voice was quiet—too quiet to be real.

"Take whatever ya need from the store, Snit. I don't know the prices of things yet, but ya can have whatever ya need, an' settle later. Sure, we been good friends—come through a lot of times together, you an' me. Sure one helluva hailstorm, eh—betcha it flattened everything fer miles! Come on—take whatever ya need—act the same way like ya always acted before, fer Christ's sake!" His tone rose slightly on the last words.

I had found the knob now, and opened the door quietly behind me.

"I didn't want nothin', Johnny. Was just lookin' fer ya—to give ya the money we split. Here—that's yore share!" I pulled the handful of bills out of my pocket and threw them on the counter before him. He stopped chewing then, and the bread fell out of his hands. Momentarily, I saw fear freeze his face—the most terrible kind of fear a man can know. Then he seemed to get hold of himself.

"Like I said, Snit—take whatever ya need—there's lots of things in this store. Come on—take something!"

I threw the door open and backed outside.

"Ya don't hafta pay me—just take something like ya was gonna buy from any other store! Goddam ya—take somethin'!"

I ran like I never run before, through the yard and out on the road. When I looked back, I saw Johnny standing outside Whittles' store, staring after me, but he didn't follow. Still, I ran until I felt my heart would burst right out of my chest.

"He's mad, Aunt Matilda. If ya seen his eyes an' face like I seen them, ya'd a knowed he was mad. Whittles is in that store—either killed or hurt bad— he had no time to get him out. What we gonna do?"

It was getting dusky in the kitchen now, but neither of us rose to light the lamp. Aunt Matilda had moved her bench in front of the stove, and sitting on it, she rocked gently back and forth, looking at me and past me.

"You're sure you're not just tired an' excited—you're sure about what you think you know from seein' Johnny?" she asked.

"He was in a fight—his clothes is torn. An' he said he bought the store from Tom Whittles—what with? He didn't have no money on him. When I give him the cash, he was scared like I never seen him scared before."

"I suppose you should go tell Kane. Although I have no feelin' for folks who go telling cops against their own neighbours," Aunt Matilda said with anxiety.

"It's either gonna be me or somebody else. An' the way I see it, if someone else says or does the wrong thing to excite Johnny, who knows what he might do?"

"All right, Snit. You go an' tell Kane."

I rose to my feet.

"Snit—not tonight! Stay home tonight!"

"Ya ain't scared, are ya, Aunt Matilda?"

I could feel her eyes on me in the gathering darkness.

"Yes, Snit—I'm scared. I'm so scared it makes me cold all over!"

I had to have some fresh air to clear the numb pressure from my stomach.

"Go to bed, Aunt Matilda. I'll go close the pasture gate on the cattle, an' I'll come into the house to sleep. Then tomorrow, I'll go see Kane in town."

"All right, Snit."

The sky was clear and a faint trace of moon was showing over the eastern rim of hills. The air felt like the first frost of the year would come tonight. My feet were still wet, and a short distance from the house I felt the coolness of the ground seeping through the moist leather. So I hurried to the pasture. When I had secured both gates, I stopped for a moment to look around me before returning to the house.

It was then I saw the high sparks and flames from the south. For a moment, I thought it was the church, but the moon rose now, and I saw it outline the church just slightly to the left of the fire.

Whittles' store was burning.

My first inclination was to run directly across the fields to the fire. Then I became wary; whatever was happening, I had better stay out of it. Still watching the fire, I began walking to the house.

Before I reached the yard, I saw some people running down the road from north of us, carrying a storm lantern between them. As they came nearer, I picked out two men with buckets in their hands. Minutes later, Shnitka came over the hill from his farmhouse, also carrying a lantern and a bucket. Our house was in darkness, so nobody called in to take us to fight the fire. The neighbours passed down the road in the direction of the store, and soon the countryside and road were again quiet and undisturbed. I was about to turn into the house, when I saw someone moving in a crouch along the ditch, then turn into our yard.

"Who's there?" I called.

Whoever it was stopped, then straightened and approached.

"Who's there?"

"It's me, Snit!" Johnny spoke, and I gasped. The moonlight glinted off a small pickaxe he carried in his hand.

"Ya better stay away, Johnny—ya know what my Aunt Matilda said to ya!"

"To hell with what she said—ya gotta listen to me tell ya what kind trouble I'm in. Somebody's gotta know—an' yo're my pal, Snit—we been through thick an' thin together."

"Stay where yo're at, Johnny—don't come no closer!" I started to back away to the house, for he was near now, near enough for me to see the chalk-white outline of his face, and to hear his heavy breath.

"Ya said in the store ya didn't believe what I told ya about Whittles sellin' to me."

"I was only talkin', Johnny. I didn't mean nothin'.'"

"Sure, Snit—ya knowed everythin'—ya knowed I was lyin' to ya. Ya knowed Whittles was lyin' in the other room, dead!"

"No, Johnny—I don't know nothin'!" My arms and feet felt like they were tight against my body and I would never move them again.

"Yo're the only person come to the store today—the only person who knows everythin', Snit." He came a step nearer, but now he was crouching like he was aiming to jump at me.

"I told my aunt," I said out of despair.

"Ya told the kook? Ya shouldn't a done that, Snit—she didn't like me none, but she never done me dirt nohow. Ya wanna hear what happened?"

"No!" I cried. Another step—how many more before I had my back against the wall of the house?

"I was in his store," Johnny spoke quickly now, his voice thick and heavy with some inner passion. "An' this storm come up. I was tryin' to get some grub an' tobacco on credit—an' Whittles won't give me none. Says I'd never get credit in his store. Then he tells me to get out. Ya hear me, Snit—he pushed me an' I fell. Then he come at me with his boot—that's the livin' truth, he did!

"I got to my feet and grabbed this barrel pick off the counter. He didn't see me holdin' it, an' when he come at me, I hit him across the head. He jus' fell an' never come up. I was gonna go out an' run so nobody'd ever catch me, but this hail was outside. So I waited, draggin' Whittles into his room. I tried to close his eyes from lookin'—but they wouldn't stay closed! He jus' kept them open fer mean, the dirty sonofabitch!"

"Stop it, Johnny!" I tried to keep the panic I felt out of my voice. "Let's be friends an' forget about it—forget we seen each other tonight!"

"It ain't hard to kill a man, Snit—only ya gotta run or bury the dead. Ya can't live in the same place as the man ya kill. I tried to close his eyes—but they won't stop lookin'—only he don't see nothin'!"

"Johnny, yo're sick! Leave me alone!"

"Ya ever see a dead man—an' knowin' ya made him that way? It makes ya short of breath, ya feel that good—an' then the creeps sets in."

"Johnny—no!"

"I gotta kill ya, Snit—or I'll never know what ya'd do when ya got the chance."

"For the love of God!" I could retreat no further. My back was against the wall of the house, and I sucked my body into my spine to make myself as small as possible. Johnny approached, slowly inching his way with his feet, the pick held ready before his face.

As if through a set of senses other than my own, I heard the muffled explosion and the splinter of glass. As if through another set of eyes, I saw Johnny grow rigid, then straighten with the poised, slow movements of a diver under water. His head went back, and his mouth opened in a silent cry of agony. Then he fell.

It seemed a long time later when I mustered enough courage to bend over him and feel for a heartbeat in his chest. He was dead. Behind me, the lamp flared and lit in the kitchen. I looked up through the shattered slivers of window glass and saw my aunt, still holding my father's rifle, standing erect before the kitchen table, and weeping.

"Have a good cry, Aunt Matilda—cry for both of us, because we gotta cry a lot if we gonna live," I said as I took her in my arms, gun and all.

Still later in that moment which is the heart of all mortal time, I heard footsteps and voices outside.

"What the hell's happened here? Jesus, Jesus! It's the Swift boy! Who's gonna get the cops?"

"It's all right—Shnitka's gone to tell Kane about Whittles."

"Don't touch nothin'—just leave everythin' as it is!"

Then the door was pushed open and footsteps came over our threshold.

"What about those two?"

"Leave 'em alone—they can talk to the cops—we got no more business here!"

"What a helluva night—Jesus, Jesus!"

The footsteps and voices departed. Aunt Matilda and I were left alone again.

BALLAD OF A STONEPICKER

Now what is it you've come to see me about? I have your letter—it came on Tuesday. I was going to reply, but there is so much to do here ... Yes, you wrote about Jim, having known him as a friend.

I agree it was something for him to become a Rhodes scholar. Not many of those around, and damned few ever make it from a place such as this. Oh, it's not a bad place as places go. Not a helluva lot for the mind, but when it rains like it's been doing the past two days there's bound to be things growing. Maybe I exaggerate saying that, but I've got to believe in something.

Yes, I know in a couple of months it'll be that time of year again when he died. Always someone or something to remind me ... I wonder if it will ever end? From what you said in your letter, I understand you will be writing a story or article for some magazine about my brother—yes? And you want me to tell you everything! In two hours ... maybe three if I talk slow!

Don't look at me that way. I'm not angry. I'm just tired. You see, there's nothing more to tell. The way I see it, the two things which made my brother Jim important to guys like yourself is that he came from such a place as this, and that he died when he did. That's all. I can't tell you more than you already know about him. If you were his friend, you know more than I do. If you want to know what sort of people Jim came up from—what it cost the family to educate him and what his death did to them and to me— that's another story. You see ... I want to leave this place but I can't. His death did that to me. I'm all that's left, me and the debts taken out to educate him. I'm paying my brother's debts, buddy. I'll be paying them for the rest of my life. For two years now, I've been losing ground with bad health and poor crops. All I've been able to pay off is the interest on the money owing.

But it'll be better. This rain will help. And I'm feeling pretty good health-wise these days. Come on in—no sense standing out here in the rain.

On a clear day I would take you for a walk up Windy Hill. From there you could see all there is to see. You could take four pictures from there and say, "that's all there's to it." Or you might want to stay a while and have a quick look at the fields I'm working. Which isn't much, but it's better than nothing.

I shouldn't talk like that. It's a habit I have ... I get nervous talking to someone for the first time. You're not dressed for walking up any hill, and the road's too muddy for driving up there. Come inside—I'll make us tea. House is in a mess. Nothing's been done to clean it from front door to back since my mother went away. That bedroom used to be hers and it hasn't been swept since she left. Look at the tub of dishes, will you! I can't find time to keep up with them, even when it rains. I wash them on Saturdays. All week they pile up. I've got seven each of plates, spoons, forks and knives— for the seven days of the week. This time of year when the weather's warm and I'm working outside, breakfast is the only meal I eat in the house. I boil up a few eggs and take some bread and coffee to where I work. By the time I get back, it's turning dark, and most days I feel so tired from the sun and wind I don't feel like cooking. So I go to bed.

Here, have a chair.

It's not often I have visitors now. Used to be different once. This kitchen has always been a kitchen and sitting room. A lot of neighbours came visiting when my old man was around. Surrounded by people he knew, he was a good, entertaining talker. He was shy with strangers, but with people he liked—I've seen him in that chair over there carrying on three conversations with three different men at the same time, mixing up their memories of old songs, tired feet and bargains in farm machinery. When he'd got them all properly screwed up, he'd say over his shoulder—

"Hey, mama! You making tea? ... Pour my cup first if you are. That fancy new tea you bought makes my heart jump if it's brewed longer than thirty seconds!"

The men laughed and he laughed, and she poured his cup first like he asked her to. There was nothing wrong with her tea. It was his house and he wanted her to serve him first ...

While the water's warming I'll show you pictures of the old man. There's a couple taken when he still had all his teeth in. After that he had them all pulled one winter when he got this gum infection. He'd planned to buy dental plates but there was always something needed buying first. So when he laughed he used to cover his mouth with a handkerchief, and my mother put his meat through the grinder after she'd cooked it.

You get paid for coming here? ... I thought so.

No matter how hard a man works, there's never enough money to pay what's owing. Even when Jim was still here, we were always broke. Always something that hadn't been paid for and the store we bought groceries from on time was always hollering—pay up or we'll see you in court! Those memories never leave you—the shame of unworthiness, the feeling of not being able to provide food and clothing for yourself no matter how much work you do. It stays with you like a numb headache. I'm cutting wood and I still get scared of snagging my pants because it's the only pair I can afford between now and the next winter. Last few years I've been wearing canvas running shoes such as these, which I buy for a dollar and a half at the sports store in town. I walk through a pair a month, but it comes out cheaper than leather boots in the long run.

I can see in your eyes you're not really interested in my problems. Why should you be? ... Look out the window. It's nice-looking country when the rain stops. Air is fresh and when it's hot and dry there's always a smoke-haze in the atmosphere. A truck going down the gravel road into town raises dust that don't settle for half an hour. It's because of this clay—the same clay you can't walk through when it gets wet won't stay down when it dries into dust.

I met a guy once who told me parts of Australia were like that. I don't know about that. I've never been to Australia. Never been more than twenty miles from this house. Don't intend to go, either. There's enough to do and see right here. Besides, I'm too old.

Sure, I'm twenty-eight. But over here you can be old at twenty. My brother didn't age that way, but then Jim didn't have to live here all that long. My mother was grey before she reached twenty-five. And the old man lost his teeth at my age. When he died he was forty-three years old. Yet there are days when this country makes you forget all that. I've seen this blue haze on a hot day—the sun going low in the west and a blackbird flying against the evening light like it was shot from an arrow. You see a thing like that and you say to yourself there's some things in this world are all right.

I still remember the trees and scrub which grew here once. It was all taken out by hand—every branch and root. Underneath was grey earth. And in the earth the stones. They call us "dirt farmers" here in the back-lands. Not because we're dirtier than farmers anywhere else, but because we've got to keep our hands closer to the soil to keep going. Winters are cold here. At thirty-five below you can hear the poplars explode with frost. Spring turns up fresh blisters of stone which weren't there the summer before. Then comes heat, and the dust and the mud when it rains. It's not the best way to live, but it's a way ...

The last member of parliament from these parts was a lawyer who called us red bastards because he didn't get our votes. Nobody gets our votes unless he comes out here and talks to us straight off the chest in language we understand. A man don't have to do more than open his mouth and we know if he's real or not. We gave our votes one time to a man who couldn't even make a speech. He stood up in Anderson's Hall, shrugged and pawed around with his feet, then said—

"If I get in there, I'll tell 'em we got to have better roads an' a bit of education for the kids!"

We gave him all our votes. It's the only votes he got, but he got them. The guy who won was this lawyer who never even came to see us.

But you came all this way to ask about my brother ... He's dead. He's not here anymore. All that's left of his blood and memories is me. And this farm, and the people he grew up among. Maybe that's all that's left to tell. And once it's told no more need be said ever again. For you who's come all this way from the city it may not even be very interesting. It's too wet for me to do any work outside, and the dishes can wait another day. So if you want to listen, I'll tell you everything I know. But I can't tell about Jim without telling about everybody. It's the way life is lived here. There was never a lock on that door. We grew up on everybody's knee. Jim and I never really saw eye to eye on much. We couldn't. But life made us what we are, and I'm the only one left to tell about it ...

My brother was a year and a half younger than me, but he was always brighter. In school, Jim put everything he had into his books. I got my head turned around easy by a cowboy song or a dirty joke, but not Jim. By grade three, he'd got ahead of me in school. And when I got to the sixth grade he was through the eighth and was starting high school in town. My folks never *said* it was no point in me pushing on, but I knew what they thought. When I didn't go back to school for grade seven they never once spoke to me about it. I know it was my fault for quitting—but I had other reasons.

Today, as then, I wonder what was the point of me going on, if all school was doing for me was giving me a place to grow bigger than other kids in the same grade—bigger even than the teacher. I was always hungry, so I ate a lot and grew bigger and bigger. I used to slouch so I'd look smaller. I'd try only half as hard in the games to keep from winning all the time. But there were times some kid would get hurt, and I'd be blamed because I was *bigger* and was somehow responsible. I hated what was happening in my body. It was like a prison growing up around me, forcing the man inside to feel and think like the body of the man outside was expected to perform. My brother was small and you're a small man yourself— perhaps it's not important to anyone else. It's important to me because a lot of the good things and bad things in my life keep going back to that ...

Water's boiling. Would you prefer coffee to tea? I would. We'll eat together in a few hours, but coffee first—eh?

I make good coffee which you can smell as far as the road. A fistful of coffee in the pot, then scald it with boiling water and let it steep for ten minutes. Best coffee you'll ever drink! My old man made it that way—that's how I learned. He made his own coffee on nights when mama went to bed and he still stayed up talking or arguing with a neighbour. I'd wake after my first sleep—hungry, with the smell of his coffee all over the house. I wasn't allowed to get up. So I'd lay back and keep swallowing and listening. Sometimes I'd hear him humming some old song. Other times he was laughing and talking low. And one night I heard him argue with John, the wife-beater, who must've come late 'cause he hadn't been visiting when I went to bed.

"Turn yourself in before she does. You're crazy coming here!" my old man said in a loud voice. John was whining like a kid. That was how he was—first he'd whine and then he'd cry, but when his wife had to be beaten, he'd do a proper job of it.

"I can't. They'd give me three months in jail this time an' I got to get the crop in!"

I heard him cough. I sat up in bed when he kept on coughing for I knew he was crying.

"One day they'll put you in and you'll stay in—you know that!" My father's voice was lower, less angry now. "Here. Drink this."

I heard the wife-beater clink his spoon against a cup.

"You're right … you're right … "

"What'd you do this time? Put her in hospital?"

"Hell, no. It'd take three men to beat her into a hospital. I tied her up to the fence an' whipped her with a rope. Not badly—just across the back an' bottom end!"

"A rope?" My father's voice rose again. "What do you think the woman is—a goddamned cow?"

"No, she's not a cow! I just beat her with a rope … a wet rope, to teach her a lesson. What else can I do? God doesn't see what goes on, neither do you! Cold beans for supper … burned eggs for breakfast. Complain an' she's off at the mouth like a runaway hay-mower!"

A lot of men beat their wives—at least two besides him were pretty mean about it. But John always went overboard with the business. It could never be kept at home with him. After he'd almost half-kill her, he'd go out to whine and cry to somebody about it. In the meantime she'd always find the strength to crawl into town and turn him in to the police.

So John put in and took off two crops a year. One on his own farm and the other at the provincial jail farm where he served time twice a year for at least ten years.

Yet it all ended this last time he went in. For when he came out she'd run off with another man, a hired hand who was remembered for eating lots of salt with his food. I can't even remember his name now, only that he ate lots of salt. She never came back, and as far as I know, none of the neighbours have ever had a letter from her.

It changed John. He stayed out of any kind of trouble after that. In fact, he took to religion in a big way. Right now and for the past few years he's been song leader at the evangelical picnics at Canyon Creek.

The rain's stopped. Take your coffee with you. We can sit on the porch where it's cooler. Sure, take your notebook too. If I talk too fast, you just tell me. I'm not used to talking to people. When someone like you comes by and I get feeling easy, I kind of run off at the mouth in twenty different directions …

* * *

That long row of buildings there—that was Sid Malan's place before he left.

Everybody reckoned on Sid Malan coming back to her. They reckoned for—well, twenty years at least, according to what my mama remembered.

Sid's wife, Minerva, still lives just across from where the road turns north, on the same land they farmed in the beginning. She farms different than we do. With us it's wheat and barley on the better land, and what's too stony for putting a plough into we turn into potato fields. But Minerva's been putting up long rows of buildings all over her place until it looks like a village all to itself. She turned her place into a chicken ranch, and making good money at it. Not that it makes her laugh any easier, but she's fat and getting fatter all the time, and that's a change.

She put up an electricity line to her place, and last few years she's given up seeding her fields. Says it's cheaper for her to buy grain from us to feed her chickens. I even got a week of work last summer helping her build a new slaughterhouse and freezer. Now she can hold her slaughtered chickens fresh into the winter, when she gets a better price for them. Now that's good—that's using brains. But it's not the sort of thing would have kept Sid married to her. From all the stories I've heard about Sid, that new slaughterhouse would've ended him.

Sid was a tiny fellow. Never grew any taller than a school-boy.

"But his gab would make you forget the time of day!" my mama often said. "When he stood around talking to you, you'd swear that you heard flutterings like the whole sky was full of birds!"

Before he married, he already owned the land Minerva's been building on. Mind, the place was no farm. I've heard my old man tell there was nothing except a house with a railed-in porch and a woodshed in front. All the rest of his acreage was brush and wild grass. Not even a garden.

"Nice to see the flowers in spring, like the Lord poured a bucket of gold over my place!" was Sid's reply when they got on to him for letting his place go wild.

Back in those days, Sid Malan made his living trading horses and selling second-hand machinery. He was liked, listened to, and jollied around with. And he always had the right price on an old cream separator, used set of harness, or even a bent old garden hoe, if you were looking around for a cream separator, set of harness or garden hoe.

My mama and some of the other women were pushing him to marriage. They had to have something nice to do besides live and work. Today the women have church auxiliaries and home and school clubs. But during the tougher times, it was about all they could do to knit a sweater or marry somebody off.

"Wait! I'll marry! But first I've got to ripen and sweeten some!" Sid would wink at the women and they'd laugh and bounce around and get even more worked up over Sid remaining single for so long.

Then he took up with Minerva, and they began to wonder. She was from around here, which was something. But she was twice the size of Sid to begin with and her face had that rough and sour look which she still has. She wasn't the tidiest person. Sid was always dressed in a clean shirt and a bit of suit, while she wore and slept a dress to death, and it showed all the damages.

When they married, Minerva put her foot down on Sid's huckstering. She took over a rusty plough Sid had already found a buyer for, and began breaking the land. The first year of their marriage she'd turned over the best soil on the farm and seeded in a good stand of barley. Maybe something in Sid was going under, but everybody figured it was a good thing after all, for Minerva showed she was a woman of the land.

Sid still did horse-trading and machinery selling on the side, but before that first crop was harvested, she had him pulled into the farm. Like she had him help her build a fence around the property. As my old man used to say:

"For weeks you'd see them—Sid squatting close to the ground, his sleeves rolled up, holding steady a stool on which she stood as she hammered down the posts, using a twenty-pound hammer and a wood-chopper's stroke!

"'Give it a good whop for me, Minerva, me darlin'!' Sid would egg her on. When she really got sluggin', he'd start to sing—

'On the farm in the morning,
Many birds awake;
Over fields and lawning,
The sweetest music make—
Chirreep! Chirreep! Chirreep!'"

In those days Sid used to buckboard the ten or fifteen miles into town like everyone else. There were a few cars around even then, but they were expensive and a little scarey to own, since the cop in town liked horses and was even down on a kid with a bike who could make a horse bolt. Most people, my parents among them, found the speed of walking just about right. Any more speed would get you there faster, and what would you do when you got there? But Minerva was different.

She saw her first car parked by the beer parlour in town. She shook it to test its strength.

"We got to have one!" she said to Sid, who was shrinking away with surprise and fear.

And before the summer was out, Sid did some lively trading in almost useless hay-mowers and bought a battered, 1930 Chevrolet for her. Now about every second Saturday my father would have enough heavy produce to take to town to make it worth driving his team and wagon in. But on odd Saturdays he'd only have a crate of eggs to deliver, so he'd go in with a neighbour who was also travelling light. When Sid got the car, he began going over to Sid's.

"I'd no sooner reach his yard," my old man would say, "and Sid would appear with a clean rag and go over this car of his. He'd wipe the dust from the windshield first. Then he'd wipe the headlamps. After that he'd open all the doors so the car looked like a rooster after a dog had worked it over, and he'd clean the seats. He'd wipe the steering wheel an' the gearshift stick. And then he'd give the panel a dusting."

Minerva drove the car with my father sitting beside her. Sid sat in back with only the top of his head showing through the window. He sat in back because the noise and fumes of the motor sickened him with fright.

In their second year of marriage they got some livestock. My mama remembers a golden-haired cow, some pigs and a dozen chickens. She also remembers that Minerva began putting on fat.

Then one day their marriage was all over with.

"It was Friday … " was the way my old man always began telling it.

"I think it was Thursday," my mama piped in, just to give him a chance to argue by way of warming up.

"It was Friday—I know it was a Friday because one of the reasons I went to see Sid was to ask for a lift into town the next day. It'd been hot as a torch nozzle that day. I'd been working my summer fallow and had to give up for the heat. So I went over to Sid's to ask for a ride, and also get loan of a wrench I needed to tighten up my equipment."

He'd stop and stab a finger towards his cup—his way of saying to mama he was ready for a refill of tea. When the tea was poured and he'd had a sip to test it, he'd continue with this story.

"As I was saying, I walked into Sid's yard and see him there stripped of the jacket he always wore. He was bent over, his shirt dark with sweat, and he was making a commotion as he tried to corner a large red rooster where the fence around his yard joins the house. Minerva was on the porch, a tiny apron wrapped around her big middle. She'd her hands on her hips and was watching Sid trying to outsmart the rooster.

"When I went up to help, Sid an' the rooster had begun this side-stepping dance with each other—Sid would move a step this way, an' the rooster moved a step that way. When I closed in, the rooster tried to break through my legs, but I pinned him. When I picked him up and give him to Sid, the guy's hands shook and his face had gone white. He gave Minerva a pleading sort of look, his lips moving but no words coming out.

"'All right.'

"That was all she said, and she pointed with her thick finger to the wood block in front of the shed. I'm telling you that Christ God Himself carried His cross easier than Sid carried that rooster to the block. When he got there, he laid the rooster out like he was ready to give him the business. But instead of taking the axe, Sid stood looking at the fields. He stood there an' he stood there, and I could feel the time tearing my skin off a foot a minute, but Sid just stood there, looking …

"Then the porch floor creaks and I see Minerva come at him—her mouth hard and dirty, and her eyes on fire. She grabbed the rooster from Sid and give him a shove that damned near put the little man through the fence. Then she picked up the axe and with a quick stroke lopped off that rooster's head. Throwing it in the grass, she turned to Sid. He was looking at her now and talkin' in a soft and furry sounding voice, his eyes filling up with tears.

"'I'll be going now, Minerva, me darling,' he said. 'I'll be going.'

"She kind of melted a little when she heard that.

"'You don't have to go if you don't wanna,' she said.

"That was all either of them spoke. He took his jacket off the porch railing an' just walked off without once lookin' back. And she never stopped staring after him. Not once … "

* * *

Look—the rain's stopped! The sun will be out before evening!

I was ten, and it was a day like this when 'Whole Damn Cheese' Stiles first came into the community. The road was sticky after the rain. The trees were wet, and the grass smelled of wet lime and slow rot. My old man and I were putting a new roof on the chicken house. We first heard and then saw the old Ford truck growing and twisting down the road towards us like a cow gone blind.

"Who's that?" I asked, looking hard into the sun. A boy at ten can tell most of the cars and trucks in the world just by hearing them, but this one had me buffaloed. My father had a mouthful of nails bristling out. He took the nails out and not taking his eyes off the truck, rolled himself a smoke.

"Don't know," he said. "That truck's old enough to burn straw. Will you look at it!"

It was near our gate now. Its radiator was blowing steam. The box in back of the truck was wired and tied together with rope and each time the machine skidded in the mud the box squealed and leaned over to one side or another, just barely avoiding spilling its load of mattresses and bedding, paper boxes and chests of drawers. Six boys—full grown boys with black beards on their faces, sort of held the load in one place by standing all around the cargo in back of the truck and heaving left when the load shifted to the right. On the very top of the load, rocking like magpies on a windy branch, were two girls, also fully grown. They sat back to back, one facing forward, and the other in the direction from which they'd come.

"They're stopping!" my old man said with alarm and got to his feet.

And sure enough the front wheels of the truck crimped over sharp into our gateway and the whole mess slipped on top of the culvert which crossed the ditch in front of our place. As my father and I came down the chicken-coop roof, a heavy and grey-haired man came out of the truck and walked over to meet us.

"Hullo. Having trouble?" my old man spoke first.

"Yes an' no. Whole damn cheese is boiling. What's the matter, farmer— is this the best road you got hereabout?" He pushed his cap back on his head, stared meanly at my old man and spat out the corner of his mouth. I looked up at my father and saw his ears getting red as he came to a slow boil.

"Same road's been here for twenty years so all kinds of pricks can walk or ride it. You figuring on improving it tomorrow?"

The stranger shrugged with one shoulder.

"No, I won't be changing anything," he said. "But if that's a road, I don't think people should take this whole damn cheese sitting down. That's all."

The two of them stood a couple of yards apart, both mushing up mud with their shoes. My father's face got friendlier.

"We should've had better roads by now, that's true," he said, looking away quickly. "You aiming to settle?"

"Yeh—sure. Have a look around an' see if there's anything we like. Had a farm in Manville. Lost it. But I'll make out good this time—got me six boys strong as horses now. Say, neighbour you got some cold water I can have for my truck?"

"Sure," my father pointed to the house. "Well's back of there. Help yourself."

We left him to cool his truck and ourselves went back to shingling the roof.

A week or so later we learned they'd picked up a homestead some five miles north of our place. But they never got prosperous. Never made enough to eat and dress properly on. The boys worked hard, but they were a clueless bunch—the kind who pitchfork hay they're standing on. I saw the old man cutting wood once. He was handy but he couldn't be everywhere seeing to things.

You're going to write all this down? Am I talking too fast? No, it won't matter. I think better when I think slow.

One of the girls married. Not one of the two we saw on the truck, but the one who sat in the cab between 'Whole Damn Cheese' Stiles and his missus. She never had babies though.

The two on the truck knew how to cook and sew, but couldn't get themselves married nohow. Shorty Mack, whose farm begins just across the road, himself not married, thought they should have learned to play mandolins!

Now you take our Shorty—real 'sport' if there ever was a sport. He always dressed in a white shirt with cufflinks, even when he milked cows or did the spring ploughing. He wakes up in the mornings singing and doing bends from the waist down.

"You could hoe a garden with the strength you use up doing that!" my father used to holler at him. And Shorty Mack would holler back:

"It takes a good body to house a happy mind!"

I don't think Shorty had two coins to rub together, but on Sundays he walked with a cane in his hand, and wore a hat always brushed slick with the brim turned down in front and bent up at the back. Once my old man and I stood leaning on the gate, watching Shorty lead a cow to market.

Shorty didn't have enough money to buy a rope, so he led his cow by four neckties tied end to end and looped around the cow's neck. As he led the cow past he looked straight into my father's eyes. He twisted his head to look back even when he was past our gate and some distance down the road. My old man stood like he was a statue made of stone. He didn't laugh. Didn't even smile.

I've seen days made for fun. And I've seen days and people over which you've got to weep.

People like Mary and Pete Ruptash. They'd been married fifteen years before they had a kid—a girl with one missing arm. Pete had built a play-room ten years earlier for her coming. The playroom had wallpaper with rabbits on it, a small crib, rocking toys and a little desk with a chair. And then this baby came.

It had learned to walk and was able to say "Mama, I busy," and "da-da" when it caught diphtheria and died. Pete had to beat his wife with his fists to take the kid away so he could bury it.

My first teacher in school was Mr. McFarland, who was short of breath, and had a moustache which he combed when he thought nobody was watching. At school picnics he shook hands with the women and hugged the men up tight.

"It's funny, but his cheek smells—of lavender," my old man said after he'd been hugged.

"I was … an infantryman in … the British Army!" These are among the first words I remember him saying when I began school. I kept dropping my pencil one afternoon and it kept getting under his skin. Then it fell once more, careful though I was, and Mr. McFarland brought me down by suddenly aiming his yardstick at my head and making a 'pow-pow' shooting noise. I was scared—wetting-the-pants scared, for there was hate in his eyes when he did that.

He had a brother named Joseph, who split wood, brought in water and cooked meals for him in the one-roomed teacherage. At recess, Joseph would sometimes come out and play ball with us. He was very tall and always smiled. Once in a while he didn't seem to hear when you talked to him. I kept telling my father about how big Joseph was and how he had to do woman's work. And so when my father got behind with his haying, he asked Joseph to help, and he did. I was in school that day, and when I came home, Joseph was gone.

"Is Joseph finished working?" I asked.

"He's in the barn, brushing down the horses." My old man was down on one knee beside the kitchen door, wiring together a wooden keg that came apart every September. I looked up and saw the large haystack which had taken shape beside the barn.

"Sure is a strong guy, that Joseph!" I said. My father looked up at me.

"First day on a farm any man starts off good. Tomorrow he'll be flat on his back." I was hurt and my father noticed. "Can't expect a man who's never had to work on a farm to be top of the heap. Sure, Joseph's all right."

"Don't you like him?"

"I got nothing against him. And we don't talk enough to argue." He tried to shrug me off.

"He talks sometimes around school."

"He's terrible slow. Men like him end up doing women's work, if they get work at all. I'm sorry, son."

"He can do things, an' he can talk!" I was angry now, wanting to defend Joseph. My father looked at me as if he was trying to explain something I didn't know. He talked slowly to me as he held the pliers in his hand, opening and shutting them with each sentence.

"You seen the lumberman's boots he wears? Well, if he has to put them boots on, lace them and tie the laces, he could do all that quicker than tell you about it."

I saw Joseph opening the barn doors and leaving the barn in that stumbling sort of walk he had. He was very tired, his clothes wet with his sweat. He crossed the yard and left without speaking to us.

"Joseph be back tomorrow?" I asked.

"No, I paid him off."

"But you didn't bring *all* the hay in! Not with a man who doesn't work fast," I argued. My old man was looking at me with eyes that had gone dark and strange.

"I needed a man for one day. It's all I could afford a man for—one day. Any man! So I had to drive Joseph like he's never been driven before!"

"Did you hurt him?" I suddenly saw Joseph as just a big child, trapped in the fields, while my old man worked off every fury on him.

"No. But we had to bring the hay in. He got paid top wages."

Joseph worked at surrounding farms for short periods of time. Most places he got paid off before lunch. War had broken out, and one week he just drifted out of the community and into the army. He came back on furlough once and paid us a visit.

His hair was cut short and he looked good in his nicely pressed army uniform and V-cap. His back had become so straight he might've stood against a tree and his entire length would've touched the trunk. The uniform impressed even my father. He shook Joseph's hand and slapped him across the shoulders. I ran ahead to the house to tell my mother, and she put water on for tea.

After they'd settled in the kitchen and Joseph took his cap off and tucked it in his shoulder flap, my old man tapped his foot with pleasure.

"Well, Joseph—how's it going? Army treating you good?"

"Sure, Mike—treats me real good!" Joseph mumbled and grinned at us all.

My father offered him tobacco and paper and they both rolled and lit up. Leaning against the woodbox next to the stove, I stood watching Joseph and wanting to be a soldier myself. The water sputtered and warmed in the kettle on the stove. Jim came tearing in chasing the cat, once around the kitchen table without even seeing Joseph and out the door into the yard.

"You ain't scared?"

Joseph hadn't heard. I thought it was me my father had spoken to.

"Scared of what?" I asked. My father looked up at me and his ears began turning red. My mother saw and pushed me gently to the door.

"Bring some wood from the shed!" she said quietly. I moved as far as the door, but didn't go out.

"You ain't scared, are you, Joseph?"

"Scared of what?" Joseph woke up, surprised.

"The army. Fightin'—you know, guns pointed at you! Attacks! Getting hurt—maybe even dying!"

Joseph took a deep drag on his cigarette and smiled stupidly.

"I don't aim to—to do no fighting!"

"Then what in hell are you doing enlisting?" My old man suddenly turned sharp with anger. Joseph squirmed.

"Why not? Everything's … taken care of. One guy tells you when to get up. Another guy says when you go to sleep … An' they feed you good, Mike! Grapefruit juice for breakfast—ya! A glass, this big—for breakfast! Jesus! I never tasted no grapefruit juice before!"

With his brother at war, Mr. McFarland also enlisted and was given a posting guarding potato stores for the Defence Department somewhere in the south of the province. We figured with war ending they'd both come back, but they didn't.

And the years sort of whistle by, but in summer all of us boys went swimming Sunday afternoons where the creek joins the river. There was nobody to spy on us, so we'd strip naked in the sun and before going in the water would make a game of grabbing for each other's dangles. Then we'd wrestle, one hand over the crotch, and the other fighting like hell, each one defending his manhood joyfully.

The river ran swift and straight there. To cool off, I'd swim for an hour or two in the creek, where the water was still and warm. Then I'd go up on the bank and watch the rougher boys swimming against the river current. Six boys, hollering and panting, swimming like their lives depended on it, swimming half an afternoon to gain a yard against the current! Watching them, I often thought what would an ant make of human stubbornness?

If Jim had been there he might've told me, for Jim knew more about ants that way than I did.

* * *

This community is still a last outpost.

Ten miles beyond here the road ends in wilderness. If you go another fifty miles past that, you're in muskeg that would swallow you up live in summer. And they say that much further north of that begins the tundra.

There was a lot of trapping carried on here when the Hudson's Bay Company was doing big business in furs. A few trappers still pass through going south in spring and north with freeze-up in October. Whichever way they go, the poor devils are loaded right down. Coming off the trap-line in spring, they bring their pelts into town for sale. In the fall, they have to carry all their winter provisions in one load.

Now look at how big this house is—and I'm the only one here now. But when he was building, my old man planned on a big family. A spell of sickness and then the depression years, and after that the real truth that this land takes almost as much as it gives in return—well, he had a big house on his hands and a lot of silly dreams that were already dying when Jim and I were born.

Yet others made use of the house. Word got around among the trappers, and ever since I can remember they made this house an overnight stop before going on. The trappers were a queer bunch. There was one called Weasel Jack, who never said a word. He used to sit on the floor over in that corner and never blink his eyes for watching my folks and us kids. But our favourite among them all was Dan Jacobs!

Dan was skinny as a rail. But to get through that door he had to bow his head, he was that tall! His skin was dark and parched until he looked like a smoked fish. Except for his eyes—they were bright eyes and clear as water and full of fun. He didn't marry, but he used to brag that between the Pelican Rapids and the Arctic Circle he'd fathered forty-two children, most of them on Indian and half-breed women. Except one, a school-teacher in a fishing village who'd burned all the textbooks in her school and was teaching children about a world where there was no more war. The woman's name was Anita, and she was Swedish or Norwegian—Dan wasn't sure which. My father took a strong interest in her, and what Dan had to say about her.

"She sounds like the kind of woman you should marry," he said to Dan.

"She'd make a good wife, yes. But she won't have me. Takes great care of the kids—won't let me help her at all, but this school and the kids there are her life."

"Do the people like her?"

"There ain't a person in that village who wouldn't show you the road out if you said a bad thing about her. They love her—especially the kids she teaches!"

We never got to meet Anita, although she flew out to the city once a year, and one summer Dan told us she'd gone up north by motor-boat, using our river to reach the lake where her village and school is.

Dan knew each of his forty-two kids by name, and carried cartons of chocolate bars for when he would visit them with Christmas gifts that he delivered between the first of December and the end of February. I've seen him sit at this table, an open scribbler in front of him and a chunk of pencil in his hand, writing down what medicines cured colic and sore chests, and my mother talking on and on about the times Jim and I had this and that, and how she made us well.

Now here's something I never got straightened out in my head—my mother's liking for Dan. To her divorce or remarriage was a real crime. The love of one man for more than one woman was a sin that would put anyone doing this into hell for ever and a day. I've seen her get sore at one of the dances at Anderson's Hall when she saw a man dancing with a neighbour's wife.

But forty-two kids or not, she liked big Dan and washed his shawl and cap for him when he came. She mended his socks after she'd washed and dried them in front of the stove. But he'd never allow his shirt to be washed. It wasn't really a shirt—just a burlap sack turned upside down with openings cut out for the neck and arms.

"Never touch this, Josie!" Dan would warn her. "Or the fleas will come at you and kill you!"

I guess his clothes made one big flea-nest. I've sat up nights watching him open the door of that heater there, with the fire burning so you had to put your hands over your eyes to look in. He'd strip off his shirt and stand naked to the waist. Half-naked like that he didn't seem thin any more. He looked like a man must've looked when he lived in caves, his muscles jumping on his arms and back with every turn and move he made. Dan would flap his burlap shirt in front of the fire. As the fleas burst with a clicking sound in front of the heat, he would laugh.

"Listen to that! Will you listen to that!" he'd whoop and stamp his feet with joy. "Can you hear them buggers sizzle!"

I was afraid of going outside on the nights big Dan stayed over with us. I still feel ashamed and guilty for getting up on a chair and making water through my window into the snow outside. But Dan's dogs were outside, howling, snarling and chewing on their leashes which were tied to our garden fence. Dan had pulled the covered toboggan into the middle of the yard out of possible reach of his dogs, but they kept snarling and pawing snow and dirt to get at it.

"They're wild sons of bitches—tear anything apart. Even a block of wood," Dan would say as he went in among them, a length of chain in his hand.

There was the look of killers and scavengers about his dogs. Frozen eared, with yellow, rheumatic eyes and long fangs off which the dark gums had shrunk from sucking icy air on the long, hard winter trap lines.

You know, a man gets to look like that if he lives half-wild long enough. Last time Dan Jacobs was through was about five years back, and I couldn't help feeling that big Dan was carrying a wolf upon his back.

What else do you want to hear—our hatreds! Small hatreds and big ones, like the hatred of Timothy Callaghan for his ox, Bernard. Timothy had eleven or twelve kids—can't remember for certain as there were two that died, but some got born after. To dress up these kids and feed them, Timothy had to work hell out of some ten acres of ground, half of it as stony as the church wall. He could never save enough to buy himself a horse or tractor, so the work of clearing and cultivating and hauling in wood in winter was the job of Bernard.

The ox was slow, lazy, stubborn. When Timothy had to work fastest to keep his soil from drying before the first seed was planted, Bernard would grunt like he was getting sick and start limping. Sometimes he'd lie down in full harness, digging his horn into the ground, turning up his eyes and making like he was dead.

When I was younger, I used to watch Timothy from a distance—watched him lose his temper so completely that he'd take off his cap and beat the ox around the face until all the stuffing in the cloth cap came out. I've also seen him kick the ox, taking a run with each kick. I've seen him work over Bernard's backside with a willow switch, as well as a four-foot alder club. Timothy cursed the ox, and once I saw him get down on his knees and plead with him, while in the trees all around the early summer birds sang, and that was the worst time of all.

I think Timothy cried then, and told the ox everything—how he hated to live and how terrible was the work that had to be done each day.

Then one day Timothy Callaghan came to our place, running and bare-headed, his eyes bulging out of his head.

"It's the devil! He's in that ox of mine!" he shouted. "I've seen the devil in his eyes. He was laughing, teasing me to kill him! One day—one day, I will, and God help me!"

It was talk—only talk. Timothy and the ox were tied together until one or the other died naturally. Sure, they hated each other, but they also needed each other so they could carry on living and eating.

You want to see them? I'll take you over in the morning. Timothy and the ox are both grey now, and kind of too weak to do heavy work any longer. But they still hate, and maybe that's what keeps them living now. What else they got to live for?

Bernard is an ox, and Timothy's family broke up and left him.

* * *

The summer I was nine, Jim had gone to camp and my father was in hospital having an ulcer taken out of his stomach. It's a funny age, nine. It's like you suddenly hurt all over with all the stuff that's being torn away from you, and you know you'll never heal proper, which makes you all empty and sad inside. It's also a time when some morning you lift your head from the pillow and everything around you is singing and laughing with a new and stronger music!

See the farmhouse with the green roof over here? That's the Bayrack farm.

The summer I turned nine, Helen Bayrack turned eighteen, and that made such a change. She turned eighteen and she wasn't married, and I was told by my mother:

"I want you to call Helen 'Miss Bayrack' now. If I hear any more of this 'doom-doom' nonsense, you'll get a swat across the ears!"

I always called her 'doom-doom.' Used to shout it after her when she came past on her way to the store or on Saturday evenings, her hair all curled, as she walked to the dance at Anderson's Hall. I called her 'doom-doom' because of the way she sang. She liked to sing, but she couldn't remember words to songs she liked. So when she forgot words, she kept right on singing 'doom-doom-doom-doom.' She didn't mind me calling her that name. She liked it. But the summer I was nine and she came eighteen, it seemed to matter.

My mother didn't say it, but somehow I felt she was worried for a girl turned eighteen and not married. And when I got this planted in my mind, I figured I'd marry her myself if nobody else would. I didn't tell Helen Bayrack how I felt because I didn't want to make her think I was soft on her.

She was a beautiful girl. I say this now, for then she was only a girl I liked. Her hair was long and black, and hung down her neck in two thick braids. Her teeth were even and very white. And her skin was tanned deep to the colour of cinnamon from working outside in the sun and wind.

We played together a lot that summer. I teased her and she chased me. When she caught me, she'd put me over the highest branch of the nearest tree and leave me there to hang.

"Hey! Let me down!" I'd holler if she pretended she was walking away and I wasn't sure if she was really pretending or if she meant it.

"You still think I look like a goose?" she'd ask, holding her arms folded in front of her like she had all the time in the world.

"No—heck! You're nice!" I'd swear in a panic, because by now my arms were getting numb from holding on to the branch and the ground was too far down to let go. She'd take me down and laugh.

"You're sure some hero. A grasshopper could jump higher. But did *you* ever shout!"

"You—doom-doom!" I spat at her when my feet touched solid ground. "I hate you!"

I ran then, turning only once to shout over my shoulder. "You look like a goose!"

Then I am standing by our gate, whittling a birch whistle and she goes by on the way to the store, slowing down as she passes me and looking at me with her head turned under and sideways. She is changing. She no longer wears jeans, but is now wearing a blue dress. There are shoes on her feet. I don't know what to say, for I haven't any shoes and the pants I wear are patched at the knees and backside—and that's the difference as I see it then between us.

"Hello, short-stuff!" she says and smiles in a way that cuts into my heart.

I can no longer stand looking at her. I am mad at her for dressing that way. For looking like I'd never seen her before. She is walking away from me. Further and further away. I try to keep my eyes on my whittling, but my hands tremble and I throw down the knife and the piece of wood and run.

I know she has stopped and is looking after me, and I know she is sorry. But I could not return, for now she was Miss Bayrack, and she was eighteen and wanting to marry, and that was the world between us!

On other days, I tried to tell her.

Like I tried to tell her when John Zaharchuk began to court her. He looked terrible, with his dark blue chin gleaming in the sun and the hair of his chest creeping up and over the collar of his shirt. He rode his bicycle when he went to see her.

"Hullo!" he shouted and waved to my father. Then he saw me.

"Hullo, boy!"

My old man waved back, but I wouldn't even look at him. He'd never spoken to us before, and now he spoke, because we were neighbours of Helen's, no other reason. One day he even got off his bicycle and stood talking to my father. He left his bicycle on the road and climbed over the fence to where my father hoed between the cabbage rows. As they talked I slipped away from the garden and out on the road. I let the air out of his tires and they looked up when they heard the hissing. John Zaharchuk picked up a stone and threw it at me. His aim was bad.

"Why don't you kill me? Come on!" I screamed at him, wanting to die standing between him and Helen.

"Come here!" my father called. When I came, he pulled down my pants and spanked me with a bare hand until he was out of breath. Hanging over my old man's knee I saw an upside-down world in which John Zaharchuk was moving along an upside-down road, pushing an upside-down bicycle with flat tires. He was laughing. I could hear him laughing. That was how I tried to tell her, but she didn't hear me. I felt she had stopped listening.

Another day she picked wild strawberries along the fence where her farm and this one joined. I hid behind the stone-pile and made sounds to her, like those of a pheasant with a broken wing, but she didn't even look up. I cawed like a crow and whistled like an evening lark. But she was where she was, bowed to the ground picking wild strawberries. I crawled away from her and went home, hurting inside like I was going to die.

Soon John Zaharchuk was cycling to her every second day—and once on Saturday and again on Sunday. I watched from behind the barn, not being able to take my eyes away from him for hatred. What kind of a man was it would leave work to ride to a woman? She would starve to death if she married him.

Now there was an idea that pleased me! Helen Bayrack starving to death, no longer able to raise her head with hunger. Running her dry mouth over the stones and boards on which she lay, searching for a crust—and then I coming to see her, bringing a bowl of cooked oatmeal and milk! There beside her was John Zaharchuk. When I came in he tried to grab the bowl and milk with greed.

"Food! Thank God for you, boy! Give me food!" he pleaded. But with the heel of my foot against his cheek I pushed him down and kicked him. Then I lifted Helen in my arms and fed her. Quickly, she became strong again. And then she was up on her feet, running out with me and after me. We played in the sunlight, and I called her 'doom-doom' again and said she was like a goose. She chased me for it and made me apologize.

Helen's mother came to see my mother one afternoon and I heard her say, "That Zaharchuk is a good man. He will make a good husband for my Helen."

I ran out of the house and back of the barn. There I picked up a stick and beat it to pieces against the log wall.

That week the stranger came.

He was one of those guys who'd lived and worked all his life in town. McQuire was his name. Philip McQuire. He was bald and fat, and old enough to be Helen's father. He talked loud and drove a small car. And he smelled of shaving lotion and pipe tobacco.

Once my mother sent me to Helen's place to ask for some pickling salt. McQuire drove up behind me, and stopped to offer me a ride. He laughed a lot when I got in the car, and he called me 'Buster.'

When he turned the car into Helen's place, I asked him, "What for you coming here?"

"Well now, Buster—it's not easy to give you an answer to 'What for you coming here?' You get a little older and along will come a pretty girl—and you'll know. Or maybe you've got yourself a little girl friend now, you little bugger!" He laughed and poked me in the ribs with an elbow. We got out of the car and I ran ahead to tell them he'd come.

He was a plumber, which meant he had money and so was a cut above us farmers. Helen's folk were Ukrainian, and McQuire learned very soon to say 'dobra, dobra!' to anything they told him, and this went over very big.

"Understand me," Helen's father said in the grocery store one Saturday evening, his chest stuck out and his eyes shining. "Understand me please when I say this McQuire is the man for my girl! He's a plumber—a skilled man, not like our farm boys. He's got gas, water and power—important people come to see this McQuire of ours, and they call him 'Mister.' Even the mayor of the town calls him 'Mister'! Now what do you think of that?"

The group sitting around the store said nothing. But you could see who the Ukrainians were, because they were all scratching their heads in about the same places. Old man Bayrack saw this, and said to them:

"This McQuire is not like the rest of *them!* He speaks our language. He eats what we eat. Last Sunday he tasted creamed chicken and dumplings my wife made just for him and he said, 'Dobra, missus, dobra!' Now what do you think of that?" He took a deep breath, straightening his back proudly and half-closing his eyes as he went on to say, "I tell you my grandchildren will carry the name of McQuire, but they shall speak our language!"

The Ukrainians stopped scratching and looked up at him. They believed him. You could feel the change in the air of the store, and there was nothing more anyone could say.

John Zaharchuk cursed and swore there was nothing for him but the rope when he heard of this McQuire. For a while he continued visiting the Bayrack home, on the days McQuire did not call.

My mother asked Helen's mother why Zaharchuk kept courting when it was plain McQuire was the man Helen would marry.

"To finish eating the cookies I baked for our Philip the day before!" Helen's mother said angrily.

There is a saying here that a courtship is like milk. Taken fresh it gives good health and long life. But allowed to grow old, it sours. So on the first Sunday when the hay was in and no other work was pressing, Helen's people invited the neighbours for a dinner at which Helen's engagement would be announced to the world.

"If only your father was well enough to come. He never missed such a dinner before!" my mother griped as she fixed up the suspenders on the clean pants I would have to wear. I hated the way these pants smelled of P and G soap and mothballs. We used mothballs to kill potato beetles, and the smell of mothballs came to mean insect death to me. But I never got around to telling her all this, because as she was doing up the last button, McQuire arrived, hooting his car horn in the yard. He had driven over to get us.

The Bayrack house was small, hot and humming with flies who came after the sweet-smelling iced cakes.

"Here—make yourself useful, or they'll mistake you for a stool and put a glass on your head!" Helen's mother gave me a whisk of willow branches, with which to shoo out the flies through the open door and windows. From the parlour came sounds of shouting, laughter and shuffling feet. McQuire was in there, offering whiskey to the men. He'd been drinking before he came to our place, because driving over he kept steering from one edge of the road to the other, and my mother was so nervous she grabbed my knee and held on tightly all the way.

"Dobra! Dobra!" He kept hooting. "Die Bosheh—drink! God provides, and all that jazz!"

I looked around for Helen among the women in the kitchen. She wasn't there. My mother was also looking for her.

"Such a shy girl you've never seen—she's gone into the barn to think things over. Silly, silly girl! Why when I was her age and in this situation I was so cock-sure ... "

"Paraska—the boy!" One of the women cut in and pointed at me. Helen's mother looked up from the turkey she was carving, saw me, and the giggle died on her face. Then she blushed. But some woman in back by the stove cackled a dirty laugh and everybody seemed ashamed because of me.

I stopped swishing and the flies came back into the kitchen like a dark cloud. I wanted to leave and find her. But what could I say to her when I did see her? She was eighteen and about to be married, and I was somebody called 'short-stuff' from down the road. I didn't matter and there could be no friendship left for us. I still had an anger ache in me, but I wasn't sure who I was angry with.

Then I looked up and she was standing in the doorway!

"Oh, my child!" Her mother threw the meat knife to the floor and moved over to hug Helen up. Helen turned her face away, and her cheek was red and hot.

She was more beautiful than ever before, and the anger hurt got very big in me. I couldn't close my mouth as I looked at her, for my breath was choked between my ribs. Her black hair had been brushed so good it rose in deep piles over her head and down her neck. The blue dress she wore gave off a light, like water under the sun. She seemed thinner. She trembled so only I would see, and tears came to her eyes. I looked down at her hands, and saw how much she'd cried, for the knuckles were wet still from rubbing her eyes with them.

"Helen Bayrack, my dobra, dobra! Gimme a chum-chum!" Philip McQuire came roaring out of the parlour, a whiskey glass in one hand and the other pushing aside the women in his way. He pushed away Missus

Bayrack like she was a sack of potatoes and tried to get both arms around Helen. She moved back and he spilled some whiskey over her dress. She yelped with surprise and hurt.

"Hey—dobra, dobra! Die Bosheh!" McQuire turned quickly and sprayed the guests with a long sweep of the hand in which he held his whiskey glass. The crowd moved back and McQuire grinned. His eyes now swam in thick pools which bulged out of his face and threatened to burst and pour out of his head.

Helen's mother began to bawl loud. I looked around to see if my mother would go home. The people were crowded near the stove, at the back of the room by this time. They seemed mixed-up, sad—something had gone wrong and the laughter was gone from them. Then a stone came flying through the open door. It barely missed McQuire's head and fell to the floor with a wallop, then rolled under the stove.

Helen's mother stopped bawling and bent down to look under the stove after it. Helen's father hoisted his trousers like he meant business and stepped outside.

"What you want here? You got no business here! Go home—get lost!" He came back in and closed the door behind him.

"Who's there?" Helen's mother asked.

"It's that John Zaharchuk, crazy fool!"

"Is he gone for sure?"

"Naw. But he'll go. What's the matter? He's got no summer fallow to plough or something, the crazy fool?" Helen's father stuck out his chin and looked over the heads of everybody in the room.

"His whole farm is gone to pigweed. Besides, he's not the man! Here's the man!" He pointed to McQuire.

"He's got gas, water and power! And important people call him 'Mister' —even the mayor! Now that's really something, if you ask me!"

"Dobra! Dobra!" McQuire hooted, letting go of Helen and bending over with laughter. Then he threw his glass on the floor and grabbed Helen's father and pulled him fast to where he stood. He puckered and kissed Helen's father loudly on the ear. Helen lifted her hand to her eyes and began to cry.

Now the guests came alive again. They began moving around, laughing, congratulating.

"It is true what he says—important people call him Mister all right—live long!"

There was a crash, a scream, and everybody stood silent again, looking at one another. The door was split down the middle, with the blade of the wood-chopping axe coming through into the room.

"Look!" Helen's mother pointed to the axe blade. "He could've killed someone!"

"Come out and fight! I'll make mush of the town bum!" John Zaharchuk shouted in a thick voice through the window.

"Hey! Hey!" Helen's father walked over to the door and threw it open, but stayed back in the kitchen, only poking his head around the frame this time. "I said get out of here—go home! Helen is spoken for—you've no business here!"

"I want to kill the fat town-boy!" Zaharchuk was in the doorway now, frothing at the mouth and his shirt opened to the belt. His hair-matted chest jumped each time he gasped for air.

"I'll show him who gets her! I'll fight him with bare hands or an axe, whichever way he wants! Or race him on a horse to see who rides better! Or maybe he wants to show me how much man is still left in him—I'll dig a ditch with him. We'll dig from now until sundown, and who digs farther and deeper gets Helen! Okay?"

Helen's mother marched up to him and putting both hands on his chest, gave him a push. "Go away—pshaw!"

She didn't move John Zaharchuk an inch. He didn't even see her, and she walked back to the stove as if she didn't know what to do next. Zaharchuk was staring at McQuire, who was wiping the dribble off the sides of his mouth with his thumb.

"Wait! If he wants a contest, I'll give him a contest!" McQuire said drunkenly, not looking at Zaharchuk at all, but taking away the glass from Helen's father and peering around for the bottle. Zaharchuk laughed hard.

"Don't be crazy, Philip!" Helen's father started to argue. "You don't have to do it."

"You—farm boy!" Suddenly McQuire was looking straight at Zaharchuk, and his voice became strong and firm. "Those things you want to try me for—that's out. I don't fight or ride horses. Last time I dug a hole in the ground was to bury a dead budgie bird! It's like me saying to you, race you to see who can thread more pipe in half an hour. I'd have a hundred feet of pipe tied up before you'd figure out what to do with the die!"

John Zaharchuk wasn't laughing any more. He was straining to understand what McQuire was saying and what he should do about it. But McQuire had more to say.

"Let's do something fair and square to us both. Let's see who can drink five pounds of melted butter first!"

"W ... What!" Zaharchuk's blue chin was quivering with surprise.

"First guy who drinks five pounds of melted butter gets Helen. Okay?" McQuire walked away and came out of the parlour with his bottle. He poured himself a stiff drink and took it down with one swallow.

"Okay—farm boy?"

"Okay!" John Zaharchuk was suspicious as a cat, but there was no way out for him no more.

"That settles it—okay everybody—first we win Helen, then we have fun!" McQuire was refilling the men's glasses. Someone even gave Zaharchuk a glass, but he stood near the door and would not drink. The women set about melting the butter, which Helen's father brought in cold and hard from the well where it was kept from going rancid. As the butter crackled and sputtered in two pitchers on the stove, the men moved slowly to the parlour. Even Zaharchuk went in at the end, while the women returned to preparing the meal as if nothing unusual was happening.

"I'll bet a dollar on Zaharchuk! He's built bigger than you, Philip!" a man shouted from the parlour, and there was laughter.

"I bet two dollars on Philip. It took some stretching to get a gut that big!" Again there was laughter.

"Men! Dogs, that's what they are! Give a man a drink of whiskey and a chance to make some money and he'd sell his own mother!" Helen's mother complained, but she was really happy, because her house was at peace again.

I was alone and forgotten, and no one even remembered I was supposed to keep the flies away. I turned and saw Helen, sitting on a bench in a dark corner of the room, looking at me. Her eyes were large and full of pain and laughter, like those of a small girl who bangs her toe on a sharp stone just when she's having one heck of a good time playing a game.

"Doom-doom."

I formed the words with my lips. Then I forgot all the women around me and rushed to her, falling to my knees before my beautiful friend. She reached down, and putting her cool hands under my chin, lifted me up.

"Hello, short-stuff! You're a bad boy to run away from me like this!" she said, and I covered my face with my hands so she wouldn't see my happiness and shame coming all at once.

I stayed at her side as the contest took place. When Zaharchuk and McQuire stripped to their trousers and reached for their pitchers, I knew this was the end—the very end of white skies and days without hours for me. My father was in hospital, my mother worried and my brother was away. It was a sin to whittle and play when the whole world was worried and busy.

They lifted the pitchers to their lips, waiting for Helen's father to give the signal to begin, and I started to chirp like a bird— making cries like a pheasant with a crushed wing and all the other pheasants flown and none to help. Then I cawed like a crow, and whistled the gentle cry of the evening lark. My hand hurt from where Helen caught it and squeezed it in hers.

I trilled and warbled; the killdeer—the twitter of an oriole sitting on its nest with its face to the wind—and she squeezed and she squeezed until I cried aloud with this and other pains.

"Dobra!"

Shouted McQuire, and he turned his empty pitcher upside down first. And there was a cheer.

Helen Bayrack released my hand, for she was eighteen again, and she had a man to go to.

* * *

I am thinking—trying my damnedest to remember the name of the man who counts. Andrew—Andrew something or other. It was a Polish name. He was from Krakow, and the way he told it in the old days he made out like he owned the city.

"I wore white gloves, and the nobility thought I was one of them and doffed their hats to me." I still remember him saying when he was able to speak. Now he has fallen so with his silences I can't even remember his name—strange.

You can see him if you like. He's around, from the moment the sun rises and he comes out of his house, until night falls and the last turkey has found a perch on the rigs, thin and wild-looking Andrew is around counting on his fingers. Each time he says a number, he stabs the air with his arms.

He's been counting—what? Fifteen years, twenty—I don't know. He's up to four now, which is an improvement, because only a year ago he couldn't get up to the number three twice in one day.

If you're in town tomorrow, call in to the Chinese café for a coffee and you'll see Andrew there. Tomorrow is Saturday, market day in these parts. Andrew's always in town on Saturday. He goes into the Chinese café and sits at the table nearest the door. It makes no difference if somebody is already sitting at this table. He'll sit down anyway. But we know him here, and feel sorry for the poor bugger. I always buy him a coffee and a chunk of raisin pie. He's crazy about raisin pie—so crazy that if you ever eat with him he'll put you off eating for the rest of the day!

Nobody talks to him. But it doesn't matter, even if he butts in on you while you're talking to someone else. It doesn't matter.

"One ... two ... two ... One ... two ... two ... THREE!"

With that he'll wallop the table with his fist so hard all the dishes jump a foot, because he's made it again! Like I say, you get to feel sorry for the poor bugger.

My old man knew him well from way back before Jim or I were born. He tells that Andrew did some farming in those days. Used to fight a lot too.

You wouldn't guess it to see him now, because he doesn't stand taller than five feet and his weight is somewhere about … oh, a hundred and ten pounds at most.

"Andrew was a mean sonofagun when he got sore," my old man used to say.

"How could he fight? There isn't much man to him?"

"Hudson's Bay rules, boy. Andrew fought by Hudson's Bay rules!"

"What's Hudson's Bay rules?"

"Dirty rules—meanest fighting a man can do. Biting, scratching, kicking, fingers-in-the-eye and knee-in-the-crotch sort of thing. If you was to bundle all the dirty, sneaky tricks into one man, that man would be Andrew!" my father said with an angry grunt.

"He must've lost some fights!"

"Some, but not many." My old man tried to explain a fact of life very slowly so I'd understand. "If a guy got tangled with Andrew he'd do as well to lose. Because if he roughed Andrew up fair and square, that pint-sized little bugger would get his own back by clubbing from behind whoever had beat him."

"Then maybe he's lucky he's in the shape he is now. If he'd stayed strong and fighting, by now somebody would've killed him," I said, feeling wise as hell. My old man sort of looked at me and through me.

"You figure that would've been worse than what Andrew's got now?" he asked, then answered himself, "Maybe it would at that."

Andrew got the way he is by hoeing a carrot patch on a hot day and not wearing a hat on his head. His head got so hot from the sun he passed out. When they found him and poured enough cold water on him to bring him around, he'd lost most of his memory and speech. He didn't know his name, although he seemed to have no trouble finding where he lived. The municipality voted him a small tobacco pension and he's been counting up to four since.

There are others half-in and half-out of life as life might be. Like Stanley, our horse-trader. He comes through every August selling horses which he leads tied to one long rope back of his wagon. When you see him leading eight or ten horses down the road that way you'd almost expect to hear a guitar playing and someone singing about the wind and the long, lonesome road, just like they do in the movies!

Stanley was short-sighted, so much so that when two horses on the tail end of eight broke free, he drove twelve miles before he stopped, counted them and learned he'd lost the two. Farmers traded mean stock off on him, throwing in five or ten dollars in conscience money, because some of the horses turned over to Stanley were so mean they would kick or chew a stall to pieces. Anybody else but Stanley would've been killed by these brutes long ago. Yet Stanley didn't know the danger he lived with every day.

With my own eyes I've seen him put up a dozen horses into stalls lining opposite sides of the corridor in our barn. Now our barn is narrow. A horse could kick right across the corridor and into the next stall if he'd a mind to. Like I say, I've seen Stanley walk down that corridor and the horses leaving the floor with their rear legs as they sent out volley after volley of kicks at where they heard him walk. Any one of those kicks should've killed him— but they always missed! He was like Christ Himself walking through the waters!

He never even suspected they were out to get him.

My mother was with me when I saw him walk through all those kicks, and she crossed herself and sat down on the barn-door ramp. After Stanley was gone into the house, I sat down beside her and watched her chew a long piece of straw until she made a little round ball of it in her mouth. She spat it out and got to her feet.

"If those were my horses," she said, looking back into the barn, "I'd lock this barn up, pour two gallons of coal oil around it and set fire to it. There's more evil stabled there tonight than I've seen in a lifetime of living!"

Here—let me warm up some more coffee! How about a can of meat and some bread?

You want to know about love? What can I tell you? Of Nancy Burla? Or Marta? Later, when the sky clears altogether so that I can walk as I tell you, for I must have air and soil under my feet to tell of those loves.

Love could be a cat's tooth, like that one that bit Clem, the blacksmith. He was so honest and good you couldn't really talk to the guy without sounding rougher than you meant to be. If he'd been born five or six hundred years ago, he'd have made it as a saint.

Jim was still around when my old man and I called on Clem, bringing an iron wagon-tire between us for him to shorten. The old man had bought this wagon from some farmer selling out, but when he brought it home, he found the wheels all shrunken. We ended up with more trouble and expense on our hands than a more costly, newer wagon would've cost in the first place.

When we got there, Clem was in the smoke-black smithy. It's still there, about four miles this side of town—you might've seen it when you came up. Clem's clothes were always glued to him with sweat, and his beard and long hair jiggled each time he brought his hammer down on the anvil. He looked up when we rolled in the tire, and gave us one of those beautiful white-tooth grins only he has.

"Well, men—what can I do for you?"

My old man explained what he wanted done and Clem nodded.

"I'll get on it soon's I have breakfast."

"Breakfast? You mean to say you haven't eaten yet?" My father stared at him. "It's noon already."

"No! Working alone like this, I eat when I get hungry, and I just haven't eaten today." He picked up his hammer and balanced it like it weighed no more than a paint brush. My father was thinking pretty deeply as he looked at Clem.

"'No need for a man to be alone," he said. "Clem—you been pounding that anvil on to ten years now. When you going to take a break? Get out and meet people? Do a bit of drinking and rolling around with the girls? This kind of life isn't natural. You're still young and it's not right for a man to work like this!"

Clem was staring at my old man as if what he heard was said in a foreign language.

"I'm happy like this. If I wasn't happy, what could I do? I haven't seen a girl who needs me." He spoke with surprise and something like bitterness in his voice.

"A girl needing you—why a girl that needs you? Don't you need a woman for a wife?" My father leaned back against Clem's tool-bench, ready to argue anything just to keep from having to go home and do work that was endless. I picked up a pair of pliers and pretended to be straightening a bit of copper wire. Clem turned to his anvil, but he seemed worried now.

"I want a woman—true, it bothers me so I can hardly sleep some nights. But a man must give happiness to the woman who needs his help. There is so much unhappiness in this world we live in."

He lowered his head, and again I say he looked like a saint in one of those religious calendars you see in homes where they got crucifixes hanging on every wall. My old man coughed one of those rolling 'harrumph' coughs of his and said, "We'll see about that!"

"What sort of woman would you marry?" he asked after a while.

"I never really thought it out, but it'd have to be some girl who needed my help and understanding ... an unfortunate girl." Clem looked at my father with clear, trusting eyes, almost like the eyes Jim had when he was a kid.

"Aw, come on off the fancy baloney! You know the difference between a woman and a man—they're built different—you know that! Talk about women and you've got to talk about stuff that makes kids—the other's for the birds!" My old man got quite a kick out of pushing Clem that way. Clem blushed deep red and gave his anvil a hard whop with the hammer. He left the hammer lying on the anvil and turned to my father, but not looking at him any more.

"Suppose," he began quietly, "suppose I was to see a young woman—about to be a mother, let's say, and she's standing on a bridge, wanting to jump over into the river and end it all."

Clem stuttered now and the colour came up high in his face.

"I ... I would run to her. And ... and carry her away with me! I would work for her. Make her laugh again and keep her and her child happy and alive!"

Clem was still talking when my father touched me and nodded for us to go. We were at our buggy and getting ready to drive away when Clem came out and called for us to wait and hear what he had to say.

"Get a woman—a lumberman's whore if you like, and lock yourself up with her for three days! Then I'll listen to you!" my old man shouted back and turned our team homeward. I turned to see Clem holding out his thick arms to us, as in benediction. My father never bothered to look back.

"I'll be back for the tire tomorrow!" he barked over his shoulder.

"Right!" Clem called from a distance now. As we rounded the bend in the road, I could hear his hammer ringing on the anvil again.

Clem did get married to a girl from town.

She wasn't a mother-to-be as you might expect. And she wasn't found on a bridge planning to end her life. She wasn't all that young, but neither was Clem when I think of it.

They met outside the town hotel—Clem walking along minding his business, and she pulling up her dress to show where the policeman arresting her had first grabbed for her—and was this legal? A few men gathered around her, asking to show them again, and the cop laughing into his fist. When she saw she was being led on, she told them all in a high whiskey voice to go to hell and leave her alone.

Clem sat through her trial, during which she was charged with disorderly conduct. After she was sentenced, he went over to tell her who he was. Then he paid her fine and took her to the Chinese café for supper. And a week later they married in the magistrate's office.

Clem continued working in his smithy after his marriage, only now he whistled while working, which made all the men and some of the women in the community smile. Curtains appeared in the windows of his shack back of the shed, and for the first time since anyone could remember, he cleared up the junk mouldering around the place and mowed down the grass. This nice life lasted about three weeks. Then she went into town and got herself roaring drunk.

Jim and I were running down the sidewalk, carrying the cream cheque we'd been sent to collect for our mother from the creamery. We were alongside the hotel when the beer parlour door was thrown open and one of the bartenders pushed Clem's wife outside.

"This is a nice place—quiet farmers, root pickers and lumberjacks drink here!" he shouted at her. "So don't you ever come back again!"

Mother came around the corner of the building and tried to make Jim and me go with her, but the two of us locked our hands together and pretended we didn't hear or see her. A crowd was gathering quickly. Then Clem pushed his way through to her.

"Let's go home," he said quietly. He was worried and looked up at all of us as if asking us why we stayed and what we saw that we had to stand open-mouthed. Yet we stayed.

"Take your goddamned paws off, you queer!" She pushed Clem away. "He never had a woman before! Would you believe it, the blacksmith never laid with a woman before me—he didn't know anythin'!"

She wagged her finger under his nose and laughed viciously. Clem slapped her hand down, and taking hold of her wrist yanked her through the crowd and around the corner of the hotel. She was digging her heels down and yelling for him to let her go or she'd put him in jail. By this time mother got Jim and me by the ears and marched us away from the hotel.

"Shame on you standing like that watching!" I did feel ashamed. But when I looked over at Jim, he was grinning and looking down at his feet.

Clem's smithy stayed shut for a couple of weeks after that. We came to collect our wagon tire and had to knock many times on Clem's door. It was finally opened by his wife, whose face was swollen and bruised.

"What do you want?" she rasped at my old man.

"Is Clem around? I've some repair work to pick up."

"I don't know where he is. Go away!"

She slammed the door shut in our faces. As we walked past the shop we saw the growing pile of ploughshares and broken rods and pieces of machines brought to be welded and then left for when Clem would re-open.

Jim, my father and I were among the first in the place when Clem did open up. I was surprised at how thin he'd got, and how grey his hair and beard seemed now. Other neighbours started arriving and watching him fire his forge. He picked up his hammer, held it for a moment, then turned to all of us.

"It's all over now. I'll be working again—it's finished. She's gone. The marriage is kaput! She's giving me a divorce ... " He turned away from us.

"She's giving you a divorce?" my father piped in. "How much is that favour costing you, Clem?"

Clem blew his nose and kept his face turned away from the men in the shed.

"Thirty dollars a month! It's all right—I agreed to that. I'd of given her even more if she'd wanted."

"On top of that, you're paying for the divorce?"

"Yah." Clem nodded.

"You're going to keep paying her until you fall dead at your anvil?" Another man asked this.

"Get out—all of you! How can I work with you blocking out my light? You farmers have nothing to do with your time?" Clem glared at all of us now. He pointed to the door with his hammer and one by one we all drifted out.

Clem got more tired and grey-looking. His eyes became dull and dead, and he never seemed to even wash any more. Anyone could tell he wasn't making the money to pay her, because he was selling out tools from the shop.

Two years after divorcing, she married a shyster selling stocks with get-rich-quick prospects to farmers. By this time the blacksmith shop was stripped down to little more than the forge, anvil and hammer Clem used all the time. He'd even hawked his acetylene welding cart. But even after she re-married, Clem continued to go downhill. I was with my old man the day he stopped before the shed and went roaring off at Clem for splicing a disc axle that didn't hold a damn.

"Look here, Clem!" I heard him argue. "It's none of my business, but I'm not going to bring my work to you no more if you keep paying off that woman of yours and welding axles for me with spit and wire! You can't sell all your equipment for her sake and expect to stay in business! She's married now, and you're still paying for the keep of that pimp of hers and her. Look at you, man! You're still wearing the clothes you bought before your own wedding. And look at your shop—how can you work with what's left? I'm telling you now—either stand up on your feet, or I'm taking my business to the repair shop in town!"

With that my father came stamping out of the smithy, his toothless mouth clamped tight. Clem came out right after him. He was smiling sadly, and brushing his white hair back from his sticky forehead.

"Take your business elsewhere if you wish," he said. "Let her have what happiness God can give her now. Let her have this—I don't care. I can't eat. I can't sleep without her. Soon it will end—soon I will be an old man and it won't matter."

"You damned fool—you're killing yourself! You're killing her! Your money only makes it easier for her to drink and brawl her life away!" My old man was fighting mad now.

"Look neighbour." Clem became sad, far-away. "Stay out of this—do that for me. You don't understand how I feel. My love ... the way I wish it to be ..."

Slowly, as if it were the hardest thing he could do that day, he turned his back on us and went back into his shed to work.

* * *

You ever eat honey? Me—I can't eat it.

Mike Sadownik keeps a bee-farm in these parts. He has a large tumour on the back of his neck—big as his fist. He never buttons his shirt all the way up, and he can't push his hat to the back of his head for his lump. I don't know how or why, but I came to think he got this lump from eating honey. I started to think that way as a kid. I've never been able to forget and think different.

I've never been able to eat honey.

When you're born poor, the price of learning a lot and getting away from it is too high. Because you can't do it alone, that's why. Someone has to help, and you can't stop taking once you begin. Jim kept needing more and more help—and we kept paying and paying. Even now there is still so much has to be paid for, and that's the worst thing, because Jim can't put it to use and it's all lost.

Towards the end, he realized how much it cost to make him the great student he was. He wrote one letter to me while he was walking through Hammersmith in London at night. He wrote it against the side of a wall, using a street lamp for light. It was a sad letter. He was a young man who lost one world and never felt at home in another. He said it that way in his letter. I burned the letter. It was mine to read and remember—only mine.

No, Jim did not ride motorcycles. He didn't own one in Canada. He was not the person to enjoy it. I could, if I had one handy, but not Jim. And not at eighty miles an hour on a winding English road like they say. Yes, I think Jim took his life, but don't write that in your story. If my mother should hear of it she would never forgive me for saying so.

I loved him, I hated him—what's the difference now?

I never saw him ploughing fields or walking between the rows of barley, gathering stones in his arms. From the time I remember fields and every-thing on them, I begin to forget Jim. We walked as kids down some roads together—we even danced once. At times we sat in the Chinese café and chewed ice-cream cones. Then he followed his books where they took him and I opened the land. After he'd gone I hated him, because he left me with torn pants and a thin shirt on my back. Yet I'd give it all to him double if he was around now and I could ask him to tell me why a mother leaves her son to look for God. Or why love should hurt so much.

Maybe we're both forever kids—him and me! Maybe all the pain and bleeding never took place—it was all a dream, and my old man will come out of that room there, rubbing the sleep out of his eyes and chewing on his toothless gums. And my mother will show up pretty soon with the milk-buckets full of froth and say if one of us will separate the cream from the milk, she'll put on some rice pudding for supper!

Man, I sure wish my old man was alive! I sure need him now!

She always felt I hated him, but he and I worked together. You work with a man, even if he's your father and you don't see eye to eye with him. He's still your chum as long as you pull the same saw or heave stones off the same field. We worked together that way.

But I was young, and once I tried to shake a weight someone else placed on my neck. I quarrelled, and through the quarrel, I began killing my own father.

"How come Jim's not helping us cut? He's been home from school a week and a half and he's not put down his books and come out to help!" I cut into my old man when we were in the creek hollow, cutting frozen spruce for cordwood. Jim was home for Christmas holidays, but we only saw him at meals. Even then he brought a book down and buried his face in it as he ate. He'd only put on his jacket and go outside when he had to go to the john next to the barn. And when he came back into the house, he never brought an armload of wood with him.

"How come?" I asked. The old man turned to me. He was trying to look angry, but his eyes were sad.

"You leave Jim alone—he's working same's you. Only he's working with his head! You understand that? With his head! There's gonna be some good come out of it—so leave him alone!"

"Why do I have to leave him alone?" I asked biting back the tears, sure that Jim had never been told to leave *me* alone. "He's been in town getting school since he finished grade eight. I never did get to grade eight."

I could see how I was hurting him, and I felt glad of it. I still felt sorry for myself—still tried to keep the tears from coming. Watching him squirm helped me. The old man gripped his axe so tight the knuckles of his hands stood out like white knots in wood.

"Don't ever talk like that, son. I'll make it up to you after Jim's all fixed up. Jim's not as strong or as big as you. But he's smart. Our help now is going to make something of him. Your mama and me are thinking of you. There'll be a farm for you to work for yourself, don't worry … "

He spat, and I knew he felt better too.

Maybe you want to see Jim's room? It's behind that door—go ahead. I don't want to go in there. Go ahead, open the door! It hasn't changed in ten years—the same yellow bedspread on the bed. Jim and I chipped in the nickels and dimes we earned on errands to buy that for her for Mother's Day—and you know, she gave it to him before he went away.

"It's the nicest spread in the house. It belongs on his bed for when he comes home!" she said smiling like a mother.

Look past the lamp and up the wall. See the lousy medal hanging there? Jim got that in school for knowing how to spell, and for something called citizenship. What's this thing, citizenship? You know? Being the good joe all the time? Who decides that?

This is the part of Jim I hated. The hoarding of tin and paper. A callus on a hand tells its own story. When a bright man speaks, it's the same. I don't like people who take medals as if they had to have it proven to them they were good. And I don't like the people who give out these medals. By giving out a medal they make out like they are better than the best of us. Medals meant a lot to my mother. It gave her something to look up to. And that's yet another reason I hate medals.

Anyway, the lousy thing's up there on the wall. She used to take it down to polish at Christmas and Easter.

The summer Jim was sixteen he came home for a week. The other summers he got work in the school for all the holidays. But this year a new job came up in the library and the person holding it had a week to go before leaving and letting Jim in. So Jim came home. He bought me one of those turtle-neck sweaters—matching one he already had. We didn't say much to one another, but we seemed to be laughing a lot then, and mother was so happy about this that she broke her neck trying to find things for both of us to do together. There wasn't much to do. It was the spell between haying and discing up the summer fallow, so we were all sort of laying around.

There was a dance, and I said to Jim we should go. He agreed. It was over at Anderson's Hall. The same crowd came out, liquored up just as much as every other dance.

About midnight someone lets out a whoop and throws a stick at the lamp. Like always, he missed. Someone else sent an empty beer bottle sailing to where the orchestra was playing on the stage. Sammy Wallis, the long kid who played the piano, tumbled off his seat before he even saw the bottle coming for his head. The bottle hit the far wall, and Sammy is back on the stool without missing a note of music on his piano. Down on the floor they stopped dancing. A guy figures he knew who threw the bottle, and without a word of warning goes over and punches this sleepy farmer in the kisser. The farmer shakes his head with surprise, sees the man who hit him, and just as quick hits him back in the nose. By now the fight has spread. Sammy has taken his backend off the piano stool with excitement and is speeding up the music to keep time to the punching, kicking and cussing going on below him.

The ladies are squealing and backing up against the walls. A fat lady backed into the stove, knocking it over, bringing down twelve feet of stovepipe and all with a cloud of soot. It makes one hell of a noise, and two jokers grab a stovepipe each and start bashing each other across the heads, making dirty sounds with their lips each time they hit or get hit.

I catch sight of Jim walking quickly to the door. He never made it on his own steam. A big fellow fresh from the lumber-mills catches him, lifts him over his head and throws him. As aims go, this one was pretty good. Other than clipping an elbow against the door frame, Jim sailed through that door like it was cut out just for him to be pitched through. I was tangled with a kid who didn't want to fight, so I broke off and went after my brother.

Jim was on his feet, his pullover pulled up around his chest, when I saw him outside. He was brushing dirt off his pants and face.

"Attaboy, Jim!" I was happy and shook him by the shoulder, for I was in the heat of the fight and really full of it.

"You hurt?" I asked, because he was looking around like he'd lost his directions.

"No. I'm not hurt. Let's go home." And he started to walk away.

"Go home? You're crazy! Tell you what, Jim," I came up behind him and caught him by the hand. "Let's you and me go back and clean up on the smart guy who threw you. I saw everything—I know who it was! Come on!"

Jim tore his hand out of my grip. He was suddenly so mad he was trembling all over.

"I'll go home alone!" he snapped at me. "As for you—you go right ahead back into that pigsty and enjoy yourself with those dirty, smelly hogs on a night out! I've had enough of this sort of thing!"

He turned and was gone. I didn't go back into the hall, but followed slowly after him. The music was playing a waltz now, so I knew the fight had ended. Nobody really had that much heart to keep it going any longer. I followed Jim slowly, letting him stay ahead. I was feeling guilty and wondering what was wrong with me—why there was no contact or pride in what Jim felt important, and which I never saw. And why I could never tell him how I felt because he was too far away to hear me now. That was the end of our laughter that summer. Even the two matching pullover sweaters we wore seemed like a silly joke now.

Too far away to hear me? He's gone—there won't be our day of sitting by a ditch as old men and talking about a fight we took part in one hundred years ago. Maybe it's as well.

I think of old Hector Winslow, eighty-four years of age and dying, running a message on radio and in the newspapers to find his one sister to visit him before he passed on. He hadn't seen her since the First World War when he came west from New Brunswick.

He'd no idea if she'd married, or if she was even alive. Two letters came to him—one from Vancouver and the other from Winnipeg. Both claimed to be his sister, and both excused themselves from visiting him because of the distance. We all felt both letters were frauds, written by small crooks who make a business of writing letters to sick, weary people. But old Hector made out a will right there in hospital, splitting his property two ways and saying it was to be given to the two women who wrote him.

If Jim only knew how we bought a cow at an auction sale, I think he would have laughed and known why we were as we were.

Auctions are still held once a week on the willow flats just the other side of town. My father and I went at least once a month. Most times we didn't bid on anything. But this one time we had money for a cow, so we walked into town, planning to walk the cow home and so save transport costs.

The auction mart was an old, sagging barn with a plank platform out front. The thin, hunched auctioneer used to stand on the platform surrounded by heaps of junk, used furniture, old crockery, leaning clothes pillars loaded with second and third-hand clothing. There was sacks of meal, salt and left-over fertilizer. Much of the stuff was stained and damaged by being left out in the rain all week.

My old man and I pushed our way through the morning crowd of yawning farmers, run-down spectators who didn't have thirty cents to take in the movie in town, and kids who made a million-dollar bid and ran like hell before the auctioneer or his clerk could catch them! A wind blew up in our faces and I pulled down my cap to cut off the smell of wet ammonia fertilizer and rotting upholstered furniture. Nobody said much, and when the auctioneer came on the platform all muttering petered out and there was silence.

The auctioneer fixed up his glasses, cleared his throat and clapped his hands together twice. This was his signal that the auction had begun. Lame Willy, his clerk, immediately led a cow from the barn behind up in front of the platform where we could see it.

"Now what am I bid for this lovely, three-year-old Jersey ... " the auctioneer fired off, leaning forward as if sniffing the air for how things would go this morning.

"That's no Jersey—that's a Shorthorn!" A big man with a handlebar moustache hollered at him roughly. There was a tired 'haw-hawing' of laughter from all over, and then silence once more.

"Oh!" The auctioneer took off his glasses and cleaned them with his thumb, then put them back on his head. He bent over for a closer look at the cow in front and below him.

"That's the head you're looking at—ass is on the other end!" snorted the moustache, and there was more 'haw-hawing' than before. The auctioneer acted like he'd come across the surprise of his day.

"Well, goddamn isn't that something! It *is* a Shorthorn ... what do you know! A lovely three-year-old Shorthorn. What do I hear? What am I bid?

Come on, gentlemen—what offers do I hear? Don't just think a bid—speak up!"

My old man stabbed his fist into the air and shouted:

"A hundred dollars!"

"A hundred dollars from the man with the check shirt and grey hat!" The auctioneer turned quickly to us then away without slowing his patter.

"A hundred dollars for this lovely, three-year-old Shorthorn! Do I hear any offers? Gentlemen—this would be a giveaway! For a hundred dollars I'd buy the cow myself! A hundred dollars is the bid—what do I hear?"

"A hundred and ten!" The bicycle moustache coughed out, his shoulders coming up as if he was squaring for a fight.

"A hundred and ten! I am bid a hundred and ten ... who'll raise that to a hundred and twenty? She's worth every cent of that and more than a bargain—do I hear a hundred and twenty?" The auctioneer was swinging now. He was on fire, bending to us as if to catch us all in his hands and squeeze all the sense out of us. I saw little beads of sweat break out on his face and run down his neck.

"A hundred and fifteen!" Again my old man.

The auctioneer smiled just a little.

"A hundred and fifteen—the man with the check shirt and grey hat! Gentlemen—quickly now! Let's move this beautiful Shorthorn to meadow— quickly! Who'll give me a hundred and twenty? Do I hear a hundred and twenty? No further bids? Come now—no further bidding? A hundred and fifteen once ... twice ... SOLD! To the gentleman in the check shirt and grey hat for a hundred and fifteen dollars!"

The moustache spat a big oyster into the dust, stared hard at my father, and grunting like a wounded boar, walked away.

That wasn't the end of the business, however.

When my old man went up to pay for the cow, he first made a thing of pinching and feeling its legs, prodding its rump with his thumb, kneading under the neck. Then he took the cow's mouth into his hands and opened it. Lame Willy was fidgeting behind with his open ledger, waiting for the money. Even the auctioneer was standing still now, looking down at this inspection with a puzzled frown. I watched my father shake his head slowly and nod for Willy to come over. They had a short talk. Willy seemed scared. He closed his ledger and went over to call the auctioneer himself down.

By now my old man seemed like he was working up into a proper small fury. He started lipping off at the auctioneer while the guy was still coming down off the platform. Then he opened the cow's mouth to show Willie and the auctioneer something. They looked into the cow's mouth, and the auctioneer caught his head in his hands as if trying to hold back a sudden headache. He said something to my father, who made a 'to hell with it' motion with his hand and started walking away. The auctioneer came after him, tapping him on the shoulder. They stopped, talked some more, then shook hands. My father then dug into his pocket, paid Willie, and called me over to take the cow away. The auctioneer was back on the stand now, and the sale continued.

"What was wrong? What happened?" I asked as we led the cow through the willow flats on the way to town. My old man threw his head back and laughed until tears came into his eyes.

"Serves the stupid bastard right," he said, wiping his eyes and fanning his face with his hat.

"What'd you do?"

"I knocked fifteen dollars off the price of this milk sack, that's what I've done!" He started to laugh again.

"We got it for a hundred—is that it?"

"Sure, we got it for a hundred! You remember he didn't know the difference between a Jersey and a Shorthorn?"

"Yeh—but ... "

"I was counting on him not knowing anything else about stock. So I points out to him he was taking me by selling me a bad cow. A cow that didn't have teeth in its top jaw!"

"You mean to say this cow got no teeth in its top jaw?" I was wondering what mama would say when she found out. My old man grinned.

"No, boy—no cow got teeth in its top jaw! Here—you get behind and drive her faster. We've got to get through town before he finds out an' comes after us ... "

So you see, while my brother was away learning about music, history, electricity and law—I was here learning how to buy a cow for less.

* * *

The most beautiful girl between here and town is Sophie Makar. She never married, and she won't marry. Hers is the kind of beauty that don't ever marry. It's meant for something else, and here there's nothing else but to marry, farm and raise kids, so she's out.

I knew her as a kid. Even then she'd stand back and watch. Her father, Dan Makar, was a widower and a better farmer than any for miles around. So when she stood back as a kid, I figured at the time it was because she was putting on airs and not wanting to mix with roughs like us.

Then she got older and her great breasts pressed hard against her clothes and her eyes got clear and wild, then we all began to step away from her. Her white skin turned dark with a touch of far-off gypsy, and her hair went uncut until she could wrap it around her long neck. She was wild, strange … and so beautiful you got so you'd be afraid to look her in the eye because you knew she could do something to you if she wanted. The women, my mother among them, stepped aside when Sophie approached on the road. It was almost as if she were the queen—the very best among them.

Then dumb Freddy, the idiot, came around.

I was still a kid the summer he came. It was the year we got a good oats crop and everyone took to raising hogs to use up the extra feed the oats made. It was a Sunday afternoon at the general store, and on Sundays when the weather was warm and a nice wind blowing from the south, there were always a few people around the store.

We saw the rug pedlar coming up the road. He pulled up at the store, honking the horn of his car and waving. We stood around watching as he came out of the car. He was a small man, with a Hitler moustache under his nose and whiskey pouches under his eyes. His chin was small and came down quickly to his neck from his lips. It wasn't the kind of face you wanted to talk to or do business with. But he came out, carrying a short polished walking stick in his hand.

"And how are all you good people today?" he asked in too-loud a voice, and then he had himself a loud laugh when no one said anything in reply.

"Hey—any of you want to see a monkey?"

He pointed the stick at me and I crossed my eyes to watch the end of it. This really broke him up with laughter. He had to take out a handkerchief and blow his nose before he could speak again.

Now isolated as we are here, a lot of characters have come around promising to show us things. Some promised to show rain during a dry spell, others said they could bring back a dead mother. This one had his monkey, but nobody was biting. And then Sophie Makar took a step towards the pedlar and stared at him, her eyes wide open and steady as those of a cat.

The pedlar saw her and the smile left his face as he looked around to see if someone was trying a fast one on him. When he saw everyone was half-asleep and not caring if he was here or gone, he unlocked the trunk of his car and took a few pokes inside with his stick.

"Come out!" he called.

I heard a grunt, and then a pair of worn, cracked boots came out on the ends of thin, scarred legs. We all crowded closer now, and watched this man push himself out of the car trunk. He was dressed in tight, patched and repatched jeans and in a shirt from which his elbows came out. His hair looked as if it hadn't been cut from the winter before and a patchy beard sprouted here and there on his face.

His eyes must've hurt in the sun, because he blinked hard and they watered. Then he began to see us standing watching him and the pedlar, and his face broke into the loose grin of an idiot. His eyes were grey, dull and dead.

"Dance for the people, monkey!" the pedlar ordered.

The idiot didn't seem to hear him, and the pedlar swung his stick and hit him across the knees. The idiot staggered under the blow and pressed himself against the car, putting one hand up in front of his face.

"See—you've got yourself a monkey to look at! If you stand close you'd say he looks a bit like a man, even speaks like a man, but he has the brain of a monkey." The pedlar was swinging his stick like a fan in front of his face as he spoke in his loud sing-song voice. He turned to the idiot again.

"All right, monkey, dance for the people. Tra-la-la-la—like this! Dance!"

The pedlar did a quick-step in front of the idiot, who now squinted like he had a pain in his head. One of the farm women among us laughed nervously. The pedlar heard and suddenly got mad. Raising his hand he slapped the idiot so hard the poor devil lost his balance and fell on the dust of the road, where he lay quivering and covering his head with his large, twisted hands.

The pedlar turned to us again and tried to smile, but his eyes were bloodshot with anger.

"Sorry, folks—guess there won't be a show today. To keep a monkey obedient you got to cut back on his food. This one's fed too much. And now if you ladies will come up to the car I'll show you rugs such as you've never seen before! Colours? My, I've got rugs in colours you've never even seen!"

He opened the car door and brought out his sample bag. He had to step over the idiot to get back to us and doing so he kicked the lying man in the ribs. The idiot twisted slowly with pain.

"No ... " He groaned pitiably. At that moment I was shoved to one side and Dan Makar stepped out of the crowd and reached out to grab the pedlar by the arm.

"Ouch! Lemme go!" The pedlar dropped his samples and tore at Dan's hand. But Dan was a big man with iron wrists and the sad head of Abe Lincoln. The rug man looked up at him and wilted like a little girl.

"Now you git into this car of yours, turn around and beat it just as fast as it can go before you make me more sore than I am right now!" Dan said softly, but his voice had an edge to it I'd never heard before.

"Sure, sure. I've got no argument with you, brother!" the pedlar whimpered and broke away from Dan. "Come on, monkey—back in your cage! People don't like fun here!"

The pedlar picked up his case and stick and stood over the idiot, who lay on the road, but now with his head lifted. He was watching an army of ants creep through the dust in front of his face and he did not hear the pedlar.

"Come on, monkey!" the pedlar repeated, throwing his samples roughly into the car. The idiot was chuckling now and putting his finger in front of the ants, trying to stop them. They moved over his finger and he laughed like a kid.

"Come on!" the pedlar's anger busted out and he came at the idiot with boots and stick.

"Father! Stop him!" Sophie Makar shouted, herself jumping forward and pulling at the pedlar. Then Dan Makar was at her side. With one hand he picked the pedlar a foot off the ground by his shirt front. He swung and threw him against the car. The huckster was scared now, with all the stuffing shaken in him. Picking himself up carefully, he moved around to his door of the car and drove off, forgetting to close the trunk lid, which bobbed up and down like the tail of a galloping horse.

"Now, Dan—what we going to do with *him*?" Pete Wilson, the storekeeper asked, pointing to the idiot. Dan scratched his chin and squatted down beside the fellow.

"No one's going to hurt you now. What's your name?" he asked.

"Freddy," the idiot replied, sitting up.

"Freddy what?"

"Freddy what ... " the idiot repeated and laughed. Dan got to his feet and turned to the storekeeper. "I'll take him. He'll earn his food and keep at my place. Here—give him a bottle of Orange Crush."

Dan handed Wilson the money for a bottle of pop.

When evening came and Dan walked home with Sophie, Freddy followed ten or fifteen steps behind. My folks and I walked as far behind Freddy, and we were followed by the Bayracks. Once in a while Dan and Sophie would turn and tell Freddy to hurry up and walk with them. He'd smile and run a few steps like they wanted. But his boots hurt his feet, and half-limping he'd slow down, looking around and listening all the time to the sounds of a country evening. Soon he was walking alongside my father. Another mile and he was behind us.

Freddy took his time learning work. But he learned to do simple jobs as good as anyone else. He was passed from farm to farm and there was always work for him cutting wood, cleaning barns or repairing fences. He even learned to milk cows. He took his meals wherever he worked, and slept in empty granaries and in haylofts of barns. People he worked for would chip in money and buy him clothes, and kids were warned not to tease him or throw things at him.

He was stubborn, but farmers found they could break him from sulking by seeming to give in to him when he got sore at something. Even my old man did it once and Freddy melted like butter.

"Doggone it, Freddy, you're right. Don't know what got into me to say you were lining up those fenceposts wrong!"

The next year Freddy started to get wages for his work when people thought he'd learned how to buy his own clothes and tobacco. The wages were nothing much—the odd buck here and there, but Freddy dressed and seemed to have enough left over for chocolates and soft drinks on Sundays.

He became quite a guy for soft drinks. I've seen him open a bottle in Wilson's store, take a long sip from it, closing his eyes and letting the liquid run down the sides of his mouth. Then he'd look around and hoot, "Goot! Goot! You want?"

And he'd offer the bottle to anyone near him.

The second summer Freddy was among us, Sophie Makar got stranger than she'd ever been before. Maybe this was the time she should've married, but like I've told you, Sophie could never marry. Where does one find a man for a woman like her?

Day after day she'd comb her long, heavy hair until it shone with fire in the sun. Then she'd show up one Sunday or on a Saturday in town dressed in the roughest, oldest overalls and man's shirt, her head low and her cheeks dark and angry. She wouldn't speak to anyone. The following day she might come over to borrow a crescent wrench for Dan, and she'd be laughing, her big eyes full of life and fun.

One evening the moon was up and it was too hot to sleep. I heard my folks get up, make themselves a cup of tea and go out into the yard to drink it. I got up and went to sit with them. As we sat there, listening and thinking of nothing, we heard footsteps of someone running. In a moment she was dashing past that gate, her long hair trailing in the breeze, her head thrown back and her white teeth gleaming in the night.

"What's that?" my old man asked in a whisper.

"Come to sleep." My mother gathered the cups and there was a bit of fear in her voice when she spoke. "It's Dan's girl—she walks and runs by herself nights. It's dangerous—something will happen!"

"How do you know?"

"I just feel it will, that's all." My mother shook her head and went in.

One Sunday soon after, Freddy bought a chocolate bar and after biting it himself, offered it to Sophie, who happened to be standing behind him in the store waiting to buy herself an ice-cream cone. Sophie laughed lightly and took the entire bar and ate it. Then to the surprise of everyone she said:

"You're sweet on me, aren't you, Freddy? You like your little Sophie, no? Bet you're dying inside to cuddle up to her and give her a squeeze! You're a dear boy, Freddy!"

And just like that she takes Freddy's face in her hands and kisses both his cheeks. The idiot blew the rest of his money on chocolates and gave them all to her.

It was here at our place that Freddy was called in the week after to help butcher our meat for the winter. We only had a hog to butcher, but it's always wise to have an extra hand in case the hog breaks his rope or gets frightened before he's tied down properly. Nothing happened so Freddy just hung around. But during the killing itself, he came up so close we had to get him to move back. When we were bleeding the carcass, he stepped right up to the bucket. Dipping his finger in the warm blood, he licked on it. Then he turned sick, and my old man had to lead him away while mama and I started the dressing down.

The next Sunday, Freddy was at the store again. He bought himself a straw hat, and when Sophie showed up, he stuck close behind her.

"Come on ... play ball." He invited her, and covered his face as he laughed with pleasure when she stepped outside the store. They played catch-ball most of the afternoon. I was sitting on the steps outside the store. My father and Dan Makar came out and stood above me to share a smoke.

"It's wrong, Dan," my old man said. "It's wrong for Sophie to carry on with the fellow. He's spending all he earns on her. It's asking for trouble."

"Don't I know it," Dan growled. "I could spank her into sense when she was a kid—but now, I can't do anything. You've seen enough to know she'll always get her way. It's my fault. The kid should've had a mother—any mother. Too late now ... "

Sophie stepped on a sharp stone just then and gave a little cry of pain. She limped away from the game she and Freddy were having and went into the store. Freddy stood outside for a long while, then his lower lip hung down sullenly. He moved past me and the two men above me and followed Sophie into the store. I asked my old man for a nickel and went in myself.

Freddy was standing right behind Sophie, staring at her neck. His face was red with anger and he was breathing quickly, his breath bubbling at the corners of his mouth.

"Come on—play!" He spoke loudly. She moved among the women. He stayed right behind her.

"Come on—play!"

"Go away!" she almost shouted as she turned on him. "What you sniffing at me like that for?"

Then she was heading for the door. He jumped in front of her.

"I buy you chocolate—okay?" He bent his head to her, his lower lip covering his top one with stubbornness.

"No! I don't want your damned chocolate!" Sophie clenched her fists. "Now get out of my way!"

"I buy you chocolate—sure! I buy you pop drink … sure! You love me? Okay?" His face crinkled like that of a cornered, hurt dog. "I take you home. Come on."

He reached out and caught her arm. Sophie screamed and tore out of his grasp. She was quivering with rage now, and her eyes were bright and sharp.

"Leave me alone, will you!"

"I walk you home. Come on!" Freddy reached for her again, but she jumped back. Only now she was backed against the counter. I saw Wilson moving to the back door to call for help among the men outside and around the front.

"Go shovel manure or split wood, you crazy fool!" Sophie spat at him. "Go on! You're stupid as a sack of potatoes! You want me to walk with you? I hate the sight of your ugly, stupid face, you know that!"

Freddy bit his lips and blood spurted and trickled down his chin.

"She think—I crazy! She laugh at me! I fix her!" He was a baby kid now, bawling. Dan opened the door behind me. Freddy saw him, ducked and slipped out before Dan was able to figure out what was going on.

"What's the matter here?" he asked. The women looked at him, but none seemed able to explain to him.

Freddy worked and stayed at the Tippets' that week. When Mrs. Tippet got home that evening, she saw Freddy out in the garden, honing the bread-knife on a stone. She asked what he was doing.

"Something," the idiot replied and walked away from her, still sharpening the knife.

The rest happened quickly.

That night, Dan Makar heard his daughter rise and dress in her room, as she had risen and dressed every night for months past. Then she left the house for her nightly run.

And this night when Sophie came down the road near the store where there was a tall border of poplar and alder, Freddy suddenly jumped out from behind a poplar. He stood in front of her, holding a long breadknife belonging to the Tippets.

"Now, Freddy … you know I love you and you're a dear boy!" Sophie was scared and started walking backwards. She tried to remember if she'd seen any lights nearby so if she shouted for help there were people up and around to hear her. But she couldn't remember. And Freddy was gaining on her, his arms apart and his movement like those of a wild animal stalking for the kill.

"You … not love! You love! You laugh! I do—what I see do to pig!" Then he lunged. Sophie's heel caught in a rut and she fell backwards. She screamed, but her cries were choked in Freddy's sweat-drenched shirt which fell over her mouth. She tried to fight, but the idiot had the strength of another man in his passion. Then she froze as he lowered the razor-sharp blade to her face.

She said she never felt the pain of the blade cut deep into her cheek.

Then Freddy stopped cutting, and with the fingers of his free hand he reached up to touch her injured face. When he felt the blood he had drawn, he lifted his fingers to his lips and licked at them. Then with a terrible cry he sprang to his feet, dropping the knife. She watched him run off the road on to the fields and become lost in the silent night.

He ran, and he ran, and he ran. In the morning they found him where the creek meets the river, in the place I swam every summer. Here Freddy died of a heart burst with exhaustion. The tears were still wet on his swollen face. His fingers, like some twisted hooks, hung in the clear water of the creek.

Sophie is still around, more beautiful than ever. More woman, and more strange, distant and fiery. I saw her last Easter—watched her in church. She didn't know I was watching and thinking of all that happened. So I saw her forget herself and absent-mindedly brush a finger along the thin, white scar which runs from just under her eye down her cheek to her throat. It's a strange scar—once you saw it you'd never forget it.

For it gives her beautiful face just a touch of cruelty.

* * *

You ever cup the face of a dog or cat you liked and pressed your own nose against it? The odour of the face or hair is the odour of the love you had for that animal. The same with touch. I'll close my eyes and you put an axe or hammer handle into my hand and I'll tell you if it's been used one, two, three or ten years. Bring it up to your nose and you can smell work in the wood. It's the scent of sweat, tobacco, iron and earth. Maybe those are the things all work is made of.

I've gone through a life touching objects Jim never knew existed. In fact, there are things I've touched my parents never knew, and they lived longer. But because I touched them, they belonged to all of us.

I've stood by the church and run my hand over the red brick of its walls and learned a truth few books tell about. The truth of dedication.

The kind of dedication hunch-backed Joe had when he cycled the countryside at seventy years of age, pleading, arguing, humbling himself like a damned beggar to find labour and money with which to build his church.

"If I die without my church it'll be like I never lived at all. What is land or a house? They can burn or be buried under a dust storm. But a church! It is the house of God, and He will watch over it and protect it!"

Tone-deaf himself, Joe led a band of women carollers up and down the drifted roads each Christmas, singing at every house they could reach. If the farmer didn't give as much as he might, Joe would stop to argue, and threaten to sing more carols by himself if the donation couldn't be bettered!

In summer, when the neighbourhood came out for the few ball-games, there would be hunch-backed Joe canvassing among the people.

It took Joe seventeen years to lift his church from the soil—and you'd have to see it to understand at seven cents a brick how much went into it. We all came out to see it opened for services—all of us, believers or not. It was for Joe's sake we had to go.

Joe was there at the door, his eyes wet with tears he was so proud. He wore a nice black suit and white shirt that must have been his son's because it was too big around the neck. My folks shook his hand and told him it was a good thing to see this day and they knew how happy he was.

The minister came late. We'd all been sitting around for about an hour, although I didn't mind it. I was looking at the coloured glass windows the sun was shining into. Wax candles were lit all over, and I liked their smell. Mother sat with her eyes closed, and my old man was looking and touching the wooden seats and floor—feeling the wood and finish with his fingers and pricing it. He kept turning and fidgeting a lot. When he put his foot on a floorboard under his seat and found it squeaked, he was happy and sat still.

When the minister finally came he turned out to be a young kid from the city. You could tell from his face, eyes and way of looking at all of us that he'd never missed a square meal in his life, and that he really didn't give a damn for anything in particular. Joe walked beside him to the pulpit, trying to touch his arm. But this kid preacher never even gave the old man as much as a look or a smile.

He gets himself standing in the pulpit, and without so much as explaining why he's late, he gets right down to business:

"Before I begin the opening service, I would first like to collect the certificate of ownership. Is the chairman of the building committee here?"

As he asked this, he took out a pair of glasses and set them on his soft nose. Nobody moved or spoke. Simply because there was no such thing as a building committee. There was only old Joe, riding his bicycle, collecting, singing. He was standing in front of the pulpit now, looking foolish and not knowing what was happening.

"The chairman of the building committee? Or doesn't he go to church?" The kid preacher asks again, a wise little smile on his face now. Joe cleared his throat and spoke.

"What is it you wish, Reverend? Maybe I can help."

The preacher kept smiling as he looked down at the hunched old man.

"Did you build this church yourself, my friend?" he asked, like he was talking to a kind of countryside funny-boy.

"Why—yes! Yes, I did!"

The grin went.

"Oh, I see … I must explain that if I'm to preach here as minister of our faith, I will require ownership of the church to be turned over to the area council. Otherwise, anybody could just walk in and preach a service!"

"I wouldn't let them!" Joe stuck his chin out like he meant it. The preacher began to pick up his satchel and move down from the pulpit.

"In that case I'm afraid there will be no opening service today!"

There was a bit of a growl among the people in the church, which Joe mistook as anger against him.

"Wait! Wait!" he called out. "Whatever you want—if I got to sign something … "

There was a paper to sign all right. They used the pulpit to sign it on. When it was over with, the preacher started to look holy, but Joe was beaten. He walked out with his head down and his hands gripping the bottom of his suit coat. When the service was over, we found the old man standing by the church gate, crying like his heart was breaking apart. The preacher walked past and drove away in his nice new Chevrolet car like Joe never existed. But we all stopped to hear him when he raised his head and saw us.

"As God is my witness, I renounce this church and what faith I had that made me build it! I'd sooner pray in the bush than enter a place where— where business is made on the pulpit!" He brought each word up like it was wrapped in barbed wire, tearing his throat to shreds. Then he walked away from the churchyard. All the neighbours started talking out the rights and wrongs of what happened, but Joe's wife and family were having none of this foolishness.

"It's our business—so stop it!" His wife had a high voice that cut you wherever you stood. She had her hair curled in town for this day, and seeing her I could tell how worked up she'd gotten over Joe's humiliation. At home she must've had three or four fried chickens to feed the new preacher, and new curtains on the windows and cloth on the table. Now the preacher was gone, and she somehow felt Joe was to blame for it all.

"Joe! Don't disgrace us!" she called after him. He didn't turn, so she went after him, her sons and daughters trailing in a long line behind her.

When we drove past their gate on our way home, Joe was sitting on the porch, holding his head in his hands. She was giving him her tongue. He waved for her to go away.

"I have said what I had to say, now leave me be!" he pleaded.

"Such shame you have brought down on us! Ask those people to stop and eat with us!" She pointed to us. "Our children have to live here—and I have to blush for you. Say to somebody you didn't mean what you said and you'll do what the preacher asks!"

With all his nice clothes on, Joe went to bed. He lay in bed two days without rising or asking for food. On the third day he died of a broken heart.

At Easter of that year they raffled off his bicycle to help buy a bell for the church tower.

* * *

I like mushrooms. In all the years I have lived here I must've gathered and eaten a ton of mushrooms. Times are changing. They say mushroom picking now is taking too much time for what one gets out of it. I continue to pick, even when others no longer do so. There is really no one who picks in this neighbourhood, and the last two years I have had full run on all mushrooms in a two-mile area around this house. I have my favourite spots, like the other side of the meadow, where you'll find plenty an hour or two after a light shower. When these heavy rains pass, there'll be at least four places they'll be coming up thick as buttons. If you stay until tomorrow, I'll take you along.

To reach one of the mushroom patches, I follow an old cowpath that goes across what was once a pasture for everybody's cattle. A few years ago, some cows got hoof and mouth disease and the cattle were taken away and pastured at home to keep it from spreading. I like this meadow, although since they stopped grazing it, there's a new crop of young alders coming up. The meadow was once an old and dry stream bed. It's not far from here, and a nice walk when you feel like a walk.

I'm not a good or heavy thinker. But I can think a lot when I'm alone searching for mushrooms. I even talk to myself knowing there's no one to hear me. Can you tell me why talking to yourself is wrong? Have you never done it? I've talked to stones I rolled and trees I cut. I've talked to our cattle and horses. Farmers, lonely men, talk to themselves—they have to.

If you knew her you'd say Marta Walker would never talk to herself. She's married to Eric Walker, and that's their house over there—first neighbours to the south of here. Marta was a teacher at our school for a few years before she married Eric. He's quite a bit older than she and had worked too hard to take time to marry—but that's before she came here.

I don't know how they met, but soon they were going around a bit, and when she finished teaching she went over to his house. My old man said when he saw her once she'd said she was housekeeping for Eric for the summer months. Then we heard they'd married. When school opened in the fall, she didn't apply to go back to teaching.

I've told you that Eric was older, but Marta looked older than she really was. She'd come from an unemployed coal-mining family in Drumheller. Some kind of operation when she was a young girl made her hair grey. A lot of hard times at home and getting through school made her face tight and serious. She would look you in the eye and act like she saw right through you. Yet one day I saw her in town walking along with Eric, and I was in for quite a surprise.

She'd let her hair down and had used some lipstick on her mouth—and damned if that didn't make her look a grey-haired eighteen! Nice, too. Eric looked like he was her father, and he seemed to know it, because she nodded to me a "hello" but he didn't even look my way. Now if you want to see a sour face any day of the week, you need only look at Eric Walker.

"He smiled once only," my old man used to say. "And that was the time Swift's made a mistake and paid him for three steers when he'd only shipped one to them. But they found out and he had to give the money back, and he's never smiled since!"

The story may be true, it may not. But I saw another story much later which told me everything about them, and a lot about myself. I was picking mushrooms and thinking a lot because I'd been working hard and was put off with how little money I was making and getting more and more tired because my stomach wasn't right. I was getting pains that brought me to my knees in a sweat.

"It's something you ate," my old man reckoned.

My mother figured it was growing pains. I kept on working, but the pain wasn't getting better. So I had a lot to think about. Which is why I walked right on Marta without hearing or seeing her first. She was sitting under an alder just off the cowpath, holding her face in her hands and moaning to herself. Her hair hadn't been combed and was hanging down over her face and fingers.

"Mother of God!" she was saying in a pleading, sad voice. "What have I done? No childhood … no happiness ever, and now I have this. Four pots to wash every day—two beds to make. And then I should find him some place in the fields … a man? Eric! Eric! A stuffed sack would be no different! Not a word since Thursday morning. If he isn't working, he is eating or sleeping. Why did I marry? Why?"

I stood over her, wanting to run for my face burned with shame at finding her—so undressed. I couldn't move. I knew if I moved she would see me right off and I could never run from her, and her knowing that I heard all. What was there to do? I got down on my knees in front of her and gave her my handkerchief.

"It ain't clean," I told her. "But it's good for a wipe yet."

She was on her feet like a deer that's been shot at and missed. Her face turned white, and her eyes became big and scared.

"You've been standing—listening to me?" she asked in a whisper. I nodded. The colour was coming back to her cheeks now and her eyes were mad.

"What business you got listening? Do you look into windows when people sleep? Is that the kind of boy you are?"

"I didn't hear what you said!" I lied, and she knew I lied. She laughed.

"I didn't really," I kept on. I sounded foolish listening to myself speak, and I was getting hot and prickly all over. She laughed again and then *I* got sore.

"So what's funny?" I almost shouted at her. "You think I want to hear all this crap about you and your old man? I been walking this path before you even came here, so it's not my fault! Anyway, what I heard don't matter. I won't say nothing to nobody."

"I know you wouldn't, or I'll put you in jail!" She was going to throw everything in my face now—I could see it in her eyes and her face—angry, hurt and a little bit frightened. "You want to see something?"

Right then she reaches up to her throat and grabs the collar of her dress. With one pull she tears it open down to her stomach, showing me one of her naked breasts. Then she seems scared of what she did and pulls the dress together with both hands.

"If you say anything, I'll tell you did that to me! If not, I'll say it caught on a branch and tore!" She turned away and looked as if she was going to cry or run screaming from me. But now I was scared. I ran before she did. When I got back to this yard, I couldn't come in because I was on fire. So I pulled up a bucket of icy water from the well and splashed it over my head until my eyes hurt with the cold.

* * *

Yes, the last few years I've been working this farm, but there's nothing in it for me. Between the bank, grocery store and this religious hostel that's been milking me ever since my mama went to work for them, I don't get enough left to buy myself shoelaces when the crop's sold! If I get the debts cleared, if I live that long—then it might be different.

I still do some stone-picking, like I did for years before. I used to move from farm to farm as new land was broken, and I'd lift the stones and boulders from freshly-turned soil and haul them off the fields. Here behind my belt I carried a small hatchet to cut out long roots that the plough hadn't turned. You'd have to get as many roots out as you could find, or they'd tangle in other machinery when the farmer tried to work the new fields down for seeding.

I once read a book on American prisoners working on chain gangs busting rocks for roads. Compared to stone-picking here, a chain-gang was a holiday. There's no hotter, harder or dirtier work going. It stoops your back and turns your hands into claws which take years to straighten out again. And you're lucky if that's all the damage you got off with. I've known guys with hernias operated on so many times there was hardly anything left to stitch together any more.

Why did I work like this? Same reason I still do a spell of stone-picking— it's about the only job around that pays money for wages and lasts more than a day or two. Oh, there's some work on road repairs but you've got to have pull for those jobs, like you got to be a bit of a hammer-boy for the Social Credit party, because we're still an improvement district and every-thing we get here we get because the party wants it that way. When I see a farmer riding a road maintainer, I know how he voted last time in the provincial elections, or how he sold his vote and the votes of all his family for the next election. Even though he swears on a stack of Bibles it's not so.

Hey—you ever meet anyone who *admits* he votes Social Credit? I've never. It's like a disease they won't talk about. Yet they got forty-six votes here two years back. So we've got forty-six liars living here, or somebody's mighty handy with opening and closing ballot-boxes between the time of voting and the time the ballots are counted.

We work as stonepickers for money. Big money. Four dollars a day with grub thrown in. Sometimes, even a place to sleep.

We work alone. We work in pairs. For a while I worked by myself, because I was still a kid and scared and needing to find my own feet. But about the time of the business with Marta Walker, I began working with a partner. His name was Hank. He was a German and he stood over six feet tall and weighed two hundred and fifty pounds. He was a heavy work machine, lifting and carrying away boulders I couldn't even roll.

"You take little vons, I take the big!"

We worked like that, and pretty soon we were on piecework and making six dollars a day each. But we couldn't work through the summer together. We quarrelled over women.

Hank had ugly things to say about women. I listened, and one day told him about the afternoon I found Marta Walker. He got a big laugh out of that.

"If it vas me, boy, I'd of give her a couple in the mouth! She'd stay home then!"

"She didn't know I was there."

"If voman takes dress off in front of me like dat, I kill her!"

"Why?" Again I was choking and my face burned.

"Vot's the matter, kid? You tink woman is like man? You tink?" He growled like a dog.

"They hurt like men, Hank. They're no different!"

"Voman is noting! Noting at all!" Hank snarled and his eyes got mean and small. "Voman is veak, small. Cry like baby. Take dress off. Man don't cry! Man is everytink because he don't cry! Man is like mountain—can take vind, snow, rain! Never change! Alvays the same—alvays strong!"

"Do you hate women?"

"Dat's right—I hate the sonofabitch! Dey try veaken me—ruin me ... take avay my man-juice an' den my teeth an' hair! Never! I kill her first. Voman never do dat to me!"

I was afraid of him now because he wasn't talking to me. He was shouting at the wind—as if arguing back something he'd done or was going to do. For a moment I was scared for Marta, thinking that he knew her and was going on like this because of what I said about her. Then he stood over me like a giant.

"I hate voman!"

He picked up a two-hundred pound chunk of granite and with a grunt threw it ten feet in the air, his muscles snapping like snakes up his arms and down his legs. The rock hit the earth with a whomp and drove itself completely into the ploughed ground. Hank bared his teeth and laughed a wild stallion whinny. I never went back to stone-picking with him. He was fair enough to leave my half of the money with the farmer we'd worked for, and the guy brought it to me after Hank quit and went on.

I worked alone for a couple of weeks after breaking off with Hank. And then this shrivelled little sonofagun Walt showed up. I was clearing a field and suddenly he was there working with me and I didn't have the heart to say move on for I was here first.

Walt was a terrible man for cursing. Either he never learned to speak properly, or proper speaking couldn't get across what he meant. For he cursed when he was happy, he cursed when he was hungry, and he cursed when he was down and sad. He'd been out to sea. He'd worked on grape and cotton picking in New Mexico and California. He'd followed the tobacco harvest route for many years.

"But my damned luck broke and I end up on stones. This damned dyin'—a little every damned minute. But what the hell—everything's dyin' in this country." He looked up straight into the sun and spat.

"We're making a living, Walt," I said.

"Living? Kid—you don't live here. It's a damned graveyard, that's what it is. The place of the blasted and dead back in the pines! Will you look at the bloody country? Grey, an' thirsty and hot. Same's the farmers I've seen here. Damn, but I wouldn't stay here if I was paid a million dollars!" He spat again and his skinny face twitched he was that cheesed off.

I pulled off my cap and mopped the muddy sweat on my forehead.

"I've had my fun here."

"Fun?" He looked at me as if I'd lost my bolts. "I've been here since June and I haven't seen or heard anyone laugh, that's how much fun you all have! Hell—whole damned place is for the birds. As soon's I clean this field and the other one I promised, I'm gone—gone for good!"

I came home to sleep at nights, unless I worked more than four miles away. I told Walt to come home with me and we'd throw up a cot for him. But he always went his way at sundown. He didn't even turn into the empty granary that stood on the edge of the field. He brought his grub with him each day—a can of cold beans which he poured over a few slices of bread, washing the mess down with coffee he had asked the boss to bring down in a jar each morning.

But at night he'd throw this old blanket roll that came with him everywhere over his shoulder and march away to his sleeping place. I soon learned this was a strawstack of the most vicious barley anyone had grown in these parts for years. Walt showed up for work in the morning with clothes and hair bristling with glass-like barley spikes.

"What you sleeping in a barley stack for, Walt?" I wanted to know. "Those spikes will dig your eyes out."

"I don't mind the spikes. When I sleep, I damned well want to be left alone, an' when I sleep in a barley stack, I'm left alone!" He took his shirt off and picked it clean. I was watching, and wondering how any shirt could pick up and hold so much dirt, for it was shiny black.

"You being bothered in your sleep, Walt?"

"Not now. But other times I've been."

"What do folks want to bother a man for?"

"Not damned folks—it's the cows come nosing around that gives me the bloody willies! You ever been waked by a cow licking your face? It's like a wet rasp file!"

"I never been licked by a cow. Once by a calf, but never a cow. Funny a cow should want to lick you. I never had that happen to me."

"It's the damned salt they're after, boy. They can smell the salt before they see you," he said, looking wise and old.

"Why don't you wash, Walt?" It'd take the salt off you."

"Aw, for the love of Christ! Talk to a kid … " He spat a fast zipper through his teeth and, putting his shirt on, went back to work. I liked him, dirty clothes and all. He was what a lifetime of living on road-dust had made him, and it wasn't all bad, the way I saw it. We build roads, canals, tall buildings and airfields, as well as pulling in every harvest going. And in the end we wear a shirt and pants to death on ourselves for there is neither the place nor the time to wash and change any more. I'm afraid of filth, for I know when I find it I shall be at first walking and then running downhill. Filth finds us—sometimes on the kitchen floor or the pillowcase, at other times in back of the heart. It is not pain, but in pain one has time to see the filth he has let gather. I've already seen the filth I've gathered, and some of it's worse than Walt's.

I walked with Walt as far as the road when he left. Watched him limp away, going as empty-handed as when he came, with the blanket roll and lunch bag over his shoulder. Going south for the warmer autumn and some tobacco fields he'll find there, and after that the next year and the next on cotton.

Sometimes I bartered my work when money for wages was hard to come by. People barter their hours of labour when there's need to help and be helped, but payment in cash is not possible. Even when the harvest is in and sold, there are taxes and bank loans to settle, clothes to buy for winter. I've had to ask men to help me—yet how do I pay? Last year I come out with thirty dollars to the good—the year's farming, and I got thirty dollars left! You still want to know how our half of the world lives? Smells in our houses will tell you—soap, fried grub and cheap wallpaper.

I bartered my work years ago, even when I was no more than a kid. We all had to. I used to work on harvesting crews, or cutting wood, or putting up fences. I've even dug potatoes. My old man kept count how many days I worked here and there, and when the time came to settle, we'd get a quarter of beef as payment from one neighbour, two days use of a tractor from someone else, and a couple loads of hay when we went short ourselves.

When I was just about full-grown, but not yet a man, Sam Topilko pulled off a stunt which was part of barter living. Sam had a face blue as a piece of suit-cloth. Some liver disease did that to him. He always liked a good argument, particularly if he felt it might save him money or work.

"Now look here," he says to my father. "The kid put in three days stooking oats for me. Now I'll work it back helping to grind hog feed for you—but not three days, no sireee! I'll work back *one* day, and I think that's fair and square!"

He stuck out his chin like he was planning to make a fast fight of it. My old man is no slouch at this game himself. He rammed his hands into his pants pockets and stuck out *his* chin at Sam.

"What in hell you talking about, Topilko?"

Sam stepped back a little. "I'm saying me working a day evens up the three your kid worked for me. That's what I'm saying!"

"Like hell it does, is what *I'm* saying! I got three days coming from you and three days work I'm going to get!" My old man was loud, wide-mouthed, knowing he was going to get his way, and making all the noise he could in the meantime.

Sam Topilko began scratching at his crotch.

"He's only a kid. He can't put in the work a man can. Not that I've any complaints about him, but he's a kid."

My father had Sam, and he was playing with him the way a cat plays a mouse. He narrowed his eyes and snorted at Sam: "Come on now—what in hell you talking about? That kid is stronger than I am. Hey—son!"

I looked up.

"Show this fat prick how you throw a grain-bag full of wheat over your shoulder. Come on—show him!"

Our wagon was standing in the yard, fully loaded with grain to grind. I went over and lifted a sack of wheat down.

"Now lift it as high as you can and put it back on the wagon," my old man ordered. I took it up over my head, turned twice with it, then heaved it back on the load.

"See that? Did you see that, eh?' he gloated, wagging his finger in front of Sam's blue face. "You had a good look. That kid's made of muscle and bone!"

Sam bit his lip and looked at our wagon. Then we began work. He put in three days for the time he owed us, and never said another word about my worth. I was worth as much as the next man.

Dealing with men, it worked out this way: a man working with a team of horses, as at haying or threshing time, was worth the work of two men. So when I took our team and hayrick, each day I worked out made up two days of some neighbour having to do hand labour in return.

I was getting bigger and stronger every day. Then one day I had to use my strength to hurt. But only once, because word got around and I didn't have to do it again. Yet I was scared sick when it happened.

My old man had taken the team to another farm, leaving me to field-pitch on the farm of Sidney Danzer. Sidney was a nervous, tightened-up sort of guy who went hairy when things weren't going his way. The year I was helping him harvest, they sure weren't going his way at all. The crop was poor, and the machine threshing for him was putting a lot of grain into the straw. He wasn't sleeping good, and on the third day of threshing, he was getting dark rings under his eyes and a guy was taking his life in his hands even talking to Sidney any more.

So I was field pitching for him. The day started hot and dry. By ten o'clock in the morning, the sun was a grey fire dancing up and down with heat waves. The men coming and going were edgy, silent, hot. Soon they drank the water-jug dry and kept going to it even when they knew it was empty. But it gave them a chance to walk away from work and have a bit of a swear to ease up on. The threshing machine was laying down a cloud of brown dust, and soon it would spread and we'd have to breathe it instead of air in the field.

"Li'l bit too hot to work today, no?" said the Indian teamster I was helping to load up. I said it sure was. Then the commotion started near the threshing machine.

We stopped loading and looked over to see Sidney's team bolt, and him hanging on hard and being thrown from one side of the rick to the other as the wagon bounced and whipped over the rough field. Then he got hold of the reins and began lashing the horses into a controlled runaway. I'd seen this done before—giving the runaway team the head until they tired out. But Sidney was wild and was walloping the daylights out of his team.

"If wagon-pole break, they kill him for sure!" the Indian said with a bit of fear in his voice. His team started to snort nervously, and putting down his pitchfork he went to them and held their bridles. Meanwhile, Sidney was keeping his team galloping in a wide circle which he began tightening in to where we were. The team took at least a dozen turns before he brought them up to us and pulled them to a stop. The two dark mares were lathered in their own sweat. I went over to help him load up first so he'd have more time to rest his team before taking the load in.

"What do you want? Get the hell out!" he hollered at me, his hands shaking like he was about to throw a fit. "Get out or I'll put a fork through you! I don't need your bastard help!"

He jumped off the wagon and began loading two and three sheaves at a time, grunting like it was busting his back. I sort of stood around wondering if I should go back to the Indian, or give Sidney a minute to cool off and help him first. Then I saw a pool of blood gathering under the hoof of the horse nearest me. I went over and saw that she'd jumped the trace, which had torn a deep cut into the inside of her leg. I started to talk to her and slowly undid the trace, bringing it around the outside and fastening it again.

"What you doing?" I looked up to see Sidney standing over me, his eyes red and squinted. The Indian was still standing by his team, staring at us as if we weren't there at all.

"Your horse is hurt." I pointed at the blood.

"It's her or me today! She'll go like that until she drops, and that won't be no loss. Put the trace back where it was!" he ordered.

"No," I said and didn't move. I watched his hands tighten on the handle of his fork.

"You heard me!"

I couldn't and wouldn't move. I tried to swallow the sickness rising up from my stomach and choking my throat.

"You little bastard! I'll put her down with you—if that's what you want! I'm an old man—got piles so bad I can't walk! But don't fool yourself! I'm not too old or weak to bring ya to your knees—I'll teach you I can!"

He stepped back and lifted his fork to stab at me. The acid in my throat was now burning the back of my nose. I took my handkerchief from my pocket and wrapped it around my right fist, for my knuckles were swollen big and painful with work. My knees felt like they'd give. I tried to speak, but the sick fear was on my tongue now, gagging me.

I watched him run at me, the fork held high. He came fast, but I saw every step he took—the hate flowering in his eyes—the pitchfork coming at my head. I saw him bare his teeth for the feel of the steel tines going into my skull. And just before this happened, I came alive—one hundred percent alive! I jumped at him and hit him with all my strength to the side of his cheek. I could feel his jawbone break and saw him fall away, spinning round and round and round. And then he fell beside his wagon and lay still. I turned away and vomited long and painfully.

"You sure hit 'im hard! Betcha he never been hit like dat before!" The Indian was in front of me now, grinning with excitement. I wiped the sour phlegm from my lips with my sleeve.

Then I took my pitchfork and ran all the way home.

* * *

I've been telling you before about this pain I was having in my stomach. It was nothing at first, just a pain that felt like I'd eaten too much of the wrong kind of grub. But pretty soon it was bothering my work, and towards the end it hurt so I had to bite my lips and I was seeing floating specks before my eyes.

"It's just growing pains," my mother kept saying, but I saw her getting worried. Then one day my old man and I went into town to see the doctor. I had to go into hospital a week later and they made an operation to take out a stomach ulcer. When I came around, I saw a nurse standing by my bed. I thought she was laughing, but it must've been the gas playing hell with my ears and eyes, because when I asked her what was funny, I saw her face clear and she wasn't laughing or even smiling.

"What's your name?" I asked, not really wanting to know because I was that weak. I felt I had to keep talking to fight back the weakness and sleep that sat like a black cat under the window.

"Nancy Burla."

"So you're my nurse. You going to make me strong again?"

"I'll try." She came around with a tray from which she gave me some white pills and a glass of water. I took them and went to sleep. During the night I kept waking, burning with thirst. I thought she was by my bed some-times. At other times I knew how alone I was. I thought I was going to die, not from pain but from a feeling of death and loneliness that I felt would get the best of me before morning.

And then … and then it was morning again! Outside the hospital window a spruce branch rocked in the wind and blue clouds moved across the sky. I was alive, and outside the building neither the tree nor the milk truck I heard squealing to a stop knew how close to death I had been. This is the scare of death—knowing that your going isn't going to make it rain that day or change a highway you might have helped to build. A few friends around you might know a little of the truth you had to live with one night, many weeks—or that half-second you come up for air and know it is too late—you shall never make it. A little of that truth of your death and nothing else. It's the way it should be. The dead should have no grip on the living. Never, never!

I once watched a neighbour build a tomb for himself in our cemetery. He built it of cement, reinforced with four-inch steel. The damned thing is good for a thousand years. Inside he made a dozen shelves for a dozen coffins to rest in. The coffins were to be left open, so that as more of the family were placed inside, someone would have a chance to see the faces of the ones gone earlier. He and his wife lie in this tomb now. A thousand years—some-one will find them, blackened and dried like rotten leather—or prunes.

What is the meaning of this sick sin? Is a man who builds a tomb for himself any better than a guy caught doing something dirty in public? You tell me—you look like you had a half-assed education! Or don't you know nothing about things that hurt, frighten or mix us up?

I'm asking you, you bum!

I've got a right to know what it is you've learned in your schools that I cannot find here to answer my questions! Jim never talked but in one letter, and then he was only a sad kid, and what he had to say wasn't important to me, because I'd already lived through that kind of doubt and it would never make me think of taking my life.

Tell me something from yourself. You can't just be educated to make new machines that take work away from me without telling me what you are doing and how you are going to help me live! Tell me! You've got ears and mouth the same size I got, yet I'm doing the talking and you the listening! Or, don't you know either? Or are you going to give us a pension and a small hut to sit in, like we've been giving our old ones and the crippled. You're not going to, you know, because I'm going to fight you as I'd of fought Jim. You won't take the world away from me that easy! You haven't proven to me you deserve it.

Ah—don't worry—it's not you I'm shouting at.

Let's see where was I—yes, Nancy Burla was there when I came back to life. And as I sucked up more and more life into me, she seemed to be there giving it out! The clean white uniform, the fast, powerful walk—her way of coping with every problem quickly and gently—she was a world apart from the farm that was killing me. She was life! That is why I felt rotten and mad when my folks came to see me. I didn't talk—wouldn't even look at them.

When I coughed, the stitched wound in my belly hurt so I had to feel down to make sure it hadn't torn open. I couldn't hold back the tears from coming with the pain. They saw this and said nothing.

"We'll be killing a hog for when you come back home, so you get fattened up," my old man said. As he got up to leave he warned me, "Don't let them feed you any peanuts here. Peanuts can kill you after an operation."

"What have peanuts to do with how I am?" I asked. He only shrugged, like he didn't know why, but only that one mustn't. That's another thing about our people—our heads are full of things we mustn't do. We mustn't steal; we mustn't tell lies; we mustn't want what we can't afford; we mustn't tell anyone how poor we are.

I'm going to ask you something—how many people are there in Canada in the same boat as me? Living on a farm off which they'll never make a thousand dollars a year? And how big are their families that have to be raised on so little? You don't know, because the poorer a man gets the less he wants to talk about how little he's got.

You'll find out if you wanted to stick around for a few weeks. Watch and see what a man with a family eats—how old his furniture and dishes are—how many blankets per bed does he have. Or watch the mortgage men at work, if you've the stomach for that sort of thing. I still chew my lip until I taste blood every time I see the mortgage man come out to a farm where an old man's died.

He's there to sell the place, pay himself and the tax office off, then throw what's left for the family to fight over. Land has to sell at so much per acre. Then there's stock and unsold grain. The furniture and household goods will sell for very little. It all totals up to around four or five thousand dollars. Which sounds like a lot of money, even when half of it goes to paying taxes and loans at the bank. But remember that a man worked thirty-two years of his life to set aside that much, and that he had nothing at all besides this to carry him through sickness, or when he gets too old to work. To get any money at all towards the end of his life, he had to stand back and see his home, farm and family torn apart just to have a few measly dollars come to him.

It makes people cheesed off until sometimes they let go of the rope for a few hours and do the craziest things imaginable. I've seen two men—a white and an Indian—both so drunk they were blind. Each loaded up a .22-

calibre rifle and went staggering out into a field of clover. There they started to play war, shooting at each other and ducking down from the shots being returned. The clover field was on a corner of this farm. I climbed into the barnloft and watched. I was afraid they'd kill each other and too afraid to go out and try to stop them. There was always the chance the white man would think me the Indian or the other way around, and both open fire at me and not miss. They shot it out until they reached the end of the supply of shells. Then the white man rolled over and went to sleep. The Indian went stalking through the clover for a while, trying to find him, and then he too lay down and slept. I ran out then and collected both their guns and hid them in the cellar under this house. I'll bet neither of them today remember what they did that day when they both got too cheesed off with living.

At the hospital—when I came to leaving, I had the most awful time. First, they wanted money which I didn't have—to pay for the operation. The doctor seemed more concerned about this than checking out the dressing on my belly. In fact, he never did look at it that day. And I was sort of weak, and worried that nobody had come out to get me. But it was in the middle of haying, a hot, clear day—and the folks just couldn't afford the time to come into town. I'd have to walk home, and I didn't feel up to it. Then this damned doctor was wearing me down.

"How soon can you make a payment on your bill?" he asked, looking at me over his glasses.

"Next time I get into town I'll bring some money."

"How much will that be?"

Nancy Burla came into the doorway. I could smell and feel her all over the room. She didn't speak.

"Have you no idea how much you will pay?"

He made me mad. He had no right rubbing me down in front of the girl. My family and I had done without, but we always paid our way. Any other time wouldn't have mattered so much, but not in front of that girl.

There was a sun-room at the end of the ward, and at night I went there to sit in the dark and listen to the wind in the spruces outside. Most of the nights were cloudy, and once the wind was so strong it carried dust that chinked against the windows. I used to dream all sorts of crazy dreams in that room. Once I imagined I was a shoe with no lace, and I walked around unbuttoned and coming apart like Hattie Winslow, when her girdle didn't dry in time for the Hallowe'en dance—her clothes just weren't big enough to hold her together!

"A few feet of binder twine would do the job—through the crotch and over both shoulders!" I heard my old man saying to one of the neighbours, but when he saw me he acted like he hadn't said it at all.

So I sat there thinking I was a shoe, and Nancy Burla came in, bringing me a bottle of soft drink.

"How did you know I was here?" I asked.

"Don't have to have high school to know where anybody is in this hospital." She laughed when she said that, and I laughed with her because it really sounded funny.

When we'd laughed ourselves out, we didn't say anything for a long while. We drank our soft drinks. I heard her get up from her chair to go. I could smell her skin with the movement of her clothes, and I felt both angry and happy—wild and tired—all at the same time.

"Pay you back tomorrow," I said. "Haven't got any change with me now."

"That's all right."

I watched her in the lit ward. Her hair bounced as she walked, and she clicked the two empty bottles against each other as she carried them. Before turning the corner down the hall, she threw back her shoulders, half-turned and waved to me. Her body pushed hard against the blouse of her uniform when she did that, and when I went back to bed I couldn't hold back the dream which exploded out of me that night.

"You've got no right saying that!" I said to the doctor, holding my breath back as I spoke so as not to sound too angry.

"Well now, I don't think you're in any position to argue with me, young man. We expect prompt payment, just as you expect prompt treatment when you come to us!" He had this oily, smart-aleck smile on his face now, knowing he was digging where it hurt the most. Some people are like that—they just have to ride somebody to feel complete themselves. I've got a thick callus on the palm of my hand, and when I slammed the table between us a bottle of ink rolled off and broke on the floor, but I didn't feel my hand hurt at all.

"You shut your pig-mouth or I'm going to shut it for you good!" I heard myself holler. The doctor didn't even move his eyes from me. I left him sitting there like he was made of wood.

I paid him off as soon as I could but I didn't go back to have my dressing changed. I did it myself here in this kitchen over a basin of salt water. Yet the next time I was in town, I walked to the hospital soon's I got away from the folks. I didn't see the doctor's car, so I hung around in front, hoping to see Nancy again. She didn't show up that time, but the next trip into town I was in front of the hospital again, and saw her. She was dressed in her ordinary clothes when she came out of the place. Without the white on she looked smaller, more shy. She saw me and came over to where I stood under the spruce tree. She smiled, and then we walked up the hill overlooking the town. We reached a ledge of rock and she said she wanted to sit awhile.

"How's your stomach?" she asked.

"All right." I pitched a small pebble playfully at her ankle. She quickly pulled it back under her skirt. But she didn't smile.

"What's eating you?"

"My father's drinking again," she said quietly. She never told me of her father before.

"That's bad, eh?"

"Yes, it's bad. Two years ago he took a pledge. He'll lose the farm if he doesn't stop now, mama says." Then she started to cry. I leaned over to touch her, because I felt so damned sorry for her that I had to show it some way. But when I put my hand on her shoulder, she moved away and got to her feet. She seemed afraid.

"I'm sorry—you mustn't cry. You're so beautiful, Nancy!" I wasn't making any more sense than her tears. I was just that close to tears myself. She only got more scared and started walking downhill in a hurry. I came after her, saying again how sorry I was.

"Leave me alone!" she said in a crying voice. Then she began to run. I stayed alone behind, looking after her until the path turned on the way to the hospital. Then I looked at the town, hot and dusty, with a sign made of white stones imbedded in the hill across the river saying to watch and not start forest fires.

Behind me on this hill was a small farm. I heard a woman holler from the barnyard. A dog barked and a hog squealed long and loud, as if the dog was tearing off its ear with his teeth. Then there was no sound, and I walked down the hill back to town.

* * *

Before you return, we will be sure to visit Sergei Pushkin. Every year there was a big party at his house. It happened just before harvest time, when the hay was in and the barley was a bleached mat on the fields, ready for cutting. Sergei would appear at the gate and shout, "Come to my place tomorrow! We have something to drink and little bit to eat!"

He is a white-Russian émigré, who came to Canada about the time of the Russian Revolution. He likes his food and he likes his drink. On Saturday nights you can still hear him coming down the road from town, beered-up to the eyes, hollering at his team and the wagon creaking and rattling as he drives along.

"Amerika all right! Gidyap straight ahead, sonsofabitches together!"

If you were to meet him in town or at church and he was thinking about life, he would say:

"Boy, if we was rich, we could go to British Columbia and grow apples! But we are poor, so we stay in the muskeg an' grow weeds and taxes. But that's all right—never have crop failure that way, what you say, boy?"

The day of the yearly party at Sergei's place was in honour of some Russian saint whose name I never learned. It was a special day in Sergei's life, and he once sold a cow to pay for the food and whiskey to make a good party for everyone.

It would be sundown by the time we reached his house, and he would stand outside the door with his wife by his side. He'd shake everybody's hand and say, "Welcome to my place, my good friends! Have a good time, please!"

Inside, the main room would already be half-full of his children and grandchildren, who'd also rise and welcome you in. It was ten times more polite than any church party I've gone to, and these people meant every bit of it too.

Always there were candles on the table, surrounded by enough grub to feed an army. Roast beef and pork, sweetbreads, pickles, headcheese, dumplings and holopchi. As we made our way to our seats, his children and grandchildren would wait until we'd all settled down before moving up and taking their places. But before they sat down, they'd wait for Sergei and his wife to seat themselves first.

Like I say, there were candles on the table. They lit up the proud smile Sergei had on his face. Then he'd reach for the whiskey bottle in front of him, rise and go around the table, filling all the glasses to the brim. Ending up back at his chair, he'd fill his own glass last and raise it.

"For this year an' next year—and next year after that, an' maybe lots more years if we lucky—good luck and everything be all right for everybody!" he'd propose a toast.

We'd all drink, every man and woman and child over ten. Then we would begin to eat, cold food first to put out the whiskey fire in our throats. Everybody was talking now—some laughing, some teasing, and all agreeing about the heat of the whiskey and the good taste of the food.

Sergei didn't eat much, for he talked a lot—to us and to his children and grandchildren. In between his talking he drank from the bottle in front of him. Sometimes he broke from his halting English into phrases of Russian. And he drank and asked us all to drink with him. Then he laughed, and after he laughed he wept a little and put his arms around people nearest to him.

"We work like dogs—sometimes go hungry, but I tell you, Amerika all right! Drink, my friends, an' be happy!"

We drank and ate all we could hold. We talked to each other and listened to Sergei talk. And always I had a sad feeling that this was a time of departure—a sort of last supper after which we would all scatter to the four winds and life would change and there would never again be another supper at the home of Sergei Pushkin.

Because of this, it was the one evening of the year when I listened in a greedy sort of way to all that was happening and spoken around me, trying so hard to take in everything possible and never forget a word or gesture.

* * *

I can't help coming back to an old thought that eats away at me night and day. We did so much, and yet it was I who said, "No!" to borrowing more money to have Jim shipped home from England for burial here. It was I who said no, and it was they who suffered, for without knowing myself then, I accused them for failing Jim, me and themselves.

If only Jim had not written what he thought that night—if only he stood beside the wall in Hammersmith and said, "I am here, fresh and ready to work. Nothing important happened before this—all that means anything is about to happen to me now!"

If only he'd said this and carried on with his studies and his almost child-like loves. But he tried to reach me, and it was a desperate thing to do. For he should have known the letter would come to me when the first snow was falling outside and mama was sitting in the chair you're in. She was patching over last year's clothes for the winter ahead. My old man was staring out the window, not having the guts to ask who the letter was from or what it said. He had his large, flat hands hooked behind his belt and he was thinking pretty deep, because his brows were crinkled up.

"What's wrong?" I asked her after I'd put the letter into the stove and watched it flare up. "Didn't we make any money this year that we're back on the same clothes we wore last year this time?"

"Sure we made money, kid—lots of money!" My old man said this with a short laugh, but he didn't look at me.

"Then it's gone out to Jim again—Rhodes scholarship or not. No one said it was gone so quick!"

Now he turned to me, and he was so mad one of his cheeks was jerking with a jumpy nerve.

"I don't want to hear another word about your brother, you hear me? Jim's going to make it up to us. A couple more years in school and there'll be more than just his picture in the papers—there'll be money to pay us back with—big money such as we never had a chance to make ourselves! You'll see I'm telling the truth! So don't talk nonsense! Better still, don't even think nonsense!"

We faced each other a long time—the father gone greedy on some kind of hope, and me, the son. Already the stonepicker, threatening brother-hatred as I killed land and brought it back to life with my hands and sunshine from the sky.

When had my boyhood gone, and when did the man take over in me? Forgetting was a wild horse, galloping away from me, taking on its back the memory of weeks without end when I kept to myself and felt beard grow and the heart become changed. I laughed sometimes, then and now, but not very much.

I remember laughing like hell watching Pete Wilson trying to sell my old man three sacks of flour at his store. All my old man wanted and could afford was one sack. Pete's gone now—the store where Sophie Makar met Freddy burned down, and Pete went south to set up a hardware business outside of Calgary. Pete and my old man never got along. After the fire, he started at least one story that damned near got Pete in trouble.

This story had it that Pete forgot he had to get out of the building, so when he was pouring coal oil all over his stock, he poured a mess right across the doorway. After he was supposed to have lit the match and got the fire started, he had one hell of a job finding where the door was and getting outside before getting himself trapped for good in there. My old man set this story going, saying he'd been walking past the store and saw Pete come out the door, kerosene tin in his hand and his clothes full of smoke.

"It's a damned lie!" Pete Wilson swore. "I've lost my business and someone's trying to ruin my insurance claim!"

It was a lie, because the day of the fire my old man and I were working together. He never saw Pete that day. And Pete Wilson didn't have his insurance claim ruined. His pigsty of a store was heavily insured. But I began telling about the sacks of flour ...

"Take three sacks," Pete says to my old man. "Winter's long, and it'll save you coming back when the snow is up to your earholes."

"One will do. I only got money for one sack of flour."

Pete Wilson chewed on a stray chunk of moustache that hung over his mouth and he looked my father over carefully. Like I say, there was no love between those two and this time both of them were ripe for a bit of argument. So it was starting.

"Hell, take three!" Pete goes on. "I'll give you credit. I'd give you half the store on your word, I trust you."

This was the kind of talk that got my old man going. He didn't mind being damned for his business dealings and he didn't mind praise. But when Pete Wilson started in with this praise that wasn't really praise, he started tugging his ear.

"What're you driving at?" he demanded. Pete shrugged.

"Nothing. I think you should take three bags of flour and save yourself bother later on."

"What's the point of going into debt when all I need is one damned sack of your flour? I came in here to buy a sack of flour, so if you can't sell it to me, say so and I'll go some place else!"

Which was just talk, because some place else was in town, and he wasn't going into town for a sack of flour that cost twenty cents more than what Pete was charging.

"Do whatever you like. I'm overstocked. Haven't got place to store too much flour without mice getting at it in a week or two. So take three bags and I'll throw in ten pounds of sugar for the same price." The storekeeper slammed his hand down on the counter as if he was throwing down a high card in a game. It sounded like a good deal, but because they couldn't agree on anything, my old man became more stubborn.

"Nope. When I need more flour, I'll come and get another sack!"

"Well," Pete slowly took out a cigarette and his eyes crinkled with worry before he lit up. "Well, I hope so. But supposing you can't come back—you ever think of that?"

I saw my father's ears come up.

"What do you mean by that?" he wanted to know.

"What I was going to say was supposing you took sick and died—nothing like that will happen, of course. But just suppose it did. Imagine that you're a neighbour and it happened to him, not you. If you took sick and died, would you want your wife and boy to go hungry without flour? I'm not saying this will happen to you, only to a neighbour of yours!"

"All right! So you said already!" He had my old man with that one. "Stop that kind of talk, will you! Nobody's going to die tomorrow—not me, not any of my neighbours!"

"How can anyone say when he's going to die? You don't know and I don't know." Pete Wilson was smiling now and blowing smoke-rings into a shelf of peanut brittle. "Besides, if your wife's got to choose between going hungry and ... well, remarrying. Look now, you can't blame a woman, can you? You know as well as I do that sometimes a woman has to do these things."

"What things?" My old man tried to make his voice threatening, but it didn't come off. Pete kept blowing smoke-rings.

"Why," he was talking lazily now as if speaking to nobody but himself, "she might even marry a lumberjack because of tough times. Just think— how would you like your wife to be screwed by a lumberjack because you didn't leave her any flour before you died?"

My old man bought the three sacks of flour, and as we drove home that afternoon he spoke only once to me. He said if I was to repeat a word of what went on at the store, he'd kick my ass up into my shoulders. I said I'd never tell, but I had to cough some to kill the laughing that was starting up inside of me.

* * *

So many men come and go. Only a short time ago I was a kid, and I never gave a thought to death. How could a man die whose eyes were on fire and whose arm muscles stood out high and sharp? Or who ate the way some of the men in our neighbourhood ate? A guy named MacDonald who lived close in used to eat with two hands—a slab of bread in one hand and a piece of meat in the other. First the meat, and then the bread. In between chewing he talked. He was hard, tough. His mouth was scarred and busted up from fighting.

"So I shoot this deer! It was as tall as a house. The biggest deer I've ever killed and it was a hundred years old, it was that tough. First night on the hunt I tried to eat it, but it wouldn't chew. So I boiled it for three hours. Still it would break your teeth. So I cut a chunk out of the shank—enough to make a good sized steak, and putting it over a log, I worked it over with the butt-end of my axe. Goddamn it, but it was like beating rubber! I worked it over until I began to sweat. Then I says to myself, this way I'd die of hunger on this hunt. Got to forget the deer and eat something else, or I'll use up more strength softening the meat than I get back from eating it!"

He stuffed his mouth with more bread, chewed for a moment, then continued.

"I said to hell with it, and ate a can of pork and beans."

"Don't remember you bringing a deer home from last year's hunt." My mother wasn't believing his story.

"No, I didn't. I buried it right out there in the bush. You think it'd rot being that tough?" he asked my old man.

"Don't know."

"What makes meat rot?" MacDonald took another bite of the pickled ham he held. "Eh—what makes meat rot, you know?"

Nobody knew, so nobody said anything.

MacDonald did a bit of farming, and fall and winter he was out in the backwoods shooting anything that had meat on its bones and walked. He used to cut cordwood once, but he's been too old for that quite a few years now.

He had a son, Sammy, who was a year older than I and about thirty pounds heavier. The guy was a bully, shoving smaller kids over with a bunt of his shoulder. He was always eating prunes and dribbling out the pits over his shirt front. In a lot of ways he resembled a young pig. I tried not to have any mix-ups with him.

Then one day we were playing tag in school and he was around. I caught him when he stopped near the schoolyard fence to dig up some prunes from his pocket. I tagged him.

"Beat it!" he hollered at me.

"You're it!" I shouted and waved at the others to run. He hauled off and hit me across my lips, making my front teeth bleed. At first I was too scared to do anything. Then he came at me and knocked me down with his shoulder and I started to cry. This was way back when I was a kid still in school.

"What the hell you crying for, you baby?" By now he was mad and scared himself. Instead of leaving me alone, he was so scared he started to kick me. The school bell rang then, ending our recess. Instead of going back to school, I got up and went home. My mother wanted to know what was the matter, and I told her I fell on my face and was sick.

When Jim got home that evening, he told the folks I had run away from school and that Sammy MacDonald was tattled on for hitting me and got strapped before the class. My old lady was all ready to go over to the MacDonald farm right then and complain to Sammy's old man about Sammy. But I kept shouting at her not to, and finally she made out like she wouldn't do it that day, but if it ever happened again, it would be a different story.

Sammy didn't take the strapping like any gentleman. I didn't expect him to. The next morning he came part way up the road to meet me. I was walking to school with Jim, and when he saw Sammy coming like that, Jim turned around and high-tailed it back home. I couldn't run. I wasn't going to run. But I was scared.

"You told the teacher on me!" Sammy said when he got to where I was standing. He spat out two prune pits.

"I didn't so tell."

"You did too. Bet you laughed when I got the strap!"

"I was home," I admitted kind of weakly.

"Chicken-shit!" But he didn't wait for a reply to that. He hit me across the mouth again like he'd done the day before. I fell and reached for my cap to put back on my head before I tried to get up. He took it out of my hand and threw it across the road. And while I tried to rub the tears out of my eyes, he walked over to the cap and with his back to me peed into it. I grabbed for a stone and threw it at him, then ran off the road along a cowpath, thinking I could lose him in the heavy bush.

But there was no losing Sammy. Fat and big as he was, he was fast on his feet. Soon I heard him panting just behind me. Then I fell, tearing my cheek open on a rosebush that grew wild beside the path.

It might've been the cut, or maybe I was scared enough to do anything by now, but next thing I remember is kneeling beside Sammy, clubbing him over the head with a chunk of alder root. He wasn't moving now, and there was blood coming out of one of his ears.

"Say you got enough! Say it!" I was shouting at him. He didn't move or make a sound.

"PLEASE say it!"

Then I threw the root away and tried to lift him up, but he weighed a ton. I left him then and kept walking, sometimes running. I didn't sit down until I was by the river, here I ate my carrot-jam sandwich which I carried behind my shirt, drinking down some river water after I'd eaten. I waited until dark before I turned home. Nobody seemed to notice me arriving. I told my mama I didn't want supper and went to bed.

I dreamed Sammy's father came to our house. I saw him talking to my folks in the dream. They talked so low nobody could hear what was said, but once in a while all of them turned to look at me, so I knew they were talking about my fight with Sammy. Then I dreamed they all came towards me, their faces angry.

"You killed Sammy!" MacDonald said like it didn't matter, but he had to do what was to be done.

I thought I shouted at him that I didn't mean it, but I'm not sure. Then the three of them, MacDonald, my old man and old lady, took me out of the house into the barn and hung me from a girder beam.

Anyway, what I started to say was that since those days, MacDonald has more or less given up his winter hunting, because he's had a bad run of rheumatics. Sammy went to a trade school where he learned to weld and got himself a job in a garage in Vegreville or some place near there.

No, I didn't hurt him all that bad. He was pretty sick for a few days after our fight, but we never tangled again. We didn't play or speak to one another either. Sometimes I'd turn quickly and see him watching me from a distance, as if trying to figure something out. And there were times I stood watching him, remembering him lying on the path. Only I stopped looking at him this way, because it made me shiver.

* * *

There's always been dancing at Anderson's Hall. Summers back there were three guys—one with a guitar, the other with a fiddle and a third with a drum—came all the way from Clyde every second Saturday to play a dance here. They brought half the crowd with them, and the hall used to get so packed you'd have to drink your coffee standing up when the lunch break came. My folks decided to go a few times, but they weren't used to so many people they didn't know, so they stopped going. It was tough for them to understand that because most everybody owned a car outside of this area after the war, people were moving farther, faster. They sort of looked upon the outsider coming here to dance as someone out to have a wild time where he wasn't known. There were wild times, but it was we who made them.

I got into the back seat of a car with three guys I knew who'd come in from the lumber camps. We drank gin out of a bottle, and the four of us got so drunk we all passed out in a heap back of the hall. Next morning old man Anderson himself found us and gave us holy hell for being stupid.

Before I forget, one other reason my folks didn't come dancing was because Marta Walker started coming alone. Not only my mother, but other married women as well, stared at her as if she didn't belong, but she stayed. For the first few dances she mostly stood back along the wall, watching us. Some were kids who'd been students of hers in school. She didn't seem to want to do any dancing or anything, just stand there and look. So the next time the three lumberjack friends of mine and I got drinking, we dared one of the boys to go ask Marta to dance. Hector braced himself with a stiff drink and went, and she danced with him.

The rest of us watched from near the door. We giggled when they didn't break apart after the first dance, but kept on dancing again. This time they were talking a little bit to one another. Two weeks later, Hector asked her without us daring, and this time he danced four dances with her. During lunch at midnight, they went outside together and I sort of snooped around but couldn't find them.

"Where you been with that woman?" I asked Hector when the dancing started up again and he came back. Hector looked right past me and his mouth was shut tight and stayed shut tight. I asked again.

"Keep your dirty nose out of my business," he said.

"I'm not interested in your business. You can do what you want with her. You can even ... " He looked at me now, his fist brought up and his eyes hot and wild.

That romance built up steam pretty quickly. To get from Anderson's Hall to here, the quickest way is across Eric Walker's farm. I ordinarily chose the longer way, following the road, because Walker had this damned German Shepherd dog that would just as soon take your leg off as sleep. I didn't hear talk of him bothering the neighbours, but one night after a dance I took a short-cut through Eric's yard and the dog came out of nowhere and had me down and shouting, and I decided to stay away from walking this way again. I would've too.

But Nancy Burla came to the dance with a couple of nurses one time. One of the nurses had a boyfriend with a car, and as I stood in the stagline, I looked up and saw her smiling at me. Meeting her outside the hospital like this threw me. Instead of letting my surprise come and go, I had to try and cover it by being smart-alecky.

"Didn't know you danced," I said to her. "Didn't even think you could walk very good!"

The smile faltered on her face and she got beet-red. One of the nurses with her giggled. I hated myself when I did these things. It was a thing with my nerves. When I get excited in a happy sort of way, I say the damnedest things to people. I want to stop myself when I hear me saying them, but I can't. Nancy moved away from where I stood, and soon I saw her dancing with one of the boys who'd come from Clyde. I sat and watched and felt miserable.

Yet when the dance ended she came over and sat by me and I couldn't think of anything to say to her. So I kept my mouth shut, which was as well for it kept me from insulting her. She seemed to understand how I felt, for when the next dance was played, she got up the same time I did and we danced without me asking her to. She smelled of sweet perfume and woman's soap, and her hands were warm and moist. With my hand over the back of her dress, I could feel her back muscles, firm and tugging as we moved across the floor. I felt sad and happy all at the same time. When the dance finished for the night, I walked to the car which had brought her and the other nurses.

"So awright—so give 'im a kiss an' let's go!" The loud-mouth who owned the car rolled down his window to tease her. The crazy things I do—without holding myself back, I pulled her to me and kissed her on the mouth, and her friends looking on. Then I turned away and went home, blind, because my eyes were full of tears and I couldn't stop them coming.

I wanted to reach home quickly and get into bed so I could dream of a different kind of life, with Nancy Burla beside me. A house of my own. A few chickens and some meadow with a cow that had enough to eat and give milk on. We'd get by on very little. People can, and do.

One of the few times my old man and I could talk and understand each other was when we talked about farm people—peasants, and how nothing could break them.

"Give a man like you or me a shovel and a bit of dirt and he'll grow grub no matter what happens—atomic bombs or no!" he'd say proudly, and I knew he was right. People born generations to earth know about seed, water and sun without being told. They can suffer the kind of pain that sends a city-bred man to suicide, and they come out of it a little more bent and wrinkled, but still doing those things that give food and shelter to themselves and their children.

Not that I like this. I'd give all this away a thousand times over for a year of the kind of joy I know a man can have. Sometimes I feel I can see Jim as clear as if his soul and heart were made of glass, and everything inside was written out to be read. He's saying to me: "I don't hate you. I love you. I'll never be older than you. But I've seen so much I would show you if I could. It came too soon for me and too much. I'm a child … you'll have to care for me!"

And then I cry. Believe me, man—I drop my head down and cry. I cry for every goddamned day I've spent here, rooted to a hundred and sixty acres of mud, rock and bush. I cry for Jim and not hearing *his* story before he decided there'd never be anyone to hear him. I cry because I've lost her, and with her gone, I've lost life itself. I'm not even as useful as a second-hand tractor you can buy for two hundred dollars. I cost more to keep and I can't do as much work. I thought once I'd write a long poem where I'd tell everything. Or make up a cowboy song to sing. But the words never came. I've stood for hours out there in the field, the wind blowing all around me, drying the soil and sapping the water out of my flesh. I've felt it all, but could never tell others how it felt.

That night I left her I wanted to get home as quickly as possible. I crossed Eric Walker's barley-field and began walking through his yard as quietly as I could so's not to surprise the dog. The house was dark. The path in front of me was dark. Marta had been at the dance, again dancing with Hector a lot of the time, but I didn't see her when the dance finished. Neither did I see Hector.

Even before I heard her giggle and sigh, I knew they were near me, making love. I stopped in the middle of the Walker yard and looked around. Darkness was cut only by the stars. Then I knew where they were. Over in the feed-shed by the barn. The door of the shed was open, and I heard Marta laugh again and Hector pleading with her.

I forgot about the dog and my fear of him. I began to hurry away, my footsteps kicking up pebbles, but I was too shamed and excited to care how much noise I made in my retreat. Then I stopped, wanting to steal over to the shed and spy on them, to share by listening to them in their sinful pleasure. No—I mustn't! I had to run away from here. Then my foot kicked the dog and I fell over him.

I was on my feet in a flash and ready to protect myself. But nothing happened. I knelt beside him and reached out to touch him. He was still warm and wet. I touched him again, this time exploring. When I found the hot hole in his ribs I almost became sick. After coming here they had to kill the dog to have each other.

And in the dark house, Eric Walker, who never laughed, was having himself a good sleep.

* * *

There is the palm and the back of the hand. And so it is with a community. Some are known for the work they do, others for the way they can enjoy themselves. Let me tell you about a woman who could dance a whole story she could tell no other way.

Elizabeth Junco was her name, but I grew up knowing her by her first name. As I suppose my folks did before me. You go three miles towards town down this road. At three miles you turn off and go another mile towards the river. This last mile is hardly more than a footpath, and at the end of the path is Elizabeth's place.

She's about seventy now, but smart as a whip. She's never changed. Always grey-haired, skin parched and brown, and hands that are thin and small as a kid's. Her clothes don't have any colour or shape to them any more, she's worn the same things so long now. Winter and summer she's got the same skirt and jacket on, with wads of other clothing underneath. But she can bake an apple pie like nobody else can bake an apple pie here. And she smokes a pipe.

If you ask her why, she'll say, "For me asthma."

We have farmers' picnics every year on the school playground. In the old days, neighbours walked to the picnic, carrying kids on their shoulders. Now they drive in, with their cars and half-ton trucks all washed and waxed for the day. But they get dusty fast, and there's always a few brats moving around drawing pumpkin heads with crazy mouths over the dust that's settled on the waxed metal. Some write dirty words, but that's only some, and I chase them away myself when I see them ready to write.

Anyhow—at the picnics they've always had a baking contest. My old lady took the best bread prize two years in a row. For prizes, she once got that set of glassware you can see up there on the shelf. The second time she got a cushion cover, but that's long gone.

Every year Elizabeth brought her apple pie, and every year she's taken a prize. You've never seen apple pie like the one she bakes. Rich, thick, spiced so you can smell it a mile off, and covered with whipped cream this thick! It makes your mouth water just to see it stand on the table during the judging. I once had a small spoon of it after the judging, and it was something to remember! It got so no woman brought pies to put against the one Elizabeth entered. Part of this was a dislike the women felt for Elizabeth. For after all this old woman lived without a man or means and beat them at their own game.

Elizabeth had hardly enough land for a garden, at the back of which was a tiny shack and a clothes-line. Next to the shack, planted in such a way that it could be covered with a big canvas sheet attached to the roof for winter, was a small sour-apple tree. It was the small green apples she got from this tree that she baked the pies out of. That was all—no cattle, no dog or cat. My old lady knew how poorly Elizabeth lived, and one summer she tried to pull a dirty one on her at the picnic. When a crowd of women were standing around, she says to Elizabeth:

"Tell me, dearie, with no cows of your own, how do you manage to get whipped cream? If you tried to bring it from town, or even from another farm, surely it'd sour before you got it home! But there's a pasture meadow near your place ... and Russell Jones keeps four milk cows there now ... I wonder if it's possible you might be milking one of these cows when nobody was looking!"

My mama had no right doing that. A kid could figure out Elizabeth was stealing milk for cream to cover her pie, but it didn't have to be talked about with the old woman standing there.

"Now what makes you think that's the kind of dirty work I'd do, huh? Or have you seen me doing it?" she asked my mother quietly, then she continued: "You surprise me, Josie—all dressed up so nice and thinkin' such thoughts of other people less lucky than you!"

My old lady did feel ashamed. It served her right to have her nose put out of joint for what she tried to do.

"Oh, forget it!" she said. Old Elizabeth wasn't going to let her off that easy though.

"Forget what? You telling these good women that I'm a thief?"

"I didn't say any such thing! I'd never think of it, and if you think I said it, I'm sorry."

Elizabeth smiled and looked squarely at my mother.

"I'm sure glad of that, Josie, an' no hard feelings," she said. "You're such a fine, upstanding woman, with a good man an' two boys of your own. Always somebody around to see to you and take care of you. That's nice."

She looked around as if wanting the judging to be over and done with quickly.

"If they don't come to judge, I'm invitin' you ladies to have the pie with me," Elizabeth grinned and began packing her pipe. When the judges did come up to choose the best baking that summer, Elizabeth again got first prize for her pie.

Elizabeth was there every time when they held regular dances at Anderson's Hall. She never stayed the whole night because she wouldn't light her pipe for fear of offending someone in a closed building. A few dances to get things going, and she'd be gone. When she danced, it was like lecturing us not to forget there was more to living than stones, barley, and debts.

She was like a deer on her feet. When every man who'd dance with her got too tired to go on, and no fresh ones came forward, they would clear the floor and old Elizabeth went at it alone—holding her skirts like a girl, and her legs moving so fast it made you dizzy watching her.

"Turkey in the straw—fast!" If the orchestra didn't know the music, they had to come in with as good a tune quickly, or they'd be booed off the stage.

Now there were handclaps in time to the music. And in the middle of the big floor was Elizabeth, her white hair flying and her mouth slightly open with pure joy in the music and speed of the dance. Applause, and some man from the back of the hall shouting, "Bravo, Elizabeth!"

Another would shout from nearer to her, "If it wasn't for a wife and five kids already, I'd run away with you tonight, that's for sure!"

The music played on, but she stopped, brushing down her threadbare clothing over her thin old body and looking down at herself. Faint droplets of sweat made her forehead and cheeks shine. There'd be some laughter among the women, and Elizabeth would look up at the man in front of her and say:

"Shame on you for even thinking such thoughts—with a wife and five kids of your own! You ought to be ashamed."

The man would argue back that he meant it, and devil take the consequences. But would she dance some more?

Elizabeth shook her head as if to say it wasn't the same any more—not until the next time. As the dancing started up again, with younger people coming on the floor, Elizabeth would pull her clothes more snugly around her and leave to walk home all by herself.

* * *

We had a grey cat called Mike, who sat and slept on the chair you're on. Can't say for sure if he came to us as a kitten, or if he was born right on the property from one of the strays that came and went. He seemed to have been with us for years, and always boss of the barnyard. Cows stepped aside when he came down the path from the house to the barn. I'm not surprised, because even I gave him the road when we met. There was something wise and firm about the way he walked and held his head. Like if he was a man, you'd call him "sir" without thinking. He earned his respect as far as the family was concerned, because Mike was a good mouser and kept our cellar and granaries free of mice and squirrels.

In the house, the chair you're in was his to sit or sleep in. Nobody ever thought of lifting him out. Partly because Mike left the farm once in a while. Four times in all he was gone for as long as eight months.

Each time he went, we were sure he was gone for good, especially since nobody in the neighbourhood saw or heard of him. It's easy to lose a cat in the bush around here. A weasel or cougar could kill him. Or if he was able to survive wild animals, he could easily freeze to death in winter, when temperatures can drop to forty below-zero and worse for weeks at a time. Then one spring or summer morning when you'd almost forgotten him, Mike would be there on the porch, sunning himself and yawning when you picked him up!

We made a lot of him on his returns. He got plenty of fresh milk, and if we'd slaughtered pork, mama would fry a bit of liver for him to eat. Jim and I played and patted him a lot for a few days until we were sure he understood how much he'd been missed.

But each time Mike came back, he was changed in a way that shocked us. The same kind of changes you'd likely get with old soldiers who go from one war to the next, or saints who take it on themselves to tame a fierce world and never quite make it.

The first time, part of his right ear was missing, and the tip of his tail had frozen or been bitten off. The next time he took off, he came back with his left ear completely off and part of a front paw torn off by a trap. The third time, all the hair off one side of his stomach was gone, showing a large patch of white, dry skin. The fourth time, he lost one eye.

I took it on myself to save him from more damage, by taking him inside the house at nights and closing all the windows to keep him in. For I felt the next time he left, he would not return. There was only a small part of old Mike left then, and the spirit of a cat is no stronger than the spirit of a man.

I was right. For he took off in broad daylight once and never did come back.

* * *

Have you ever heard of Calling Lake?

It's only an hour and a half by car when the roads are dry. When there wasn't a proper road ten years ago, it took us a day to get there by sled and horse in winter. For every winter some of us went to Calling Lake to fish through the ice. If you were low on money, one way to keep a family fed was to fall back on fish and potatoes in the winter.

One winter I drove out with Wally Pantaluk, who was at that time one of the strongest men around. He was short and solid muscled. I think he was about twice my age then, but he could still break ice and pull in a net with the strength of two men.

We got to the lake as it was turning dark. By what light was left and the help of a bonfire on the beach, we sank our nets and had supper and warm tea before rolling in under blankets and hay on the sled to sleep. With the first grey of morning, we were pulling the net out of the thin channel in the ice.

It was cold, but we had to work fast to dump the heavy catch of whitefish and pickerel before they froze into the net once it was lifted out of the water. Our mitts crackled with ice. Our breath froze in white puffs as we panted with the strain, and soon the sun was up, but it gave no warmth. We were almost finished now, and I began rolling up the net while Wally took out the last few fish. He was drenched with water from the net and from his own perspiration.

"Hey—boy! Get this done and we take five! I feel like I'm on fire!" he shouted to me over his shoulder. Then he tossed up the last fish on the snow and stood up.

"I'll fold the net myself," I said to him. "You go on the sled and rest."

"The way I feel the last place I want to rest is the sled. I'm gonna lay me down right here and cool off first!"

He began to settle down on the ice, and I started feeling afraid.

"Don't lay on the ice, Wally! You'll catch cold!" He grinned at me.

"When Wally Pantaluk gets hot, Wally Pantaluk has to cool down before he can work some more! Leave the fish to freeze hard. I'll help you load them right away."

He was still looking at me as he stretched out on a spot of ice that was windswept bare. He lay on his right side, his head resting on his hand. In five minutes a small pool of water had formed under him. When he rose, I saw that he staggered a little as he came to the sled where I'd been loading the half-frozen fish. The colour was gone from his face. He had himself a cup of coffee we'd kept warm in a jar wrapped in newspaper, as I harnessed the horses to the sled. When I was done and had the net tied down to the back of the sled, Wally climbed slowly to his seat, wrapping himself in a blanket while I put up our food box. He shivered a lot as we drove back home.

That was the end of Wally Pantaluk as a workman. Even as we drove in, he suddenly took a scare of something only he felt or knew, and he whimpered and shivered like that all the way. I asked him what was wrong, but he wouldn't talk. When I happened to look into his face, I noticed his eyes had gone bloodshot and were running tears.

I got around to visiting him once at his home that winter. He'd lost a lot of weight, and was laying in bed smelling powerful strong of mustard and camphor. By spring he was up and around, but it was as if the side on which he had lain on the ice had shrunk on him. He walked bent over in that direction. He wasn't able to turn his head without shuffling his whole body around. And he couldn't walk without a stick. He tried to put in his own crop on his farm that spring, then ended up hiring men to do it for him.

The winter following, Wally got married. His woman was older than he by quite a few years and she had this real heavy moustache on her lip, so I don't think he was very happy.

* * *

Some of the other things that happened you already know. My old lady got her first stroke in time for Christmas—she was in hospital a month then, and that ended our Christmas that year and every year after.

A young kid called Steve Swanson came from Edmonton and paid a two year lease on an acre of land just downhill from the garden right on this farm. He built himself a shack. After he left, we kept the shack open a while, thinking he'd come back. When he didn't come, we finally turned it into a chicken coop.

But first, you'll want to know about my mother's stroke.

When we heard of Jim's death it didn't come through to us for a while. Being killed in a motorcycle crash—at high-speed, in England? You know the way it felt? It seemed like so far away and such an unlikely way for Jim to go after all these years of books and schools, that I really think we believed it wasn't Jim at all. It was a mistake and somebody else got killed and we'd hear the true story in an hour or two. But when I tuned in to the radio and they repeated what the telegram from his school said over the news, we knew then.

My old lady just kept puttering around the stove.

"Well, what the hell do we say to all that? What the hell do we say?" My father was sitting over there when I shut the radio off, and he muttered and then whacked the table with his fist.

Then Dan Makar came, bringing another telegram from town. He left after saying how sorry he was about Jim, and my old man opened the new telegram. It was from Jim's student fraternity, saying he'd requested they bury him through some insurance they had for this sort of thing in his school. But if we wanted Jim's body home, then—

"Yes, we must!" My old lady dropped a saucepan on the stove as she turned. My father nodded and got to his feet. He was on the way to the bedroom to change.

"What're you doing?" I asked.

"Changing to go into town, boy," he said. "See if we can raise more money to bring Jim home and bury him."

"From the bank?" I wanted to know.

"What's it to you? You finished cleaning the barn and doing your chores for the day? Get on with it!" Suddenly he got hard and mean with me, not really attacking, but defending himself in a way that hurt me worse than him. Maybe if I hadn't done this I would have let all this go. But I felt an anger—hot and wicked—shaping up inside me, edging closer to an explosion. My mother moved to the table and sat down.

"Your father knows what he's doing ... " she began to say.

"No!" I shouted at him. "You're not borrowing a damned penny more and that's that!"

"Stop it—both of you!" my old lady whimpered. He stood glaring at me for a moment, then came over quick and slapped me hard. I kept watching him and saw his eyes look away with shame. Then we heard her fall off the chair and the fight ended.

We stood over her for maybe five minutes, both of us thinking she wasn't lying there—we were both imagining it. Then we came to life—I, running for the barn to get horses and sled for taking her to hospital, and he sponging her head with vinegar and pleading with her to forgive all and live.

We learned all the bad news about her soon's we got her into the hospital. On the way home, the old man asked me to wait while he went into the liquor store.

At home that night, he sat up by himself after I went to bed and got himself blind drunk. He staggered into my room towards morning, mumbling about us understanding each other. By the time I was awake enough to raise myself in bed, he'd gone to sleep sitting on the edge. I put him down, covered him, and got dressed to begin the day three hours earlier than usual.

* * *

Steve Swanson had four toes to each foot. He never drank water from a well. In summer he caught rain-water, and in winter he melted down snow to make his soup and tea.

He was only a year or two older than me, and he could play a fiddle like nobody I'd ever heard play before. Not just dance tunes, but heavier stuff also. Opera and things like that.

"Where'd you learn all that kind of stuff, Steve?" I asked when we first worked on his shack. My old man charged him forty dollars a year for lease of an acre of land, and I thought that was high if a man was also to build a place for himself to live in. So I helped Steve put up his eight-by-twelve foot frame but, wondering all the time why he came from Edmonton to live like this.

"From records. I played records and learned by ear."

He showed me the box of records he'd brought with him. He also brought a record player to play them on, but it was no use to him here for it had to have electric power to work. If he'd lived here now he could've carried the player to one of the farms where they've got power. But when Steve was here, the powerline was still about fifteen miles away and any farm wanting power had to have eleven hundred dollars to shell out in advance. Eleven hundred dollars is more than a farm such as this can produce in the best year, and there hasn't been a best year since I've lived here. And even if you got that much, you'd still have to pay off taxes, seed, fertilizer, repairs to machinery—and in my case, hospital bills and loan repayments, plus some for her missionary work among the bums, and what'd be left.

But Steve—yes ... I asked him finally what made him come out here. He didn't say a word, but picked up his fiddle and started tuning it. After a while he looked as if he was going to put it down.

"A woman?" I asked.

He picked up the fiddle again and started playing "Buffalo Girls" and stamping his stockinged foot on the rough plank floor we'd put into the shack. That was the first time I saw his feet and noticed something peculiar about them. They were pointed and long at the toe.

"How come?" I touched his foot with my boot and immediately felt foolish for doing it.

"Four toes." And he stopped playing and pulled off a sock to show me. "Ever seen a guy with four toes before?"

I said I hadn't and he laughed. Then we got back to work finishing the door and setting in his window, for the first snow had fallen and the wind could turn icy within hours this late in the year.

It was a few weeks later and well into cold weather when I saw Steve again—just around Christmas it was. I saw Eric Walker drive over to his shack after the last heavy snow to deliver a bigger stove. And a few times I saw Steve going out axe in hand to cut up a bit of fallen log for firewood. I'd always stop in the barnyard to listen to him chop wood with the short "chick-chick" axe blows of a city man!

I was milking cows one evening by lantern light in the barn when Steve came in to see me. I never heard him open the barn door, because my old man was giving me enough worries to think about, and when Steve touched me on the shoulder, I almost come off the milking stool with surprise.

"What the hell's the matter with you, creeping up on a guy like that?"

My father was getting just about useless since my mother's stroke, and I didn't know what to do about him. He started drinking pretty heavily. He got another bottle of whiskey from town the next time we drove in to her. When he drank that, he went out once on foot and came back with a gallon jug of moonshine he'd got some place in the neighbourhood. Drink wasn't making him any happier. For one thing, he didn't eat much any more. For another, it started to make him turn grey. The month the old lady was away sick, he became an old man, and that's no lie. I was too busy keeping the place going single-handedly to stop and figure out why everything was going to pot. Jim was buried in England by now, and as far as I know, my father never even got around to replying to the second telegram. I started the whole mess moving this way, but at that time I couldn't see further than the next chore so the guilt didn't come until later—half a year later.

Anyway, Steve scared the hell out of me.

"I didn't mean to. Sorry." He shuffled around a little beside me before asking, "You think old Anderson would let me play dances at his hall?"

I'd told Steve some time earlier about the dances, and how Anderson often took different players in for music.

"I don't know," I said. "Why don't you go over and ask him tomorrow?"

"I'd rather you asked him for me."

"What the hell! It's your problem—if you want to play, go talk to Anderson. I've enough to do around here. Besides, how can you play a dance with just a fiddle? You've got to find someone to play guitar with you."

"I can't just go up to him and say I play a violin good! It'd be better if you told him!" Steve looked like he was making to go out and not say any more to me. But he stopped, but didn't look at me.

"I've no money," he said quietly. "I'm broke, and I've only got grub to last a week an' no more!"

I didn't believe him. He said it so straight out that I was sure he was having me on.

"Tough!" I said, and started to laugh. He sort of let out a groan, and before I could speak to him again, he'd left the barn and was gone in the night. Next morning, I went over to see him at his shack, but he was gone, and a nail had been driven into the frame of the door to keep it shut.

Week after Christmas—second of January, my old lady was ready to come out of hospital. My old man cut out the booze all New Year's Day and had himself a bath. Except for being thin and grey, he seemed more cheerful than I'd seen him the month before. But we hadn't talked, and now it was hard to begin. So we loaded up blankets and two hot water bottles into the sleigh and drove into town with hardly a word said. It was just before noon when we got in, the time the old doctor would be gone for lunch. There was a new doctor in town—he'd come from Australia, but when my mother went in, he was up north, so she had the same Doctor Brent who'd operated on my ulcer a year before. Because he was in the hospital the afternoons a person could visit, I didn't see my old lady during the month she was in. I hung around the pool-hall and Chinese café while my father went to her.

Before we could get mama out, the old man had to sign forms and arrange how he'd pay. I paced around the front office and next thing I was in the corridor and headed to the ward where Nancy would be at this hour. I hadn't seen her for a few months—no, less than that—six weeks! But I was older by a year now, supporting a sick mother and a father who was turning to putty on me. I had to stop in the corridor and take a deep breath to catch up with myself—to know what to tell her. An older nurse who was big as a house came over to me and asked what I wanted. I told her.

"Miss Burla isn't working here any longer. She's with Doctor Helsen now, working in his office."

"The new doctor?"

She nodded and then herded me back to the front of the building. My mother was down now, thin and rattly as a ghost, but smiling from where she sat on a bench waiting for me. I kissed her and then we led her out.

Our horses snorted steam on the winter air. As we drove away the sleigh runners squealed on the frozen snow. The Christmas lights were still up in town, some of them staying lit right through the day.

"What did you men do over the holiday?" Mama asked in a tired voice.

"Nothing," I said.

"Nothing," the old man repeated and looked away from me, for I wondered if he'd tell her about his drinking. I think she knew, for after we were out of town he gave me the reins to drive and himself bent down to kiss her. When his mouth touched hers, I saw her eyes flutter open with surprise.

"You going to live now, Josie. I was scared you wouldn't." He kept saying that over and over to her, like he still wasn't sure it was so. She didn't say anything back to him. When we got home I lifted her off the sleigh and carried her in. Her breath smelled of hospital, and when I was putting her down and she reached up to hold my neck and help steady herself, her hands were icy cold.

Affairs didn't improve between my old man and myself. Even with her back home, we still couldn't get around to speaking again. He had his odd shot of whiskey with tea now, but he did cut back on what he'd drunk during the time she was away. But the strangest change was in her. She'd somehow become very resigned and quiet. She was still too weak to get up, but she didn't seem to mind the filth filling up the house, and once when we missed a meal, she didn't mention it to the old man or me.

What really threw me was to see John the wife-beater now turned evangelist stopping by. It'd been years since he'd come around, and that was during the time he was bad. This time it wasn't the old man he came to see, but her. While we hung around the kitchen, drinking tea and wondering what the hell was going on, John went into the bedroom where she was and stayed talking to her for about an hour. When he left, I looked in and saw he'd left her lap full of his magazines and little religious booklets.

"Is she—taking religion?" I whispered to my father. He looked past me as he lifted his shoulders in the most weary shrug.

"Who cares?" he said.

Steve came back two weeks later. I heard his violin one morning as I was busy carrying hay off the stack into the barn to feed some cows which were due to calve shortly. It was a clear, frosty morning, and the fiddle sound carried right into the barn. He was playing his heavy music. I finished feeding quickly and went over to see him. He wore a new suit, and had a nice sheepskin hat on his head. He had his feet on a stool in front of the blazing stove and played with his eyes closed. When I came in, he jumped up.

"Close that door, stupid peasant!" he shouted at me. "You're putting me out of tune!"

I'd brought in a cloud of icy air with me, which kept billowing in as I tried to kick my rubber overboots off, holding the door open because I couldn't keep my mind on two things at one time. He put his fiddle on the bed and covered it with a pillow.

"Close the door!"

"I'm sorry about laughing when you asked for money," I said.

"I never asked for money!"

"Well, you know, when you were broke and wanted me to talk to Anderson about playing!"

"Forget it. I've got all kinds of money." He took out a roll from his pocket. There must've been a couple hundred in it. By now the shack was warm again, and he took the fiddle out and started playing, but something was worrying him, because he couldn't play more than a few notes without going off. I hung around, but he only sat with a long look on his face and his fiddle on his lap, so I went back to my work.

Like I told you, Steve paid two years lease and put this shack up. But he didn't stay out that first winter. Next time the old man and I were in town to shop the mountie stopped us on the street.

"You got a guy called Swanson living at your place?" he asked. We said yes, and asked what was wrong. The mountie said he wasn't sure, and walked away without saying anything more.

When we got home, we saw the door of Steve's shack hanging open and no sign of Steve. I ran over and found some of his stuff still there, except for his clothes and his fiddle. The records in the box were busted, and he'd put the axe through the middle of the record player, so there was nothing left except the stove, a half dozen pocketbooks and the bed and bedding, and two small cooking pots and spoons.

My old man came in then and looked the place over.

"The kid say anything about being in trouble?" he asked me.

"He needed money once."

"You give him some?"

"No."

He gave me a sad, long smile.

"Too bad you didn't," he said, and walked out.

I talked to the mountie about Steve, and was told he'd got six months for theft in Edmonton. So I took his stuff out and put it in a corner of the back porch in case he comes back to collect it. Then I made a chicken-coop out of the shack.

* * *

It was early June—spring. The crops were in the ground and winter-born calves were as full of devil as seven-year-old children. Much work of picking stones off the fields had to be done. At home, an unreal kind of happiness was driving my mother to John's evangelical meetings, and my father had gotten as thin and bug-eyed as a man with a killing disease. I now knew he was being driven by some secret worry he wasn't telling about. He drank openly as he had when she was away, but he was never drunk.

One day I got so damned sad I couldn't go on working. Blackbirds walked beside me like they knew what was going on in my head and heart. I had to get out and see her—tell her, or if I got nervous and said things I didn't mean, make her look at me and understand.

She was working for this Doctor Helsen, the fellow I told you about, who'd come from Australia last fall. During a farm union meeting for the whole region, they said he came out to speak about state-controlled medicine for everyone. I wasn't at the meeting, but Sergei Pushkin said the doctor stood for the farmer and worker, and we could learn a lot from him. Word was also going around that he and Doctor Brent weren't hitting it off too well at the hospital because Doctor Helsen wasn't charging anywhere near the old fees for visits and surgery.

He'd been away when my mother had her stroke, so he hadn't treated her. But I'd seen him around town, and liked what I saw. He was a big guy, sandy-haired and with this voice that sounded like a deep horn down inside his stomach.

I walked into town, dressed just the way I was coming off the fields and so goddarned sad I didn't know which way to turn. It was a long walk and I got in just before lunch. I hadn't seen Nancy Burla to talk to going on eight or nine months. She seemed both surprised and happy to have me walk into the new office this Doctor Helsen had. There were two other people waiting to see the doctor.

"How are you, Nancy? I ... want to see you by yourself," I said to her.

"Is there anything wrong with you?" she asked, and she was worried.

"No, no! But I don't know if there is or isn't!" I felt the two women waiting for the doctor looking at me with the blank stares of farmers who hear every word and don't forget a thing. "Can we ... "

I pointed to the drugstore across the street. She smiled at the two women and came from behind the desk. She'd gotten thinner than she'd been at the hospital and there was a slight slouch to her shoulders.

"But only a minute. Doctor Helsen will be back any time."

In the drugstore, a few high school kids were reading comics and magazines at the rack. A little girl with a twisted shoulder and dressed in white, as Nancy was dressed, brought us coffee at the bar, then hung around, looking at me without seeming to. I wanted her to go away, but she wouldn't.

"I've only a minute." Nancy spoke, then looked up at the girl of the bar. "How are tricks today, Sadie?"

"Fine."

"Nancy, I want to say something to you, so will you listen ... " I started off that way, and felt wretched as hell because it was all going wrong.

"Well?" She was looking at me now, laughter in her eyes. First laughter, then anger, for the little bitch back of the bar giggled.

"I don't know what I'll do—unless you marry me!"

It was out, and in such a loud, fast voice I could hear the students at the magazine rack crumple their magazines to listen for more. I wanted to run from the place, but I couldn't move off the stool. Sweat was trickling down the sides of my face, and I felt like some grimy, sweaty, smelly-armpitted joker grunting at the slaughter table. My hand was bigger than the cup I held, but the cup was too heavy to keep up and I spilled hot coffee over my wrist before I dropped it. A long shudder went through Nancy. Her eyes turned away, shocked, and she put down her coffee very carefully. When she spoke, her voice was so soft only I could hear her.

"It's not going to be. A year ago, maybe. But now you're crazy to ask. It's not going to be!"

"But I love you, and I thought ... "

"It doesn't matter!" She was on her feet now. "What's love anyhow? You think I don't know how it'd be? Smarten up! Just kids and tough times ... my old man's a drunk because of it—I ever tell you how much of a drunk he is?"

She was gone out the door, her legs knotted like those of a runner. Outside the door, she did run across the street. Before she turned away, I saw her face once through the window. She brushed away at her eyes with both hands and then she started running. The waitress giggled again and took my cup away.

Then one day my old man says to me, "That Doc Helsen got married—anyone tell you? Married the nurse in his office, that nice Burla girl! He's smart—still have a nurse and he won't have to pay her wages!"

* * *

Days came and then nights. I remained in the field with a horse and low stoneboat, loading up what stones I could find and taking them to the big white stone-pile, where I threw them off. In the darkness my mother came to me, talking in this new holy-water voice she used.

"It's night-time. You can't see what you're doing. Come on home and stop trampling the new barley shoots. The horse hasn't been out of harness since morning and father said you should have her home. So please come on!"

I felt a headache coming on, and through its scream I could hear myself shout. "So what? Drop dead, why don't you? Who's doing all the work anyway?"

She was gone, and my head cleared. I worked some more and then I slept, and when I woke up, the fields were grey with morning. My body was numb with cold. The horse had pulled the stoneboat with me on it to the haystack and was feeding.

* * *

I pushed my old man and he fell like a sack of potatoes, his cap rolling across the kitchen under the stove there. The old lady got down on her hands and knees to get it for him, while he lay on the floor looking at me, his toothless gums chewing on his anger. Then I started laughing and calling him names.

"You drunken old bastard! You fell by yourself—I didn't push you that hard!"

That was after Johnson, the bank manager, came over to talk to him. They went into a huddle in the corner. My old lady was going out for water, but I took the bucket from her and got it myself. When I came back into the house, my father and the banker were at it loud and wild.

"I can't pay last month's note! What in hell can I pay you with?" he was shouting at the banker.

"Then you should have thought of that before you borrowed! The bank can't afford to keep all types of bums floating! I understand there's been money for whiskey, or am I wrong?"

He didn't wait for a reply, but pushed by me out the door and drove away. I asked my old man what sort of money we owed and how far behind we were in repaying. I swear that I was talking nice to him at the time—nice and low, and I was worried enough to want to get the mess straightened out somehow.

But he just looked at me like I wasn't there.

"Is it Jim?" I asked, my headache blinding me again. "Has goddamned Jim sunk us so low we've got to pay forever for it and never have a life of our own? Tell me?"

"You just keep your mouth shut where Jim's concerned! He was a good son. You're not fit to speak his name!"

He just got that out of his mouth when I gave him a shove and over he went. I might've hit him, but I can't remember. A bit of blood was coming from his mouth, and he kept looking at me.

"You fell by yourself! I didn't push you that hard!" I hollered again. She handed him his cap. I saw her hands as she was doing it, and they were shaking to beat hell. I started to cry, and when I finished they'd left the house and I felt tired enough to die.

* * *

There was nothing the matter with him that I could see, but he stayed in bed and wouldn't get up. My mother took meals in to him, but he wouldn't eat.

One night she went in to him without his supper. I'd eaten some, and was sitting at this table, knowing it was all my fault. Then I heard them arguing with her sounding off pretty strong and him only mumbling. I couldn't hear what was said because the door was shut, but I think she was throwing some of this new religious stuff at him by way of arguing something else. When she came out, I asked her to sit with me.

"I may as well go into town tomorrow and have the doctor come out to see him," I suggested. "I'll do it first thing in the morning."

"A doctor?" She looked at me as if I were crazy.

"Yes—a doctor. He hasn't eaten in three days. I was going to help get him to lunch, but he wouldn't even look at me yesterday."

She started to laugh when I said that.

"What's so funny?"

She caught her breath and choked on it.

"You're funny! A doctor for your father—there's nothing wrong with him that a doctor can cure. And because he's not sick, I won't let money be wasted on doctors for him! There shall be no more waste!"

"He's sick!"

"His sickness is in not facing up to being wrong. He's failed, and now he's scared he won't live long enough to make up for it."

"I didn't mean to push him!" I said, almost begging her to forgive. Her tired face and hunched walk that was left after the stroke seemed gone now as she stood in trembling anger. Even her breath smelled hot and furious.

"Don't you know what I'm saying?" she asked, and suddenly her voice was soft, motherly. She reached out as if to touch my face, but instead pulled back and got at the stove, throwing things here and there before she opened the fire door to put in more wood. Her back became bent again and the angry fever left her cheeks. When I next saw her face, it was again filled with her new-found religion that gave her the harmless look of the blind.

To get away from it all I figured to bury myself so deep in work that I wouldn't have the time or strength to think of anything else. When I'd finished picking stones for the season, I began putting new fences around the pasture, and getting the machinery repaired and mower sharpened for the first hay cutting. My mother didn't come out to help any more, so I was left completely alone. I only wished I could die before either of them did, to get out of it all first. I even put off going into town for grub to avoid seeing Nancy by some accident. Not that we needed that much grub—the old man did no more than nibble something every second or third day.

I tried to get through to him after she refused a doctor for him. The light was bad in his room, but it was scarey how thin and haunted he'd become even in the first few days.

"Look," I said. "I want to talk to you."

He turned away from me, and kept staring with wide-opened eyes at the wall on the other side of his bed.

"You listening?"

He didn't make like he heard me at all. I could smell the sour odour of the clothes he'd never taken off since he laid himself down.

"You planning to go like old Joe went when his church got lost on him?" I asked, trying to get him to argue at least. "I thought you said once that nothing busts a farmer down. I didn't mean to shove you—you know that!"

Still he kept staring away, and then I got sore.

"I guess if I was Jim talking, you'd listen, wouldn't you?"

I didn't want to hit him with that, but it did make him turn. The look he gave me was both angry and lost as hell itself. I felt just as sick of it all.

"Can I take you to hospital?" I was begging now. That was the last time I spoke to him.

I used to sit at this table after supper, and watch the old lady bring in her Bible. In the past, the old Bible hadn't been opened once in all the years I've lived. But now she was in it every night, following page by page, word by word with her finger, while the grease on the dishes hardened and the floor got swept only on Saturday mornings.

"What's it say that's so interesting?" I asked her one evening. She looked up at me and gave a smile I'd never seen on her face before. It was the smile of a tired woman who's going to bed at last and knows she'll not have to get up until she's had a good sleep. It was also a smile that sort of looked down at me, if you know what I mean, and I found it cutting more skin. But I didn't say anything, not even when she said:

"Each one of us must live to find the Word of God on our own, son!"

So I worked from dawn to dusk, seven days a week, trying by sheer labour to clean away the filth and guilt that weighed me down like a ten-foot logging chain. And as I worked, I thought of the life I had lived and all those that had peopled it, much as I've been telling you. It made time pass, and there were moments I could smile a bit.

Nancy Burla kept troubling me in my thoughts. The more tired I became, the more she appeared to me as a Nancy Burla I did not know. She had become a temptress with no face I could recognize as belonging to her, only a body with a strong animal scent. And her body swelled until it split her clothes wide open and I had to waken and grasp my manhood in both hands and hurt it to keep from shaming myself further.

I would get out of bed gasping for air, dress myself and walk like a demon through the night, sucking in the sweat off my face through my wide-open nostrils. But even when I hurt so much that my leg and arm muscles jumped at the slightest sound, I could not help but think of her, and all I had lost with her gone from me.

Then my father died.

I guess I'd known all along he was dying, for when it happened it didn't seem to bother me at all. I felt I was in a strange town, like the cowboy song says, trying to find the gates to the country—all confused. He had passed on in his sleep, and my old lady told me before breakfast. I sat at the table and said nothing. She brought the food, and I ate like any other morning. I even had another cup of coffee. Then I went into the room to see him.

When I came out, she'd gone to tell the neighbours, or at least those that were in her new faith, as I later suspected.

I left the house then and climbed into the barn hayloft. There was a wide black poplar plank curing under the hay for I don't know how many years. It was straight as anything, hard and shiny. We'd kept it to make a new water-trough for the cattle for the time when the old one began to leak from rot.

I moved the hay over and pulled the plank down. Then I measured it carefully back and forth and sideways. The way it figured out, by cutting it short so that his head and feet touched the ends, there was enough plank there to make a casket for my father.

I began to saw away, and by night time had a crude wooden box built for him.

My mother didn't come back, so all this time I was alone with my hammering, and the blood pounding heavy in my ears. I had no hunger or thirst—no sensation of the body. Only loneliness and a desire to reach the end of whatever was to come. Once my mind began to waver and I felt I was carrying the casket on my shoulders, tripping and falling on the way to the cemetery, and the neighbours running beside me and shouting insults in my ears …

Hammer still in hand, I went outside. The fields seemed to fall away, turned to ashes, and the trees parched and wilted as with some great heat. Yet the air was cold and made my hot skin ache.

Night came like a silent mist, without sound or substance. I lit the lantern in the shed and worked on. By morning, my nails were broken and my fingers bled, but the casket was polished and glowing like some holy thing in the dim shed.

Still my mother did not come back.

Now I went outside, and had to shield my eyes against the red heat of the sun. I turned to the house, and saw it listing and scaley, as if it too had perished with him and had begun to rot over the decomposing body of my old man. Around me, the countryside was a desert. Not a soul came over to help or talk to me. I felt frightened as I stared at the homes dotting the ends of fields, the same houses you can see through this window and that one.

They seemed like something grown out of the dirt, as if no human had lived or loved in any of them. Sheep, cattle and dogs wandered stupidly over fields and pastures, but they seemed wild now, as if they always moved that way without master or purpose. I felt tears of panic, but choked them back. I wanted to shout out loud, "Enough!" But I had no voice anymore.

Still, like Johnson the banker, nobody tore themselves from the world beyond mine to come to me. I knew now this was the way it had to be. This was my end, and his end, and probably the same end Jim saw in that last half second before his body was broken against an English tree.

I got a shovel from the barn and started walking down the road to the burying grounds. Again I felt I had walked here before, carrying a terrible load that shifted and rolled on my shoulders. I stopped and laid down the shovel in the dust and pinched myself. I also bit my tongue.

There was pain—sharp and sweet! I was alive!

I dug wide and deep into the solid clay—through the day and into a night and then another day. A kid came off the road, leaned over to look down at me, then ran away. Now there were no thoughts of Nancy Burla.

"I have killed the animal in me!" I whispered to myself over and over, knowing it was so and feeling good for it. "Now I can bury my father without shame!"

Then there were no thoughts at all, only a strange dizziness and the taste of salt in my mouth. I saw my arms, big and flashing with sweat in the sun, but not seeming to belong to me anymore.

Then it came to me—the truth I had never realized before—the truth Nancy Burla saw when she married the doctor. These arms were all I had and all that anybody had ever wanted. Anybody—my mother, those who hired stonepickers, and Nancy Burla. They were the reason for my life. Here was my strength and my food and my bed. There was no other part of me worth anything—never had been. In so short a time they raised their Jims, their babies, their invalid mothers and fathers—and then they shrivelled and brought unhappiness to the man willing to work but not able because his visions twisted downwards into a patch of earth no larger than a grave.

What price a stonepicker's ballad? What curse is his dream? What I saw and felt all these years was real—only to you, out there, was it wasted shadows on a landscape that had never been painted.

The burial casket came towards me, carried by all the neighbours who filled the road for a quarter mile as they came in twos and threes, through the cemetery gate and to the fresh grave I had dug.

Everybody was there—Wally Pantaluk, limping and leaning heavily on his stick; John, the wife-beater, carrying a trunk-sized Bible under his arm and followed by my mother who had a sacred look on her face now that she had made peace with her conscience; Shorty Mack, still dressed in a white shirt with cufflinks, and wearing a blue jacket for mourning; Mary and Pete Ruptash, who stood well back against the fence, weeping with a greater sorrow than I knew; Clem, the blacksmith, long-haired and with the tortured face of a poet-saint. They even brought dumb Andrew, who shivered as with cold and pulled his collar high around his throat. Stanley, the horse-trader came, but stayed outside the cemetery grounds. He stopped his new team of horses on the road, currying them woodenly and staring through his blind eyes in our direction. The auctioneer, who brought a fistful of paper flowers, which he dropped carelessly on the nailed-down box.

Marta Walker was there, alone with growing belly, where the child of Hector grew. Hector had gone since winter up north to Smith, where he married a farm-girl about Easter time. So Marta came alone, and I saw her staring at me with the eyes of someone who's come to a wedding rather than a funeral. For the longest time I could not break away from her eyes, in which I again saw the promise of a darkened shed and a dead dog in the yard. Big Dan Makar and Sophie, both grown handsome as statues; Minerva Malan, dark and overfed; the Bayracks came up and stood behind a few faces grown blurry to me. Then I looked to the gate, and saw Nancy Burla and Doctor Helsen coming up. By now I felt cold towards them, like a stranger grown grey.

Sergei Pushkin came and embraced my mother. He and his wife held her hands all through the burial. Pete Wilson, the storekeeper, came farthest, all the way from Calgary. Then a few people from town. There were farmers I had worked for from as far away as ten miles—some others only my folks must've known. But Pete Wilson came from farthest away …

I was still dressed in the milk-stained jeans and torn shirt I had worked in for over a week. I smelled of cream and straw, dust, grain and stones. But it didn't matter. It was for others to stand beside my mother now and do all the nice things that must be done. None saw me or spoke to me, except Marta, burning her sinful stare into my skull.

John droned on and on about what a good man my father had been. How he'd raised a good, God-fearing family, and how the Lord would fix up a goose-feather bed for him in paradise. Then he closed the book, and I moved forward, pushing through the small crowd over the grave, carrying my shovel in my hands. It had to end here—in this way. I heard a commotion start around and behind me, but I struggled on, my eyes on the shiny dark casket now lowered to the bottom of the hole I had dug for it.

"Stop him! He's going to throw the first sods on his father!" some woman called out. Then a man stepped in front of me.

"Hey, boy! Enough's enough—you're not to do this. Go stand by your mother an' let me do this! It's not for you to do this!"

"What's wrong?" I argued as through a dream. "I've got nothing else to do. I can do this as quick as anybody."

My voice sounded old and rusted to me.

"At a time like this you don't help. No son buries his father when there's others to help. We didn't know before today. Go over to your mother an' take it easy!"

He tried to be a friendly and good neighbour. Before I knew what he was doing, he took my shovel from my hands, leaving me naked and useless. I grabbed for it and twisted it away from him. His eyes opened wide with surprise and then he stepped back. I heard a loud gasp from behind me as I walked over to the open grave. I began filling in the pit. If there were others helping, I do not remember, for time and memory stopped for me then.

When I looked up again, the sun was high and hot, and I ached so I straightened with terrible difficulty. Now memory came back, and feeling and hearing. I heard my old lady crying like she'd never stop. The Pushkins had left her and were standing alone. How small she looked and how pathetic! I began moving to her, to take her arm and tell her it had all ended. That we would begin as equals and try to rebuild from what was left us.

But her broken health was being fed by new spirits strange and distant to me. John, the evangelist, tried to hold me back, but I brushed him to one side. Then she saw me, and from her crying came this sharp, high scream. She turned and left the cemetery at a run, even though the doctor had said she was never to run again.

Yes, running, with her head thrown back, out the gate and up the road towards our home. The crowd moved nearer the gate, but nobody went through. As I came up, they parted to let me through first. John came up behind me, wrestling the big Bible in his arms.

"She's going to work in our hostel—it's all decided!" he said to me. I turned to him, the shovel in my hand, and he stepped away. I walked on.

"So there was no one to tell us the day he died!" an angry voice said out of the crowd. "Damn you, anyway!"

Then a woman in a soft, gentle voice: "You've done a dark and terrible thing today!"

"Shush now, that's not so!" a man scolded her.

"Don't hold no grudge now, no matter what they've done to you. Take care of your mother and do what's right." Now it was the voice of Dan Makar, standing near the gate. I wanted to cry out that I hadn't reached the end of living. It was only the frightening beginning of another afternoon.

"You've got neighbours, boy. Where there's neighbours there's love and belonging!"

And then a voice that might've been Marta Walker. Or was it Helen Bayrack?

"It's love that'll make it all wonderful. Find love quickly—today!"

"Good luck, kid!"

I was out the gate … the road … I hurried home. Behind me the voices had had their silences for the day and now rose in louder, everyday talk. I hurried on, and the trees, fields and piles of stone along the roadside danced through the tears pouring out of my head.

That was how the day ended.

NIGHT DESK

PROLOGUE

He came into my life, stayed for a winter, and vanished. No, that's not true. It was I who vanished from *his* world. I left it at a run, a bundle of manuscripts under my arm. And a headful of memories I have wrestled with all these years. I fled into the university, searching for shelter and the safety of refined literature of other lands, where human affairs are orderly and predictable. Where lecturers spoke to students in words and metaphors never heard on a dusty prairie roadside, or in mining towns where all hope has a coating of grime. In time, the students spoke like their teachers. We were expected to, and obliged our tutors by writing theses on Renaissance poetry, the Restoration novel. Even on the effects of the American Civil War on the literature of the new world.

It was, and continues to be, academic rubbish. But it was warmth and security, and kept us from facing a bare-fanged, gaunt reality moving like wind shadows across the landscape of the country.

I had fled from the night desk and from the towering presence of a man who harangued, terrified and excited me in ways I still cannot describe, but I never fully escaped him.

Strangely fearful of losing his words and gestures, I carried with me the manuscripts I feverishly wrote during that winter. I had virtually memorized all I had written, yet I was haunted by a fear that once they were stolen, or burned, they would somehow be likewise destroyed in my memory. Like a damnation, I heard them laugh in that massive voice of his at the intellectual games, the smoothly turned phrases, the self-indulgences of borrowed life and experiences which in time would have to be repaid—with what? With the impressions of a barren non-existence?

But somewhere in this also lay my salvation. For he was the raucous guardian of the gate to fields of thistles, stones, hunger.

He never called me by my name. His name was important to him, and he restated it at every opportunity. I was simply called "kid." When I knew him, I had yet to earn my name. Until I did, I had the protection of his. This I now understand. As I understand now I must return to the beginning of things to find my own integrity—an integrity he offered to me with a smile on his face and tears trickling from his eyes. An offer I refused in the most profound fear I have ever known. A cowardly refusal, which all the trappings of scholarly accomplishments cannot erase or alter.

Gleaning through this portion of the manuscript I wrote so quickly that long winter many years ago, I blush with the realization that despite many published articles on the craft of communion through the written word, I am a better copyist than I am a creator of fantasy and wonder. For in truth, there is much in this story I still do not understand. There are passages which upset me, and others which make me chafe at the futility of my own existence.

I am in the story somewhere, but not through choice or design. I was only drawn into the vortex, as were others, of his consuming restlessness. He gave what he had freely. I tried to take only that which was useful or fascinating to me. It was a futile exercise, and I quickly realized my time would be better served by recording him, even if the work I was employed to do at the hotel was neglected.

It was. There were two of us dismissed that April morning. Myself, and a bartender who stole seventy dollars from the till. The bartender returned the money in exchange for a letter of recommendation and the dropping of possible charges against him. I did not return to ask for support in finding employment elsewhere. I did not think Romeo Kuchmir would have approved of such an act of humiliation. I already felt his disapproval in other things, so I moved as quickly as I could towards the opposite horizon.

ONE

Iwent to the ballet at eight o'clock. Yes sir, I went to the ballet tonight!

Does that surprise you? I'm not a barrel of water ... or a stack of hay. I'm a man! An' I want the best for myself, an' the same for you. So I dress up in my grey suit, polish my shoes an' go to the ballet to sit among women who smell like a flower garden dyin' of frost ...

Let me tell you about it, kid. But then, how can I tell you a ballet? You can't tell it, or sing it ... you've got to *dance* it! I could dance it for you if you liked, but then there'd be parts missing ... an' the garden smell of dyin' flowers would be gone ... an' that's somehow part of it too.

There's this little Italian broad called Juliet. She can't make it out of this garden, so she swallows some poison. The same with the guy she's goin' around with. They're in bed, but they're not doin' anything in bed together—they're never gonna be able to. That's sad. An' that's what's beautiful ... they can't do nothin' because they're *dead*. The women sitting around me start heating up. Itchin' in their seats. But the smell they give off is like a funeral. Because it's *their* fault, an' the fault of Juliet's goddamned family, an' the fault of the family of the kid she's goin' around with. Everyone knows healthy kids got to run an' play an' screw when they get the chance. If they don't, they're gonna die, an' it's somebody's fault ... always somebody's fault.

I went to the ballet at eight o'clock, an' I cried until half-past nine. The last time I did that was when my mother died, may the angels give her wings that never wear out. She was a good woman, even after she married my father.

He killed her, you know. The old bastard ran a poolhall in a small town that's since been eaten up by Calgary. In the evenings he'd stand around with his hands in his pockets keeping young punks from lifting the table felts with their cue sticks.

"Hey, weasel-face! This is expensive property! You remember that, or I'll kick your butt into your shoulders!" He spoke like that when he was feelin' good an' was being nice to the kids.

He also sold French safes under the counter to any boy having trouble with his root. For an extra dollar, he'd fix it up so the kid could get in the backdoor of Sweet Mabel's place. Sweet Mabel ran a candy store with a one-woman cathouse in the back. She'd let a man in the way he was an' for nothin' because "they know the proper thing to do." But young punks taking the dip for the first or second time had to have the swelling packed in rubber.

"They go off all over the place, an' some of them got eczema," she says to me once. "I handle candy for the kids. I can't risk spreading eczema."

When my old man wasn't at the poolhall, he was home. I mean he was at *home*—like a big stone in the garden, or a boil on your ass. Nothing moved him. She had to lift his feet to sweep around his chair. She had to cook, clean, plant a garden, clear the snow. For he was Fedyor Kuchmir, descendant of the Don Cossacks. An' when he talked to me, which wasn't often, he told me his ancestors had cut off heads of Turks.

"When you gonna cut off a Turk's head?" I asked him one day in the winter when both of us stood at the window in the warm kitchen watching her outside, up to her knees in snow, splitting wood for the fire.

"When it sticks up high enough to get in my way," he said.

He had shoeboxes full of medals. When he pinned them on, he looked like Herman Goering. They came from service clubs where he drank whiskey an' made loud speeches about how much he loved the Queen of England. He made it as a mayor once … yeah. The same time Sweet Mabel was elected to the council. She got her sidewalk paved, the decision for that being made the night of November 15th, 1957, when she invited the mayor an' three men on the council to her back room for a vote.

Here kid, this is a sports coat an' three shirts I want you to put through for overnight cleaning. Put a note to tell them not to starch the collars. There's bums workin' in the laundries now would put starch in socks. An' they got hair like women. The world's fillin' up with men who never cut their hair!

Some of them work in restaurants as cooks. I once ordered a doughnut an' a cup of coffee in a café up the street. A little broad with blue eyes two tables down does the same. The waitress brings both our orders an' sets them down. The little broad picks up her doughnut an' puckers to bite it. Mine slides off my plate. I grab for it, an' it jerks the other one out of the little broad's mouth. We're friends now, connected by a seven-foot long hair cooked into our doughnuts an' strong as piano wire! I move to her table, believin' as I do god has more ways than four of bringin' a woman to a man.

Put the cleaning on my bill. If you've got a Saskatchewan pig farmer stayin' in the hotel, put it on his bill. Pig farmers don't argue over hotel bills. There's only so low a man sinks before his suffering is silent.

How much do I owe? ... Look it up, then. There's somethin', somewhere, written down about every man who lives. Half the Bible was written around Moses. A man like me has to settle for a laundry an' hotel bill.

That much, eh? You haven't heard them say anything about planning to evict me? Naw, don't tell me—don't depress me.

I've been around this hotel on an' off for fifteen years. Came here the first time in the back of a second-hand hearse, six other wrestlers an' me. The guy drivin' the hearse was old Ross, the promoter. Built like a brick shithouse an' dumb as he was big. We used to wrestle in towns with only one grain elevator, times were that bad. One night seven of us wrestled for five people. Ross gave us two-bits an' an apple each for our work that night!

I've been poor, kid, but never down. I left Ross when I seen him fight a city bus. He was crossin' Jasper Avenue, just two blocks down from here. Along comes this diesel bus an' boom! It hits Ross. Ross picks himself off the street, hits himself here an' there to check for broken bones—nothin'! He's in good shape. But the front of the bus is caved in an' the windshield busted. Any other day, that might've been that. But the bus driver is the kind who don't even let a cripple ride for free.

"Why in hell don't you watch where you're goin', farmer?" he hollers at Ross. Which was the wrong thing to do.

Ross shakes himself, stares at the driver an' the bus, spits an' takes a run at it. He hits the side of the bus with his shoulder. It rocks from side to side like a cradle. People inside are screamin' an' climbing over one another to get out. The driver goes out the window an' hightails it out of there. Other passengers have now kicked out emergency escape windows an' are pouring out like wild cattle from a broken corral. Because old Ross is now poundin' the bus to crap, putting dents into it, smashing windows with his elbows.

Fellows with small brains are meaner than guys with big brains once they get worked up. That's why I don't like fascists. I knew a Polish fascist who beat his dog to death with a shoe when he'd heard on the radio that Hitler had lost the war.

"Hey—quit it!" I hollered at old Ross. "The fuzz will arrest you for bus slaughter. That's enough!"

The old prick stopped and turned to glare at me an' the other wrestlers he had workin' for him.

"Useless, no-good grub sacks!"

An' he's charging us, like a bull, head first. By now we'd all had our problems with Ross. Being driven like dead meat from town to town in his goddamned hearse was one thing—no money was another. An' we were young an' horny, needin' women in the worst sort of way, but all he'd given us was draught. A good promoter looks after his boys. Kids need lollipops— grown men need nooky! So we beat him up. Just before we knocked him out, with four of us holdin' him up an' three others punchin' the hell out of him, we told him we'd quit. Then we put him out an' stuck him behind the wheel of his hearse. One of the wrestlers with a sense of humour put a cigarette in old Ross' mouth an' straightened his necktie. Then we took his wallet containin' twenty-eight dollars, which we split seven ways an' took off to make our fortunes in this world.

Yeah, I've been poor ...

Before you worked here, years ago, I only had one suit of clothes to my name. I'd come down like I done tonight, to leave my clothes for overnight cleaning. Only then when I came down I was wearin' nothing but my undershorts.

There used to be a drunk sleeping in that chair by the door. A funny old bastard with a sheepskin cap on his head, flaps tied down under his chin like an immigrant from Peru. Looked like Father Christmas with no teeth. One night I'm down here, talkin' to the night clerk who worked here before you. Another old tit who'd fought in the first war an' could never stop serving. He was a company man an' a drunk himself, but that's another story ... Anyway, I'm breezin' with Sam—Sam was his name—an' the guy with the sheepskin cap in the chair starts to sing:

"Oh, the cow kicked Nellie in the belly in the barn ... " he sings.

"Go back to sleep, old timer," I says to him. "Your train's left the station. Next one in comes through at four ... "

I'm just joshin' him along. He's harmless an' I'm feeling well disposed to anythin' smaller than me.

"Thank you, captain," an' he kind of bowed to me like I was somebody important. Almost fell out of the chair doing it. Then he sort of twitches up an' slaps the leather arms of the chair with both hands.

"Oh, the cow kicked Nellie ... "

That's as far as he got with singin', for it petered out into a kind of bubbling snore, his head fallin' to one side, his toothless mouth opening in a dumb grin. I tapped him nicely on the cheek, for he wasn't anything you wanted to look at while believin' man could aspire to somethin' beyond this life.

"Hey, old timer!" I says.

He's awake, his small eyes starin' at nothing, his mouth chewin' on itself. "Yeh?"

"How come you wasn't born a general … or a waiter in a French café?" I ask him. He grins at me and points his finger at my crotch.

"You got no pants … You is bare-assed nekkid, boy!" An' he pokes me with a mittened finger in the dink. Then he's up on his feet, slappin' his hands and twitchin' his shoulders, laughin', singing his way out into a thirty-below night:

"Oh, the cow kicked Nellie in the belly in the barn … "

You know, there are men, an' women in this hotel an' other places I know, who ask about you. An' I tell them. I tell 'em, "The kid on the night desk is writin' down what we do an' say—about who we are an' what we might've been. The trumpet of the night. That's what you are." Don't be surprised or frightened. Praise me or condemn me. I'll protect you. You're all we have between us an' the grave.

When you write about this time an' the way we were, do me a favor, kid. Ask the world a question—one question. Ask why some poor woman long ago pooched herself inside out to give birth to that old punk who sat in that chair, when she might've popped a saint. Or a jet pilot. Ask why, an' if someone tells you, but I'm dead by then, you go find my grave an' you dig a hole until you reach my ear. An' when you've dug the earth out of my earhole with your finger, you holler loud the answer so I can sleep forever, happy that I know everything!

I seen a ballet at eight o'clock tonight. They danced it for me—only me. Because I was on fire—my face an' hair in flames, begging for the truth of who died an' why so that I might avenge them!

Anyway, that other night when I was here in the lobby dressed in nothin' but my undershorts, two old women came through the street door. Before I could run, they seen me. I had to act. I'm an actor—a performer. A good one.

"Look at me! Look at what a burglar did!" I shouted, tears comin' to my eyes an' the old bum soldier of a night desk clerk rushing for a towel to wrap around my ass.

"I'm an honest man. I believe in god an' god's mother an' all the angels an' saints he's got workin' for him. I'm an honest man. I sleep like an honest man: my door unlocked, my wallet on the table, my shoes beside the door. I'm sleepin', dreaming of my mother—god protect her from the rain! A burglar comes into my room. He takes everything I own, ladies! My shirt, my pants, my socks, my wallet, a photograph of my wife an' children, my prayerbook! Here I stand before you, ladies, forty-seven years old an' naked as the day I was born! Another man—a burglar, a child of god like myself, did it to me!"

When I'm finished, those two mothers, one short, one tall, one ugly an' the other homely, each took five dollars from their handbags an' handed the money over to me. Such is the power of the word!

"Sir," the taller one says, "we're sorry about what happened. We work with retarded children an' the pay is little. But we hope this will help to restore your confidence in mankind!"

I took the money. Oh, I kissed the hands offering it to me an' ran upstairs. I went to bed an' lay there, trembling. I was guilty, but I could also see the possibilities of a new career. Any punk with half a brain can trade or sell a house, a wheelbarrow or a wet puppy. But to exchange human yearnings for cash—*that* was something else! As I'm sweating, turnin', thinkin' of these things, my telephone rings. It's the desk clerk, an' he wants a cut of the money.

"Stretch out an' die! You scurvied dog!" I yell at him. "I went to their rooms an' gave the money back—how does that grab you?"

He had nothin' to say, but I kept shoutin' at him, squeezin' the telephone until I heard it crack an' then crumble in my hand.

"Nothin's black an' white," I says to him. "Life's not like that. Life's as grey as a thousand miles of prairie in the winter, an' you're a one-eyed gopher staring at a black thistle an' thinking you've just seen a pillar ten miles high!"

I'm an outlaw, kid, a stallion. I'm goin' where I'm goin' an' no one asks me why.

After I seen that ballet tonight, I says to myself, "I've got to keep screwin' because I'm alive, an' because it feels good an' because I don't want to die an' smell like a flower garden in November ... "

What makes some women missionaries an' others hookers, do you know? Sometimes I think there's no difference. They're both the same. It's got somethin' to do with the need to serve. Don't laugh, kid. I'm serious. I know you're a good Catholic boy, but you'll outgrow it. If you don't, all that scribblin' you're doing won't save your soul or mine, an' I'll stand behind you all the way.

Here's somethin' else for you to think about: when I was a kid your age, I had a cousin called Stella, who took to religion like a calf takes to the milk bucket. I was a big muscled village punk, razzin' cops, breathin' heavy when my old man got too near. Family didn't like me. Called me corrupt. After Stella, they disowned me. Called me a degenerate.

And because I, Romeo Kuchmir, was ruined, Stella saw herself as my redeemer, ready to bring me back on the road to salvation.

One summer afternoon, we went for a walk. Past town, through fields of barley, down to the river where a lot of willows grew. At first we weren't sayin' much, but in the willows, she starts pleadin' with me to cut the booze an' broads, get myself together, let god an' her be my friends. While she talked like that, I started takin' off my clothes. I flexed my muscles an' danced around her—kind of slow at first, but building up steam as I went along. She had to keep turnin' to follow me, her little ass twisting this way an' that, because she wore high heels an' the ground was soft.

In a big but helpless voice I says to her, "It's no use." I was the devil, except in one place, where god was tryin' to get out. "See how he's pushin'," I shouted at her, "see how he's pushin', he's tryin' to get out but he can't!"

"Get hold of his door-handle, Stella!"

She's bug-eyed with fear, but she reaches out an' gets hold of my root. First with one hand, then with two …

"That's it!" I holler. "That's it! The devil's got me, an' god's tryin' to get out—Help him!"

Jesus, Jesus—she's sayin', an' pretty soon she's not afraid no more. She's got my wang in both hands, an' while I'm dancin' around her, she's pushin', pullin', twistin', laughin', like a kid with a new red wagon. Then she's down on her knees, dizzy, her face red, her eyes dreamin' …

I didn't tell anyone, but Stella, well, I don't know because she got sent to Africa by her group. An' my uncle Nick an' my father both told me to get my ass out of the house an' family an' never come back again. My mother? Well, she didn't say anything. She only looked worried when all this happened, but she never said a word to me one way or the other …

But that's not what I started to tell you, no. What I wanted to say is what started as a bit of crackerjack down by the river became a religious experience for me. I've never forgotten it. I've never asked Stella or anyone for forgiveness, because I've never felt what happened there was bad or hurtful.

TWO

You sweep the lobby floor even when it's clean—why? It's not the shiny floor or the polish on the desk that brings me down to talk to you. It's the feel of men, the sound of things not said.

Look at the clock—it's after midnight. I just got one day older, kid—one day nearer to my death. It's the same for you, even if you try to sweep away the truth off an empty floor. The bricks an' waterpipes know. The wind knows. The stars know.

I've been readin' what you wrote here while you were upstairs checking for fires an' whores. Perhaps what you say is pretty good, but who am I to tell? I'm not an educated man. I can't read truth—I smell it! What you have there has a feeble smell, but in time, who knows?

I'd give my last shirt to an honest man. I'd *give* it! But how many have come to take it without asking? I don't like that, an' I'm not talkin' about burglars. If a burglar comes into my room, I'll take care of him—I'm no cripple, an' I weigh two hundred an' fifty pounds. But crooks with words scare me. The ones who come into my life with talk of love an' brotherhood. The ones who write up papers which take my land away from me or my kids. The worst kinds—men an' women—are the ones who rob me of my feelings, who can persuade me that love is business, that the poor should be grateful Jesus died for them! That everything I feel an' say is selfish. That I will never rise above the level of a mindless animal!

I don't like that, kid. Don't ever write that about me. For when I read, I read aloud, my fingers following the lines, every word an enemy unless it makes me laugh—or cry!

Do you sing?

Ah, kid—you should learn to sing. It's the sound of blood welcoming the sun! I was born with a lump of happiness jammed into my throat—listen!

La donna mobile …

Try it! ... No, not like that! It's got to start down in the balls an' if you turn your face up, it hits the clouds an' brings down rain! Put away your pen an' the ledgers of the thieves who own this place. I'll give you a drink of whiskey in my room an' we'll go out into the street an' sing—you an' I! It's twenty-five below out there. Will this winter ever really end if we don't sing?

I know good singers. Jan Peerce is a friend of mine. We were punks together long ago, in cheap hotels from San Francisco to Dallas. Me wrestlin', him singin'. Once, on the coast of Maine, we walked together through a storm, both singin' arias from Puccini. He forgot the words, but *I* remembered them. Hey, but we sang! The wind an' rain howlin' in from the cold Atlantic ... an' there was Peerce an' me, bent into the wind, singin' for the broads asleep with other men. But that's alright, the silent ones are brothers too.

He came to Edmonton in November. You were off that night. He sends a ticket to me, an' I go to hear him. But he didn't make me happy. I came back drunk I was that mad. Jan Peerce is dead—I don't know him! He's a fat prick now, singin' for the rich an' dumb. He knew it—I'd gone backstage to tell him.

"Take your 'Bluebird of Happiness' an' shove it up your ass, amigo," I says to him. "Romeo Kuchmir came all the way across town to hear you, an' you betrayed me. I didn't hear Jan Peerce. I heard a three-grand-a-night punk doin' exercises. I've heard you singin' better warmin' up in a baggage car on the way to Tulsa. Here's half your ticket back. I just wasted the other half they tore off to let me in!"

So I get back here an' go to bed. He phones me from the MacDonald, the hotel with class. He don't stay in workingmen's hotels no more.

"Romeo," he says, "I'm sorry about tonight. I want to make it up to you. Get over an' we'll kill a bottle of scotch together, for the sake of old times, buddy."

"Fall down a shithole," I says to him. "To make up for tonight, it'll cost you *two* bottles of scotch an' you're comin' *here* to drink it. Right here, where the fire system don't work, an' people still screw an' hit each other like they once did."

He came. An' we got drunk together. An' we talked about the old days, an' how we sang together on the coast of Maine. An' then we cried a little about time passing, an' what had happened to us. I stopped cryin' first. He cried a bit longer, which made me think he was worse off than me.

There was this little woman long ago. She played piano in country towns with two grain elevators an' one poolhall. She played a Brahms recital in my town, what a night that was! It was winter outside, snow two feet deep, car exhausts steaming. But inside there was summer, with joy, green trees, cattle grazing on stone-speckled pastures. Learn to sing, kid, or at least learn to play music even if it's no more than bangin' a pot lid to the rhythm of your heart.

La donna mobile ...

You ever been in love? Still too young, is that it?

You're never too young. I fell in love with that pianist when I was nine. I was ten when I got laid the first time. Not by the same woman. The one who screwed me was the wife of the telegraph operator who worked in Red Deer an' only came home for three days at the end of each month.

I was runnin' home from a softball game one evening. I knew I was late. Instead of followin' the road, I crossed some fields an' gardens, tryin' to get home the shortest way. In one vacant lot, I run into some nettles, which burned my legs as I was wearing short pants. Through a fence, an' I'm crossin' this small yard surrounded by high caragana hedge. An' sittin' on the back porch, naked to the waist, combing her hair, was this woman—the wife of the telegraph operator. The first thing I seen was these large white tits, scooping out like two plow-beams. Then I look up an' see her starin' at me, her face shaded by her hair.

"What are you doin' here?" she asks, her voice low an' soft. I couldn't say a thing. I couldn't get my eyes off her tits with the pink nipples which reminded me of little rosebuds.

"What are you lookin' at?"

"Nothin'," I lied.

"Come here ... How old are you?"

"Sixteen," I lied again.

She put her comb down an' got out of her chair to put on a small jacket, which she closed an' held with one hand. It made me sad to see her do that.

"What's your name?"

"Fred Kuchmir." I gave her my father's name. She looked at me a long time, an' then she sort of looked past me, an' her face made me think she might cry.

"Would you like an apple? I got some fresh raisin pie too."

In her living room I was eatin' an apple an' scratchin' the backs of my legs against the rough couch. She sat on the coffee table in front of me. In one hand she held an apple, which she ate quickly. With the other, she held the front of her jacket closed. She was holdin' it very tight, the knuckles showin' white.

Then like she was reachin' for another apple for herself, she began to touch and squeeze me between the legs. Another kid my age might've dropped his apple an' run. I almost did, at first. But then somethin' inside me started to bloom an' heat up, like the sun comin' over a hill. I was scared, I sure was, but I couldn't run. She put her arm around me an' pulled my little short pants down. I dropped my apple an' grabbed hold of her ears in both my hands.

We laughed, we wrestled, off the coffee table an' down on the floor. The nettle burns on my legs began to itch an' burn like hell itself, spreadin' up an' all over me. Then she had me inside herself an' she was heavin' an' sighing.

"Peter! ... Oh, Peter ... do it ... DO it!"

Which was strange to me then, because my name wasn't Peter. It was Romeo, same name I have now, but I was only a kid—what did I know about these things? Then I had my first explosion, every cell in my body lettin' go, an' suddenly, I was very sad an' tired an' scared, like I was dyin'.

"Jesus, mother!" I remember sayin', an' she pushed me off her an' I fell to the floor, coverin' my head with my hands. After a while, I looked up at her, an' she was sitting up beside me, almost naked and shiverin', her head bowed between her knees. Then she straightened up an' looked at me, an' I seen the same fear an' sadness in her eyes that I felt in myself. I crawled towards her, an' she bent down an' kissed me on the forehead.

"Go home now—quickly, boy," she whispered. "And don't tell anybody about coming here, not ever!"

There are people who sit watchin' through the peephole of life. The snow falls an' piles up on their heads, but they don't move. They just sit, watchin'. As you're watchin' me, kid. Go ahead—watch! I'm a performer! I bleed, spit out teeth, I howl an' I laugh! You can't touch me! I will lie, an' I will tell the truth, but you will never know the difference. Because you're a watcher!

Come on—don't look at me that way. I'm sorry if I hurt you. It's not you. I'm talkin' through you to the dead souls with pension plans an' homes of their own. You're closer to me than my mother. I live through you. Tell me to go away an' I'll go. But if I'm stayin', then I'm here to make you my mouth, my fist, my cock!

I promoted a wrestling match last year in the building where they keep livestock for the horse an' cow shows—you know the place—east end of the city. The place smells of shit an' popcorn.

The wrestlers I hired were old an' fat. Two of them were senile. I had no bread, so I took what nobody wanted. I put these two dumbos into a warmup event. They each took a fall, then became confused. They couldn't find each other, so one took on the referee, the other a corner post of the ring, which he eventually broke off. I had to throw them out. The match was a disaster, a comedy show. I figured makin' half a grand, but all I cleared was seventy dollars an' thirty-five cents!

After the match I rented the big room here for a party. Laid on some fried chicken an' beer for the boys. But these old timers wanted broads.

"Chicken an' beer are on me, you guys. Anything else you pay for!" I says to them.

"Yah … yah … sure … "

An' they started phonin'.

In half an hour, the whores were comin' in. Like they'd been dumped by a truck in front of the hotel. Bargain basement jobs with clap, bad teeth, sore feet. Except one—Margo, who come in last an' who didn't belong. She was in a different class, but times were tough.

I knew her, not as a whore, but as someone from my childhood. There was a teacher in the school I went to when I was a kid, a Missus Dayton, who was widowed or divorced an' had two little girls with her. Margo was the youngest.

Missus Dayton was sick a lot of the time. She'd have headaches which lasted three, four days at a stretch. She'd close the school when she was sick an' we'd go home. Next day we'd go back an' return home, because she wasn't there. Margo an' her sister, they hung around town a lot during summer holidays, always together, an' I thought a lot about them. I thought that maybe they'd be hungry when she was sick because if she was too sick to teach she was too sick to cook. I was a funny kind of kid, things like that bothered me. An' I'd feel sorry for them. That comes from my mother. She always felt sorry for the poor.

Mushrooms an' morels grew pretty good in those places where river birch an' poplars shaded the ground in summer. As a kid, I kept our house in mushrooms from June to September. My mother dried a few varieties for winter soup, which was black as ink when she cooked it. It had a sharp, peppery taste. I never had a cold when I ate that soup.

I worried a lot about Margo, her sister an' Missus Dayton that summer. But anyone can worry, it takes a kid with mushroom experience to do somethin' about the worry. So one Sunday mornin', I'm off with two metal pails in my hands. It's rainin', a soft rain which hangs in the trees an' on the grass, a perfect day for mushrooms. I picked the best there was—not a wormhole in any of them. I even washed the stems in the creek, somethin' I'd never done before. In the afternoon my clothes were soaking, an' my feet an' hands were scratched, but I got me two pails of the finest mushrooms in the country that day.

I could see the two kids an' Missus Dayton through the front window of their house as I approached the door an' knocked. The teacher comes to the door. Her face is white an' old lookin'. I could tell she was sick again.

"I picked them for you," I says, holdin' out the two pails of mushrooms. She looks at them, then at me. Somethin' was wrong, she wasn't sure …

"Do … you people eat this?" she asks.

"Huh?"

By now, the two kids are beside her. They looked hungry an' worried.

"Do … Ukrainians eat these?"

"Sure, all kinds of people eat mushrooms. Cows eat 'em too!" I says.

"You've eaten them yourself?"

"Yep."

"Then perhaps you had better take them home for your mother," she says, blinkin' with the pain in her head.

"No. They're for you … "

"I don't want them. I'm sorry!" Her voice gets high an' sharp all of a sudden. I'm still a kid. I don't know what to do, so I hold up the pails to her. She takes them an' marches down the steps an' to the corner of the house where a small lilac bush is growin'. She lifts the pails one at a time an' empties them around the roots of the bush. Then she kicks some dead grass an' rotten leaves over them an' hands me back the empty pails.

Like I say, I knew Margo before she was a hooker. Seein' her now, her teeth needin' repairs an' her shoulders hunched, I feel more sorry for her than ever. There's somethin' in her eyes that's still alive, but the clothes she's wearin' are worn an' look as if they'd been slept in. Her hair's not cut, an' has the sweaty look of someone who's not eatin' too good. A third-rate hooker. I take her aside an' out into the hallway.

"Margo," I says.

"Who in hell you talkin' to? My name's not Margo. My name's Millie!" She snaps an' moves away from me.

"Come on, kid. I know you. I knew your mother an' your sister … "

She's backed against the wall, as far away from me as she can get. Her eyes have gone hard, her fists clenched.

"Who in hell are you? I don't know you!" I could tell she's about to cry. Then just as quickly, the whore mask comes over her face, an' she's got a grin on, her voice goes soft.

"Look fella, if you're tryin' to get around me for some free tail, forget it. I've got a guy at my house who takes care of that. This place is business, nothin' else!"

I don't care what they say about me, there are things I would never do. I'd never take an orphan girl in out of the snow to feed her an' then screw her. I may be corrupt, but I'm not rotten. What could I say to her? What could I do?

I start walkin' away.

"Who are you? One of them wrestlers?"

"Yeh, a wrestler. Name is Kuchmir, Romeo Kuchmir."

Now she's excited an' angry an' comes at me like a spike into butter. "You're no ball of hot shit yourself, Kuchmir. Your mother did all the work, an' your old man ran a poolhall, right? You were so poor you walked around in short pants, when other kids had long pants and jackets. Oh yes, I remember you. You were nothin' special! My mom used to say you ate mushrooms that grew on manure piles, you were that poor. An' you're not very smart to end up a wrestler. Wrestlers aren't exactly god's answer to women. I've known all of you, an' none of you are much better than pigs!"

Sayin' all that, she turned an' walked out. Walked out of my party, walked out of this hotel, walked out of my life.

It's not true what she said about wrestlers, kid. A great wrestler's got to be sad … an' heroic. The last of the gladiators. A body bigger than ordinary men—trained to fight, to tear the heart out of a livin' bull, to walk across the world, performin' for peanuts an' sandwich money. No place he comes from, an' no place to go. No home or nooky of his own—all he gets belongs to other men, second-hand an' worn out.

Long ago, a hundred of us might've taken on the world, an' won! Today there's motors an' chainsaws an' machine-guns can cut us up like paper.

You know what's sad about all that? What's sad is that we continue to live. That we've become clowns playin' for laughs! An' who's laughin' at us? Every prune-prick with ulcers in his guts an' arthritis in his balls. He's sittin' out there in the bleachers, laughin', gettin' it off because he's on top now an' we're on the bottom lookin' up. The same guys who took away our clubs, our horses, our houses an' our iron overcoats—they're up there laughin'! With gunpowder, they shot our swords to shit. They got everybody votin', an' we were put out to pasture. Watchin' over us in the pasture at first was a cripple. Then a kid. An' pretty soon it's gonna be women with theatre school training!

Sure, before long the women are gonna manage us, tell us when to sleep, what to eat, when to rest, what clothes to wear, how to speak nice an' how to speak mean. A hundred years from now, the last laugh will be ours, an' you know why? Because all the sickies will start to die. They're dyin' already!

Cancer an' heart attacks an' malaria aren't spreadin' like the papers say— no sir! What's happening is that people who should've died as kids, would've died if it wasn't for vitamins an' antibiotics an' incubators, they're *livin'*. They're livin' with death inside of them. There's more of them now than anybody, making packaged foods, car accidents an' kids with the same sickness they've got. I'm healthy, but I've got to live like the sick, think like the sick, smell like the sick.

It's the advantages they've made that kill them. Kid, I love the world an' everythin' living on it—especially people. But I'm afraid, not of nuclear weapons, that's nothin'. Wars are made for land, cities an' prisoners. Nobody—not even a madman would reduce what he wants to ashes. No, I'm afraid it'll come from the way we live, from the panic of the weak an' sick. It won't be hunger that'll make us look at a camel-driver as a brother, it'll be some bug or virus no more serious than a bad cold to a goatherd in Syria who's never known anything except hard times. It's dumb, an' there's nothin' we can do about it now.

You know the dumbest thing I ever seen?

I was in Winnipeg … winter … three o'clock in the morning. Thirty-four below zero with a twenty miles north wind. No cars, no pedestrians within twenty miles of each other. An' there's this old punk standin' at an intersection, freezin' his stub off, waiting for the traffic light to change! I come up behind him, an' liftin' him up by the armpits, carry him across the red light. He kicks an' bitches, so halfway across the street, I let him down. Goddamn if he didn't turn back to where he'd stood. An' he waits there until the light turns green, then starts to cross. I come towards him, laughin'.

"Hey, old timer," I says to him, "what would happen if the light froze an' didn't change all night?"

He's grinnin' and dodgin' to get by me, for I have my arms spread out to catch him an' give the old bastard a hug. I could see he was a flat-faced old Uke, same's me, the solid kind who'd think nothin' of pullin' a plow if his horse fell an' died in the field during the depression.

"If the light froze an' stayed froze the rest of your life—would you stand there like you was made of stone?"

"No. I'd of turned around an' gone home. I'm not the Queen of England. If I break the law, I pay a fine!" he says. I grab him an' hold him tight against me.

"The Queen of England is our queen," I says to him. "When she learns to ride a moose side-saddle, we'll make her boss of everything!"

"Don't say that!"

"Why not?"

"What in hell are you—a bolshevik?" He was pushin' an' kickin' to get away from me. "If you're a bolshevik, I don't want to know you."

"Come on, what've the bolsheviks done to you?"

"They raped my mother an' took her egg basket!"

When an old man says that in the middle of a Manitoba blizzard, you've got to let him go. He stood in front of me, grinnin', like a shoemaker in paradise.

"My mother was carrying a basket of eggs to the village market in the old country long ago. She bent down to take a pine needle out from between her toes. Two bolsheviks came from behind, an' while she was bent over like that, they raped her, then took her basket of eggs. I'll never forgive them for that."

"When did this happen?"

"Nineteen-fifteen," he says to me.

"Were you there? Did you see it happen? How do you know all that?"

"No. I was born nine months later. But she told me lots of times why I should hate bolsheviks!" The old bugger was still grinnin'. I took him by the back of the neck an' shook him like a pillow as we walked, the icy wind to our backs.

"I had a wife an' a couple of kids," he was tellin' me. "Wife died, kids are grown up. The boy drives a cat for the highways department in Ontario. The girl's a nurse. Nice lookin' kid, but she's got no time for her father—not her. Both kids don't like me very much. When I'm feelin' bad, I walk a lot. An' I drink a bit when I'm feelin' good, and then I like to play cards, for money. A little bit of money—just enough to feel the old excitement warm my bones."

"Do you win at cards?"

"No. Sometimes I lose my whole pension cheque in one night an' then I'm pretty hungry for the rest of the month. But that's alright. At least I've *lived* for a few hours!" he says, an' giggles an' rubs his mittened hands together.

"You dumb old tit! Come on—I'll buy you a drink."

We found a bootlegger who was open night an' day, an' who sold us a bottle of rye an' a bowl of onion soup, which we ate standin' up, holding the bowls in our hands. Then we drank the whiskey. The Winnipeg winter night didn't seem as cold anymore. The old punk was laughin' an' wantin' me to go to his house. But I was tired of his company. I was startin' to burn, an' he was a fire extinguisher.

So I left, walkin' fast, because it was freezin', the wind cutting into my face. He ran after me, cacklin' like a rooster who'd just found three willin' hens.

"Hey, rassler! I've got lots of likker in my house. We could drink until morning. We could drink all day tomorrow!"

"Go away," I holler at him. "You're too timid for me. I don't believe your mother got knocked up by bolsheviks!"

"They made me. What other proof do you need?"

"You weren't made by a bolshevik. You were made by a coward, a wife-beater, a drunkard who played cards for pennies once a month. Go home!"

He got sad an' stopped followin' me. I looked at him an' saw tears in his eyes.

"Teach me to be brave, rassler," he begged.

"C'mere," I wagged my finger an' he approached, his oversized boots shufflin'. I pointed down the windy, grey, frozen street.

"See them parkin' meters, old timer? There's five hundred miles of parkin' meters in Winnipeg."

"Yah."

"They're the law, an' we're the bandits, you an' I, old timer!"

"Yeh—we're the bandits!" He pushed the fur cap back on his head, an' his eyes were bright with excitement.

"Let's piss into the money slots of the parkin' meters an' screw the law by freezin' it until spring."

He was game. We unzipped ourselves, but he was slow an' a born follower. I'd dribbled into five meters, which steamed for a moment, an' then froze solid before he overtook me an' took on the sixth meter. I passed him, my stub in my hand, an' went to the seventh meter an' the eighth. When I looked back I seen he was emptyin' his bladder into the one meter.

"Hey!" I shouted. "Just a squirt, an' on to the next one. You don't have to fill the pipestand—just a squirt to freeze the mechanism where the money goes in!"

"I can't make it stop! When I start to piss, it just keeps comin'!"

I hit another six meters before I was empty. Zippin' up, I waited for him. He was still at the same meter, soakin' it down, so to speak. He was laughin', an' I was laughin'.

"It feels good, eh?"

"Yeh, it feels good," he says. "We sure pissed the system to a stop, rassler!"

Behind him, a police cruiser turns from a side street. The old punk didn't see it. He was laughin' as he shook the last drops from his pipe. But the two cops inside the car saw him. They threw on the roof light an' the siren an' came screamin' down at him.

"Run!" I hollered, but he couldn't hear me. He just stood there, holdin' his soft old dink in his mittened hands. I slipped into a doorway an' watched them grab an' throw the old punker into the back of the wagon.

I was laughin'. But I also understood why some men should never do things which are against their nature. They're beat before they start, an' nothin' on earth or in heaven will change that ... nothin' ...

THREE

> ... I know who I love
> An' I know who I'll marry,
> Fairest of them all
> Is my handsome, winsome Johnny ...

The tune to that song is Irish, kid. They're good singers an' makers of songs, the Irish. I didn't sing that right. My voice is too low, it's coloured like my skin with a mishmash of Tartars, Mongols, Cossacks. Turks an' blue-eyed northerners that's the bloodstream of the Slav. Every part wantin' to get out of the stream an' go home. There's somethin' sad about a heart that bleeds for an' with everybody, all the races of the world. So we sing dirges in minor key an' low voices.

But not the Irish. A good Irish man who sings does so with the voice of a happy Russian mother!

They're good fighters, mean fighters, but only for a short time. Ring a churchbell an' they're off to confession. A Slav is different. He takes longer to heat up, but when he does, there's no time limit to a fight. He'll fight even when he's got too old to remember why ...

See this gold-capped tooth? An Irishman broke that in a fight. He was tough, big, with ears like garden shovels. I was laughin' when he hit me. I was still laughin' when he hit me the second time, an' I spat out a tooth. Then I got mad. For five minutes he fought good. Gave me a bloody nose an' a cut across the cheek—you can still see it here. By then I'd made up my mind I'd have to kick the shit out of him. He knew it too ... I could see it showin' in his eyes. He comes at me again, with both fists an' a knee.

"Fall down, why don't you?" he's shoutin' at me. "I don't want to hurt you any more than this!"

Those were his last words that day. Because I'd got hold of a wooden chair, which I broke across my knee. An' with the legs an' seat in one hand, an' the heavy back slab in the other, I began to soften him up. It took some time, but when I'd finished with him, he was rolled up on the floor, his knees up to his chin an' his hands wrapped around his head, the fingers locked together like steel clamps.

Saint Patrick ... he wasn't Irish, you know. He was a Bukovinian shoe-maker from a small mountain village in the Carpathians. My grandfather knew the village—four barns an' six small houses. Nothin' good ever came from it.

This man who became Saint Patrick was the worst shoemaker in the world. You know how your left shoe is different from your right shoe? This prick didn't, an' made them both the same, because he'd never seen a proper shoe made by anyone before. He also made them big because he wasn't good at trimmin' leather. He made them so big that when the Austrians took the village in a war, they found a pair of these shoes an' developed them into skis. That's how that business of comin' down the snow in the Alps got started! But the Bukovinians were people same's anyone else. They needed shoes, not skids for a snowy day, so they ran the shoemaker out of the country an' waited around for another one to be born. He left for Poland, but even the Poles couldn't use him, so he was told to keep movin'.

There was no welfare in them days, kid. Today, he'd live like a king, maybe even run a restaurant where they cook meat different. You can kill good meat seventeen different ways today, an' still find somebody who'd eat it, providin' you got a fancy name to put on the mess a starvin' dog would avoid!

Take chicken wings. We used to throw chicken wings out when I was a kid. Who in hell would put up with chewin' dead chicken skin on a bone dipped in honey? Today, I know a hundred guys who'd eat the feathers off the wings if they'd been left unplucked!

It was downhill all the way for this Saint Patrick. He went to Germany, tried for a job tyin' up bundles of flax. But he'd get the sleeves of his coat tied in with the straw. So they fired him. He went to Norway then, or Sweden, where the broads are good-lookin', but men look like they'd been axe-chopped out of blocks of wood. They used him there to walk dogs for the rich. But the pay wasn't much.

Then he hears there's a job open for a saint in Ireland, where it's warmer an' you don't have to know much to live.

When I was a kid an' kicked out of home, I came here, to Edmonton. First home I had in this city was a roomin' house. A room of my own, just a little smaller than the cells of some jails I've done time in, an' it cost me twenty dollars a month. I had to share a crapper an' sink with eight other people. I was lonely. Jesus, I was lonely. All day I'd work at the railway yards, loadin' cement bags into trucks. At night, I'd come into this roomin' house, eat an' go to my room. I'd sit in a chair an' listen to waterpipes, the furnace an' every radio wherever it was playin' in the house.

Bein' lonely makes me horny. I had a hard-on day an' night, like a pick handle. I could hang a wet towel on it for an hour while I thought of how I'd die or have my teeth pulled by a blacksmith, or how my mother might kill my father an' then hang herself in the basement. An' still that thing would stand up. No remorse, no shame, a mind an' life of its own. If a good cock goes into politics one day, I'll vote for it. It don't give up.

There was nobody to help me, kid. The two girls who lived in the roomin' house were school teachers who shared a room with a hot-plate an' kept to themselves. I spoke to one of them—Agnes, in the hallway once.

"Hullo," I says to her in a loud voice. "You want to go to a movie? I'm goin' an' don't mind if you come."

She looked at me like I had one eye an' two cowtits painted on my chest. She don't say nothin', she just walks by me an' out into the street. I go into the kitchen to have my supper of peanut butter sandwiches an' a glass of milk, an' there's two guys from other rooms in the house, eatin' the same thing. I tell them about askin' Agnes to the movie.

"Jesus Chris', boy … you're lucky she didn't say yes. They're dykes!" the guy with buck teeth who worked in a barbershop says to me, then laughs, his mouth an' teeth full of bread an' peanut butter. But the other guy at the table starts to argue.

"No sir, they're not dykes. They're from Egremont. I know Egremont. There's no dykes in Egremont!" he says.

"Not anymore there ain't. They're both in Edmonton now!" An' the barber's helper laughs a high whinny, like a young stallion comin' in for a feed of evening oats.

"You're full of shit, Jake," his buddy says in a way a professor with a lot on his mind might speak to a student. "Dykes don't get monthlies. These broads do. I seen some rags they left in the garbage on Friday. There was blood there, like with normal broads. They're not dykes."

Sometimes I run low on bread, but don't mention it to the bandits around this place. Especially the ones who say they're my friends. I've never been lucky with friends. All I gather around me are bandits waitin' for Romeo to trip an' fall on his face. They'd pick my pockets if I broke a leg. Which is alright, because I'd do the same to them!

Like Mark, the head clerk in this place. He's a dumb punk who reads by pointin' at the words with his finger. Dresses in a brown suit, an' then wears a black hat an' white shoes with perforations in 'em. He's a rube, it's written on his face an' back … RUBE … here comes the rube! Big as a Coca-Cola sign. He's no good at anythin'. He's too lazy to work, an' too stupid to get by without workin'. So he steals an' pretends he's in charge of staff here, when actually everybody else makes decisions for him, from the maids to the bellhops. So he steals, but only up to his own level, like shakin' down the cigarette machine, pocketin' tips left for maids in rooms. He'd never put his hand in the till, because he can't count, an' is afraid of anyone who can. You got nothin' to fear from Mark, kid.

I know Matt, the manager, good too. He stole another man's wife an' money to buy this hotel. Thirty years ago the prick was a junk dealer. Twice a year, in the spring an' fall he took lame horses an' contaminated army surplus canned food to sell to Indians on the reservations. In summer, on Sundays, he worked a tent revival, with faith healin' on the side. Him an' his "angels of mercy"—four teenaged hookers who'd give arthritic old farm bachelors a rub around the knockers in exchange for what pocket money these jokers carried on them.

They used to do that in four old teepee tents they'd set up back of the big tent, where Matt was scarin' the shit out of the poor with a description of hell that was a bit like the depression of the '30s, with polio an' bushfires thrown in for good measure.

Then we got Clapper, the bell-captain, the prize specimen of the lot! I gave him that name—Clapper, about five years ago. His real name's Willie, but he can't remember that anymore. He's got the sift so bad it's cooked his brain to a prune. He'd die if he ate a hot turkey sandwich with pepper sauce. Even a cup of coffee makes his face red as a railroad signal light.

How'd he get it? I don't know. I've heard he cupped it from a young broad he wanted to marry once, who got it from a Hungarian sailor. But I think he got it from his aunt Trudy, who runs a cigar store about six blocks from here. She'd put it out to any burglar on his coffee break.

Some years back, I seen Clapper behind this desk, drinkin' a hot cup of tea through a straw. His head was swollen like a balloon, his lips purple, hands shakin' …

"What's the matter? You fall into a cement mixer?" I says to him, happy-like, because I was feelin' pretty good. He pulls the straw carefully out of his mouth an' grins, an' I never seen a sadder expression of happiness. His gums were thick, an' his tongue was like a plug of raw liver he was tryin' to chew down.

"Tetracycline, Romeo," he says to me. "I'm allergic to tetracycline."

"He's got an infection in his lungs," dumb Mark, who's standin' beside him, tells me. Now I know the kind of doctors Clapper goes to, an' why. An' when they prescribe tetracycline it's for somethin' lower down than where a man's lungs got a business to be.

"Sure makes a mess of your kisser," I says to Clapper in a concerned kind of voice. He nods, pleased as hell for any sympathy he can get, an' begins to push the straw back into his mouth. Then I says, "But all the same, it's not hurtin' as much when you pee, an' the dribblin' has slowed down a lot, eh?"

He nods again. "Yeh, it's better than it was ... "

It takes Mark about a minute to realize his bell-captain is curin' a bad case of clap on the job. When he gets this to register in his small mind, he also thinks he's got to take action because there's three well-dressed people comin' through the door to register for rooms.

"Keep your hands out of the ice when preparin' ice buckets for customers," he tells his bell-captain. "Use ice-tongs!"

Those three gangsters barred me out of here for six months at one time. I'd run up a bill for seven or eight hundred, an' Matt was tryin' different ways of collectin' it. At first they were threatening, hinting my luggage could be seized an' the lock changed on my door. I laughed at them, sayin' if they was to do that, I'd consider my account settled with a plastic suitcase an' twenty dollars worth of socks an' underwear. So another time, Mark phones my room, coverin' the telephone mouthpiece with a handkerchief an' sayin' he was a collection agency. If I don't pay, they'll put me in jail, he says. I came down those stairs over there roarin'. When I get up to this desk, I take the edge of this tabletop an' tear out a four-foot strip of oak shelving, which I throw after Mark as he ducks out the side door.

I don't mind them tryin' to collect from me, it's their hotel. But show me some quality of thought, even in a den of fools. I despise dumb, cheap threats like, "You pay me, or I'll burn your house down!"

They intercepted mail comin' to me, lookin' for cheques. My mail always got to me, but I knew it'd been handled over electric lights because of finger smudges on the envelopes. Matt never washes his hands. No cheques came, an' after two weeks of this Dick Tracy lark, they gave up.

I always pay my debts, kid. But for the first time in my life, them hoods began to bother me. I started wonderin' just what did I really owe them. You seen for yourself the hotel rooms I get—the worst rooms in the house for Romeo Kuchmir, because when he's in place it's home to him, an' he stays for six months. Okay, so I get a twenty percent discount, but twenty percent of what? What's my room worth when it's a hundred percent? The plaster's peelin', windows haven't been washed since the war ended, waterpipes play like an organ when I turn a tap to brush my teeth. I hear the languages of half the world through the walls, floor an' ceiling. An' when I need to crap, it's a half-mile walk down the corridor to the men's john, which is occupied half the times I need it.

Listen—the old punk who was night clerk before you walked through the buildin' every hour, lookin' for fires, an' free tail an' booze for himself. One night I'm waitin' at the door of the crapper, been waitin' like that for twenty minutes. Sam comes around the bend in the hallway, makin' his rounds.

"Sam," I says, "open this door with your passkey."

"There's someone in there. I can't do that. It's against regulations."

He was big on regulations, having served in the army. There's men who spend a few years in the army an' if they're lucky not to get themselves killed, go back home an' do useful things. There's another kind of man who learns to read regulations in the army. He spends the rest of his life polishin' his shoes an' bein' a cop to a garbage dump or a stack of two-by-four lumber joists. It's against regulations to piss in the sink. A broad who smokes in the airport will set a plane on fire. Beat the boy who pulls his wire ...

"It's against hotel regulations, Romeo. I won't open the door."

"Don't make me mad, Sam. I can kick the feet out from under you an' take your keys an' your false teeth away from you. So you open this door, or I'm gonna rough you up!" Sayin' that, I give him a slight shove, enough to make him hit the corridor wall with his shoulder an' the back of his head. Right away I saw in his eyes that he was about to bend one regulation a bit. He took the passkey out of his pocket an' handed it to me.

"If anyone asks me, I'll say you forced me," he whines an' starts walkin' away. But I catch his arm an' pull him back.

"Hey, I want you to see this," I says to him.

I've got this one face you see, but in my profession I've learned to work it for myself like a hundred masks. I'm a good actor. I can cry, fake laughter, pain—anything. If your father died an' you had to work the day of his funeral, for ten dollars I could go an' cry for you. For you, for everybody in the family, two hours of solid cryin' of such a quality as to make people remember it five years after they'd buried him.

So, as I unlocked the door of the john, I twisted up my face to resemble that of a dinosaur with indigestion. Kickin' the door open so it hit the side wall with a wallop, I stepped into the doorframe, breathin' in deep an' spreadin' my elbows so I looked half again as big as I really am.

An' sittin' on the pot in that washroom was a constipated little barley farmer from Lac La Biche ... peaked cap on his head, eyes waterin' with bowel strain ... a day's growth of grey bristle on his face.

Good actin', kid, is a matter of power an' timing. When you come in like gang-busters, save on the sounds until all the other terror has sunk in. Then you let go. I bared my teeth an' growled before I moved to stand over him.

"Shit!" I commanded in the biggest voice I got. "You've been here twenty minutes—now shit!"

He did. What Exlax couldn't touch, fear drove through him like a blast from an air compressor. He was out of there in thirty seconds, empty an' white-faced. I patted him on the back as he went out the door, bucklin' his pants. But when I did that, he yelped like he'd been touched by a brandin' iron.

It says in the Bible the meek shall inherit the earth. I don't believe it, kid. All the meek will inherit is bad breath an' a hollow wind aroun' the heart.

I've been down an' out on my luck. But I've never begged, an' what I've borrowed, I've repaid with interest. When the wrestling game got slow, I used to be in business sellin' sacks of cement to gangsters who build houses for the poor in this country. I never had a warehouse or an office. Yet they always knew when I had surplus cement stacked up in some farmer's field with a plastic sheet over it.

Where did it come from, you ask? It was stolen. Not by me—by others. It was stolen from construction projects an' city supply sheds, but mostly from the government. You see, the way the system works, government buildings are supposed to be built to last. The same's bank buildings. Politically, it has to be that way. Wouldn't look good to have a government building fall under four feet of snow while the bank stands. Why vote for a government then? Go vote for a bank. There was a sayin' in my town that all roads in the world ended up at a gravel pile owned by a government minister … or his wife … or his brother. The gravel was there to build other roads to other gravel piles, but that's another story.

The smart contractor assures the government he's buildin' better. Oh, it'll cost a bit more, but it'll be a better building. For every two bags of cement, he'll see a third one gets put in the mixer. So he gets the contract. What goes into the buildin' after that is somethin' else. Cement disappears, carpets grow wings, government-bought panelling ends up on the walls of the best homes in the west end.

So I buy cement from one crook for a dollar a bag an' resell it to another for a dollar-fifty. I only deal when I'm hard up, so I can't afford a warehouse. God provides me with an open field somewhere, an' from Woodwards I get a hundred yards of plastic sheet for ten bucks to cover my loot an' I'm in business for myself!

When I make a sale, the guy who buys sends a trucker to collect the load. The truckers they send are bums. They've got all kinds of reasons why they can't load cement bags by hand. So I usually end up loadin' it myself, or gettin' some kid to help for ten bucks an' a steak dinner in town when the job's done. But the money's good, an' I always come out ahead of the game.

The worst trucker I met in my business looked like one of them kodiak bears. Big shoulders, yellow fangs for teeth, an' hairy all over. You couldn't see the skin on his hands or fingers for this black hair. An' on his head it come down to meet his eyebrows. Neanderthal … the kind of animal who'd eat a suitcase if it contained raw meat.

"Hey, sport—how about helpin' out," I says to him after I'd carried four sacks into the truck, an' he's still hangin' around, kicking the tires on the back wheels of his truck.

"Can't."

"Why not?"

"I'm a sick man. I should be in bed. I'll die if I lift anythin'.'"

"What's hurtin'?"

"I'm sittin' on a Volkswagen inner tube to drive here—did you know that?"

"No, I didn't."

"I should be in hospital. I'm that sick. Or sittin' home in a hot bath."

He was beginning to bitch me off.

"What the hell's wrong with you? If you're a cripple then why come here? I need a healthy man to load this stuff!"

He looked up at me out of the bluest piggy eyes I ever seen in a dark hairy face. Christ, he was ugly.

"Well sir, I went to the store on Thursday an' bought me a pineapple. I had a cravin' for pineapple on Thursday. Would've done better if I'd bought a can of juice an' drunk that instead. But I cut the pineapple in two an' ate half of it. Never do that again ... "

Right then I knew he wasn't as dumb as I thought he was. That he was spreadin' a good layer of bull under me, around me, an' over me. That he'd already spread it an' I was standin' in the middle in it up to my ankles.

"I've eaten a whole pineapple on a hot day. It's good for you. Lots of vitamins in a pineapple," he continues. Then he spits on the endgate where I'm standin'. He thinks for a moment, an' then goes on. "But not on a *cold* day. Never eat pineapple on a cold day. I ate half that pineapple an' within an hour, it blew my arsehole out!"

He had me. I made one desperate attempt to stop him.

"Friend, I've never met you before," I says to him. "I don't know your name or where you come from. You're a stranger to me. I don't want to know you. I'm not interested in your asshole. My religion don't allow that. I don't wanna hear about it."

But that bastard wasn't listenin' to me.

"I came outa there on my hands an' knees. First guy I seen was the shop foreman. 'Get me a Volkswagen inner tube an' blow it up!' I yell at him. The same inner tube I got here in the truck with me now. 'Put it in a car for me to sit on, an' drive me to hospital,' I holler at him again."

He cleared his throat an' spat at the endgate again.

"Well, sir, they got me in alright, an' two doctors worked for an hour scrapin', cuttin' away the damages an' then sewin' my blow hole back together again. I was sicker'n a dog for weeks after. Had to learn to crap standin' up, careful not to poop on my pantlegs like a baby."

"I don't want to hear about it—piss off! Get your goddamned truck out of here—G'wan!" I wasn't shoutin' at him so much as pleadin', but it was like askin' a locomotive the time of day.

"A guy like you takes his arsehole for granted. You abuse it, sand it down with toilet paper, sit on ice or dive into water feet first, an' legs apart. You wouldn't do that if you'd a woman's equipment! You wouldn't do that to your nostril, would you? They're both the same, you know. You blow shit an' air outa both of them!"

"Okay, okay—when I next put Vicks up my nose I'll do the same for my ass to keep it from feelin' bad, you sonofabitch!" I says to him. "They got you all fixed up, so give me a hand with the cement. What you know won't make you a senator or a school teacher, but it shouldn't stop you carryin' cement like other men!"

The last thing he had in mind was helpin' me.

"I'll never be the man I was, no sir. I should be walkin' with a stick up the long hill to my death now. But I'm a poor man, got to keep drivin' this fuckin' truck," he says. "A month after I come out of hospital I'm walkin' down a city street, bent over, me legs so wide apart a kid on a trike could drive through them. An old lady comes up behind me, walkin' stick in her hands, her knees thick as footballs with arthritis, her back humped over, mouth all shrivelled up, she's maybe a hundred an' ten years old. But she passes me goin' uphill like I was standin' still! How do you think that made me feel, eh? How do you think I felt? Go load cement yourself. I'm gonna rest in the cab. When you've loaded up, knock three times on the endgate so I'll know when to go."

Like you were tellin' me yesterday, kid—with computers an' new machines, life gets easier for the workin' man. I think it's good it's gettin' that way. I don't want my kids livin' like I lived. But what's gonna happen to guys like that trucker? If he gets an asshole pension, who's he goin' to fight? What purpose will his life have?

What's it goin' to be like for the rest of us, when we're left with no stories to tell? I read somewhere in a book that there's no sorrow in the just society. If there's no sorrow, where's the joy comin' from? I can't imagine anythin' more sad than a world where there's no sorrow. Because there'll be no room in such a world for a punk like that trucker.

FOUR

You can teach dogs to listen, an' magpies to speak.

When I was a kid, my uncle Vladimir had a Saint Bernard dog whose name was Valentine Number Two. The name was too long to say if you were callin' him in a hurry. So instead he was called "boy." He was a big, stupid dog. With eye pouches too big for his eyes, lips too big for his mouth. He drank the toilet bowl dry at my uncle's house. He slept a lot in the shade of a poplar tree which grows in my uncle's front yard. Car rides excited "boy," an' when he was excited, he kept breakin' wind.

My uncle Vladimir drove his Chevrolet sedan with all windows open, winter an' summer, an' "boy" on the front seat beside him. Even so, for an hour after my uncle came home from a car trip with the dog, the car an' my uncle both smelled of dog fart.

When "boy" slept an' I wanted him to be up on his feet an' goin', all I had to say was, "Go, boy—go!"

"Boy" would be awake an' on his feet like he'd been spring loaded ... tearin' up gravel an' runnin' this way an' that, growling, his eyes wild in their watery pouches tryin' to find what it was he was expected to chase.

"Go, boy—go!" I'd call an' point. He'd see the way I was pointin' an' go like hell in that direction until he'd hit a board fence. Then he'd reverse directions an' run like hell the other way, his rear end poppin' like bursts of rocket fire!

"Go, boy—go!"

An' he's off, woofin' an' snortin', over-turning buckets of water, garden rakes, upsettin' wheelbarrows an' rocking chairs until my uncle would catch him by the collar an' rassle his dumb dog to the ground.

"What the hell's the matter with you anyway?" he'd say an' pat "boy" on the head until he cooled off. Pretty soon he'd go to sleep, his big lips spread out like a puddin' around his mouth. The top of his eyes shut, but the bottom eye pouches extended like two meaty shoehorns.

I'd creep up behind the trees, an' makin' sure my uncle wasn't around to see me, would cough softly. Just like that, the stupid dog's eyes opened an' the head comes up, the curtain of lips followin', drooling saliva like a fishnet.

"Go … "

An' the dog's rear end is up, back paws dug into the ground.

"Leave boy alone, you goddamned bastard!"

My uncle Vladimir was in a corner of his garden where I hadn't expected him to be. He came towards me, his eyes hangin' from the tops of his sockets, his lips loose. He looked like "boy." I climbed the fence just ahead of a handful of pebbles he threw at me.

The followin' spring, I found a baby magpie that'd been chewed up by a cat. I kept him in a paper box an' fed him cornmeal, bits of hamburger an' milk. I began teachin' him to speak. You don't have to split a magpie's tongue to understand words he learns, that's not true. He won't learn many words. Even if he had a mouthful of tongue, he'd never learn the Lord's Prayer, but there's some things you can teach a magpie, split tongue or not.

When he was strong enough to fly, I let him out of the paper box. When I went for a walk, he'd fly to one side of me, then the other. Sometimes he'd fly ahead an' wait in a tree until I caught up to him.

"Go, boy—go!" he was shoutin' in a funny kind of voice, like you some-times hear on an old recording. One day we're on a walk, an' approachin' my uncle's house. My uncle's gone to work in the lumberyard, his car's gone. An' "boy" is sleepin' on the sidewalk, beside the garden gate. The magpie flies ahead, glidin' past the dog an' settlin' on a picket of the fence. He kind of caws once an' flutters his wings. "Boy" lifts his head, looks up at the bird with one eye an' rolls over for more sleep.

"Go boy—go!"

The stupid dog's feet was awake before the rest of him. They dig into the ground an' he's off down the street. The magpie tips his head, watchin' him go, then flies after him.

"Go, boy—go!"

"Woof! Woof!"

The dog's in high gear now, layin' down a cloud of dust mixed with the stench of dog fart behind him. A kid comin' around the corner on his bike is sent flyin' into a hedge. An' Missus Donnel's low-slung clothesline full of wet washing goes "plunk" as "boy" takes a shortcut through her yard an' clothesline into the next street.

That was the last I seen of either "boy" or my magpie. If they found enough to eat, they're probably to the bottom of South America now, for they were headin' that way when they left town. I felt it was like kind of a marriage. Each found what the other was lookin' for. An' because I was a kid then an' had time on my hands, I accidentally turned out to be a kind of marriage broker between them ...

Marriage ...

I've been married myself, kid. Had one baby—a boy. He's a teenager now. He's not like me—not at all. He wears thick glasses an' turtleneck sweaters. He wears sandals all summer an' needs a haircut. He doesn't live, he sits an' reads these big books on how wars were fought. It makes me laugh, seein' this half-blind little bugger readin' about how to kill! An' it's my kid, my seed made that one, that's for sure. Although there's a helluva lot of his mother there too. She had big, flat feet, same's him. An' a habit of rubbin' her left eye when she was worried. She rubbed that eye a lot when we were together.

When I'm worried, I laugh. I'm laughin' in the wrestlin' ring. I laugh when a letter from the bank tells me I'm poorer now than I was the day I was born. I'll tell you somethin' else, kid—I'll be laughin' the day I die!

I laugh at what the heart an' wang of a man takes him to when he's lonely—a woman. Especially a *good* woman. Nancy was one of them—a *good* woman. What a helluva thing to say about a broad! They're condemned before they're tried. Who cares if a man tells his friends he married a good woman.

"Hey, guys—I got married!"

"Yeh? Who'd you marry?"

"A broad called Janet, but that don't matter. She's a whore an' a shoplifter!"

In five minutes, every guy in the plant is pumpin' your hand, askin' you to a party, slappin' your shoulder. You're somebody, an' so's your Janet! The world's too full of good people. We need bastards now to liven things up, or we'll sink in a puddle of goodness.

We were nothin' when we married, Nancy an' me. But hand in hand, from spoon to mouth, as they say, we first collected a rockpile an' then built a house. An' after that, the start of a life. Nothin' of value comes easy. Not a marriage. Not a child. Not even knowin' what's inside of you.

We began as muck, along with the mosquitoes an' lice. The bugs went their way, doin' what bugs do. But someone put his lips to our earhole an' whispered somethin' about god, about becomin' god ourselves. An' we're just stubborn an' tough enough not to forget that. But it's no four-lane highway gettin' there, believe me.

You know what eats up a man from the inside out? It's the curse of withholdin'. No man trusts another. Leave two men in a room for ten minutes an' you've got two liars layin' down bullshit.

"I killed the biggest moose in the world two years ago, up by Fort Saint John!"

"Oh, yeh? But I've got the thickest cock on the prairies!"

Never do they say—"Brother, help me. I'm small an' mean an' I don't know what I'm doin', can you help me?"

Women are different. They tell each other everythin'. They trust each other, even when they're enemies. They hate an' love an' call to each other for help. An' each one gives love an' support to the other. They withhold nothin'. I've been told there's cases where the wife of a man, an' another woman he's been screwin' on the side, they'll meet, an' talk, an' cry while holdin' on to each other like sisters. Now if that's true, an' I don't know if it is, but if that's true, then it's special! That's two hills an' a mountain above us. It tells *me*, a punk who's never learned to speak one language well enough to be understood, that women are up there. Near enough to get the almighty by his ankle an' ask him—"See this, boss? Is it good enough? Is this what you wanted?"

Not so with men. They're afraid to confide an' cry an' kiss an' hold each other. A friend of mine, a Greek wrestler who reads books, an' who liked to eat hot sauerkraut an' stewed rabbit, he once told me he read somewhere that Greek soldiers in a war used to put down their guns at night an' meet the enemy soldiers to share food an' a place to sleep. In the morning, they separated to shoot at each other all day, because two kings far away said they had to. That's not the same thing as with the women. That's not love. It's despair.

Why do you look at me that way, kid? There's somethin' in your eyes that's afraid. Is it because I tell you I love men that makes you afraid? I love women, an' when I tell you about that, you smile. But with men ...

Kid, I could make a faggot out of you in an hour if I put my mind to it. An' you'd do it to the next guy you liked, so don't look at me that way. I'm a lover, not a killer. What my hands or lips touch gives life, not death.

If you were dyin', an' all the medicines couldn't help you, all that would save you was to be held or touched a certain way, count on me to help you. That's all I have to say! But let me ask you somethin', would you do the same for me? Would you ever forgive me if you did?

You can't answer me, can you? The disease is already inside of you, workin' away.

I'm sad about many things. I would like to wear rings on my hands, an' shirts with puffy sleeves, an' more gold in my teeth. An' expensive perfume ... the kind that makes people stop, turn an' smile when I'm walkin' through. Shoes of red leather like they use to bind old books. Then everybody'd notice me, eh? Then they'd say—"Hey, there goes a *man*!"

I want what I can't have. A rose behind my ear an' sexy oil on my skin. I hate Taiwan underarm anti-perspirant an' one-way sunglasses—that's for pimps an' watch thieves. I'm a man from where the pine trees grow, an' the wind burns like it's comin' from the smokestacks of hell! That's the way I am, an' that's the way I love. No holds barred, nothin' but the best, even if I know I'll never get it!

It's not my fault if I scare you talkin' like this. It's two o'clock in the morning. The hour men die in their sleep, or think of death if they're awake. There are things which make me sad. I'm a wrestler. I could've sung opera, or been the captain of a ship.

My life wasn't much. But it's better than some lives I've known.

There was a guy called Shwartz, disabled an' on pension. He married Nina Bergman, who preached each summer just outside our town. Shwartz was thin an' tall, walkin' with a limp an' one arm frozen by his side.

Nina was a young, willowy broad with big, dark eyes an' a smile that'd turn your mind if you were a guy, any guy. But especially if you were a young punk wantin' real bad to see up a woman's skirt for the first time. Yeh, Nina had every young hood in town turnin' over an' sweatin' himself sick tryin' to fall asleep at night.

Maybe it was the age we were, an' seein' things different. She had this pubic hump showin' even when she wore a skirt an' stood up straight. The broad was made for screwin', not Bible-thumpin' an' living with a crippled man at least thirty years older than herself. She was *juicy*, an' so were we. Anyhow, she played the accordion, sang hymns an' preached. The services were held in an old school about four miles out of town. Shwartz an' she rented the school each summer, as well as the teacherage, where they lived. A week before the preachin' started, she had posters all over town … big posters, with her standin' life-size, opening her accordion, an' always that damned smile that got you so. Somewhere in the background of the poster, a Bible under his arm an' a lost prairie farmer look on his face, was Shwartz. Them were good posters. I use her ideas today in my wrestlin' promotions.

About a week after she was in business, there'd come a night when a bunch of young punks an' myself from town decided to attend her revival meeting. She'd been botherin' our dreams from the previous summer, an' it was something of a pilgrimage we had to make—a rites of puberty sort of thing. We went down in the truck I drove part-time for the feed mill that year.

There was more to it than just Nina. It was the time of year … the heat of the summer, the broads around town wearin' less an' less. Fresh summer food an' the boredom of growin' up with nothin' to do. The pressure startin' building up, an' nobody less than Nina could relieve us. She knew it—I know now she knew it—an' that promising little lump of hers pulled us in like bees to honey. We needed tail so bad we ached all over. She gave us the word of god instead!

I'll tell you this, kid: in the heat of the summer, when you're a young punk with the bud breakin' open, that rounded little hump of hers had more pull than a CPR locomotive, an' that's no lie!

So we went down, the guys all in the back of the truck, their shirt fronts open to catch the evening wind on their bodies. When we got there, the service had started. Nina was playin' her accordion at the front of the classroom, her body swayin' in a bright green dress which showed everythin' we came to see. Behind her was Shwartz, in baggy pants an' a grey shirt three sizes too large around the neck. Right up front were the young broads, an' behind them sat some old men an' women, bent over their prayerbooks like death at a picnic. We walked in an' took what seats were left at the back of the room. The young broads could smell us comin' in. They looked at us, got red-faced, giggled and turned away, because there were flames burnin' up our clothes an' rising to lick our faces an' damp hair.

"God is like a golden harvest," Nina was sayin' in her soft, breathless little voice. "God is like a summer rain, cooling our bodies, sweeping goodness an' love through winds of piety an' faith. Believe in God as I do, an' we shall all walk hand in hand down the footpaths of salvation!"

She smiled a goddamned sexual floodlight, her eyes an' mouth washin' over us like the wind of paradise. The guys around me were starin' straight ahead, their eyes glazed, mouths hangin' slack. Each one of those bastards was seein' himself hand in hand with Nina, walkin' down the road to salvation. But the road was twisted …

"The lord is my shepherd, I shall not want … "

It led up dark ladders into haymows … the back seats of cars parked in a woodlot … hot barley fields with the cunt-smell of sun an' summer earth …

"He leads me to green pastures … "

She picked up the accordion again, an' setting a beat with her hip an' foot, led the hymn singing. That goddamned red-pleated accordion flowered open an' shut in a regular kissin' motion that was makin' the punks around me start to cross their legs. Up front, the little broads in pigtails was singin' in loud voices. The punks an' myself in back sang in monotone, a sewin' machine chorus. The old timers between us couldn't follow the words fast enough, so they just stared at their books.

Then suddenly it all ends. Shwartz is at the door, his shoulders slouched an' his eyes watery like those of an old dog. He's handin' out chapters of scripture on cheap paper an' thankin' us for coming as we shuffle out the door. We walk past him, starin' past him, for *she's* out there at the bottom of the steps. She's not handin' out anything. She doesn't have to. Her smile's tired now, sweat tricklin' down her cheeks. We walk past her with our eyes down, a dull ache in the bottom of our stomachs spreadin' like a wound. Her voice is a dark whisper in the evening air.

"God bless you, brother … come again!"

The punks I came with all move to the truck. We're not sayin' anything. We lean against the side of the door an' hood an' pass cigarettes around. It's late evening now, the sky an' low spots on the ground gettin' dark. The people move away, some walking, some drivin'. We just stand there, watchin' Shwartz an' Nina go back into the school, then come out with their books. She's carryin' her accordion over her shoulder, like a rucksack.

They cross towards the teacherage, Nina in front an' the old man followin'. They don't once look over to where we're standin' beside the truck. They're talkin' … or rather, she's sayin' something, an' Shwartz just nods his head. A slight wind starts up, blowin' the sound of her voice to us. She's sore about somethin' …

"Well, you'll go tomorrow and you'll tell them to go screw themselves. I've got enough to worry about!"

We heard her say it—we heard her say it loud an' clear. An' yet, we didn't. She had us so tenderized from the prayer meetin' we didn't believe she would talk like we did. To this day, I was there an' I know what she said, but I don't believe I heard it. It's like being told that Christ had bad breath, or my mother gettin' clap when she was seventeen. I never asked to know, an' if you tell me, I didn't hear you!

We kept lookin' after them until they reached the teacherage, an' she unlocked the door an' went in first. He followed, but she shut the door in his face as he was about to step in. He turned away, shrugged an' sat down on the step, his head buried in his hands.

It was gettin' dark now, but we continued lookin' where Shwartz sat until it got too dark to see him clearly anymore.

"Let's go," I says, an' opened the door of the truck.

"It's alright for you sittin' on a soft seat. We got to stand in back of the truck. I got to jack off first, or the bumpin' will kill me," says Bruno Prentice, a big kid with acne on his neck. Bruno worked for the house painter in town, an' his shoes were always spattered with paint.

"Me, too," says somebody from around the front of the truck, an' we all moved down the schoolyard towards the well, which was surrounded by a willow hedge.

We were laughin' now, shovin' against each other, shovin' with our shoulders an' our hips, prisoners of one woman, but marchin' away from her—goddamned revolutionaries, that's how we felt! The well was encased in spruce planks. A round chamber sunk into the ground, with a suspended pulley from which a bucket was hangin' somewhere down in the water. Most of the well was surrounded by this willow hedge nobody planted. It just growed there.

Bruno Prentice an' a punk named Pat Gorman who fixed bicycles in the Esso garage was hunched over in the middle of the clearin', talkin' in a whisper an' laughin'. We heard them unzip themselves. The rest of us kind of stood around on one foot, scratchin' the back of our ankles with the toe of the other foot, hands in our pockets.

"Bet you a buck I can beat you to the draw an' shoot first!"

"Betcha can't!"

An' the match was on. We couldn't see too good, it was dark now, but we heard both of them breathin' hard.

"Here's for the holy ghost in your tight little ass, Nina!" I heard Bruno say in a thick, hoarse voice. About the same time I heard the well pulley creak behind where I stood. The bucket plopped back in the water, an' old Shwartz lit his flashlight. The light picked up Bruno, who was half-squattin' now in agony an' squirtin' a stream of sperm all over Pat Gorman's bare arms, an' there was Pat holdin' his own big stub in two hands an' pumpin' for the counter-attack.

The Gorman kid was the first to run, right through the willows, still holdin' on to himself. Those of us watchin' moved away from the light, leavin' Bruno Prentice alone in the light, his face and shirt wet with perspiration, his dink still skippin', but the look in his eyes scared now.

"What the hell you lookin' at?" he says in a thin, dry voice. "You got one of these, same's me, same's everybody!"

"Filthy, corrupt pigs! May god damn every one of you," the old man says, an' droppin' the empty bucket he carried, he shuffles away into the darkness …

She bothered our dreams a lot that winter an' the summer following. But we never went back to watch her sing an' preach. Why bother?

You can't catch rain with outstretched hands, so why try the impossible? Bruno Prentice took up with a young widow that year. The rest of us hung around my old man's poolhall rememberin' summer.

FIVE

It's better to wrestle for a livin' than raise turkeys. You become famous wrestlin'. Who remembers a turkey farmer?

I *eat* turkeys, tear them apart an' eat them, an' with the strength I get from the meat, I wrestle. Someplace there's a guy in a Hong Kong shirt, rubber boots an' straw hat carryin' buckets of turkey mash all day until his ass is draggin' on the ground, feedin' his turkeys so Romeo Kuchmir can wrestle. I think about that, an' I feel good! I feel good like a king feels good, or the superintendent of a parkin' lot: things keep movin' to keep me goin'!

A man's got to crow. That's what bein' a man is all about. To ride a horse, catch a fish, wrestle another man to the ground—that's the spice of it all. I like to drive, but I don't. Because when I drive a car, it's got to go a hundred miles an hour or I'm not livin'! Sure, you can kill somebody or yourself doin' that, but it's a better way to die than sittin' watchin' Bugs Bunny on television an' worryin' about your heart stopping … or feedin' fuckin' turkeys.

So when I promote a fight, I have posters made the size of blankets. In the middle of the poster is a life-size picture of me—Romeo Kuchmir, ex-wrestler, boxer an' promoter. All around me are small pictures of the fighters I promote. That's the way I see myself, an' I'm gonna share my vision with the world!

Sure, they give me static for that. But they got to bend or they're on the breadline. They give me static because after a match, I get the best booze an' the best screwin' for myself. The others get beer an' clap. I deserve it, kid—nothin' wrong with that. I'm an enterpriser, a capitalist with forty cents in my pockets. I'm not equal to some oxhead with a thick neck who counts on his fingers! No two men are born equal. They never was an' they never will be.

So under this system, I use what I was born with. That's why I eat turkeys someone else grows for me, an' I feel good about it.

I've got nothin' against communism. If it keeps children from starvin', that's reason enough for me to believe in it. But don't fool yourself, kid—the same kind of people rise to the top. Khrushchev wore pants which hung down at the butt an' on his head he had a sheepskin cap, the super workin' man! In America he would've wore a grey suit, an' made it as president of General Motors.

A frightened man, useless in the head, will always remain frightened an' useless in the head. Don't knock on the door—kick it open if you're comin' through. An' don't talk to secretaries. Secretaries are there to talk to other secretaries. The same with clerks an' painters in the hall. Go straight to the king an' ask for money!

There's a restaurant down the street called "The Flamingo." I go there one night last winter for a feed of liver an' onions. The waitresses there know me good … nice little broads who like to laugh a lot.

As I'm goin' in, I stick a set of these Dracula teeth into my mouth. Got them for two bits at a novelty store. Used to be a time when they sold things like pocket knives with mother of pearl inlay, key rings, cheap jewellery which looked expensive for two days until the shellac wore off. Now the novelty stores sell you plastic monster teeth, rubber cocks for a well-hung stallion, spiders the size of a baseball mitt with red eyes. What's happened to the class, an' the special kind of magic they once had?

I stick these teeth into my mouth, screw up my face an' make my eyes look dead. I drop one shoulder, blow out my stomach, make my feet drag like they was made of cement. I come through the door of "The Flamingo" an' sit at the counter. Patsy, the red-haired waitress with green eyes is leanin' on the counter across from me, readin' about Elizabeth Taylor in a magazine.

"Yes," she says, still readin'.

"I'm lookin' for the girl who made me sick," I says in a thick voice.

"This isn't a hospital," she replies without lookin' up. "This is a restaurant. Do you want coffee?"

"Yah … They said to come here for the business. I don't see no business. They got a business room in the back, maybe?"

She looks up at me now, an' jumps back against the wall. The Elizabeth Taylor magazine falls on the floor. I grin. She puts her hands over her mouth, an' then she knows who I am an' turns red in the face.

"Jesus Christ," she says, "that's an awful thing to do when it's not expected. Stop doin' that, Romeo. There's some cops having supper in the booth. If they see you lookin' like that, they'll pull you in."

"Send a message to them. Tell them they stink, tell them there's a man waitin' who's set fire to their car," I said an' grinned again. She looked away when I did that. A couple of seats down the counter, there's this drunk who interrupts our conversation.

"Hey, red," he hollers. "I ordered a steak! Where's my goddamn steak, lady?"

Patsy leaves me an' goes to the kitchen. She comes back with his steak plate, which she puts down in front of him. Then she goes to the urn to get him a coffee. The drunk pokes at the steak with his fork an' knife. Then he looks at Patsy, whose back is turned to us as she's pourin' coffee. That old bastard takes the steak in his hand an' before I realize what he's up to, he half-rises an' heaves it at her. It misses that little broad's head by an inch, hits the coffee machine an' falls on the floor.

"Goddamn meat ain't cooked right!" the drunk swears, his chin out, nostrils twitchin'.

No university psychologist will ever know what a broad who's five-foot-three an' works in a restaurant at night has to know to survive. This one's cool … super cool, as she carries the coffee to the drunk. She puts it in front of him, then goes back to the coffee machine. She picks up the steak in her hand, carries it back to where he's half-standin', an' slams it hard on his plate. The potatoes an' carrots on the plate fly into the old bastard's lap an' slide down the front of his pants.

"Eat!" she says. "Or your fuckin' head comes off!"

"Sure, red … sure. No need to get sore. I was only funnin' … "

He's beat. She's half his size, but he's not gonna move until she tells him to. The cops who've eaten in back of the restaurant are comin' out now. They pay Patsy.

"You should see a dentist," one of them says to me. Cops' jokes are the kind you remembered an' forgot when you were twelve.

"Your mother said that too. She was gonna break windows, so I paid a cab to take her home," I says. They look me up an' down, all three of them, an' decide it'd cost them more bruises than it was worth to extract an apology. So instead they all go "ha-ha-ha" an' leave. The drunk finishes his food, pays an' starts to stagger for the door. I wink at Patsy, an' she grins back at me.

"How … how … how … how!" I'm barkin' at the old bastard an' followin' him out.

We're on the street. It's colder now. A frozen wind, full of ice particles, has started blowin' from the north. The drunk turns to me, grinnin'.

"You're sure not pretty, you're fuckin' ugly," he says to me, an' offers his hand for a handshake. I grab it an' bite his wrist. He's goin' like hell down the sidewalk now, weavin' from side to side. I'm after him, right behind him, pickin' up speed, barkin' like hell. He turns into a doorway an' faces me. I can see he's scared now, still drunk but scared.

"A joke's a joke, buddy! Now piss off. I'm an old man an' I've been drinkin' pretty good, but I can still take care of myself!"

I'm fillin' up the doorway, growlin', my arms out like a gorilla. I roll up my eyes until only the whites are showin'. He ducks under my elbow an' is runnin' up the street.

"How! How! How!"

The snowplows have been through, leavin' piles of ice here an' there off the edge of the street. He picks up a lump of ice an' turnin' quickly, throws it at me.

"Urrr!" I flex my chest muscles an' the lump of ice bounces back.

"Goddamn sonofabitch! You're crazy!" He's shoutin' as he runs out into the street to flag a taxi that's approachin'. I'm right behind him, also wavin' my arms. The guy drivin' the cab is Lennie, the bootlegger. Lennie knows right away I'm doin' my bit for A.A., an' throwin' the back door open, he gives me a little wink. The drunk jumps in. I'm right behind him, even though he tries to yank the door shut between himself an' me.

"Where to?" asks Lennie.

"Fourth … down the hill!" the drunk squeals.

"How! How! Grr!" That's me. The drunk is sober now, an' pressed into a round lump against the cab door.

"Hey!" He changes his mind. "Drive to the police station!"

Lennie doesn't hear him. I lurch for the old fellow, an' he's climbin' up against the rear window of the car. I grab his leg an' bring the plastic teeth hard into his ankle. He screams out a kind of sound you don't expect to hear from any man—old or young—this side of hell. A kind of high bleat, like from a small animal standin' on four feet.

Lennie drives down to Fourth on the flats. It's only about two blocks of avenue there, snugged back in from the powerhouse. The old bastard throws a ten dollar bill at Lennie an' bolts out the door, runnin' for a square little house with a big front window.

"Drive around the block an' meet me back here in a minute, before the fuzz does," I tell Lennie, an' go after the drunk. He's through the front door before I get there, an' I hear the lock turn inside. The lights go on. I'm barkin' loud now an' go to the window. The lights in surrounding houses are comin' on. Inside the living room, the drunk is yellin' something up the stairs. Pretty soon I see a pissed-off old lady with curlers in her hair an' a cheap dressin' gown around her body comin' down the stairs. She's flat-footed an' walks painfully.

I'm scratchin' at the window an' poundin' the glass, growlin', the plastic teeth bared. He's pointin' at me, an' as she looks to where he's pointin', I press my face hard against the window. I can imagine what it looks like from the other side, an' I'm right. One look at me an' she's goin' right back upstairs. The dressin' gown falls off her an' the last I seen of her, she's runnin', her bare ass bouncing, runnin' with her hands an' feet to get the hell out of there. I grin at the prick an' wag my finger for him to come to me. He backs towards the fireplace. He's scared … *really* scared now.

There's a glass swan on the mantelpiece beside him. He's lookin' around, his eyes rollin' wildly, sees the swan, an' grabbin' it, he throws it at me. The window is a double sash winter window. The glass swan comes through the first glass but not the second. By now I figure he's ready to flip an' end up in a bird cage. Besides, Lennie's cab has pulled up to the sidewalk behind me. So with a last, lone-wolf howl, I back away, stampin' my feet like I'm fightin' against some invisible dog leash from inside the taxi.

Lennie drives back to "The Flamingo" an' we have hot coffee an' a few laughs with Patsy. Then we go to Lennie's place an' kill a bottle of scotch for which I pay twelve dollars. Patsy has two drinks an' wants to play, but I'm old enough to be her father, an' the worries of the world sit on my head like a sack of sand. I can't help her. Lennie's gone to drive his cab. We're in his apartment, she's sittin' on my knee an' gettin' sore because I'm starin' out the window, sad as an orphan boy.

"You bastard," she says to me. "What's wrong? Has there been another woman?"

"You ever seen flood or drought?" I ask her. "Do you know how deep a man can hurt for other men?"

She's off my knee an' in the kitchen, pourin' black coffee for herself, her face hard as stone.

"Listen to me," I say to her. "What a man an' a woman do when they're connected in the middle is a celebration. But you've got to hurt so you deserve to celebrate. We grow older, we see the years go by in the house we've built, the children we had grow into men an' women themselves."

"Piss off," she says, swallowin' hot coffee like she was dyin' of thirst.

"I'm hurtin' for the man who spends all his life, workin' at a job he hates, payin' for a home that rots away faster than he pays for it. Yet he'll work harder than if he was a slave, because in the north, winter is the enemy. Winter is like death sittin' in a corner, waitin'. But we laugh at death, by laughin' at ourselves!"

"What concern is that to me?" she asks, the cup in her small hands shakin'. "I've got a good job an' a place to live. On Saturday night, I go dancin'."

"So dance," I says to her. "Dance until your feet hurt an' your skin glows like stars in the night. That's what bein' young is all about. Dance an' holler. That black sonofabitch winter is scared of that. Have a good meal when you're hungry, an' a good lay with a man your equal when you're lonely. But remember, that's a celebration an' an 'up yours' to winter, an' the men of winter."

"What men of winter?" She looks at me with tears in her eyes.

"The men I understand an' envy, but whom I'll never join because broads like you are eatin' out my heart. The lenders an' collectors who never lift a board or mix a bucket of cement, who go to church, send their kids to college on your back."

Patsy's laughin' now an' throws her cup into the sink where it breaks into a hundred pieces.

"Jesus Christ, Romeo, I thought for a while you were sick!" she says.

"An' when that man's dyin', the newspapers show his picture an' cry. An' you, dumb, law-abidin' tit, cry with them. You cry more than his widow, because you're warm an' healthy." I get it all out an' I'm weak. She's back on my knee, stroking my hair back here behind the ears.

"I'd cry for you if you died, Romeo," she says. "I'd cry for you one year without stoppin'. Because I'm soft-hearted like my mother. She cried all day when she heard the King of England died."

Me, I don't cry for anyone, kid. To cry is to forgive. I get so sad I can't catch my breath sometimes, but I'll never forgive. So I'm an enterpriser, a freewheelin' bandit who follows the big bully an' picks up scraps of what's left without bendin' a knee to get it. I'll never work for another man, an' I'll never work for wages. There's people who call me nothin' but a well-dressed bum. I owe to hotels an' restaurants, but nobody burns me for that, or I'll drive a size-ten boot up their ass!

I've been kicked out of this hotel. Told never to come back. Six months later, I'm promotin' a big fight here. A contender for the world heavyweight title has come in for a share of the gate, as well as four wrestlers famous from here to Mexico City. Good advance ticket sales. I come through that door askin' for a room. The same guys who threw me out now carry my suitcases upstairs. One afternoon, I'm carryin' twenty grand in this pocket, an' it feels like a nice, warm twat.

I show them the roll, an' they're touchin' it like it was the Virgin Mary's facecloth. Matt is sniffin' at it. Clapper has tears in his eyes he's so impressed.

I can make telephone calls to New York, papers are carryin' my ads. The clerks an' bellhops are bringin' up enough free sandwiches an' coffee to feed all the bums on skid row. The biggest businessmen in town are comin' through my door like I was a one-man massage parlour. They're offerin' to invest money, time. For two weeks the whole world knows me by first name.

"Hello, Romeo. How ya doin', boy?"

"How about a drink, Romeo, old cock? It's on me!"

"Hey, Romeo … Jesus, man, you haven't changed! You don't look a day older than when I seen you in the ring, when? Four, five years back?"

"Fifteen years ago, you prick!" I tell them. "I retired from liftin' anything heavier than my suitcase fifteen years ago!"

"Oh, yeh? Still the same old Romeo, heh, heh! You don't look a day older. How do you do it?"

"Snake liver … I eat snake livers for breakfast!"

"Come on, you've got a secret, but you're not tellin', is that it?"

They throw a dinner for me night before the match at the best restaurant in town. The mayor's there, so are the car dealers. I buy myself a white suit an' patent leather shoes. I get my hair washed in a beauty salon an' dried with an electric dryer. I buy a bottle of good French cologne an' have a sponge bath in it. When I come through the front door of that restaurant, it's like Al Capone himself comin' to a christening. Every broad in the room smells me before she sees me. I come in like a stud, gold tooth gleamin' in the biggest smile I can stretch out, my eyes sparklin' like I was on a one-thousand percent make!

They bring out the best food I've ever eaten. They make speeches, talkin' about me. They talk about me puttin' the city on the map with such big names comin' over from the United States. They talk about culture for the common man, how the country is growin' up, that work, hard work, has its rewards. How enrichin' it is for the common man to have a chance to see a good fight.

While they're talkin', I'm eatin' an' drinkin' their cognac an' laughin'. I'm laughin' as I give a couple of good-lookin' broads the feel, right under the noses of their husbands, who don't know, because they're talkin' so they can make back the money they've invested. That's the best kind of feel, somethin' with conspiracy an' danger to it, kid. Put your dink near an open weasel trap an' see it come alive!

There's more cognac an' coffee, an' the speeches are comin' from other tables now. The chief of police promises support. Two guys from trade unions, who look like chiefs of police on their days off, promise to display my posters, because they know me an' are my friends.

I never seen them before.

There's other friends I don't know … guys standin' up an' tellin' stories about when an' how they knew me … where an' for how long. I'm addin' numbers in my head, an' pretty soon I figure I'm a hundred an' twenty years old to know them all the way they say. I get up an' thank them all for comin', an' say that I wished my mother was alive to see all the friends I had. I can't say anymore because I'm laughin', an' they're all laughin' because I'm laughin'. I leave.

Outside the door of the restaurant, I lean against the wall because I'm dizzy an' confused. A bull feels dizzy an' confused when he breaks a barbed wire fence an' knows there's nothin' holdin' him. One of the broads I'd felt under the table, the wife of an advertising executive, comes toward me. She winks an' asks if there's something I'd forgotten. I reach for my wallet, but it's there, an' seein' this, she laughs.

Arm in arm we walk across the street to the first hotel, check in under phoney names an' shack up until the sun comes in through the window next day. This one's a real pro, the one-timer who burns a blister on your brain. Whose little machine workin' overtime in the proper bedrooms can send a thousand fightin' men to keep peace in Cyprus the next day! She's everywhere; in the closet, against the wall, under an' over you. The kind you'd beat at her game the second time 'round, but not the first. Only tonight, she's doin' it for fun an' practice. Tomorrow she'll be usin' it to make promotions for her husband, or her friends, but not tonight!

She's still sleepin' in the morning when I leave her. I clip a fifty dollar bill into her hair, so she's sure to see it when she goes into the bathroom. Doin' that, I paint a line between them an' me.

Doin' that leaves me free. I'm a hustler who owns nothin', an' doin' that leaves me free to burn their house down.

SIX

I can't sleep at night. I haven't slept all night in years. I wake up at noon an' then I'm up until four next mornin'. What happens to a man when he does that?

I'm not alone. There's night people in every city—newspapermen, hustlers, bootleggers, pastry cooks, guys like you on night shift, cops, burglars, taxi drivers. Sometimes I feel like my skin's been washed by stars an' black wind. Then I hear a jet up in heaven, headin' for daylight an' Honolulu where it's warm, an' I feel good an' glad to be among the night people. Because among us there's guys with the power to leave it all an' take three hundred others with them!

In the basement, back of the hotel, there's a bakery. An old punk called Simon works there at night, mixin' up dough for butterhorns an' cinnamon buns which he's baked for breakfast in the restaurant by morning. Simon's not as old as he looks. But he's old. Worried old like a Jewish saint. His oldest boy is doin' eight years in the slammer for armed robbery. Simon lost his house last summer in a poker game. When the house went, so did his wife.

So Simon lives alone in a boardin' house where his bed an' breakfast cost him seventy a month. In two years he'll get old age pension, an' he'll sit in a window with a geranium pot an' look down at the street, thinkin'.

When I see a geranium pot, I kick the fuckin' thing against a wall. Did you know that you have to work at killing a geranium? Even after it's been tipped over an' the roots have dried in the sun, a Thursday missionary can set it back in the pot again an' the goddamned thing grows? I hate the smell of geraniums; they smell like laundry in a home for incurables. An' it's the flower that's put around old people to remind them they're gonna die soon. Give me lilacs an' roses. Fuck geraniums!

Simon works down in the basement. He comes to work an hour after you do. You seldom see him. He moves in the shadows, even at night. By two o'clock he's got the sweet dough mixed. An' while it's risin', he lays down on the flour board next to the oven an' goes to sleep.

Simon is a funny kind of sleeper. There's as many different kinds of sleepers as there's people. Some sleep curled up like babies, knees under their chins. For some, sleep's the last day of their lives—they fight, grind their teeth, groan an' plead. Simon needs heat when he sleeps, an' he gets heat from the oven. The room he works in is one big heat box. An' he's not too clean. The clothes he wears under his baker's apron are caked with dough an' stink of sweat an' yeast.

I don't know what he dreams about when he's sleepin', but whatever it is, it makes him reach for his crotch. If he dreams long enough, he'll get himself unbuttoned an' his hands around the throat of the northern kangaroo with two swollen legs.

He's got an alarm clock now. But before you came to work here, he had an arrangement with the guy who had your job. Sam was to wake Simon at four in the morning, so he'd get his pastry cut an' in the oven for the seven o'clock restaurant trade. One night, Sam gets a rush of late registrations, so he gives me the key an' sends me down to wake the baker.

I find the baker spread out on the flour board, his hair an' clothes all covered in flour. His legs are apart, his shoes are off. One sock is hangin' on by the toes, while the other looks like it's just been pulled on. An' Simon's hangin' on with both hands to the purple mother what's ready to whamo if you so much as touch it with a goose feather.

"Hey!" I poke him in the ribs. "Time to wake up."

He's up on his ass, bendin' from the hips like a robot. His eyes shut, his wang still at half-mast, he's on his feet an' headin' for the vat, which has a balloon top of warm dough. No time to wash his hands of his fantasies or crotch sweat, he's into the dough, flattenin' it down so's he can roll it out into flat slabs for cutting. Once he's punched the dough down, he's awake.

"Thanks, rassler," he says. "I must've dozed off. Don't tell anyone. I'm not in the habit of sleepin' on the job, so don't say anythin', eh?"

"Don't you ever wash your hands before doin' that?" I ask him. He looks at his hands then at me. He's puzzled

"What for? They're clean."

I swallow somethin' that's come up into my throat to choke me an' turn to leave. He catches my sleeve.

"Hey," he says. "Sit down. I'm makin' some coffee. There's lots of leftover doughnuts, butterhorns, cinnamon buns. No sense payin' for them in the restaurant when I've got 'em here. Sit down."

"Screw you an' your butterhorns!" I said to him an' left.

I don't ask anyone how bread is made, or noodles, or morning hotcakes. I could starve to death if I asked.

A loaf of bread can get you into trouble. I once threw a loaf of bread out of my hotel room window. Three stories down. I aimed for an' hit a college kid in the kiester with it. I knew it was a college kid because he wore a suede leather jacket an' jeans. Only a kid with enough money for university can dress like that an' get away with it. An ordinary kid wears denim jackets with jeans.

Anyway, this punk was standin' around waitin' for a bus at eleven o'clock at night. What the hell's a kid his age doin' at a bus stop this late at night? I was feelin' low, had drunk up all my booze, didn't have money for a fresh bottle. The last twenty dollars I had I'd blown three hours ago takin' a broad with the monthlies to dinner at the steak house. She waited until she'd eaten before she told me her troubles. So what the hell. I buy this loaf of bread, just in case I can't swing breakfast in the morning.

It's summer, an' I'm sittin' at my window lookin' down an' I see this kid waitin' for his bus. I don't want breakfast, I think to myself—I want some action. So I take good aim an' fire the loaf down. It hits the kid in the mug. His little beanie flies off, an' he flips over. The loaf of bread's wrapped in plastic that's tougher than bomb casing, an' it's still in one piece. The kid picks it up, then himself, an' looks up at me. I give him a raspberry.

"Sir, did you throw this?" he asks me in the nice voice of a lawyer who's about to burn you.

"Damned right I did!" I holler down at him. "What's wrong? You want me to throw down some marmalade an' butter as well?"

"Sir, why did you throw it at me?"

Right then, somethin' inside me says—watch it. This isn't an ordinary kid goin' to college so's he can make more money. This is one of those I'll-wear-you-down-mothers who don't have to lift a hand to nail you in a corner. He'll tie you up with his mouth, providin' he's got an audience.

Just then, his audience was crossin' the street in size-twelve boots. A big, rawboned rookie of a cop with legs that start where other men have belly-buttons, an' a haircut so short his neck looks blue under it.

"You're a university punk ... I know that! Go set a school on fire, do somethin' useful!" I'm brayin' down in a voice that's sayin', "I never read a book in my life an' I'm proud of it." He smirks up at me an' then turns to the cop.

"Sir," he calls the cop over. "The gentleman in the room up there threw this loaf of bread with great velocity at me, knocking off my hat an' spectacles. I asked the gentleman politely what his reason was for this offensive behaviour and he threatened to throw marmalade and butter at me as well.

There was no provocation, sir. I stood where I stand now and have stood for the past twenty minutes, waiting for my bus to the south side."

"What you want me to do?" the flywheel of the law asks, lookin' first at the kid, then at me. He starts to withdraw his book an' a ballpoint pen from his pocket.

"Do? What can I do?" That little bastard was trowelin' it on now.

"Well, you can charge him with assault … He hit you with somethin' … That's what you said."

"Yes. With this loaf of bread. Do you wish to take it as evidence?"

"Naw … that won't be necessary. A description will suffice … " He was writin' now, slowly an' stiffly, the way a rookie writes when he can't spell too good. "One sixteen ounce loaf of McGavin's bread … "

"White bread," corrected the little bastard.

"White bread," he crosses out an' rewrites. "Now how were you hit with this … this projectile?"

"In the mouth!" I shouted down. The rookie points a law enforcement finger at me.

"You're not makin' the charge, so shut up!" he orders. Then he thinks of somethin' else.

"What's your name?"

"Joe King—son of MacKenzie King. He done it in the ladies' washroom at the Chateau Laurier after a Christmas party."

"Joe … King … " I'll be damned if he wasn't writin' it down. I started to laugh, loud, so the whole street could hear me. An' while they were conferrin' on the sidewalk under my window as to how to put me in the slammer, I filled a paper laundry bag at my sink with as much water as it would hold without tearin', then carefully I carried it over to the window. The rookie an' the university punk were now standin' close together, examinin' the way the cop had written out charges against me.

"Assault has two esses," the kid says. The cop spits an' starts erasin'.

"Did I leave one out? … Shit, I did … It's the pencil … sticks sometimes. You *think* you've written it right when it stuck an' you left somethin' important out!"

"Very good, sir. I thank you." The kid is grinnin' an' turns away from the cop. I lean over them with the bag an' let it drop.

"Timber!" I roar so loud the glass in my window rattles. Both of them look up half a second before the water bomb hits the rookie dead centre to the kisser. The bag bursts an' both of them are soaked an' covered with pieces of wet paper.

"Goddamnit!" the cop swears. Just then, the bus the kid's been waitin' for arrives an' stops with a shoosh an' whistle of the brakes. The kid gets into the bus, an' it leaves. The cop brushes his tunic, picks up his hat an' plops it hard on his square block of a head. Then he pockets his book an' looks up at me, his face mad—red mad.

"Okay, you sonofabitch! I'm takin' you in!" An' he runs for the side door into the lobby.

Now I'm movin' fast too. Slammin' the window shut. Off with my shoes, socks, pants an' shirt. In my bedside table, top drawer, I keep a self-gummin' moustache matchin' the colour of my hair. I slap it on sometimes after a wrestlin' match when I'm tired an' want to get away from all the middle-aged groupies crowdin' the ropes for a sniff of wrestle sweat. I whop this on my top lip an' dive for bed, pullin' the covers up to my chin.

One minute ... two minutes pass. An' the expected knock comes at my door. Hard, hinge-breakin'—the knock of the law comin' with a big stick after a poor man who likes to have a laugh.

I wait a minute, throw myself from side to side in bed so's he can hear the bedsprings.

"Wha ... eh? ... Who is it?" I say in a hoarse, just-waking-up voice.

"It's the police! Open up, or I'll kick the goddamned door in!"

"Police? ... What the hell!" I keep up the game, but now I put a bit of anger in my voice. "I'm in bed!"

"So's my grannie's poodle—open up!" He's wet, he's mad.

"Come in ... door's unlocked!"

That always breaks a cop's pace—an unlocked door. Those bulls are used to everythin' being locked up like silverware belongin' to the Mafia. He opens the door slowly, then jumps in, his hand on his holster. I'm lyin' in bed, rubbin' my eyes. For a moment, he's not sure. You got to remember, this punk's only a rookie.

"Where's the other guy?" he asks.

"What other guy? I'm alone in here. What the hell is this—a faggot raid?" I'm soundin' pretty browned off by now. Throwin' my bare feet out of bed, I get up an' open the window, because the room's hot. "What time is it, amigo?"

It was a mistake gettin' out of bed. There's not many guys around built like me, an' seein' me upright, he begins to think somethin's not what it appears to be.

"You're him! You're the one!" He pulls out his charge book now an' flips through it, his hands shakin' with anger. The book's wet, an' the pages stick together. "Your name's Joe somethin' or other!"

"My name's Romeo Kuchmir, you prick. What's all this about? What time is it?"

"Same time as yesterday at this time, only a day later." He's still goin' through his book.

Like I say, a cop's brain atrophies from the time he's twelve an' had his first wet dream. I could've got him goin' on a string of French-Canadian jokes if I phrased the next question right, but I didn't because I don't care for them jokes. There's lots of people here in the west who believe them. Put a ten-gallon hat on a Calgary businessman, set him up with some booze an' ten Newfie jokes an' you've got the next most deadly thing to an atom bomb goin' for you.

Oh, I know, I talk big an' bad sometimes. But if you ever tell my story, you tell it like I said it. Don't clean up anythin'. I am what I am because of the way I was born an' lived. I couldn't be different. I've done some good things because I'm human. The bad things, well, I'm comin' through the dark an' feelin' my way. If I make mistakes, I'm sure god will forgive me, even if some men can't. In heaven they will, because up there I'm gonna be a bartender!

So there's this rookie cop in my hotel room. He's beginnin' to see the light, but can't tell where it's comin' from.

"I'm arrestin' you for assault an' public mischief," he says to me.

"Hold it ... now hold on!" I caution him, puttin' my hand on his shoulder, like a brother. "You come in here wakin' me up from a good sleep, lookin' for another guy. Now you're arrestin' me—why? Because you can't find the guy you're after. Is that the way a good city constable upholds the law?"

"Cut it out. I know it was *you!*" he says.

"Then would you shut your eyes an' describe whoever it was that was supposed to do whatever it was he did?" I spoke like a father to a son. He didn't know his limitations. I could see that from the way his eyes wandered around the room now.

"Okay. From an open window, a loaf of bread was thrown down to the street, strikin' an innocent bystander," he began.

"Hold it there!" I made out like I was excited by somethin' that just came to me. "My window was shut! You seen me open my window when you came in. What else?"

He was wilting.

"Here, have a chair." I moved him to where he could sit. "You walk through a fire hose or somethin'? You're wet. What did this ... this bread thrower look like?"

"He looked like you."

"What kind of description is that—'he looked like you'? Was he bare like me? Did he have a suit on? Glasses?"

"I ... don't remember ... "

"What colour was his hair? Did he have a beard?"

"No, he didn't have a beard."

"Moustache then? What colour?"

"He didn't have no moustache," the uniformed prick was startin' to quiver at the lip.

"He didn't have a moustache? You say he didn't have a moustache?" I raised my voice in fury an' he was movin' towards the door. "He didn't have a moustache, an' you come into my room like it was a public washroom, wake me, an' accuse me of assault. What in hell do you think this is growin' under my nose? An elevated cunt?"

"I … I'm sorry." He was puttin' his book away an' helplessly brushin' at his soppin' tunic. I stepped to the door an' threw it open.

"Never mind the sorry crap. You just get your ass out of here an' don't ever let me see you again or I'll have you up for harassin' an innocent man!"

He could see by my face the last word had been spoken. Quickly, he left my room an' marched down the hallway, his pointed head bobbin', his shoulders hunched.

"Hey!" I called after him. "Watch out so a sack of water don't fall on you again! It might sprain your neck next time!"

He stops in his tracks an' spins around. But I was starin' at him like I was just offerin' some good advice which had come to me. He wasn't sure if I was shaftin' him or not, an' being only a rookie, he wasn't chancin' false arrest. I shut the door, an' this time I locked it.

Yeh, I like razzin' cops. Started in my boyhood. There was a café around the corner from my old man's poolhall. Cops used to go there for coffee. In the winter they drank a helluva lot of coffee just to stay out of the cold. A bunch of us punks would be out lookin' for trouble, especially after it got dark outside. We'd carry two blocks of twelve by twelve, cut from ends of timbers.

I was built like a brick shithouse from the time I was fourteen. I'd grab the cops' car by the back bumper, liftin' it while two other guys slipped the blocks under the wheel housings. Then we'd heave a handful of gravel against the café window, right beside where the cops sat. Bingo! They're on their feet an' runnin' for the door. We're off like shots down the street. They're out of the restaurant an' into their car. We're behind some trees that aren't lit, an' we're watchin' as they rev the engine, throw the car in gear an' let the clutch in, twistin' the steerin' wheel at the same time. But they're not goin' anywhere … the suspended wheels howl as they pick up pebbles an' fire them like bullets across the parkin' lot, across the street.

Sometimes they'd catch a kid an' rough him up for it, but it was never a kid who did it.

Why did I do it? Because the guys who became cops were refugees from the same street corners an' dried out barley fields as I was. Those on top always use the poor to hit the poor. Givin' them a uniform kept them from bustin' windows an' tellin' the world they was alive, strong, horny an' needin' things. These cops were told they now served the Queen. Not the banks, or railroads, or even people, but a Queen who wouldn't know if Wetaskiwin, Alberta was in the Sudan or in the Northwest Territories! Those punks wouldn't know a Queen if they caught her liftin' panty-hose at Woolworth's.

"I am Her Majesty, your Queen!"

"Throw her in the slammer! Some kooky broad. Imagine ... Wearin' a trike wheel rim on her head in July! Some damned middle-aged hippie, that's all she is—throw her in the slammer!"

The more ridiculous the symbol, the easier to believe in it. Always been that way. Thousands ... tens of thousands of young punks long ago died in Palestine. Walked all across Europe in their iron overcoats to get there, crossin' mountains, sinkin' in rivers, clawin' through mud an' over rock-piles—for what? To find an' bring home a fuckin' cup for their king! Not only that, but they killed off more Turks than are alive today because someone said the Turks had this cup an' were keepin' it for themselves!

Knowin' that, an knowin' cops don't bake bread or grease up electric generators, I look at a cop an' laugh.

I don't do much that's useful either. But I've learned to live with that, findin' pieces of myself wherever they've been left. That's a pretty fulltime job in itself, my friend.

Don't you agree?

SEVEN

Yeah, I've managed women wrestlers. They're just ordinary kids tryin' to make some bread. But they get pushed around a lot. They draw big in isolated minin' towns an' oil rig camps, where there's few broads comin' through. So that's where I take them. But I also take along a three-foot long lead pipe when I go.

Holdin' this lead pipe in my hand, I announce some ground rules before my wrestlers come on.

"This here pipe's full of lead. Any guy reachin' through the ropes when the ladies are rasslin' gets it across the knuckles. An' at the hotel tonight, they're sleepin' in back of my room. If you want to take your chances gettin' past me, it's your funeral they'll be holdin' on Wednesday, not mine."

To give my words a little more carryin' power, I suddenly lift the pipe an' swing it against the iron ring post, puttin' a buckle in it where none had been before. That's enough to make even the toughest cat-skinner quiet an' respectful when I bring the women out. An' only twice, if I'm careful to assert who's boss, have I had to throw punks down the staircase of a hotel.

Still, broads who wrestle get pushed around when there's nobody to help them. There's a type of guy who really gets his jollies from watchin' broads throw each other around. He's usually a small guy who sits in corners listenin' to what drinkin' men say to each other. But he drinks by himself, one glass of brandy for the whole night. He usually dresses well an' don't mix much. All I know about what goes on in his head is what I've had one of them tell me. He could've lied for all I know.

He worked in the post office an' grew begonias in his kitchen. After one match I promoted for the women, he comes up to me, offerin' three hundred bucks if I would fix him up with Lindy-Lou, one of the tougher gals I had workin' for me that time.

"What do you take me for—a pimp?" I says to him.

"No sir, I'm not suggesting that, heaven forbid. I want ... an introduction an' a chance to be alone with her for two hours. I've got money. I can pay whatever it'll cost."

I bored hard into him with my eye, but he didn't budge. He just looked back at me, his pale blue eyes innocent an' pleadin'.

"What's with you? What is it you're lookin' for?"

He shrugged an' bit his lips, but said nothing.

"Look, I've been around. I've known guys who'd steal a broad's shoe or a piece of clothin' an' sleep with it like a kid with a toy bear. Guys like that have pimples, or wide noses. You're not like that. You're not after an ordinary date like a gentleman, or you'd ask her yourself. How do you see her? What in hell is it that turns you on enough to come to me with a request to hustle for you?"

He cleared his throat an' nodded for me to follow him. We began walkin' nowhere in particular. The smell of sweat in the arena hung like smoke in the air.

"I don't know ... there's something about her ... somethin' free an' strong out of another world I can only think about. I don't want to jump into bed with her ... it's not like that at all," he says.

"No, I didn't think you would."

"There's a strength an' roughness about her that I can't escape ... I've tried, but I can't escape. I imagine she goes to her room at night, an' goes to bed with ... black undies an' jackboots. That she phones down for a man like she'd ordered a cheese sandwich. I'd pay anythin' ... just to see ... bring something for her ... say hello ... "

"You don't want to touch her?"

"No ... I just want to see her, that's all!" There was somethin' whinin' an' desperate in his voice now. I stopped walkin' an' turned him roughly by the shoulder to face me.

"You came here tonight to see her fight. Why?" I shouted an' shook him.

"Because I believe in her! She's got the sort of strength for which I'd do anything she asked!"

"Even kill?"

"Yes." The word came out of him in a whimper.

"Like for the queen of a country ... or for a goddess?"

"Yes!"

I pushed him away. Not roughly, just enough to let him know there was nothin' more to be said. I told Lindy-Lou about his proposition when we got back to the hotel. The part about him worshipping her bothered me, an' I told her all about it. That tough little broad takes out a pair of scissors an' starts clippin' her toenails while I'm talkin'.

"I've never known a man who'd say that," I'm tellin' her. "Wonder how it happened? Maybe somethin' got turned around when he was a boy."

"Fuckin' creep," she says like we were discussin' a fly fallin' in her soup. She keeps on cuttin' her toenails, her leg muscles showin' up like rope pulled tight under the skin. I look at her a long while, my eyes half-shut so I'm not seein' her, just feelin' for the atmosphere around her. She's a strong broad, not easy to sit with in a room.

"Creeps like that should be put away an' the keys thrown out the window." She's still cuttin' her toenails.

"I feel kind of sorry for him. That's not much to live for," I says. I can feel her lookin' at me now.

"Not me. Any guy who looks at me that way gets his face pushed in!"

An' damned if I didn't get a glimmer of what it was that had trapped my friend from the post office, who grew begonias in his kitchen. But I'm put together different than him, an' that sort of thing don't excite me. In fact, I had to leave her room halfway through my beer, because I knew what I came to find out, an' her toeclippin' was startin' to make me mad.

Broads who wrestle for a livin' got my respect. They're serious an' work very hard at it. The crackerjacks in the racket are the midgets!

You book two midgets on a card an' you've got nothin' but trouble from the moment they arrive in town until they leave. They're built the same way you an' I are built ... normal size heads an' dinks—the two things that matter. The rest of them's a bit haywire, but that's alright. I've never known a midget on welfare, have you?

There's one of these pint-sized boomers who calls himself the Nevada Strangler. Little bastard comes from High Prairie an' his name's Swinbourne. But that's alright with me. A name like Nevada Strangler gets you more bookings than High Prairie Choker. He's spunky as hell, an' I'm bookin' him for next November if we don't have a depression first. He's spunky. I seen him tryin' to take on Gorgeous George on the sidewalk just outside that door. George says to him that a midget's got a lopsided view of broads. The height he stands at, all he can see is the woman's crotch. When he speaks to a broad, that's what he says "Good mornin'" to! An' "Good night," an' "How're you doin', kid? How's tricks?" ...

George says to him that with this altered perspective, the questions take on another meanin', that it's bound to warp the minds of little men. That there's more to broads if only the Strangler would stand up on a stool sometimes an' take a look at other parts than those at the height of his nose.

This little boomer's been drinkin' a bit, an' all of a sudden he takes objection to the big wrestler.

"You insulted me! You apologize to me right now!" He's red-faced an' yellin'. An old Indian carryin' a cardboard suitcase is passin' by at that moment. He stops to pat the Strangler on the head.

"Kinda late to be on the street, li'l boy," he says in a father-Indian kind of way. "You better get on home before your mommy gets sore ... or worried."

"Fuck you in the earhole, daddy!" says the "li'l boy" to the old Indian, who looks down at him with the sad old face of a grocer who'd just found mice in his flour shed.

"You white kids gone all to hell," he says an' walks away. Gorgeous George is laughin', an' the Strangler is still lookin' for satisfaction.

"You apologize like I asked!" He's bleatin' like a billy-goat.

"Apologize? What the hell for? When you're mad like that, you look like a bantam rooster, you know that?"

The midget starts rollin' up the sleeves of his little boy shirt. His eyes have gone kind of hard an' small now.

"I'm gonna kick the hell out of you if you don't tell me you're sorry!"

The big wrestler's sittin' on the edge of the sidewalk, his legs way out into the street. Even so, the Strangler only came up to his shoulders. But damn if he doesn't take a run at Gorgeous George, his fists goin' like a mill, feet kickin' into the ribs of the blonde giant. George puts up his hand an' shoves the midget away. But he's back, chargin' again an' again, like a bull against a haystack.

George gets to his feet, an' reachin' out, grabs the Strangler by the back of the shirt. He puts him under his arm, like a duffle bag.

"Hell, Swinbourne, I came out for some fresh air. What you got against the big people, anyway? What's got into you?" he says, as he walks into the hotel.

"You'll burn for this! You'll hear from my lawyer! Don't think you've heard the last of this one! You'll know who you've tangled with before I'm finished with you ... " He's fightin' all the way as the big wrestler carries him upstairs an' to his room.

An hour later, he's in fresh trouble with a broad who's called down to the desk to complain about him. The call's transferred to my room, as I'm responsible for the little bugger so long's he's in the vicinity of greater Edmonton. I promised the cops that.

"Yeh ... what's up?" I ask.

"I'm charging him with indecent exposure!" The broad on the other end of the line is sore.

"Don't do nothin', I'm on the way. Which room you in?"

"Three-nineteen," she says an' hangs up.

I go up to the third floor, an' there's the Strangler runnin' up an' down the hallway, naked except for a small towel he's wrapped around his bottom like a diaper. He's had a shower, his hair is still wet.

"What are you up to? You want to get us all in the slammer? Or thrown out on the street? Jesus, you're like a stuck jack-hammer! Get your clothes on. What room you in?" I was mad at him for makin' trouble.

"I don't remember ... I want my mudder!"

An' he's off down the hallway at a run. I come after him, but damned if I could catch him. Them stubby little legs of his were like two little bangers, goin' to beat hell. At the end of the hallway, he's through the fire door an' goin' down the stairs to the second floor. I've got difficulty runnin' down stairs—right leg sometimes buckles under me, so I was delayed gettin' to the landing. When I pushed the hallway door open, I was worked up enough to nail him against the ceiling once I'd caught him.

But now he'd found himself a friend—a woman about fifty with a bust this big! The kind whose name an' picture appears in newspapers as co-ordinator of fund drives for the benefit of things that are sick, lame or poor. She's holdin' him around the neck, an' bugger him if he isn't snugged up against her, his nose in her crotch.

"I want my mudder!" he's wailin' an' snortin' through his nose. Without lookin', he's pointin' at me. "That's a bad man that one, missus. Gave me two candies, an' said there was more in his room, Took my clothes off an' took me to the shower with him. I want my mudder!"

"Swinbourne!" I roars at him. "I've left a bond with the cops to get you in. If I lose that money, I'm gonna kill you!"

The woman gives me a stare that would frost the tit on a saint.

"You degenerate old animal! Shame on you!" she snaps at me.

"I want my mudder. I gotta wee-wee!" He's at it again, jumpin' up an' down now an' crossin' his legs over one another.

"Swinbourne! ... "

"Go away! Men like you belong in cages!" She's a defender of little boys now, all the furies of hell together with a strong dose of Presbyterian right-eousness burning in her eyes.

"Myehh!" says the little bastard, using every advantage he's got. She's all mother all of a sudden as she pets the monster on the head.

"You poor child, come with me. I'll help you ... There now ... There's a place to wee-wee in my room! Come along."

She opens her door an' leads the way in, the Strangler hangin' on to her skirt. The door shuts. I take a few paces so I'm opposite the door. Then facing it, I lean against the wall, my hands in my pockets. All I have to do now is wait ...

I don't have to wait long. Ten seconds maybe. There's one helluva commotion in the room. A door bangs open an' shuts. She's yellin' something, then I hear her clear sayin', "No, you stop that! Please—I'm not kiddin'. You do that again an' I'm gonna scream! Get out ... You bastard!"

I heard the midget laughin', then I hear a lamp fall an' break. He lets out a "yippee!" an' she screams.

"You ever seen one like that before, eh? It's a prize, ain't it?" he says, an' laughs again.

I don't hear anymore after that, because now the door's thrown open, an' out comes the Strangler, naked an' stumblin' to regain his balance. The woman's right behind him, her skirt twisted, hair mussed up. She throws the towel after him. Her face is red an' she's breathin' hard. Then she sees me.

"You!" she hollers as she points a finger at me. The finger has two rings, an' the nail is painted the same red colour you see on new barn shingles. "You ... set him up to this! Admit it!"

"Lady," I says, "when I first seen you, I was tryin' to apprehend this monster from doin' what he did. It was you who stopped me takin' him."

"I want my mudder!" The Strangler's at it again, stampin' his foot an' chewin' on his towel.

"Swinbourne," I says to him in as casual a voice as I could muster. "You stop that right now or I'm gonna kick your butt right out the top of your head!"

"No, you won't! I will!" says the dowager queen from the fund-raisin' committees. I agreed, an' we parted on that, me bowin' to her from the hip like a perfect gentleman, an' she slammin' the door in my face while I'm doin' my bit for peace an' understandin'.

"Hey, that was a pretty good bit of fun. Let's go do it some more ... "

I didn't let him finish what he was sayin'. Because the moment that door shut, I had that little bastard by the hair an' my other fist up against his nose.

"One more word, Swinbourne, an' you're gettin' this! Then I'm takin' you to your room an' puttin' you inside, where you'll stay until your bus leaves town!"

"I've locked myself out," he says.

"Don't worry. We'll break the door open ... with your head!"

As it turned out, the midget never locked any door through which he came or went. What could he lose? What sort of person would enter a room an' remove a little boy suit? Or a pair of little boy shoes?

I've known them all in the wrestling game. Pete the Swede, the broken-nosed, flop-eared, pot-bellied old prize fighter who turned to wrestlin' for retirement money. The day I met Pete was the day I decided to promote rather than fight. You keep fightin' an' eventually you get to look a bit like him. Then where in hell are you?

No broad wants to go to bed with a face like that, even if she's paid to do it. An' the day I pay for tail is the day I want you to put a rope aroun' my neck an' take me to some little meadow where there's crows cawin' an' nobody to see. I'll dig my own grave. An' when I'm done, I want you to shoot me, push me down the hole an' cover me. In a meadow where there's only crows an' magpies. It's worse than havin' a disease for which there's no cure, livin' like that.

Hey! What is worse—havin' a chronic bladder infection, or carryin' a criminal record? You don't know? Well, I'll tell you if you don't know. You can't leave the country or work for the post office with a record. You can't even work as a dog catcher, because that's government work. A leaky bladder is your own personal problem, but time in the slammer is everybody's business.

I learned all that from Klondike Karl, who had that kind of infection. He told me he got it in the war, but I never asked how. You never asked that bushman anythin' that couldn't be answered with a grunt.

It'd be forty below outside an' you know what he'd do to attract attention? He'd go out with no jacket, his shirt sleeves rolled up, barefoot an' lickin' an ice-cream cone! Whenever I booked him for a fight, I didn't need posters or TV publicity. All I had to do was bring him in three days before a fight durin' the coldest part of winter, park him in front of the hotel for an hour each evening, an' he'd fill the house night of the match!

But I did that only when I was flat. If I had the loot, I kept him out of town because when he was here, he insisted on stayin' with me in my room. He wasn't the best kind of dinner companion, I'll tell you. When I'd take him out for a steak, he insisted they only warm it up in the pan. He'd take this slab of raw meat in his hands an' eat it like he was a fuckin' coyote!

"Why don't you order a moose lung next time?" I says to him one evening when he'd put me off any eating. "It's slippery an' goes down without chewin'."

"Yah. But it gives you gas!"

In my room he'd jump for the phone any time it rang, an' answer all my calls, his ugly mug all happy, because nobody ever phoned *him*.

"Hullo! ... Speak up you sonofabitch—I can't hear you! Yah, sure ... he's here. What for you want to talk to him? Listen ... anythin' you got to say to my boss you can say to me—we're just like that, him an' me!" ...

By the time I tore the phone out of his mitt, I stood a fifty-fifty chance of losin' a backer. A social caller had usually hung up by then.

He couldn't read time, an' one night when I'd parked him in front of the hotel barefoot in the snow, I went in an' placed a long distance call to a bum in Florida, forgettin' all about him. It was an hour an' forty-five minutes later that I remembered he was still there. When I went out to call him in, his feet had froze to the pavement. The last guy who worked on your job an' I worked for ten minutes pourin' warm water over his feet, before we thawed him loose. After that, he wore these Jesus-big padded caribou moccasins when he went out.

"Sometimes you're no good, Romeo," he says to me. "You get too busy an' forget about friends you got workin' for you. In the Klondike, you don't telephone another friend when you've got one already!"

An' you know, to this day I'm not sure if he was the best actor I met or whether he looked that hurt for real as he stared at me with them yellow timberwolf eyes of his. It got to me, right in the heart. An' after that I never treated Klondike Karl the same way I treat other wrestlers.

Mind you, I didn't book him too much either. He was hard to take more than one time a year.

EIGHT

I would like to be a good man. A man people love an' look up to. But I was born an' raised in the shadow of a poolhall. Even though I loved my mother—an' I loved her in ways I can't explain, where I grew up, a woman was a broad. A noisy man was the leader of a gang. So I talk an' think like I was trained to do.

I've loved as many women as there's stars in the sky. An army of women, enough to settle a small city. Fat women, thin ones, old, young, white, black an' yellow. No remorse. Only hope that life gives me more of the same. The root of a man is democratic as hell … Class an' colour mean nothin'. Reason is the enemy. Wake up in the mornin', an' she's puttin' on a face for other people, mostly men.

"Hey, let's stay here a week! I hear birds in the trees. Everything's laughin'!"

"Yes, Romeo, it was beautiful. But we must be reasonable. If my family or friends knew of this, my job is finished and so is my integrity."

I laughed. But she dressed her body like it was made of ice, an' pretty soon, I wasn't laughin' anymore.

I once knew a broad who was as moral as Saint Peter's gatekeeper. She once says to me that Bertrand Russell was a "marvellous man," except that he slept with many women. Which wasn't moral in her eyes. One curiosity cancels out another, an' that's that. I went to the library an' got a book by Bertrand Russell. I read it slow, tastin' every word. Right from the first page I understood—an' she didn't—that the old man's brain an' cock were part of the same body. The brilliant man an' the lover were the same person. That neither god nor the devil had any special privileges once the old man's motors were started up an' goin'.

This same moral broad was a swimmer. A good swimmer—Olympic calibre stuff. She'd invite city workin' girls to the pool to give them instructions on how to dive an' swim—but only once. The next time they wanted to come, they'd have to pay money to join a club she owned.

"That's immoral!" I shout at her when she tells me. "A talent like you got is a gift from god himself! Share it with the poor. It's no fault of hers that some broad was born more stupid than you, goddamn you!"

An' you know what she says to me?

"I wish you wouldn't swear," she says. "I'm not arguin' with you. It's undignified to argue with someone who swears an' shouts like an animal."

She turns on her heel an' walks away from me. She's a rich little broad today, owns two health spas an' goes on African safaris in September with punks in the jet set. I never went to bed with her ... I couldn't. I can screw a whore an' laugh with joy. But I can't screw an immoral woman.

I couldn't hold a marriage together, kid. Even though I could help any friend I had with his or her marriage. But not for myself, not for me. Because the woman I married also grew up in the shadow of a poolhall. We inherited each other, like a family, or an old book full of faded pictures. There were no surprises. Only the same memories. I didn't want them memories comin' at me like a winter frost, an' me standin' around in a summer jacket.

"You've spent more on telephone calls than I've spent on rent an' groceries, Romeo," she says. "And your clothes ... I seen a suit on sale for forty dollars that I could've taken in to fit you."

A good woman, but with a touch of death in the way she spoke an' moved. *My* death. Then the kid was born, but even that was a piss-off. Lots of talcum powder an' oil, an' the juices of life dryin'; her rubbin' her left eye more an' more until I'd have to leave the house an' go somewhere quiet to cry.

An' you know somethin' else, kid? There's no end to it. When I get old an' fitted with porcelain teeth an' a walkin' stick, I'll go back to her. I'll have to go home to die with her. She knows that, an' she's waitin'. Like a hungry crow on a barbwire fence, she's waitin'.

Why do I depress you an' myself with such thoughts? There's an hour of the night, maybe the hour of night we'll die, when we start thinkin' about how we become less than we might've been.

Take me—a man. A lot of time was spent—a million years an' a lot of reckonin' by the master Manmaker how to put me together. Good eyes an' ears, this bone attached to that one. The heart an' lungs just so ... Feet that run, an' an elbow that's the right height for leanin' on a bar! Eh? Then after so many years, most of them spent learnin' how to speak an' walk without fallin', I die. An' I'm put in the ground, like a sack of carrots. An' from the ground I push up grass which some prick with a lawnmower cuts an' rakes away as so much rubbish. That's my blood an' bones an' brains he's rakin' away—but does he care?

Or worse still, a dumb Holstein cow comes over me an' eats me up. An' everything I was is reduced to one lump of cowshit an' a pint of milk, which can be worked down by some dairy genius into half an ounce of sour cheese!

So ... after all them millions of years, I become a bit of cheese which someone eats in one swallow while he's worryin' if his car will start!

Yet ... I'm optimistic. Yesterday, I seen a young broad with a baby come into the hotel. While I'm standin' around, she registers for a room. Then she goes into the restaurant. I follow her, an' sit at the table beside her. She doesn't know I'm there. She opens her blouse an' gives her baby a tit to suck. There's the kid, drinkin' her life an' strength, its little arms goin' this way an' that, while she's rockin' in her chair and softly singin'. An' I think to myself—it's a goddamn miracle, that's what it is—all this givin' an' takin'.

I know who I love. An' I know who I'll marry ...

It will take another seven or eight months for that little bugger to get up on its feet an' stand without fallin' ... a trick the calf or colt learns in the first day of life.

But fifteen years from now, that kid will forget the difficulty of standin' up. It will be sittin' in school doin' physics. While the goddamn horse will still only have learned how to use its feet. That's a miracle, an' it's happening millions of times every day all over the world! What's wrong with us that we can't be grateful for this miracle we call life? That we can still take food away from starvin' children? An' kill other lives like our own for a piece of extra soil, or a political difference of opinion that is of no help at all growing a crop of potatoes or an apple tree!

I had a friend who was a killer. His name was Blackball Stinsman. He prospected an' he trapped—the only occupations left which had no respect for property boundaries or the right to life of other species. Blackball would go through your house lawn if he thought he'd find gold there. An' in the bush, anythin' that moved got shot.

It got shot because it had fur he could skin an' sell for money. What was left, he an' his dog, Hurricane, ate. Stinsman stood a good six inches taller than me. An' the dog, who was part wolf, came up to my belt buckle. So between the two of them they could put away a lot of porcupines, squirrels, deer shanks an' muskrats in a winter. When he came into town from his hunt an' prospect, the dog an' Blackball took a room together. Then they'd throw the hotel window open an' roar. Blackball roared because he'd generally had a bottle of rye whiskey an' had started on a second an' was feelin' pretty good. The dog roared for the hell of it.

"When I go through the bush I kick the trees until they shake so they fuckin' well know that I'm alive an' comin' through!" he says, spittle flyin' out of his bearded big mouth, his eyes blinkin' hard with every word, which was spoken at full voice.

"I heard you, I heard you! Goddamn, but a man has to have an umbrella talkin' to you!"

"What's wrong with my talkin'?" he hollers at me.

"Your teeth are goin'," I says to him. "An' because you never learned to speak normal, you're drivin' a shower of spit when you make a speech. Why don't you see a dentist?"

"What the hell for?"

"You'll never be a good-lookin' man, but you can cut back a bit on the ugly," I says. "An' have a bath sometime. You an' your damned dog smell the same!"

He started laughin' then—a wild man's laugh rattlin' the windows an' goin' right through the hotel like a loose water pipe.

"I lift my arms an' everybody in the house is runnin' for cover, eh? Not like you, Kuchmir, with the sweet whore perfume, not like you! But who's got more money, you or me? Come on, guess!"

He puts down the whiskey bottle an' digs into his pockets with both hands, pullin' out two huge wads tied with twine. He drops the money on the bed.

"There it is—twenty grand, my son! I can buy anythin' with twenty grand—whiskey, a rifle, hotel rooms, nooky. Even if I never have a bath. I just drop the cash on the table an' holler. 'Gimme!' If it don't come to me like that, I take the money back. If you've got more money than me—show me!"

"Naw. You win. I'm busted. Maybe you can make me a loan. You don't need money doin' what you're doin'. So give it to me an' I'll spend it in a civilized way."

Again, he laughs. The dog bares his teeth, hops on the window ledge with his front paws scrapin' the glass an' lets out an excited howl towards the street.

"Take it from me!" Blackball shouts. "There it is on the bed—wrestle me for it! Kill me for it. Kill my dog too. *I'd* kill for twenty grand! I'd kill a man, his wife an' his kids for it, then burn his house down with everybody in it! But I'm leavin' with the stuff that buys everythin'!"

"Get yourself a woman for the night. You're bushed," I says to him.

He got sort of thoughtful then.

"Naw. I can't do it, son."

"Why not? You been through a bad frost with your pants down?"

"Well, if someone was to fix me up, he'd have to fix up Hurricane here as well. We been together a long time. Wouldn't be fair me funnin' an' him sittin' outside the door, listenin'."

"It was a friendly suggestion, that's all. But the deal's off." I says. "I'm not pimpin' for your goddamn dog, that's for sure."

"Don't say that. It puts him off. He's sensitive, you know. If I moved a finger now, he'd take your arm off for sayin' that. He's like people, Romeo. He laughs sometimes, you know."

"Laughs?"

"Yeh, he likes fun. Same's me! One evening, we're out in the bush. I've been trackin' this bull moose, whose ass I've shot off but can't bring him down. Hurricane wants to take him, but I hold him back. No, this one's mine. The moose is mad with pain. They've got very small brains, the moose. But when one has a grudge, he'll get you. This one I'm shootin' has a grudge the size of a warehouse.

"I get him out into a clearin'. His back end is all bloodied. He's makin' angry sounds an' tossin' his head from side to side as he turns to me. I put my rifle down beside a tree an' rip off a sheet of birch bark. Then I take my lighter out, an' sheet of birch bark in one hand an' Ronson lighter in the other, I step out into the clearin' …

"'Come on, you sonofabitch! … You can get me if luck's on your side … Come on!' I'm shoutin'. He tosses his horns again, lowers his head an' starts to paw up ground. Hurricane yelps, an' I turn to look at him. The dog's grinnin'. He knows the odds an' he's enjoyin' it, same's me!

"Then suddenly, the goddamn moose charges. He's comin' straight for me, enough weight there to pulverize a CPR station! I stand where I am, legs wide apart, hootin'. 'Come on, you sonofabitch! It's you an' me now! No guns, just you against me!'

"When he's only yards away, hot an' troubled so I can smell his need to kill, I flick the lighter an' bring it over to the birch bark I'm holdin' in the other hand. I hold my breath as it sputters, then catches fire, fast.

"'Ha!' I holler at the top of my voice an' run towards the moose with the birch bark torch held in front of me. There's a look in his eyes as he comes to a quick stop—panic, pain … death. Just that glimmer of intelligence before the end that tells him he's lost, that I'll kill him now on my own terms, in my own way. He lets out this terrible cry an' turns. But he's not runnin', not doin' anything except breathin' heavy. I back away an' pick up my rifle.

"The look on my dog's face is the happiest thing I ever seen. I lift up the rifle an' blow out the heart an' lungs of that moose at point-blank range. Hurricane lets out a yelp an' he's grinnin' from ear to ear. Because he knows he's on the winnin' side again."

"What if … the lighter … hadn't lit?" I asked.

Blackball stared at me as if I was speakin' some language he didn't understand. Hurricane was also starin' at me, with the same expression. Then the dog barked at me, an' Blackball threw his head back an' laughed.

"What if the lighter hadn't lit? ... Eh, Hurricane? Did you hear that? ... What would've happened if the lighter hadn't lit?" He laughed some more, then, suckin' in the contents of his nose with a burbling noise, he rises to his feet, goes to open the window, an' spits out what he's sucked down.

"I'd of been killed dead if that lighter hadn't lit, that's what would've happened!"

"Pick up your money an' put it away," I says to him.

"Why?"

"Somethin' about you an' money makes me nervous. Like life an' death rentin' a hotel room together."

"You think I'm crazy, don't you, Kuchmir?" he asks me quietly, very seriously.

"You've no respect for life. You're like that dog of yours—kill anythin' to survive."

"Nope. He's grinnin' when I'm takin' chances. If that moose had rammed me to kingdom come, you know what Hurricane would've done?"

"No."

"Eaten me up. Just like he ate what I left of that moose. I'm different than Hurricane. I kill. He stands around, his tongue hangin' out, waitin' for someone else to kill for him. He's more like you than me, Kuchmir! He grins because he's probably heard of Jesus Christ an' the ten commandments. Someone might've read a book to him once on how to set things up so they work for you, even when you're sleepin'!"

There was a strange look comin' over Blackball's face which I didn't like.

"Leave the dog here an' come with me, Stinsman. I'm buyin' you a drink, an' then I'll fix you up with a degenerate sailor who'll suck your eyeballs dry!" I tried to cheer him up like that. But he wasn't listening. He scooped up his money an' shoves it into his jacket pocket. Then he goes to the door an' looks both ways along the hallway.

"Yeh, that's what it's all about," he says, an' closes the door. Hurricane is nervous now, movin' towards the window. But Blackball is there ahead of him, an' slammin' the window down hard. Hurricane is whinin' an' lickin' his lips with fear.

"Come on, Blackball—let's go!" I says to him.

"Yeh—now I understand!" He pushes me aside an', hunching over, follows the dog. "I step out into the world in hobnailed boots. I shoot anythin' that's movin', kick in doors of trappers' cabins, rip the guts out of mountain creeks, lookin' for gold. Another man like me comes too near an' I shoot his drinkin' cup out of his hand. Nobody takes Blackball Stinsman—

I holler every mornin'! Nobody gets a free fuck on me! I don't ask for a fixed address or a pension plan. When I get sick, I either get better by myself or die. An' if I get too old to take care of myself, I'll always keep a spare shell in my rifle to choose the day an' the place I put a stop to gettin' older!"

"Cut it out, for Christ's sake! You're sprayin' spit like a rain machine. The dog's scared of you. You're gonna wake up the whole hotel. This isn't the bush, Blackball. It's night time in the city, man!" I try arguin' with, him, because he's goin' queer on me.

"Yeah ... Now I understand everything there's to know ... "

He's crossin' the room this way an' that. An' the dog is dodging, his tail between his long wolf legs, teeth bared in panic, eyes never off the face of his owner.

"Never *ask*, or you got to *give*! For twenty years I've been an outlaw, killin' enough game to start a packin' plant of me own. I also killed three men who got in my way. They was victims an' evidence. I burned two of them to ashes in fires I cut poplars down to make, the third one went down the river with the spring runoff. If you've got a job to do, do it right by doin' it yourself, I always say! I never voted, never dressed up to go to a party. The first an' the last free man on earth. Twenty years of this, an' half an hour with a wrestler who's become a bum turns the world I know to shit!"

The old bastard is ragin' now, froth bubblin' on his lips. I'm gettin' worried, because there's a smell in the room I don't know—like somethin' you taste when you've been hit hard in the mouth.

"What the hell's wrong with you? You're gonna give yourself a heart attack. Let's get out of here!" I reached for his arm, but he whacked me across the wrist with his other hand, an' I was surprised at how strong he was. It hurt, but I wasn't goin' to show pain.

"You start gettin' rough with me, Stinsman, an' I'll put you in the hospital." It was a bluff, you know. I couldn't put him anywhere if he'd taken me on. But he wasn't listenin' ...

"A dog ... A goddamned, louse-infested, stinkin', piss-legged dog is usin' me! What the mounties couldn't find, what yankee minin' companies couldn't touch, my 3, this thing has eaten an' turned to wolf fart when I wasn't lookin'! I'm killin' him, Kuchmir!"

I sat down in a chair an' lit a cigarette. There's things a civilized man who goes to see opera an' ballet doesn't meddle in. I sat in a chair an' watched Blackball Stinsman an' the dog circle each other, both of them growlin'. The dog was the first to snap. He comes at Blackball fast an' hard, his claws rippin' through the front of the prospector's jacket an' shirt like it was paper, opening long cuts on his chest. At the same time, his jaws snapped at the man's head. Blackball ducked, but I saw that Hurricane had taken off half of his left ear, which he chewed once or twice an' dropped on the carpet. Just as quick as he'd attacked, the dog jumped back.

Blackball was movin' more quickly now, his nose drippin' with pain. His eyes were no longer those of a man. He was a wild animal, bent over, his hands curved like claws which cut through the air, openin' an' shutting as he moved closer an' closer to the dog, who slung away behind a sofa. It was like a dance—Blackball liftin' one end of the sofa an' throwin' it aside. The dog cornered, his teeth bared from nostrils to bottom gums.

Blackball let out a cry, more like a howl, and was on him. Bits of fur an' animal spittle flew across the lampshade as the dog threw his head from side to side, his legs rippin' at Blackball's body, then at air. For the prospector now had him around the throat an' was shakin' him like a piece of cloth.

"Lucifer or Jesus Christ ... whichever! ... You're dead now!" he says in a thick voice.

In a moment it was over. The hot smell of killer animals was nauseating an' everywhere in the room. Blackball pulled the dead body of Hurricane to the window. He opened the window, then reconsidered an' let the dog drop to the floor. Cool air blew into the room, cold an' sweet like the breath of a livin' garden. Blackball rested at the open window for a long while, breathin' hard an' noisy.

"Wash up an' I'll bring you some clothes," I says to him. "Then we'll go out an' have that drink."

"No."

"If anybody sees you like this, they'll take you away to the cuckoo farm, you crazy bastard. Once you're in there, you'll never get out. You're out of your head, you know that."

"Sure, I know," he agrees with me but doesn't move away from that window. I try to cheer him up a little.

"I once knew a guy who had a third cousin who got himself caught screwin' a Jersey cow. He got put away, Blackball. Nobody could get him out again. We even arranged for a letter from the cow, sayin' she didn't mind, that she kind of liked it the times he used a solid step-ladder. It was the other times when he used an upside-down milk bucket that made her nervous ... "

But Blackball was reachin' for his cap an' pushin' past me for the door.

"Cut out the shit, Kuchie. Get me a cab for the airport. I'm leavin' this town," he says. An' that was the last time I seen him.

He stays in my head, kid. The older I get, the more I find him inside my memories, especially when I read the newspapers. When I read about all them politicians who steal, or lawyers who lie defendin' men who kill thousands of people slowly, with poisoned food an' untested drugs, cars which fall apart, an' television sets that castrate you an' then burn your house down ...

The worst time is when I see a baby suckin' its mother an' somethin' about that makes me think of Blackball Stinsman. That's scary. Because when that happens, I don't know what's brought it on or what it means. I'm a simple man. If I met Freud, I'd throw him in the crapper because if a man can't express himself simply so the whole world understands, then he's got nothin' worth listenin' to.

NINE

Me father was hung for sheep stealin'
Me mother is grey-haired an' poor
Me brother is set up in business
Procurin' for bikers next door …

You should learn to sing songs like that at five in the mornin'. It beats stumblin' around in the dark lookin' for a sink to spit the taste of sleep into.

In the mornings, my uncle Vladimir used to open his eyes an' say, "Another day, another dollar!"

Which woke my aunt Sophie beside him. She opened her eyes, looked at him an' said, "Thank God, another day closer to death."

On the outskirts of my town, there was a coalshed when I was a kid. One winter, my old man's poolhall wasn't payin' for what we ate. So the old man built me a sled. It was built of pine with a plank deck on top. He attached a long rope to the runners.

"Go steal some coal, like a good boy," he says to me. "If the police catch you, say it was a joke. No, better still, say it's for the widow Hughes down the street. It makes you a thief. It also makes you a good boy."

So I haul this sleigh out when it's dark, six empty burlap sacks, the sled an' me goin' through the night. I pry off the lock on the coalshed door, fill the sacks an' load them on the sled. The snow's six inches deep, sleigh's easy to pull. Even pullin' it three miles is easy.

But while I'm at the coalshed, a chinook blows up from the west. It's suddenly warm. After the first mile, I take my jacket off. I'm sweatin'. Next mile, the snow's become soft an' the sleigh runners are cuttin' through. The pulling's heavy now. I do a lot of fallin' an' slippin'. Third mile home, I'm pullin' a sled with six sacks of coal through patches of mud.

Mountie car picks me up in its headlights.

"Hey, punk! What in hell you got there?" a queen's cowboy hollers at me. "What're you doin' out this time of night?"

"I'm deliverin' coal for the widow Hughes, sir," I say. An' I lean into the rope, pullin' a load that's heavy as the boulders of paradise by now.

"Good boy," says the cop. "Good to see a kid workin' his ass off for a widow! Now get on with it before I nail you for operatin' a transport business with no licence!"

They drive away, an' through the next two hours of night, I'm pullin' the heaviest load of my life. Two years before, my mother had me move a rock-pile from the garden into a slough at the bottom of the street. I carried two rocks at a time. It would've taken me ninety years to move those rocks that way.

There's a small metal wagon belonged to a kid called Dinty Maynor halfway down the block. Dinty's in for lunch. Wagon is left on the sidewalk. I nip the wagon an' load it with rocks. I'm big for my age—kids an' their wagons are nothin' to me—I should be loadin' flatdeck trucks. So I pile on the rocks, grab the handle an' go. I pull the wagon about six feet an' all four wheels fall off. I'm mad. I yank the handle, an' *it* comes off.

Little Dinty Maynor, with a face like pink jello, cried six months over that wagon. I stole tobacco from my old man's pouch, an' sat beside Dinty an' smoked while he cried.

Both of us was eight years old then.

There was another kid, Jiggy Monroe. I'd grown up, gone to work an' come back to town for a visit, but stayin' at the hotel, because my mother had died an' the old man said he'd cut my hands off if I returned. Jiggy was fifteen when I got back. He was curly-haired an' dressed in a white shirt an' blue pants, always the same combination. He grew up on wieners an' sauerkraut, the same punk food I grew up on, except he was built like a dancer, an' I come out lookin' like a brick crapper.

A homegrown kid—but he could give a man the best blow-job to be had between Fort Smith an' the yankee border! The first time he took my anchor in his lips I thought my skull was goin' to pop open. We were both under a spruce in an open field a mile out of town. I remember hearin' meadowlarks somewhere … an' a sound, somethin' like a moan, comin' up from the black skin of the earth …

He was an artist! He was an angel! His white shirt open at the throat, skin soft as silk! Imagine—a homegrown kid who got that way before he was shavin'!

The first time he blew me, he racked up my legs. I was walkin' like a cowboy with saddle-burn for three days before I could straighten out. A couple of days later, the mounties came to my hotel room an' invited me to pack an' leave town in ten minutes or face a charge of contributin' to juvenile delinquency. But Jiggy Monroe didn't get off as easy. He was caught in the alley back of the poolhall an' rapped with a morals conviction. Into the slammer with him, where the hammerboys of the jock world went to work on him.

When they'd finished with him six months later, his face was all scarred an' there was a wild stare in his eyes I'd never seen before. Wild an' haunted, like a beautiful animal what had got itself caught an' tangled in a mile of snare wire.

"Jiggy—what'd they do to you?" I asks when I see him next.

"They impressed upon me that screwin' for joy was forbidden. They've convinced me!"

"You're kiddin'!"

"Try to tell me otherwise an' I'll punch you in the mouth!" he said sharply an' walked away.

Jiggy tried to work in small towns around Calgary—first at a service station an' then in a clothing store. But he didn't last in either place. There was too much talk about him.

Next time I heard of him, he'd joined the American army an' gone to fight a war for the yanks in Korea. I had a letter from him from Seoul, describin' how he was spendin' all his time on sick leave in the cathouses of Tokyo.

"Women aren't as much fun—but they keep me out of trouble," he says in his letter. Then he described how he managed to stay sick. Breakin' a leg gettin' out of bed, or another time he burned his hands stealin' gas for a jeep. He never fought. All his time in Korea was spent gettin' better.

I'm in Vancouver promotin' a small fight a couple of years later an' I run into him on Granville. He'd just come back from the war. He'd put on weight on yankee war food. That made me mad, an' I lace into him.

"What the hell's happened to you? You depress me. You look like you could sell used cars, or real estate!"

"It's that noticeable, eh?" That lost, wild look returned to his eyes, but only for a flicker.

"You're gettin' fat, old. Man, you were lightnin' an' rainbows together one time. You made somethin' sing inside me just to see you cross a street!"

"You haven't heard the worst yet." He drops his head an' looks away from me. "Romeo, I'm diseased … "

"Diseased?"

"Yeh, I copped it two weeks ago. Went to a bar, then for a walk. It felt good to be back on home soil, to smell the north again. I thought the Orient had milked my balls dry. The last six months were hell. I used to go to a whore house an' recite Walt Whitman to guys restin' up between bangs. The delicacy of my life came to me at such times … also, the futility. So I'm walkin' down Hastings. I stop to look at Chinese ivory carvings in a shop window. Beside me is a girl with pigtails, white socks an' a pile of books on her arm. She smiles at me, an' suddenly all the rages come back, like I'd never been away. I'm all set to oblige the world—I feel this extra flesh meltin' off my body, the blood hurtin' my eyes … "

"I know the feelin'," I says, "I know the feelin' … "

"We both walk, apart at first, then arm in am. I tell her of death an' bomb craters I've seen. She tells me of Friday choir practice, an' a twenty-fourth of May trip she took to Victoria. We walk a long distance. It gets dark. I love her so I can no longer walk without pain. She says—'What's wrong?'

"I tell her … She laughs, an' turnin' to me, kisses me. I begin to burn, the flames lickin' up my thighs, over my chest an' face. My mouth tastes like charcoal. I stumble, blind now. We turned into someone's garden, an' finding a dark place under a rhododendron bush … we did it … divinely, Romeo, like two saints in a wilderness. She had the body of a child. Tiny breasts just comin' into bloom, skin still scented with the sour-sweet odour of the infant."

"How old was she?"

"I don't know. I never asked. After all I'd been through since I saw you, I always came out clean an' refreshed—reborn. Other guys got clap just leavin' camp for coffee."

"Don't tell me the kid gave you a dose!"

"A dose is nothin'. A four day cure cleans it up. This was worse. Siberian cankers an' the sift! I'm so low now I could cry. I don't even know if I'll ever be well again … "

I put my am around him an' we went down the street lookin' for a bar. We got drunk together, but the fat on his face didn't get thinner. In fact, he seemed to puff up more the harder we tried to be happy.

"After all I've done an' lived through, this happens with the last person I love … a child," he starts to say. Which was my signal for movin' him on to the next bar, an' the next.

My fighters were in town, livin' in a rundown fleanest of a hotel which still rented rooms for under five bucks a night. As a last resort, I flagged a cab an' took Jiggy over to meet the boys, hopin' it might cheer him. Only two of them were in—an oxhead from Arkansas named Tiny, an' Ripper, an oldtimer from Toronto. Tiny was scheduled to wrestle in the preliminaries.

The room smelled of unwashed clothes an' too much beer. Ripper let us in.

"Yeh, you're just in time, Romeo," Ripper grunted as he showed us in. "We was just gettin' ready to stretch old Arkansas."

Tiny Arkansas was sittin' on the bed, his glasses on an' his enormous belly restin' on his knees. He had a torn tee shirt on, an' his socks. Bottom half of him had no pants or shorts. I looked at Jiggy, who was frowning, his eyes half-closed.

"Sorry, old buddy," I says to him. "I didn't set this up as a joke."

"I know you didn't," he replied softly.

Ripper sat down on a chair in front of Tiny Arkansas an' lifted a contraption off the floor. It was a hand pump attached to a rubber hose, at the end of which was a glass jar, like a two-quart sealer my mother used for cannin' pickles.

"We was gonna stretch old Arkansas here, but this fuckin' gizmo won't work."

"You grease the neck of the bottle with vaseline, or you won't get an airlock on the thing," Jiggy said quietly, then went to the window which he threw open. He leaned out to get some air.

"What the hell's that?" I asked.

"Hey—that's right. I should've thought of that myself!" Ripper was laughin'. He reached for a Brylcream tube on the dirty table behind him an' applied a coating of hair-grease to the rim of the bottle.

"What is it?" I asked again.

"A cock-stretcher," Jiggy said without turning. "Use it often enough an' you'll end up with a flab hangin' in front of you the size of a deflated football … "

"How big's it get when it stands up?" Arkansas asked in a voice which was closer to a bulldog bark than anything human.

"Gimme that!"

I wanted to have a closer look at the thing.

"Enormous the first few times. Then the ruptures heal. The scars close off the blood supply an' it won't stand up any more," Jiggy was talkin' to Arkansas, who wasn't listenin'. I'd picked up the equipment an' had a good look at it. The goddamned thing was a vacuum pump.

"It's like a milkin' machine for a man," I said. "Come on, Arkansas—get it on. Let's pump you up an' see what happens!"

The old wrestler took the jar an' jammed it over his tiny root. Then he leaned back in bed so he could watch the action over his stomach.

"Tiny figures the reason he can't get laid is because for a big man he's got an awful small one. I figured this would help. I got an extra inch out of mine with the pump," Ripper was enthusiastic as hell as he started to work the pump.

"Yah, another inch would help!" the big-bellied man was sayin'.

Jiggy turned his face back into the room an' leaned against the windowsill to watch. There was a tired smile on his face. He looked ten years older than when I'd met him a few hours before.

The room was silent now, except for the sound of the pump squishing as Ripper worked it, slowly at first, then more quickly. Inside the bottle, somethin' was stirrin', as the old sayin' goes.

"Is it the stretcher, or you gettin' it on by yourself?" Ripper asks, pausin' in his work.

"Keep pumpin'! The air's leakin' back in!" Arkansas bellows at him.

I pushed Ripper away an' took over the pump handle myself. I worked that damned thing so fast the cylinder got warm. Suddenly the suction leak sealed, an' I seen Arkansas' eyes bulge as the thing inside the bottle popped open. It didn't get longer, however. It just got thicker.

"Think of a broad, Arkansas! You got to help ... My arm's gettin' sore!"

But Arkansas wasn't worried. He was laughin'.

"Hey—looky here!" he's pointin' with a finger that's thick as a pitchfork handle. He's propped himself up on his elbows an' starin' over his stomach at the glass jar. I worked the pump faster.

"Slow down, Romeo," he says. "It's startin' to hurt a bit ... "

"Your cord's too short then. What the hell use is this if what you got there's wired tight?" I says to him. I stopped pumpin' for the thing was gettin' bigger on its own, blooming out in a jerky sort of way. Arkansas was sweatin' with pain, but he was happy.

"Never see it like that before!" he exclaims. "You can hold 'er there! Anythin' bigger's no use to me anyway!"

For half a minute he admired it, his eyes shinin'. As a cock, it was an awful specimen—thick, stubby, with a bend to the left side. I've seen better fixtures on dead horses. But I couldn't disappoint old Arkansas.

"Yep, you got yourself a winner there, Arkansas," I says to him.

"They can keep callin' you Tiny, but you'll know it's not because of that, eh?" Ripper was doin' his best to please his partner.

"Naw, never again."

The old man wiggled to get a better look at his prize. Just then there was a sizzling sound, followed by an obscene raspberry as the rubber hose connectin' the pump to the bottle split. Arkansas sat up an' bent over to see into the bottle. What had been a respectable root a moment before wilted down an' almost disappeared into the folds of skin under his stomach.

Jiggy moved away from the window an' quickly left the room. I followed, an' caught up with him on the street outside the hotel. He was hangin' on to a light post, an' laughin' until the tears were runnin' down his face. I grabbed hold of the same pole an' laughed with him.

An' you know somethin', kid? Under that streetlight the face I seen was of the Jiggy Monroe I knew way back as a young punk before he hit the slammer. He was young again, elegant, a sweet devil glowin' in his dark eyes. His lips full an' red as on the most beautiful woman!

"Hey, Jiggy! You gonna live!" I yells at him.

"Damn right I'm gonna live!" he hollers back at me, liftin' his hand to his lips an' then touching mine.

We were both laughin', dancin' down the street.

In opposite directions …

TEN

It's almost morning again. How quickly the nights an' days pass, from cradle to the death van. We begin an' end ridin' on wheels. If I was king, I'd make the wheel a thing to worship. Hang used tires around every flagpole an' make the boy scouts stand an' salute it! Bearded old priests would be guys hangin' around garbage dumps full of old truck rims. Wars would be fought between punks loyal to Goodyear inner tubes takin' on savages with Sieberling on their side. Anyone caught pissin' on a car hubcap gets shot without trial!

Why have trials anyway? What's it got to do with justice? It costs money to have a trial—so justice is a commodity that sells the same way as eggs, shoes or half a freezer beef. You pay for what you get. If you don't pay, you get an earful of wind, a kick in the butt an' time in the slammer.

It's all a game with winners holdin' trumps before they enter. If you're poor, or walk with a slouch, or speak with a stutter, you've lost before you make your first move. If you're a man takin' on a broad, you're also beat. Broads an' Indians get all the breaks now. The ones who lost out in the trade-off were Pakistanis. Old age pensioners got things good too—but arthritics still got to beg for money.

When I left my wife, she kept on workin' as a cashier in a supermarket in Calgary. For a while, before I found my feet, I lived with women who were like my wife. Spent a year in Vancouver with a broad called Jennie, who was a cashier in a supermarket. She was stronger than my wife an' a bit rounder, but that's probably because she hadn't had a kid to drain her out. She's makin' good bread, this Jennie, but I always get stuck with rent an' taxi fares. If we go out to eat, I pay, even when it's on my birthday. What she gives me don't cost her nothin', or so she makes it seem.

One day, she goes to a doctor. A doctor who looks after women's problems. She's back at work the same day, but a week later, I get this bill for twelve dollars an' seventy cents.

It's made out to me, so I says to her, "What the hell's this?"

"It's the bill for my examination," she says.

"This geek looks at your twat an' I get charged twelve-seventy—what in hell makes you think I'm payin' for this?"

"You broke it, you fix it," she says an' walks out the door. I had a good laugh about it, but five years later I got thinkin' about it, an' I didn't find it funny at all ...

Shadows an' lights move across the land. The wind moves them. But never is it the same wind, an' I've never seen the same clouds or swath of sun. Why is that? God spends a lot of time makin' variations on one theme. Seems to me he could do better workin' on makin' a bigger cabbage head, or a fish a man can catch with his hands.

I've got to go out pretty soon. Should have gone seven hours ago, but two guys start talkin' an' before half of what's got to be said is said, the night's gone an' it's another day. Well, what difference does it make, eh? In life, everythin' moves around enough to balance off everythin' else ... justice, broads, or havin' a friend who'll listen to you.

But this is gettin' too serious. Morning's comin' into the city ridin' white frost. The only warmth left is the love of two, ten or fifty people. The more the better!

I got to tell you about women, kid, or you'll always be an animal, an' that's no good to you or anybody. There's different kinds of screwin'. I know guys who do it out of boredom, others for duty. Then there's small guys who do it to tall broads out of vengeance—the one-shot slam-bam-thank-you-ma'am hobos who plant a scrawny kid like themselves inside a big woman every time they get a chance. Screwin' out of love is so rare I can't talk about it. I only seen it explained to me in the ballet I seen last night, an' that don't help you or me much. The closest thing to that I know is screwin' out of pity. To find that, you've got to have pity for everythin' that lives. You can laugh at life, punch it in the teeth, kiss it an' beat it in the ass. But at sundown, somethin' in you has to make you stop an' think, an' cry if it helps about what we do an' what is done to us.

There's two sisters that I know—Elizabeth an' Myrna. They've got an apartment in town, overlookin' the river valley. A quiet apartment; rugs on the floor, grey furniture made in Germany, a kitchen with copper pans, two bedrooms an' a bathroom with coloured fixtures. Both broads make good money. Elizabeth is a nurse. Her sister's a broadcaster workin' for television. She interviews me one night before a fight.

"Do you enjoy the violence of the ring?" she asks.

"Sure … "

"Why?"

"I was raised mean … When I was a baby, my mother fed me with a slingshot an' my father … "

She turns away an' makes a motion with her hand to stop the filming. Everybody's grinnin': the cameraman, soundman an' joe-boys carryin' cable around the studio. She turns back to me, an' she's not laughin'. Her large brown eyes are lookin' into mine … She leans forward, lookin' into my skull. I'm not sure I want a broad lookin' into such places.

"Have you nothing to say?" she asks me in a low voice.

"Lady, I've got a helluva lot to say. But not everythin' I know or wish for can be put into words!" I says to her. She nods, raising an eyebrow …

"Do it! Show me what you know—in any language. I'll get out of your way if that's necessary, but prove to me you're awake. That everything around us here has some sense! That death is someplace over there, but we're here, living, moving, maybe even singing!"

Them words were like fire, kid, sputtering on my skin—inside my brain.

"No, you sit there!" I says. An' I get up in that pokey little room with lights everywhere burnin' out my eyes All this body of mine's been trained to do is fight for a payin' public. I can sing, an' because I can sing, I can hear music in my head. Sometimes it's soft an' distant, like a thousand flutes playin' in a valley twenty miles away. Other times it's like drums of war beatin' so loud my ears ring an' my jawbones ache. This night, I'm hearin' both. I spit in my hands an' grin at her, an' she's on her feet now an' circling back into the shadows, watchin' me, but her eyes alive an' on fire. The lackeys in the room are starin' like zombies, but they don't matter. I don't see them anymore.

All I see through the lights an' darkness is what I might've been, what we all might've been, a burnin' dart, fallin' through the sky. Fire an' ice. My arms stretching out collectin' dreams an' dust. Then with my hands, I make a world. When it's made, I stamp on it with my foot, an' it don't fall apart. To the sound of flutes, I make trees an' mountains. Then the drums start to hammer, an' I'm down on my knees, makin' a woman. I'm singin' to her as I make her of the softest mud I can find. I'm singin' to her as I take my clothes off an' mount her. I'm still singin' as I lean back on my elbow an' watch the children we've made run away, punchin' an' pushin' at each other as they go to take over the fields an' mountains I made. A few have made themselves slip-willow whistles an' are playin' music. A lot more have picked up clubs an' are cornerin' land, broads an' hilltops from which they can control things. I laugh, an' the woman I've made laughs …

I'm in Myrna's apartment later that night. We've had each other twice, an' are now sittin' in the kitchen, slowly drinkin' wine. She's only wearin' a dressin' gown. Her skin is dark an' hot. Elizabeth, dressed in white like a nun, is makin' coffee. Both broads have the same face, the same bodies. But there's a difference.

In Elizabeth's bedroom, there's a picture of a man on the dressing table. A boy-man, curly-haired an' squintin' as if he'd just woke up an' was lookin' into bright light.

"He drowned in a sea-dive exploring marine specimens. A stupid death. Faulty equipment an' bad support staff. We were very happy together ... " she tells me, then her voice trails off. She stretches out beside me, her head fallin' back on my arm. The young widow waitin' for the hurt to go. I reach up an' turn the boy-man's face to the wall. Then I turn out the light ...

Two sisters, two halves of one woman. Myrna risin', Elizabeth fallin'. In the heat of things a man an' woman do together, one laughs, the other cries, her face turned away.

For Myrna I dance an' sing, for she's out to draw all the juices from a man through every open window—the eyes, ears an' mouth. With Elizabeth, I'm prayin' inside me, I'm lamentin', for everything which leaves me to go to her goes to die. I can't have one without the other, so I screw them both out of pity.

It isn't as bad or as good as it sounds, kid. I don't know how it sounds to you. Maybe you're too young to understand. So I'm just tellin' you so you'll remember ...

Now call me a cab. I'm goin' over to see them. What use is a life if you can't do some good with it? Who'll cry for you when you die?

I've known guys who don't care, but that's another story. We're both feelin' pretty good right now, so let's not worry about them.

Call me a cab ...